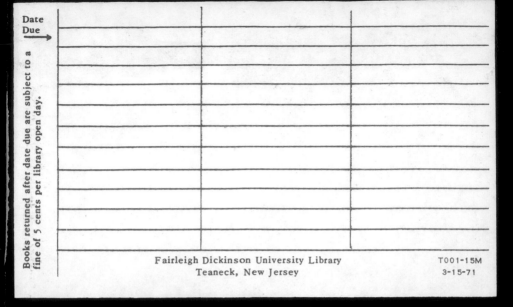

D0906192

# THE JOURNAL
### of
## MADAME GIOVANNI

# THE JOURNAL

OF

# Madame Giovanni

BY

# ALEXANDRE DUMAS

*Translated from the French Edition* (1856)
BY

# MARGUERITE E. WILBUR

*With a Foreword by*
FRANK W. REED

LIVERIGHT
PUBLISHING CORPORATION
NEW YORK

BLACK & GOLD EDITION

NOVEMBER, 1945

## FOREWORD

ALEXANDRE DUMAS, whose *Three Musketeers* and *Monte Cristo* we all know and have enjoyed,—is it to him that we owe *The Journal of Madame Giovanni?* To him most certainly, though admittedly a little explanation may be expected.

Many literary men have been amazing workers, but few can have equalled Dumas, and in the front rank assuredly none have surpassed him. It is true he had his own literary gifts and methods, and he so trained and developed these that they were supremely amenable to his every need and call. It may be that the most important of all was his invariable habit of completely composing story, drama or other work in his mind before penning a single line. Imagine the whole details: plot, order, chapter or scene arrangement, of such works as *Twenty Years After* or *Le Chevalier de Maison-Rouge* or *Mademoiselle de Belle Isle* being fully elaborated in that fine brain before one word of their lengthy brilliance was placed upon paper. These are named—and there are others which could be—because there are full accounts of his having related the first and the last, and had them accepted by an editor or the Comédie Française ere proceeding to write them out; while the *Chevalier de Maison-Rouge* had its first volume, 30,000 words or more, for a wager, written in sixty-six hours, this time including that necessary for meals and sleep. So much then for the first of his customary methods. Another, its concomitant surely, was his ability to visualize all of which he wrote: he had an astonishing gift of being able to picture to himself other lands and other times, other habits, customs and manners, and by simple and unstrained diction could place them with equal clarity before his readers. Indeed perhaps few writers have excelled him in this notable ability to convey what he desired to describe in plain language. His vocabulary was by no means an

unusually extensive one, though at need he could supply the uncommon word, but he had such a command over it that the result
surpassed the attainments of others who needed to ransack the
dictionary to clothe their thoughts.

Let it be remarked also how tireless he was. Twelve hours at his
plain deal writing-table was but a very ordinary day's work; not in-
frequently he would extend this to as much as sixteen, and even
for days together. There is good proof that in his greatest period he
was producing, from day to day, five if not six of his most famous
romances simultaneously, yet never with any confusion of characters, periods, or atmosphere. It is true that after some months this
proved too much, and there came a time when he suddenly had to
drop all and seek relaxation in travel. One sees, however, that he
was an immense and tireless worker. Romances and dramas, to say
nothing of lesser things, flowed from his pen with astonishing speed
and assurance. His memory was prodigious, and very rarely did he
need to pause for reference or for a forgotten fact. What he had
once mentally absorbed, that was always at instant call.

There, then, is the man, the author, in love with his task, and
thoroughly at home with its procedure. The one thing he asked
was to be left undisturbed to carry it out without break or
hindrance; and yet, incurably good-hearted and anxious not to dis-
appoint, it is likely that never was a man in his position more subject to interruptions, for all came to him, all desired his help, all
wished to clasp his hand and chat with him, if only for a few moments, all felt him a friend, however little they really knew him.
This unceasing stream of visitors produced in him the astonishing
ability instantly to pick up once more the thread of whatever he
might be writing when again left in peace, even though this should
chance to be in mid-sentence: no moment was needed for thought,
the plan was clear in his mind, it but needed the driving of his pen.
Here, too, he was most fortunate: from earliest youth to his last
days he wrote fluently, easily, with no strain on fingers or wrist,
hour closely following hour, and in a beautiful hand, as easy to
read as print, a veritable joy to type-setters and proof-readers. Even
when his dog Mouton, suddenly turning on its master, so mangled
his right hand that one of the bones was displaced, rendering it

powerless for a week or two, he still proceeded to write with his left.

It needs not to refer to the volume of his accumulated productions. So great was this, that men refused to believe it came from a single pen, even though an assistant had prepared a first brief draft from the master's plan. They circulated rumour upon rumour, even to the length of stating that there was no Alexandre Dumas, but that the name merely indicated a syndicate of hack-writers employed by grudging publishers. Dumas laughed, as we today laugh at it; but then men found the quantity of matter produced too astonishing for ready acceptance.

And his recreations? Before all, he found recreation in his work itself; but after, in travel, in a day or two spent in shooting over the fields or in the woods; and, finally, in conversation. Nothing, he has declared, stimulated his imagination like clever and enjoyable conversation, and of this art—as at best it is—he himself was one of the best and most enthralling exemplars. Once, when a visitor, enchanted by his lively and ceaseless flow of wit, realized, with a sudden qualm, that he had occupied more than an hour of the master's time, and rose to leave full of apologies: "Do not distress yourself," said Dumas, "why, my dear fellow, our conversation has given me matter sufficient for a couple of volumes."

The fact is that nothing quickened Dumas' gifts like congenial conversation, by which one means any repartee which was witty, sparkling, entertaining. He could sharpen his genius and imagination upon another's mind and thoughts to an astonishing degree. Houssaye tells us how, in the hours after dinner one evening, Dumas, amid an endless stream of conversation and laughter composed with Houssaye, and his secretary Verteuil, those amazingly amusing interludes for the performance, on Molière's birthday, of *L'Amour Médecin*—an innovation which because of its very cleverness and penetration prevented the success deserved. The audience was completely confused as to what was Molière and what was Dumas, and ended by hissing in the wrong places (thinking it attacked the new additions) and by finally damning the whole piece, being thoroughly exasperated at its own ignorance or lack of perception.

Bibliographical matters in connection with the works of Dumas are unusually interesting—for those who care for such things. This is not the place to discuss them, beyond stating that one never can surmise what unexpected thing will next leap at one out of the blue. Those who have read *The Journal de Madame Giovanni* in the original will certainly have remarked the abrupt and unexpected conclusion, just at a moment when the little group of travellers crossing Mexico have aroused fresh interest. In those days of the mid-nineteenth century it was customary for a contract to be signed with the editor of a newspaper for so many "volumes" of a romance or other work. Apparently in the case of the lady's narrative it was to be four. When that amount had appeared we must infer that printing was brought to this abrupt conclusion, perhaps because other material was awaiting use. Readers generally accepted this sudden ending without too much question, and regarded the matter as finalized. Not so Mrs. Wilbur. For her it was not sufficient that there should be so inadequate a conclusion. She believed there must be more if it could but be discovered. When she made this suggestion to me by letter I could only express doubt as to the possibility of the existence of such additions. No mention of any such thing, and no knowledge of the original MS., if still extant, seemed known. However Mrs. Wilbur persisted in making enquiries wherever she thought it possible some information might be forthcoming. Then eventuated what had seemed to me so unlikely as to verge upon the impossible: she discovered a German issue by Dr. J. L. Rödiger, which contained some one hundred pages additional to that printed in the French. It was a splendid piece of perseverance on her part which brought to light that of which there was no record and no clue for following. Right well has she deserved the success so won. It gave me a thrill to hear of it, and I am sure that a much greater one must have been hers. Thanks to a fine gesture of generosity on her part I have had the pleasure of reading—and retaining—a typed copy of these additional pages, and very grateful am I for that enjoyment and privilege. Readers of the following translation will also enjoy the whole, I am sure.

It is particularly pleasing and suitable that this work should be given to Californian and to American readers generally—and to others who are also inheritors of the same language—by Mrs. Mar-

guerite Eyer Wilbur. Already she has given them admirable trans-
lations, delightfully printed and produced, of a number of other
French originals dealing with the Pacific Coast: Dumas' *A Gil
Blas in California,* de Massey's *A Frenchman in the Gold Rush,*
and Duflot de Mofras' *Travels on the Pacific Coast.* Who then
could better and more worthily present such a work as this, an admirable example of the editorial work of a supreme master in the
art of pleasing narrative and delightful and often dramatic word
picturing—in fine, of Alexandre Dumas père. That he himself, that
great Alexandre, would have been right well pleased and satisfied
with his latest interpreter I am fully assured, and, saying that, believe no more should be needed.

                                                   F. W. REED

New Zealand

# INTRODUCTION

Among the many brilliant plays, historical novels, and romances that poured from the prolific pen of Dumas père, there appears a unique and comparatively unknown record of the travels of a Parisian lady to New Zealand, Tahiti, New Caledonia, the Hawaiian Islands, California, and Mexico, called *The Journal of Madame Giovanni*.

This delightful travel-journal, like many of the works of Alexandre Davy de la Pailleterie Dumas, is somewhat of an enigma, for the account is so amazingly accurate even to the minutest details of its historic setting and local color as to leave no doubt that the work was based on the actual experiences of a traveler who had visited these regions. Yet, since Dumas' travels did not extend to the Pacific, the work appears to have followed the classic Dumas procedure and to have been either rewritten by him from some travel diary of that period, or prepared with the aid of a large staff of research workers who furnished him with historic data around which the genius wove his own local color.

The amusing, albeit enigmatic tale of travel and adventure, *The Journal of Madame Giovanni,* records the unique experiences of an alert young Frenchwoman who, at the age of twenty, married an Italian merchant whom she accompanied on a semi-business and semi-pleasure trip of ten years' duration around the Horn to Australia, the South Seas, and the gold fields of California.

Although the feminine touch is always present and unmistakable throughout the narrative, yet there is a stressing of dramatic situations, a vigor and style, that raises it immediately from the typical feminine travel-narrative into the realm of a work touched by the hand of genius, wherein the interest, sustained, prolonged, and constantly varied, never flags. There is, as well, much of the style, the local color, and the masterly handling of situations, that definitely links it with the other Dumas contribution of this same character, *A Gil Blas in California.*

To understand even superficially the literary genius of Dumas, it is essential to have at least a slight knowledge of his background, his technique, and his age. Born in the Napoleonic era, while the crushing effects of the French Revolution were still apparent in the intellectual life of France, Dumas rode to fame on the crest of a great wave of literary activity—the romantic movement—that shortly after 1830 literally engulfed France. This movement contributed to French life, art, and letters, a new vigor, a fresh current of thought that formed a connection between the classical age of the past century and the modernistic and semi-scholastic era that followed.

By this full tide of romanticism, French classicism, so long supreme in France, was submerged. The classic writers were succeeded by a galaxy of brilliant young novelists, poets, and dramatists such as Victor Hugo, Gustave Flaubert, Théophile Gautier, Alfred de Vigny, Alphonse Lamartine, François Joseph Méry, Prosper Mérimée, Roger de Beauvoir, the Comtesse Dash, and a host of other writers, who created the age of literary opulence in France in which Dumas moved and lived, and from which he derived his inspiration.

Dumas ranks, with his close friend, Victor Hugo, as the leader of this romantic movement. Like all writers, he was the child of his heritage, his upbringing, and his age. And like his writings, his background was both colorful and dramatic. Through his veins ran an incongruous but dynamic mixture of French and mulatto blood, from which developed one of the great masters of romantic literature.

To the hybrid tree of the Dumas family belonged a prominent French nobleman, the Marquis de la Pailleterie, and the mulatto, Marie Cessete of San Domingo—the grandparents of the novelist— their military son, known as General Alexandre Dumas, and his plebeian wife, Marie Labouret, being the father and mother of the great writer.

On July 24, 1802, at Villiers Cotterets, some forty miles from

Paris on the main road to Belgium, General Alexandre Dumas' son and namesake, Alexandre Dumas, was born. Although instructed for a time by the village abbé, young Dumas received, on the whole, little formal schooling. At the age of twenty-one, he had the satisfaction of having one of his plays, written in collaboration with a young friend, produced at a local theatre. Its success started him on his literary career, a career that was soon launched by a series of popular dramas written by Dumas at this period. After his success with these dramas, Dumas tried his hand at romances, historical novels, and books of travel, producing before the age of forty volume after volume at a speed that is almost unrivaled in literary annals.

His literary characteristics were soon obvious. From his contemporary, Sir Walter Scott, he first derived the idea of popularizing history, of bringing into an historico-romantic setting the great figures that had guided the destinies of France. This resulted in a cycle of romances which, based on facts supplied by the erudite writer and historian, Auguste Maquet, gave to the world at large such amazing volumes as *Les Trois Mousquetaires, Vingt Ans Après,* and the purely historical studies known as the *Chroniques de France* and *Les Grandes Hommes en robe de chambre.*

At the same time a series of volumes of travel, pure fiction, and miscellaneous articles came from his fertile brain, volumes that soon brought him into the foreground of the great romantic movement in French literature. This amazing output was possible only through the medium of the literary machine brought into play and perfected by Alexandre Dumas—the use of a vast army of research writers, collaborators, and what are known today as "ghost writers." To what extent these mysterious figures participated, where their work ended and that of Dumas began, has long proved one of the baffling aspects of Dumas' literary career.

The years between 1840 and 1850 represent the apex of Dumas' literary, financial, and social ascendancy. This was the decade of his travels to Italy, Spain, and Algiers, of his vast income estimated at one hundred thousand dollars annually, of the erection of his grotesque palace, "Monte Cristo," at Saint Germain, of the publication of his *Comte de Monte Cristo,* the building and sponsoring of the Théâtre Historique, and of the horde of psuedo-friends and acquaintances, who dined at his bountiful table, sapped his vitality, and drained his purse. The lavishness of the Dumas household was the talk of Paris; his spaghetti, the toast of the town.

The crisis entailed by his extravagances led to the loss of his château, a calamity that was followed by a self-imposed exile to Brussels. To Dumas, Brussels represented a kind of literary parting of the ways. The flamboyant, utterly extravagant Monte Cristo days were definitely over. At Number 73, Boulevard Waterloo, in Brussels, where he resided, there were still servants in livery, an abundant table, a lavish cellar, and guests everywhere; but the master himself, held in check by his able secretary, Noel Parfait, and cloistered in his commodious attic, wrote prodigiously in his newly found freedom. From his fluent pen there now poured his monumental *Mémoires,* and *A Gil Blas in California.*

Two years of this sober regime sufficed for the pleasure-loving Parisian romantic. Yielding to the lure of France, he returned, toward the end of 1853, to his old haunts on the boulevards of Paris, full of enthusiastic plans for a new and untried venture. This was the launching of a daily journal to be known as *Le Mousquetaire,* which was announced on November 12, 1853. In his capacity as editor, Dumas aspired to create a paper that would be not only entertaining, spirited, and humorous, but chaste enough to be read in the most puritanical family circles. The leading writers of the Dumas group were engaged at this time to contribute articles and stories to *Le Mousquetaire,* which soon proved to be one of the most popular journals in Paris.

The offices of *Le Mousquetaire* were housed in two small rooms in what became known as the Maison d'Or, located in a courtyard opening off Rue Lafitte. Contemporary writers portray Dumas, toiling in his office from dawn until dusk, coatless, collarless, and with shirt sleeves rolled up to the elbow, seated at a simple pine table, unadorned except for a vase holding a single rose, or a fragrant spray of lilac. "No admittance" signs on the office door failed to keep off bill collectors, embryonic writers, friends, and hangers-on, who invariably formed part of the Dumas entourage.

Despite the gloomy prognostications of friends, enemies, and critics, *Le Mousquetaire* soon rallied to its subscription list no less than ten thousand enthusiastic readers. This success merely stimulated Dumas to fresh efforts, his goal being at least twenty-five thousand subscribers. The list of contributors and collaborators to the young Dumas journal of this period includes the leading writers of contemporary Paris: François Joseph Méry, Roger de Beauvoir, the Comtesse Dash, and many others. Dumas himself admits that he had thirty-nine assistants who toiled laboriously at the command of their indefatigable leader.

The *Giovanni Journal* is the fruit of this period of Dumas' literary activities, a time when Dumas was not only editing his own journal, but contributing to other periodicals as well; it first appeared in the pages of *Le Siècle,* a contemporary Parisian paper, early in 1855.

Dumas himself gives an interesting clue to the personality of Madame Giovanni and to the origin of the *Journal* in the column that appeared on April 4, 1855, in his own paper, *Le Mousquetaire,* called "Dumas' chats with his readers," which runs as follows:

"Dear Readers:

"I told you I would tell you what I have been doing during the two weeks' rest I have just taken. I shall keep my promise. I have traveled about eight or nine thousand leagues. This may lead you to think that I have been traveling in the famous boots worn by the ogre in *Tom Thumb*. Not at all. I embarked in a whaling ship with Dr. Maynard, and on board a trading brig with Madame Giovanni....

"With Madame Giovanni I traveled forty-five hundred leagues.

"'You ran off with Madame Giovanni?'

"Why no, Madame Giovanni ran off with me.

"'Who, is this Madame Giovanni?' you may ask.

"I shall tell you in a few words: physically, Madame Giovanni is a young woman of thirty, of medium height, slender, pale, resembling Mademoiselle Rachel; mentally, she is a woman who is cold and grave, who occasionally laughs, but who can hold you with a glance or a word at a considerable distance.

xvi INTRODUCTION

She passed ten years of her life traveling in Australia, Tahiti, the Marquesas Islands, New Caledonia, the Sandwich Islands, California, and Mexico, and describes her experiences with a remarkable freshness and originality, which is enhanced by her British accent.

"'So she is English?'

"She was born at Auteuil, but during the ten years spent in Oceania, where she spoke nothing but English, she became quite English in accent and appearance, although at heart a French-woman.

"'And did you cover forty-five hundred leagues with Madame Giovanni?'

"I accompanied her to Australia, Van Diemen's Land, New Zealand, Tahiti, the Marquesas, the Sandwich Islands, New Caledonia, California, and Mexico.

"'So you have done for Madame Giovanni what you did for Dr. Maynard; you have sublet her travels?'

"She was extremely anxious to dictate them to me, and although she had not even made a single note, yet she remembered everything clearly; and so if what you have read in *Le Siècle,* under the title of *The Journal of Madame Giovanni in Australia, New Zealand, Tahiti, etc.,* attracts you, you must deal with your humble servant.

"'Madame Giovanni's travels are appearing in *Le Siècle?*'

"Yes, but let me say a few words about them. *Le Siècle* found Madame Giovanni's Travels so delightful that instead of commencing publication as arranged on tomorrow, it started them last Friday."

But *Le Siècle* failed to send proofs to Dumas and so many errors occurred that Dumas reprinted several chapters in *Le Mousquetaire* for April 4th and 5th, 1855.

Then again, in one of his *Causeries,* dated February 10, 1856, he writes for the information of his readers:

"Let me tell you once more that I have not lost all my time during these past five months. I have taken Madame Giovanni by the hand and conducted her from California to Mexico and from Mexico to France."

Yet, in the innumerable published editions of the *Giovanni,* the heroine is left stranded in Mexico, and, in so far as is known, an account of her return to France was never published.

The original French edition was published in four volumes by Cadot in Paris in 1856; in four volumes by Meline, Cans et Cie forming part of the Hertzel Collection in Brussels in 1855-1856; another edition was published that same year in Brussels and Leipzic by Kiessling, Schnée et Cie, and a German edition in one volume in Pest, Wien and Leipzig in 1855; the last-named edition contains several chapters on Mexico not found in the first French edition, but which appeared, apparently in *Le Siècle.* There is also a curious Danish edition dated 1856, containing only the California section. The popular demand for the work was so great that between November 17, 1859 and January 26, 1860 Dumas featured it in his own paper, the new *Monte Cristo.* Later editions were subsequently published. So far as can be ascertained neither the eminent bibliographer of Dumas, F. W. Reed, nor any other student of Dumas ever found an English edition of the *Giovanni Journal.*

The *Giovanni Journal* is now extremely rare. It is not known to Wagner, Cowan, or Bancroft, and few copies appear to be extant. In America a copy of the first French edition is available in the Library of Congress at Washington, D. C., where it is erroneously listed as the work of Madame Saint Mars. The German edition is available in the Mason Collection at Pomona College, and in the State Library at Sacramento. The brief Danish translation, which is limited to the section relating to California, is owned by the Henry E. Huntington Library and Art Gallery at San Marino, California.

For a writer like Dumas to have turned to the relatively unknown lands of the Pacific for the setting of tales of travel, to have been intrigued both by the tale of a sailor lad that formed the nucleus of the *Gil Blas,* and the amusing diary of the mysterious Madame Giovanni is not surprising. Paris, in his day, teemed with travelers bound for western America. Parisian newspapers were filled with anecdotes of California, so recently annexed by the aggressive young

United States of America, where the gold fields were rapidly making men rich beyond belief overnight. From the year 1849 on, ship after ship sailed or steamed out of French ports crowded to capacity with zealous seekers of the mundane wealth to be picked from California gulches, river beds, and mountains. Diaries, letters, and articles by gold seekers were constantly being published. Paris, in fact, was gripped by the gold fever to a greater extent than any other cosmopolitan center in Europe, and the city sent so many emigrants to the land of gold that San Francisco seemed destined for a time to become a second New Orleans.

This exodus from France was stimulated not only by the flood of literature about California that poured from the French newspapers and periodicals of the day, but also by enticing advertisements and "promotion" literature of the steamship companies selling passage to California. Another method of inducing French adventurers to seek their fortune in California was that offered by what was known as the *Société du Lingot d'Or,* a form of lottery in which the winner drew a passage to California. The first of these lottery winners reached San Francisco on February 28, 1852, and by the time Madame Giovanni left California for Mexico there were at least twenty thousand Frenchmen in California.

French interest in the Pacific Basin was not, however, purely a product of the Gold Rush era, but rather one of the phases of the colonial policy of France. From the days of Cartier, La Salle, Marquette, Joliet, the age of the trappers, traders, and explorers who acquired for France the rich lands of Canada, and the lands bordering the Mississippi, especially the Territory of Louisiana, France had been closely associated with the development of North America. The loss of these great colonial holdings had, during the time of Dumas, long been regarded as a tragedy to Frenchmen, and the urge to acquire new colonies in the Pacific motivated the policy of French diplomats.

In his day a series of important expeditions cruised along the west coast of America and among the almost unknown islands of the Pacific, the leaders of many of which, upon their return, published elaborate descriptions of the countries visited, copiously illustrated by maps and sketches. Of particular interest among these early narratives are the records of Cyrille La Place, Du Petit Thouars, Duhaut Cilly, Duflot de Mofras, P. Lesson, Saint Amant, and Hypolite Ferry.

These world travelers were alert to report to France opportunities to acquire territory, trading posts, or trade concessions. Before the acquisition by the United States of Texas, California, and Oregon Territory, some consideration was even given, in diplomatic circles, to the advisability of acquiring California for France, and a young diplomat, Duflot de Mofras, was sent to the Far West to make an official survey of the West Coast; but the rush of Americans to California after the discovery of gold abruptly terminated any thought of French expansion in America, although it tended to arouse interest in the islands of the Pacific.

Dumas experienced, in Paris, this keen awareness of the possibilities of the lands in and bordering on the Pacific; he sensed the color, mystery, and adventure to be found in this remote quarter of the globe, as revealed in the *Giovanni Journal*. In the travels of this mysterious Parisienne he follows what may be aptly termed the Dumas technique: in other words, he uses a more or less accurate historical background against which he dramatizes any local situations of importance—the warring Maoris of New Zealand, the convicts of Tasmania, the vagaries of Queen Pomaré at Tahiti, the habits and manners of King Kamehameha at Honolulu.

The New Zealand, Australian, Tahitian, and Hawaiian sections of the *Journal* are concerned not so much with colorful and extraordinary experiences as with a description of these lands in the forties. The somber and rigid rule of England over her Australian colonies, the unhappy missionary sway in Tahiti and the Sandwich Islands, the contrast of primitive native life as it meets the influx of European civilization, and the inevitable tragedy that ensues, crowd the pages of the Giovanni narrative.

But in the section dealing with San Francisco and the mines beyond Marysville, Dumas' flair for the dramatic becomes more pronounced. Here he injects into the tale the tragedy and suffering caused by the fires, the lure and color of the gambling houses, the San Francisco urge for speculation, and the dispiriting experiences of those who mined along the Yuba. He shows, too, how the mines gradually drifted into the control of the hard-working, shrewd, and at times utterly unscrupulous Yankees, leaving to the more temperamental Frenchmen the ownership and management of the hotels, cafes, theatres, shops, and mercantile houses in the embryonic cities. Dumas has caught, and, with his irresistible and magnetic touch, reproduced the spirit of San Francisco in the fifties. The city, when Madame Giovanni visited it, was growing with meteoric rapidity on the solid foundation supplied by Yankee gold; foundations to which the French emigrants, as the *Journal* reveals, added the cultural note and the inborn knowledge of the fine art of daily living.

Although the most dramatic sections of the *Giovanni Journal* are those dealing with the traveler's adventures in California, the Mexican section provides its full share of color. Whether Madame Giovanni reached Mexico at the very moment when Santa Anna and Álvarez were fighting for supremacy in Mexico, or whether Dumas merely extracted these stirring episodes from some other source, is uncertain; but the account of the journey from Acapulco to Mexico City, touching little-known towns, is so vivid and true to fact that it seems to have come directly from the lips of one who had actually experienced revolutions, bandits, gambling, and cholera, and who had loitered in the classic beauty of the Borda Gardens.

Whatever the French writer may have woven into the Giovanni narrative, yet he has retained the purely feminine viewpoint, the delicacy of thought and feeling of an intelligent Frenchwoman of the upper class. Her fastidious ways, her little airs and graces, her inconsequential pains and minor maladies, her tears, her heartaches, her simulated bravery, and beneath it all her vivid, vivacious personality, all combine to give Madame Giovanni a charm and piquancy that are well-nigh irresistible. Madame Giovanni, as the tale reveals, is at heart an aristocrat and an intellectual, a woman whose standards of conduct are above reproach; yet, withal, she is delightfully feminine. She meets the hardships, the years of travel in lands seldom visited at that time by women, the unpleasantness of crude mining camps, with a stoicism that is almost unbelievable.

But what lifts the *Giovanni Journal* above the realm of the typical traveler's diary is its admixture of historical accuracy, with an intensely human feeling and an expert handling of local color. It is written in the mood of a charming young matron, naive yet worldly, coquettish, feminine. At times, however, Madame Giovanni is almost masculine in viewpoint, with a sense of staunch comradeship and loyalty to her Venetian consort.

Madame Giovanni's travels are unique in an age when the Pacific Archipelago was almost unknown to the world at large. No other woman ever made a trip of ten years' duration in these regions, leaving so comprehensive and colorful a record of feminine experiences in the newly opened lands of the Pacific. That Dumas knew the rare value of her narration, and skilfully revised and published it under his own name, is characteristic of his genius.

Inconsistencies in the narrative are many and obvious. In the foreword the traveler is said to have returned via Cape Horn, yet the volume describes her return by way of Mexico City. Passenger lists of vessels on which Madame Giovanni, according to the *Journal,* entered and left San Francisco, fail to reveal her name among those aboard. The great fires of San Francisco did not take place on the dates mentioned, although they occurred in the same year. This mingling of fact and fiction reflects Dumas, who was always far more concerned with the color and vivacity of his tale than with its historical accuracy.

What is surprising is not these occasional inaccuracies, but the vast amount of reliable information in the narrative. Names of streets, hotels, gambling houses, cafes, and leading citizens in San Francisco; the points along the route to the mines; the references in the Hawaiian section of the travels; points of interest in New Zealand; and details of the Álvarez-Santa Anna Campaign, are so readily verified as to indicate that the traveler had actually visited and known these countries at first hand.

Theories as to the identity of the mysterious traveler who was the central figure of the *Giovanni Journal* have been many. Various writers, notably François Joseph Méry, the Comtesse Dash, and other brilliant satellites of the Dumas group all have been suspected of having had a hand in the narrative. Yet neither internal nor external evidence convincingly supports these contentions.

The most acceptable deduction as to the actual background of the

*Journal* is that of F. W. Reed,[1] the eminent bibliographer of Dumas and perhaps the greaetst authority on his writings, who believes that Dumas "had Madame Giovanni's notes, more voluminous than the text we possess, and used them freely; that at times he would abridge and omit, at other times develop and render them more picturesque; and in this way his own little mannerisms and style would be called into play."

Neither Reed nor other sources of bibliographical data regarding Dumas lists an English translation of the *Giovanni Journal,* although its popularity when it first appeared immediately aroused the interest of Belgian and German publishers, who brought out foreign editions within a year. The following English rendition has been based on the original French edition of 1855-1856, collated with the German edition of 1855 which carries the traveler beyond the incomplete French version to her journey's end.

The translator's task, which is always more laborious and critical than is outwardly apparent, is to catch and preserve the inner spirit of the original narrative, to penetrate into the inner thoughts of the author, to follow his every mood, his fine manner of feeling, his mental processes. With a master mind like that of Dumas, this is a peculiarly difficult task, for every detail of his style, in so far as possible, must be retained in the full force of its vigor, clarity, and beauty.

Among the pleasant memories of contacts made while translating the *Giovanni Journal* is the lengthy and delightful correspondence with Mr. F. W. Reed of Whangarei, New Zealand, whose cooperation and assistance have been an unending source of joy and inspiration. To him I am indebted for invaluable research about the authenticity of the *Journal* and for miscellaneous data regarding New Zealand which have been incorporated in footnotes. Mr. John Barr, Librarian of the Auckland Public Libraries of New Zealand, also furnished notes relative to the local history of that land, unprocurable elsewhere. The staff of the Public Library at Hobart Town provided historical information, likewise used in the footnotes, as did Mr. Samuel Russell of the British Consulate at Tahiti who contributed a wealth of material regarding the Society Islands.

[1] See F. W. Reed, *Bibliography of Alexandre Dumas, père,* p. 347.

Miss Caroline P. Green, Librarian of the Library of Hawaii at Honolulu, graciously supplied from the records housed in her library accounts of Honolulu in the early fifties. For the courtesies extended by Miss Ella Danielson, of the Marysville City Library, Miss Mabel K. Gillis of the State Library at Sacramento, Miss Susanne Ott and Miss Laura Cooley of the Los Angeles Public Library, Miss Marian J. Ewing, Acting Librarian of the Pomona College Library, and the staff of the Henry E. Huntingdon Library and Art Gallery at San Marino, and Mrs. Edmund Andrews of Los Angeles, I take this opportunity of expressing my gratitude. The late Miss Margaret Baker of Pasadena kindly read and criticized the entire manuscript. I am also indebted to Harvey Taylor of Los Angeles for his capable perseverance. The use of the first French edition of *The Journal of Madame Giovanni* was made possible through the courtesy of the Library of Congress at Washington, D. C., and of the German edition through the kindness of Miss Marian J. Ewing of Pomona, California.

MARGUERITE EYER WILBUR

Pasadena, California

# AUTHOR'S FOREWORD

I am of the belief that, at a time when the eyes of the future are being turned toward the West, searching, not for Marco Polo's famous Kingdom of Cathay—this kingdom was discovered by Christopher Columbus—but for places suitable for the development of our present commerce and future civilization, I am of the belief, I repeat, that the peregrinations of a woman in New Zealand, Australia, New Caledonia, the Archipelago of Tahiti, Nuka Hiva, San Francisco, the Sandwich Islands, the Sierra Nevada, and Mexico, will not be without definite interest, especially when this woman, whose rank places her high up on the social scale, had an opportunity to know governors, kings, queens, consuls, and presidents of the places visited, and when she is able to portray with impartiality and accuracy the peoples whom she visited and the leaders with whom she came frequently into contact.

These travels, so remarkably encompassed in the life of a single woman, Madame Giovanni has accomplished, usually in the company of her husband, but also, at times, alone. Today, after making a tour of the world, after rounding the Cape of Good Hope and crossing the Isthmus of Panama, she has returned to Paris, where she plans to remain a month. Then, God willing, she will depart on new pilgrimages like a leaf blown by the wind, a leaf that goes, however, only where God leads it; for wind is the breath of our Lord.

And so I begin in her own words.

ALEXANDRE DUMAS

# TABLE OF CONTENTS

## VOLUME IV

## VOLUME V

# THE JOURNAL OF MADAME GIOVANNI

I shall not disclose my true name; certain family considerations prevent me from making this public. Such publicity, furthermore, given to the name of a woman, a mother, might perhaps at times prevent me from being as frank as I might wish to be. Those who know me will readily recognize me, despite the pseudonym I have adopted. And as for those who do not know me, provided that I amuse or interest them, what does my true name matter?

As regards my style, I make no claim to being a linguist of the first order. I do not know whether my subjunctives or imperfects are always in their proper places; whether my participles should vary or remain invariable, according to the inflexible laws of grammar. But all this gives me slight concern. I am handing the notes of my journal to a friend, and shall not expect him scrupulously to respect my phraseology; neither do I expect him not to substitute a word of his for one of mine. I merely ask him to adhere to the truth; that is all. With this explanation, I shall now begin.

# THE JOURNAL
## of
# MADAME GIOVANNI

# VOLUME I

## THE DEPARTURE

AFTER a sojourn of six weeks at Mauritius[1] and after being married only eight days to a Venetian merchant, M. Giovanni, I embarked at Port Louis on the three-master, the *Pétrel,* Captain Bruce. During the six weeks passed at Mauritius, I had, in memory of Bernadin de Saint Pierre and *Paul et Virginia,* made a trip to Pamplemousse. Beyond this, my excursions were somewhat restricted, preliminary preparations and the wedding itself having absorbed the balance of my time.

The *Pétrel,* on which we traveled was, as I have said, a three-master. She was a vessel of 600 tons burden and was loaded with sugar. Her crew consisted of fourteen men, including the captain and cabin boys. The passengers, five in number, were: an English merchant called Douglas, a Monsieur Philippe, who was disconsolate because he had left his heart behind him at Bourbon, and because of seasickness from which he suffered aboard ship, and a certain Abbé L—— whose vocation I do not know but whose calling was revealed by his tonsure. The history of Sumatra, Java, Batavia, and Mauritius reveals that the musketeer's hat would have suited this other Aramis[2] better than the tricorn of an abbé. He was a remarkably handsome man, but for some inexplicable reason, my husband, at first glance, conceived a dislike for him.

Then there were my husband and myself. My first thought, after our departure had been decided upon, was to attempt to make our cabin comfortable. It was an inside room, adjoining the captain's quarters. I had two armchairs moved in, two beds installed, and a piano securely anchored to the floor. I also assembled a library, two or three scores, the waltzes and sonatas of Beethoven, the melodies of Schubert, and everything by Rossini I could locate.

My husband, for his part, brought aboard an excellent Menton

I

gun, and an assortment of tackle that was adequate to have stocked a sportsman's shop in New Zealand. Incidentally, I forgot to mention that we were bound for New Zealand. What, you may ask, did a woman twenty years of age expect to do in New Zealand? However, I think I have already said that my husband was a merchant; in any case, I shall repeat it and add that while he was not especially attracted toward the business opportunities of the French Antipodes, curiosity inspired my visit to those regions.

Our cabin, as I have said, had many extraordinary comforts. As a result, everyone gathered there for tea and to play vingt-et-un [3] in the evenings. I was the only woman on board. To me this was a matter for congratulation. I do not know why women have never seemed to care for me; in fact I have had only one genuine friendship of this nature. Can you guess with whom? With Queen Pomaré! [4] The real queen, the one at Tahiti. I have not had the honor of knowing her namesake of the Bal Mabile.

Let me describe, first of all, how my days were spent. At four o'clock in the morning I arose, appeared on deck in a large wrap, and poured three or four buckets of water over my head; then went below, dressed as quickly as possible and with head and arms bare proceeded on deck again, where I chatted with the sailors. Fortunately I spoke English as fluently as French. Today I speak French as readily as English, but my accent has become so British that I am obliged to explain that I am from Auteuil, so that everyone will not do me the honor of taking me for a subject of Her Majesty, Queen Victoria.

Having returned to the deck, I cast out my lines and chatted with the sailors, waiting for a bonito or a dorado to bite the hook, which was baited with a bit of fat or merely a small worm that my friends the sailors found for me in some damp corner of the ship.

At eight o'clock I assisted with the breakfast. I had received some letters of marque from the captain giving me certain culinary powers over the English cook, a jolly fellow with a chubby red face, who could cook nothing except boiled fish and roast meat, so I revolutionized his department by introducing fricasseed chicken, omelets, French creams, and pastries. The cook was inclined to revolt against this usurping of his rights, of which he held far more than he was capable of exercising; but a word from the captain silenced him, and without much grumbling he finally allowed me to touch his casseroles and frying pans.

We carried a large number of chickens, ducks, and turkeys, as well as seven or eight pigs which we saw disappear one by one, although the droll fellow who butchered them never once thought of making us some sausage. In addition, we had excellent preserved goods that were the equal of fresh vegetables. Obviously we had slight grounds for complaint.

After breakfast I went up on deck to watch my lines while I knitted, read, or embroidered. Then at three o'clock I inspected the dinner as I had the breakfast; I introduced side dishes, vegetables, creams, and gelatins; the coffee I made myself. Finally, at five o'clock, dinner was announced.

Evenings the passengers spent on deck enjoying the fresh air; then at ten o'clock everyone went below for tea, music, and to play vingt-et-un for high stakes. I did not play but I made grog for the players to suit each individual taste. The winner was billed with champagne to be consumed the following day.

One fine morning, either because we had reached the latitude they inhabit, or because they were migrating, flying fishes were sighted. None had been seen since the equator had been passed. This provided a fresh diversion. Flying fishes are the Mayflies of the sea; by day they are quite difficult to capture unless they fly on deck of their own accord. In the evening, however, the hunt begins. A plank three feet broad and five or six feet long is laid against the outside railing of the ship; on this a lantern is placed, and everyone waits. The flying fish, like a moth flying toward light, approaches, hurls its head against the plank, falls unconscious on the deck, and is picked up, that is all. It was quite simple, as you can see, even more simple than that famous trout-fishing episode that brought down so many recriminations on the author of the *Impressions de voyage*.[5] Furthermore, they came so readily and struck with such force—I speak now of the flying fishes—that while I was having tea or playing vingt-et-un I could hear the sound of their fall. If I went immediately up on deck I was certain to find one of my sailors moving toward the rail and extending his arm toward swooning fish.

Such diversions were interrupted at intervals by terrific squalls, one of which lasted three days; at such times, however, captain and sailors, to give them their just dues, conducted themselves admirably. Unfortunately the ship was less dependable than the crew; she sprang a leak through which the water penetrated. The sugar began to ferment and one fine day an unpleasant odor began to penetrate the vessel, as of something bitter, fetid, nauseating, like the smell of stale beer. After inhaling it for two days, a phenomenon which the storm had been unable to produce occurred—I lost my appetite. Having decided to throw the cargo overboard, the men set to work.

Then came another calamity—that eighth plague of Egypt—multitudes of cockroaches. Fastidious little Parisian ladies, my fellow compatriots, you who swoon at the sight of a cricket, faint at the sight of a spider, what would you say if you found in your work basket, in your cup of tea, in your bed, between the rims of your eyeglasses, in your hatbox, in fact everywhere, this hideous creature known as the cockroach? The cockroach situation was indeed a vital topic.

As fast as the sugar was thrown overboard, the hold began to fill with water. Drastic treatment was required aboard ship to remedy this defect. One pump was manned, then two, then three. At first the pumps were used four hours, eight hours, twelve hours out of the twenty-four, and finally worked night and day.

Notwithstanding, we proceeded on our way. We crossed the Strait, leaving on our left New Guinea and on our right Australia, and finally hove within sight of Norfolk Island. The captain told us that within two or three days we would see the coast of New Zealand. Toward the end, our task became a veritable nightmare. Everyone pumped, passengers as well as sailors. I composed a kind of tune which I played to accompany the workers.

Two days later at two o'clock in the morning, the cry was heard, "land." I dressed, went up on deck, and attempted to peer through the darkness. Since I could see nothing, I went back to bed. On toward three o'clock I heard the sharp clank of the anchor as it was being dropped. An instant later the ship came to a stop.

At daybreak an English pilot came out and led us in to moorings, where the *Pétrel* dropped anchor half a mile offshore. I confess that at first glimpse the country did not appear attractive, with its mountains, rocks, and barren stretches devoid of forests, gardens, trees, and traces of greenery!

"My dear," I said to my husband, "I hope you will not forget that this is primarily a pleasure expedition?"

"What do you mean?"

"We are not remaining long at Auckland, are we?"

"As long as you like, my dear!"

We remained there two years, and even now when I enter my furnished apartment in Rue Godot-de-Maury, I still wish I were in 34″ 37′ south latitude and 164″ 178′ east longitude. By the way, I should explain that the cargo of sugar that was thrown overboard belonged to us. This was the first of our commercial ventures.

## CHAPTER II

## THE MAORIS

AFTER an English vessel had taken us and our luggage ashore, we stood waiting for an English porter, for the local natives are not allowed to transport travelers from ship to shore or to carry their belongings from the shore to their domicile.

If the first glimpse of the island is gloomy and depressing, the view grows more and more interesting, by way of compensation, the nearer the traveler approaches the shore of Auckland, capital of Te Ika a Maui,[1] the island lying north of New Zealand, which is separated from Tavai Pounamu,[2] the southern island, by Cook Strait. Here hundreds of canoes, hewn from the trunks of trees, and varying from fifteen to one hundred feet in length, are visible. The small ones are manned by one, two, three, four, and five rowers; the large ones by twenty or even twenty-five men seated in a line. These pass in single file to and fro bringing supplies to the city; while others, who have already made the trip and are resting, are lined up along the beach like so many horses in their stalls.

Occasionally fruits and vegetables are carried in the same canoe with the rowers; but usually a canoe filled with men tows two, three, four, or even five canoes loaded with merchandise. These follow one another as if dragged by a thousand colossal paws, like great fishes swimming in the wake of a ship with head, back, and tail out of the water. All these fruits, all these vegetables, are arranged in piles on the beach, where a man or a woman guards and sells them. The market is continuous; on Saturday, however, sales are extraordinarily large.

The Maoris—it seems unnecessary to add that this is the name of the local natives who are also called Kannaks [3]—the Maoris sell maize, sweet potatoes, gourds, onions which are eaten raw, and which they bite like apples; bread of the bracken fern called *mauna* [4]; dogs, pigs, all kinds of fish, excellent oysters that are a cross between the Ostend oyster and our common oyster and sell for six or eight pence for fourteen dozen; green beans, small peas, a kind of wild currant tarter than our own, and small yellow prunes from which jam not unlike our plum marmalade is made.

Among all this rise flimsy huts where bows, arrows, feather bonnets, shell necklaces and bracelets, tomahawks and small clappers used to call dogs and pigs, the only animals that, together with the pouched rat, exist in the country are sold. Only the pouched rat [5] is indigenous, however, dogs and pigs having been brought in by Europeans. On the other hand, the bird market, which is far more remarkable than those for dogs, pigs, and vegetables, carries many species; here are displayed the marvelous nocturnal songbirds the natives call the tui, [6] and French naturalists the parson bird; mocking birds, magpies of the sea, parrots, etc.

The costumes worn by the men and women selling these wares are picturesque in the extreme. First of all, the most important garment worn is a wrap or mat cover, a kind of mantle made of native flax which is the color of straw. The right arm remains bare and uncovered outside the cape. When the wrap is open, a fringe a foot long around the waist is visible. The women dress like the men except for the fact that those who are wealthy wrap the fringe around their thighs until it reaches the lower part of the body, thus forming a loose skirt. The head, which is usually uncovered, is ornamented by large holes cut in the ears. In one of these is placed a pipe, in the other, a roll of tobacco. The women insert purses and many of the things that our women usually carry in their pockets in their hair.

When I first landed, I thought that every woman I met was nursing a child, holding it tenderly to her breast. I believed that the vegetable, fruit, bird, and oyster markets were gathering places for nursing mothers. Curious to know what a Maori child was like, I raised the straw cape of the woman nearest me; she was nursing a dog. I raised the straw cape of another; she was nursing a pig.[7] Of fifty nurses, not four were nursing real babies, all were suckling dogs or pigs. The reason for this strange custom, which from that time on aroused in me a permanent dislike for the flesh of these two animals, is that the Maoris believe that by removing their young from sows and female dogs, they will hasten another litter and so double their merchandise. The women, in place of showing anger at my indiscreet conduct, merely smiled when I approached and said to one another: *"Oui-oui; oui-oui!"* [8]

I asked for an explanation of these two words that went the rounds when I approached, arousing curiosity and obvious sympathy. The words merely meant that I was French. The natives, who are keenly observant, heard the French reply *oui,* and even *oui-oui* to everything, and named us after the syllable we most frequently use. Thus *oui-oui* indicated that I was French. I do not know what Parisian trait disclosed my nationality. As for the smile, this mark of sympathy was the result of the sentiment we inspire in the New Zealanders; they love us as much as they detest the English who have made war on them.

The two women whose capes I raised, in addition to the strange ornaments in their ears, wore bracelets that resembled napkin rings. These are shell ornaments that mothers place on the arms of their children when they are small; as the arm grows, the bracelet remains the same, and the flesh finally forms a pad around this band, which must be extremely painful. The legs and feet are bare.

During the short time I spent at the market—my neck and arms were exposed since my shawl had fallen off—a Maori approached me and, with sparkling eyes and considerable laughter, took my arm between his thumb and index finger, clearly pronouncing the word *maki*,[9] which seemed to meet with general approbation. This man appeared to be a kind of chieftain; he wore, in addition to his cape and fringed girdle, an old regimental cap, a shirt collar, and some spurs on his bare feet. He was chatting with a kind of aide-de-camp who wore a European wrap that covered him from his neck to his wrist. I turned toward our party and saw our porters laughing at the compliment that had been paid me. I asked what the word *maki* meant.

"Extremely good," I was told.

"How can they know whether I am good or wicked?"

"Good or bad would be more correct," said an English merchant.

"What do you mean?"

"Well, the compliment paid you by the man in the hat, collar, and spurs has a physical, not a moral, implication."

"Oh, I understand; he meant to say that I am beautiful."

"Not exactly that."

"What, then?"

"That you are young, that you are tender, and that you should be excellent to eat."

"What? To eat?"

"Yes, undoubtedly; the Maoris, you know, are cannibals."

I confess that a shiver ran through my body, and I was readily persuaded to return to my hotel. The hotel was a hundred feet away and bore the sign: To the Queen Victoria. It overlooked the port. Upon reaching it, I hastened to open the window in order to look out. I admit that the sight of this market, these canoes, these men, these women, delighted me. I forgot the terrible *maki* and began to skip like a child.

I was now rid of *bibis*,[10] *robes à la vierge*,[11] all the European fashions. I did not even wish to identify my trunks and check my personal luggage, but left this task to my husband. Then, seized with a desire to explore the city, I suggested that he accompany me, but since he declined, offering the excuse of preferring to breakfast before starting out, I left without him. This was the first of my solitary peregrinations, but not the last.

I walked at random. The streets were thronged with Maoris, both men and women. The women carried in a kind of flat basket pipes, tobacco, and fruits, hawking their merchandise in poor English, or more often in New Zealandish. New Zealandish is an organized language, with its own rules and grammar. A newspaper, *The New Zealander,* is published at Auckland in Zealandish.

By walking straight ahead I found myself in the government garden. The garden was exquisite, but the palace, if I may use this hallowed word, was simply built of brick and wood. I also discovered a large Maori population living in tents. This latter group proved far more interesting to watch than those who inhabited houses which had a monotonous similarity. I entered several of the tents. This was not difficult, for the inmates paid no attention to visitors, merely continuing about their daily tasks such as weaving straw capes, eating, or nursing their dogs and pigs. The animals moved freely about the houses as if they were the true owners. I entered, sat down, and looked around. I was recognized as a Frenchwoman; the inevitable *oui-oui* was said, then no further attention was paid me. The repast of those who were eating consisted of maize in milk, boiled pumpkin, and salt fish.

In some unknown manner I came out on Queen Street,[12] the leading street of Auckland. This, like the Boulevard de Gand of Paris, the Via Larga of Florence, and the Via Toledo of Naples, is the rendezvous of the fashionable world. Incidently, I refer only to the native population. Here throng the Maori coquettes, who come to carry on their flirtations. Their hair is black as jet, they are exquisitely and neatly garbed in a wrap of brilliantly colored Scotch silk, without belt or petticoat, and their legs and feet are bare. Some of them, leaning with their backs against the wall, chat in their melodious language, laugh, and display their teeth, white as pearls; others, seated with a group of men, smoke the same pipe, each taking three or four puffs, then passing it to the nearest man or woman with a courteous gesture.

When I returned to my hotel at two o'clock, the men had already departed. I opened my window and gazed once more at the fascinating activity of the port. Thus three hours sped by like minutes, so new did each object seem. The men returned just in time for table d'hôte. They discussed what they had just seen and what they wished me to see. But I had seen everything.

That evening I slipped off again. It was then nine o'clock. By this hour the character of the city had completely changed. The warm sun, the bewitching smiles, the friendly smoking, the silk robes of brilliant hues, all had vanished. Nothing but somber, ominous, quiet figures, gliding like phantoms past the walls, their bare feet moving noiselessly on the ground, were visible. Except for these phantoms, the streets were deserted and were lighted only by European shops. Scattered here and there among them were dress shops, displaying odd and fantastic models of a type designed to suit the capricious fancy of the Maori woman and made by us with this end in view. Among them were several that carried costumes for the carnival.

I soon returned to the street leading to the hotel. A narrow lane turned into this street; down this I went. A man came over from the wall and, like the one on the beach, pinched my arm and shoulder saying *maki*. He reminded me of the gourmands with empty pockets who stop at Chevet, touching turkeys stuffed with truffles with their fingers and holding the perfumed fingers to their nostrils with the word "delectable." To the Maoris of Auckland, I was what stuffed turkey is to the gourmands of Paris. I returned somewhat frightened.

I found the men having tea and discussing the severity of the colonial laws, for they had been obliged to declare their arms: pistols, guns, swords, knives, and even penknives. All weapons not declared are confiscated, and absolutely none can be sold without a permit from the police. Whoever sells even a knife to a Maori is liable for a heavy fine. Obviously these precautions are taken to prevent the natives from arming; probably this is why they are so well armed.

We reached Auckland on a Friday. The following day, the day of the general market, I was awakened by a terrific noise on the beach. I ran to my window. From there I saw a veritable pandemonium; this is the day when five or six thousand natives, who come only on Saturdays, reach Auckland. Men and women were greeting one another by rubbing noses. Those to whom the meeting was agreeable picked up oyster shells and scratched each other's faces. Those to whom the meeting was especially agreeable found two shells and made their faces bleed. I passed the day as if I had been in a loge watching a pageant; but no pageant ever proved more amusing.

By Sunday morning everything had changed. My Maoris were unrecognizable. They had clean hands and feet, and neatly combed hair; they had donned their finest straw capes and their most elegant robes. Some went to the temple, Bible in hand; others to the Catholic church, prayer book under the arm. Bibles and Catholic prayer books, incidentally, were printed in New Zealandish. I followed my coreligionists to church. They conducted themselves admirably, singing mass with soft, gentle voices. But how to reconcile this? They have embraced Catholicism, while remaining cannibals.

## CHAPTER III

### SIR GEORGE

INASMUCH as I could not spend all my time gazing through the window, my husband and I decided to see something of what is universally known as the world. The fashionable world of Auckland at this period was still relatively unimportant and consisted of five or six persons who kept open house. Among them was Mr. Witikand, owner of copper mines at Kaoua and the most distinguished lawyer in the country, to whom we had letters; Doctor Lewis; and an Irish merchant called O'Donnell. Local society consisted of the superior officers of the ninety-ninth division and the leaders of the church. The governor, Sir George Grey,[1] lived a mile or so from Auckland and was at home only on Saturdays; however, he received no one but officers and so his social functions were primarily a kind of tea with red uniforms.

Incidentally, the customs of this society are rigid in the extreme. Everyone knows everyone else, and since there was nothing to do but slander each other, their houses had turned to glass. There was no way of sinning under cover; if a poor woman sinned openly, it was because she had decided in advance to leave the colony where all kinds of insults are showered on whoever commits an indiscretion.

The result of this unbending attitude toward public morals was a noticeable laxness in private morals. Every rich bachelor had Maori mistresses, chosen from the women of the country who, despite their copper hue, are extremely beautiful. This reddish tint, by the way, is an exquisite shade. The eyes of these native women are like velvet, their noses are straight, their teeth are magnificent, and more than one corseted lady, as they call Europeans, would be envious if they knew how little need the New Zealanders have for this by-product of our civilization.

The corset, as a matter of fact, aroused endless curiosity among the Maori women. Whenever I was ready to don my own, I usually had an audience of three or four women, who slipped into my bedroom to watch the performance—invited no doubt by my chamber maid—squatting on their heels, and exchanging glances and bursts of laughter when they saw the hooks meet and my waist grow slim.

Every unmarried European has a Maori mistress. But no matter how exemplary the conduct of these favorites with their masters, as soon as their backs are turned, they fly off like a flock of birds, in their handsome silk garments, to loiter and gossip on Queen Street, where they rest and smoke, between gusts of laughter, with their old friends.

Society, I repeat, afforded few diversions. And so my greatest pleasure continued to be in my solitary wanderings among the tents of the Maoris. My husband, who loved the comfort of the armchair and his newspapers, never thought of accompanying me; nor of feeling anxious when I was gone. I have no advice to offer husbands, but I am convinced that they would have everything to gain if they would follow the example set by M. Giovanni.

So I explored the city from morning till night, making a collection of curiosities without any competition. Here, where gold is almost unknown except among the Europeans, business in transacted with the natives by barter. Copper earrings, gilded rings, glass necklaces, and spools of thread, are the mediums of exchange. The costumes of the men in the native settlement seemed as elaborate as those of the women.

One day I was quite astonished to meet in one of the Maori tents a large blond young man who, upon seeing me, rose and with a gesture of the utmost politeness but without uttering a word, offered me his seat. From what I was able to infer from this silence, he was a rival collector. I watched him out of the corner of my eye, for representatives of the French or English aristocracy are rare in Auckland. My competitor was a man twenty-eight or thirty years of age, slender, tall, distinguished, a true gentleman, and to all appearances, rich. I was the first to leave and go to another tent. Apparently, he had arrived the previous evening, for I had not seen him before. That day I met him in three tents. At each meeting he rose, bowed, but remained silent. I departed, wondering who this strange traveler could be.

The following day I started off on my usual tour. Not only did I enjoy procuring samples of the handiwork of these good cannibals, so courteous to Europeans in the city, but who, if they met them far off in a forest would immediately make a meal of them, but I also liked to watch them work with their stone implements. The marvelous work these New Zealanders execute with a flint knife or a jade hatchet is almost unbelievable.

While I was watching a Maori work, a shadow appeared on the threshold of the tent; it proved to be my Englishman. I had intended to bargain for the strange object which the artist was completing and I had just learned that this implement already belonged to my unknown rival, when the latter entered. He bowed to me with his customary courtesy, but with the same silence of the previous evening.

I asked my merchant by the sign language if he had a second object like the one he had just completed. As none was available, I asked him how long it would take to make a duplicate. He replied by a gesture that considerable time would be required. I could not conceal the indignation that every woman unconsciously displays when she cannot have what she desires. I waited a moment. But why did I wait? As a matter of fact, I fully expected the Englishman to say what a Frenchman would have at once said: "Madame, if this trinket would please you...."

Obviously I should have refused, but at least I should have heard the sound of his voice. Not at all; he remained silent, without making an offer, and by a sign indicated that he would wait until the implement, the object of our mutual controversy, was finished. No doubt he wished to be certain that his tomahawk would not escape. I left and went out in disgust. The Englishman gave me a nod more cold than gracious to which I dryly replied *Dieu vous garde*.[2] I did not realize that, dry as my *Dieu vous garde* was, it was I who had spoken the first word to this stranger.

Yet he had a considerable advantage over me, for he had only to ask the first Maori he met the name of this *oui-oui* lady who went in and out of the tents, to receive full information about me. At the end of three days everyone knew me; after three months I was a familiar visitor. Not once that day did I meet my Englishman. Undoubtedly, he had a long wait before his tomahawk was finished.

For some trivial cause I remained at home the following day. I took advantage of this opportunity to arrange my New Zealand purchases and saw to my dismay that I did not have in my collection a single tomahawk comparable to the one the unknown collector had acquired the previous evening. The next day I sallied forth, determined to find one at any price. Luck was with me. The third Maori to whom I made my request removed from his belt a tomahawk so like the one I coveted that I could have sworn it was the same. I had decided, to satisfy my amateur jealousy—the worst of all jealousies—to give the Maori whatever he asked for his tomahawk; but he named so small a trinket that I felt embarrassed, and gave him double his price. Proudly, with tomahawk in hand, I then continued on my way.

In another tent I encountered the Englishman for whom I was searching, and showed him my tomahawk with a triumphant air as much as to say: "You see that by persevering it is possible to find one as good as yours." He nodded with an air of complete satisfaction, but as usual remained silent. The strain became too great to endure, so I decided to find out who he was. This, after all, was not impossible, for there was only one comfortable hotel in Auckland, the Queen Victoria.[3] Probably my stranger was staying there. As my husband and I had lived there for a time and I knew the manager, all that was necessary was to enter with the first pretext that came to mind and adroitly question the landlord to procure whatever information I desired.

Having reached this decision, I immediately decided to put this plan into execution. My stranger proved to be living at the Victoria Hotel; he was registered under the name of Sir George and was traveling for pleasure. I continued to encounter him the next few days; he continued to bow; but I could get nothing from him but a nod. I began to believe that he was deaf and dumb.

In the meantime, my husband told me that business would take him for several months to Van Diemen's Land[4] and asked if I wished to accompany him, inasmuch as he intended to return to New Zealand. I did not hesitate. Being constantly inspired by the desire to see something new, I decided to go with him on this second ocean voyage, although it might last only thirty or thirty-five days. To those, like ourselves, who had traveled from Paris to Bourbon[5] and from Bourbon to New Zealand, the trip was only mildly interesting.

In March, 1845, we embarked aboard the *Victoria,* leaving our house in charge of our Maoris. My last words upon leaving land and glancing for a final time behind me were: "I confess I should certainly like to know who Sir George is."

The voyage was even more rough and more dangerous than we had expected. The *Victoria* was an extremely small ship of not more than 150 tons burden—from the nautical viewpoint, little more than a tub. Her cargo consisted of cattle hides that had been recently cured, and copper ore. Within a short time these hides gave off a fetid odor, which I still recall with horror and which nauseated us to a point where we could scarcely eat. Furthermore, the ore, which had been carelessly stored, rolled from starboard to larboard whenever the sea grew rough, with the result that we were often in grave danger of capsizing and foundering.

Finally, however, after a journey of approximately six weeks we landed at Hobart Town, the former capital of Van Diemen's Land.

CHAPTER IV

## HOBART TOWN

TOWARD the end of November,[1] that is during the most beautiful days of the Australian summer, the *Victoria* dropped anchor opposite Hobart Town in the lee of Kangaroo Point.

Unlike Auckland, where natives are far more numerous than Europeans, here the Europeans not only outnumber the natives but have virtually replaced them. To have any idea of the colonial power of England, it is essential to see Hobart Town. Where in 1806 a tribe of hideous Alfuros thrived,[2] there now stands a magnificent city, a miniature London, with its numerous carriages, race horses, fashionable women, and elegant men, and its Derwent which, with its steamers, and sailing vessels, might be mistaken for the Thames if it did not flow under a cloudless sky and bask in the rays of the sun.

I confess that my astonishment upon reaching Hotel Gaylor [3] was intense. The hotel, surrounded by gardens, and adorned with balconies and gilded grills, was charming; the two adjoining streets, Macquarie and Murray, were far superior to what I had seen anywhere else; there were horses everywhere. Glimpses into the houses disclosed an air of affluence, ownership, and wealth that rejoiced both the eye and the heart. How different from poor Auckland!

My first words, and incidentally those of every visitor, were: "But where are the prisoners?"

The reply was that of Solitaire: [4] "Everywhere and nowhere."

I insisted on finding out and was told: "The porter who brought your luggage is a prisoner; the maid who waits on you is a prisoner; the man in the street from whom you enquired the way is a prisoner; the police agent who inspected your entry papers is a prisoner; I myself who have the honor to serve you am a prisoner; but as you see, we are prisoners without a prison." [5]

What is remarkable in the organization of these colonial penitentiaries is that the scum of European society is purified by the classification, several thousand miles from the mother country, of aptitudes ostracized in Europe because of vice and crime. In Van

Diemen's Land the highway robber becomes a night watchman; the lost woman, the children's governess; the forger becomes a cashier; even the assassin, after purification, turns farmer and laborer; in London he kills his neighbor, at Hobart Town he feeds him. The earth's span separates the past from the present life of these poor people.

The government that punishes them at the same time protects them. Every night, by the precautions taken against them, by the discipline to which they must submit, their punishment is brought to their minds. But no one has the right to reproach them for their crime; there is a heavy fine for every free man who uses the word convict in reference to those whom the government itself terms wards of the government.

Now what is this marvelous organization that achieves on every hand such remarkable results, unexpected even in Tasmania? An attempt will be made to give some idea of the system. A shipload of convicts arrives. The governor, his aides-de-camp, the head magistrates, the controller general, are obliged to go aboard and verify with their own eyes the health of the passengers. The captain delivers the ledger, a record kept on board, that states the reasons for each sentence and the culprit's conduct in prison and during the voyage. This ledger, recording his past, is then transcribed in the red book which is also used to jot down any further observations. Whenever any information about a convict is desired, this book of justice is consulted, which in proportion as good conduct surpasses bad, tends to become a book of pardon.

The secretaries read the rules; the governor delivers an appropriate address to these unfortunates, with the aim to encourage them to start a new life. The convicts listen with bared heads, some weep; then the governor, his aides-de-camp, the magistrates, and all officials retire.

The convicts remain for some time on the ship; on the day arranged for them to land, they disembark, the men being led to the penitentiary, located on Campbell Street, the women to the factory at Brickfields,[6] a kind of temporary detention house situated outside the city. In one of these places they remain for three months. This is known as a period of probation, or trial. Men or women, provided they have conducted themselves satisfactorily, are now given the first indulgence, that is the privilege of being assigned, or taken into service, by one of the free members of the community.

Every assigned person, that is, every convict, enters service at a wage of nine guineas. Three guineas is deducted by the government. The same amount is withheld for the prisoner to be credited to his account. The balance is given to him outright for his personal expenses. From the standpoint of the prisoners, an assignment is a reward; moreover, the person who secures permission to receive an assigned convict regards it as a favor. First of all, the latter pays nine guineas in place of the thirty or forty he would give a free servant. At the same time it indicates his standing with the government, since he is entrusted with the task of redeeming a lost soul. In this task, assigned by the government to a citizen, there is the satisfaction of being considered an honorable man.

When a resident presents himself either at the penitentiary or the factory with an assignment authorizing him to select a servant, before him—if he is at the penitentiary—are brought fifteen or twenty men; or, if he is at the factory, fifteen or twenty women. He has explained in advance what he requires—a cook, a man-servant, or a chambermaid. The fifteen or twenty individuals whom he interviews belong to the class indicated. He then chooses the man or woman who suits his needs.

If he is a man, and, in order to leave the penitentiary lied, in other words, if he boasted of being a cook and yet knows nothing about cooking; if he said he knew how to do housework, and yet is incapable of handling it, the one whom he has been assigned brings him back to prison and registers a complaint. The same method is followed with women. If a man has made false statements, he is sent to break stone on the main road; if a woman, she is sent to the washtub, that is, to washing clothes. Because they place the convict in the category of a liar, these two penalties are more serious than the punishment itself.

There are three classes of indulgences: the assigned probation, (just explained); the ticket-of-leave; and the conditional pardon. The assigned probationer can never go out after eight o'clock at night; whenever he leaves, he must have a pass from his master, stating that he is abroad on his business. The ticket-of-leave man enjoys the second type of indulgence, which he has earned by good conduct; he is no longer hired out by the government; he can sell his services, collect rents, if he has rents, and have servants if he is wealthy. But he must not be found in the streets after ten o'clock at night. If he has the slightest disagreement with the government, he becomes an assigned probationer and must start over again. The prisoner who enjoys the third indulgence, that is, conditional pardon, is entirely free except that he cannot leave the colony. This is the class of which the major part of the population of the village is comprised. Thus, not only is the door to rehabilitation open, but also the door to fortune. There are at Hobart Town, at Port Phillips and at Sydney, former convicts who are now millionaires.

On the other hand, if bad instincts prevail over good, the punishment is severe. An escaped convict who has fled into the forest and become a bushranger is condemned either to deportation, or to death, according to the crimes he has committed during this flight. If to deportation, he is sent to Norfolk Island; if to death, he is hanged in the prison court. If he is hanged, there is nothing more to be said, nothing more to be done. But if he is sent to Norfolk Island, what takes place?

The two major punishments of Norfolk Island, that land of banishment, are silence and the loss of tobacco. Norfolk Island, which nature created for a paradise, has become in the hands of man one of the circles of Dante's Inferno. There the judge is often cruel, the magistrate frequently tyrannical, but without the knowledge of the government, which expects a certain amount of severity, though not cruelty. No more codes, no more laws, no more protection for the criminal. Merely the pleasure of the governor of the island and the judge, that is all.

Only at Sydney is it possible to judge and condemn a man on Norfolk Island to death. But he can be struck with a lash until death results. The number of blows with the whip is determined by the judge, and instances are cited of a certain judge who condemned a man, his equal, to fifty lashes for having uttered a word after being sentenced to silence; to one hundred for having carried the

end of a roll of tobacco in the corner of his pocket, when tobacco
had been forbidden him.

This man's name might be revealed, but it would be of no value;
out there everyone knows him. Moreover, the governor punished
him. He was a man with a fatherly expression who said in his mildest tones as he pronounced sentence: "God help me to do justice,"
then added in equally mild tones: "Give the poor man one hundred
lashes."

This reminds me of another governor—the rascal, may God pardon him—the first, according to the records, who was appointed to
Norfolk. Nature, I repeat, created Norfolk Island a paradise, where
orange and lemon trees thrive in the open ground. In this torrid
climate, under the broiling sun, oranges and lemons, to the convicts working in the noon heat, were a blessing from God. Yet this
man had every orange and lemon tree removed, reserving for himself, however, a full garden; but it is rumored that, by an act of
divine justice, none of the citrus trees in his garden ever bore either
fruit or flowers.

Two instances will serve to illustrate the extremes to which this
particular governor and magistrate went in the case of certain life
convicts. One young man, eighteen years of age, had insulted an
overseer and the overseer brought him before the judge. The latter
listened to the accusation, then, according to his habit and with his
customary voice and favorite formula said: "God help me to do
justice. Give this poor man fifty lashes!"

The young man was led away, laid in the road, and given fifty
lashes, which he received without uttering a cry. He was then
untied. He rose, turned on the overseer and spit in his face. The
young man was extremely corrupt. The overseer brought him before
the judge and made a complaint. "God help me to do justice," he
said. "Give this poor man one hundred lashes."

The young man was again laid on the place of torture and received them without uttering a sound, without allowing a groan to
escape. However, his back was one vast sore. In certain places the
flesh had fallen off down to the bone. He was unbound. He rose,
turned on the overseer, and struck him. For the third time the overseer brought him before the judge. The judge gave a sigh, raised

his eyes toward heaven, besought God's aid and condemned the young man to one hundred and fifty blows. The victim fainted at the fiftieth lash. Eight days later he was dead.

According to reports, incidents like the one I have just recounted still occur. But everyone knows that the local government only sends to Norfolk Island, primarily, men who have committed major crimes; one important exception was made, however, to this rule when the celebrated and patriotic Irishman, Smith O'Brien,[7] who had been exiled to Van Diemen's Land with his brave comrades in misfortune, was sent out. Life became so insupportable to two of these unfortunate convicts that they made a pact whereby one would secretly kill the other. The murderer would then be taken to Sydney and hanged. In this way both of them would be released from exile on Norfolk Island.

So they drew lots to see which one should kill his comrade. One was killed; the other was sent to Sydney, judged, and condemned to die. This man was not the true murderer of his friend; the real murderers were the governor and judge, who at various times had punished these poor fellows too severely. No attention was paid to the words of the condemned man and he was hanged.

Their method had proved to be ingenious. Two other convicts in turn employed it, offering the same explanation to the Sydney judges. The latter believed that this was a method of defense adopted by the culprits. Then the same situation occurred again. This time the two confederates made their pact in writing. Each of them had the double signature of his companion, and the murderer brought the judge his absolution signed by the victim. He had no alternative but to believe it. A report was made to the English government and both the governor and judge were removed from office.

By comparison with the rest of the admirable system of deportation and colonization adopted by the English, Norfolk Island has been unfortunate in the methods used to punish culprits. I believe the secret is disclosed by the exclamation of a poor fellow who, for a comparatively slight fault, had just been whipped. With tears in his eyes he cried: "Now that I have submitted to the humiliation of being whipped, I can never become an honest man, for I am ashamed of myself. Hanging is all I am good for."

As a matter of fact, he was hanged, after having escaped and committed a robbery while armed.

## CHAPTER V

## MT. WELLINGTON

AFTER two or three weeks spent collecting birds with M. Veron, a naturalist sent out by the French government to the Antipodes, upon returning home one day I found a large delegation of new acquaintances who had been sent to ask me if I wished to join a jolly party they were arranging to climb Mt. Wellington.

I cannot say whether I was brought up on goat's milk or whether I derive this major hobby of mine from my parents, but I do know that whenever anyone asks me to climb up or down, invariably I accept. This time I acquiesced with unusual alacrity, since comparatively few women had made this trip. In fact only one other woman in the city was to accompany us.

The group of friends called on me in the name of France and England. M. de Malpass represented England; M. François de Bellegarde, France. I might add that the two powers have not always been so ably represented. The party was to consist of thirty persons; the rendezvous was to take place the following Wednesday at five o'clock in the morning, in front of Hotel Macquarie.

My husband made every possible effort to change the day. Wednesday would bring a new moon and there was a chance, he said, of bad weather. Notwithstanding his objections, on Wednesday we planned to start. The evening before, the maître d'hôtel departed with his cooking equipment and what provisions were needed. His horse was followed by three more animals carrying tents, and six servants. These tents were three in number. The first was to be set up at the spot selected for breakfast, that is, one-third of the distance; the second, at the stopping place for dinner, in other words, two thirds of the distance; the third at the supper-point—the summit of the mountain.

By five o'clock everyone had arrived. The previous evening, M. de Malpass asked permission to bring one of his friends, but I had not thought of asking who this friend was. Imagine my astonishment when I saw him arrive with Sir George. I confess that I nearly gave a cry of surprise. However, I restrained myself. Sir George approached and, with the stiff courtesy of the English race, after being presented by his friend, bowed to the party. I was included with the others, but not otherwise recognized. Nor did Sir George utter a word. I could not contain myself.

"Is that man your friend?" I asked M. de Malpass.

"Yes," he replied, "have you anything against him?"

"No, except that I am anxious to know ..."

"What?"

"If he ever talks."

"Rarely."

"So then he is not dumb?"

"No, thank God!"

"This reassures me. Perhaps I shall hear him speak some day."

"Immediately, if you so desire."

"Oh no, no, no!" I caught and held his arm.

M. de Malpass looked at me with an air of amazement, but when I signaled him to be silent, he acquiesced with a nod.

We delayed our departure, waiting for the lady who was to be my traveling companion to appear; she sent excuses, however, and disappointed us. M. de Bellegarde having arrived, the party departed, traveling down Macquarie Street, which led to the lower ranges of the mountain. There, on the left side of the road, stood an attractive house; it belonged to a French merchant called M. de Grave.

A league beyond M. de Grave's house, we abandoned our horses. The summit of Mt. Wellington is reached by a series of ascending peaks more or less sheer. Their names are significant: the first is called "Blow Me Up"; the second, "Crack My Side." [1] Once on foot, the men—all of whom were hunters—amused themselves looking for tracks. Wherever they stooped down, they found them. Those of the common kangaroo in particular were so thick that they almost crossed each other. The kangaroos could be distinguished by their tracks, which were more numerous than those of other animals, being identified by the nails, which are sharp as razors and capable of wounding a hunter with a blow as swiftly as a Japanese strikes with a knife. At nine o'clock we approached a stream that came down from the upper slopes of the mountain. The tent was placed on a plateau that afforded a view over Hobart Town, Kangaroo Point, and Derwent Drive [2] as far as Druny Island. [3]

An excellent breakfast awaited us, a breakfast as warm and appetizing in the French Antipodes as it would have been at the Café de Paris or the Maison d'Or. But in place of roast hare, or pheasant, we had kangaroo and parrot. I had come to dislike kangaroo; ever since landing at Van Diemen's Land I had eaten it in every sauce and had it served at every meal. This time, since there was an abundance of other food, I declined.

At the end of an hour we resumed our journey. Although somewhat steep, the trail was extremely interesting. In certain parts of the mountain it passed through a kind of thicket, twelve or fifteen feet high, that formed a luxuriant green canopy overhead. The men, while searching for animal tracks, remained behind, straying, and becoming lost. They were rallied with the Indian cry, "Halloa"; pronounced in a certain manner, it takes on, from the reverberations caused by its echo, an astonishing character in the mountains.

They also indulged in another pastime, which I watched for the first time and found extremely curious. Two or three of them placed around their waists an Indian belt with a pocket that held a sling and some stones. These stones, selected with care, were the size of a pigeon's egg and were pointed at each end. By manipulating the sling, they shot the stone in a certain way so that it rebounded with tremendous force, striking a tree at their right or left. Had the tree been a man, he might have been killed.

A delightful spot was soon reached; there a brief halt was made on a greensward that resembled a velvet carpet. The ascent had been rapid and in certain places I had been able to follow the guides only with the aid of handkerchiefs tied together.

M. de Malpass had an extremely beautiful voice; he sang several songs by Rossini, Bellini, and Meyerbeer, to the profound astonishment, I presume, of the sprites in Van Diemen's Land. Amid our chatter, Sir George was usually as still as a log; or if he spoke, he was careful to see that I should not think that I was the one for whom his words were intended.

We continued on our way; everyone felt refreshed, rested, and joyous. The rest had not been in vain. The higher we climbed, the steeper now grew the trail. Our guides warned us that the ascent was trifling compared to what we might expect to find in the upper regions of the mountain.

By two o'clock the second tent was reached. We discovered our same stream, and on its bank our dinner waiting. Champagne was already cooling in holes dug in this picturesque little stream. Everyone was extremely gallant to me, and full of little attentions. Although I am reluctant to mention it, I was the only woman in the party.

Sir George was the one man who did not afford me an opportunity to exchange a word wtih him. This silence, which ended by becoming almost impertinence, affected me in a peculiar manner; I almost wished he would meet with some accident. Unfortunately, he appeared to be accustomed to excursions of this nature and constantly displayed both strength and skill.

The dinner, like the breakfast, was delicious—almost too delicious. We should have finished breakfast in twenty minutes; we remained at the table an hour. We should have dined in half an hour; we spent an hour and a half over dinner. True, of this time I slept at least three-quarters of an hour. This was an hour and forty minutes lost. Finally, at four o'clock I was awakened, and the climb was resumed. Without any false pride, I confess that I should have preferred infinitely to have remained where I was, rather than go farther. Below, an immense panorama unfolded: city, river, country estates, the sea. I could so easily have remained there until evening, resting on moss thick as a carpet from Smyrna.

However, I was obliged to follow the party, unless I wished to appear lazy. So I walked on, although my feet gave me considerable trouble, without limping, pretending to be as impatient as the men to see the marvelous cascade that would be found at the summit of the peak, higher than Mt. Blanc, which was the goal of our excursion. The trail became more and more difficult as we proceeded and the stones more and more pointed; while we inspected our feet, which were now more or less bruised, our guides gazed off into the distance with obvious distress.

Finally one of them remarked: "We must hurry across the desert, a storm is approaching."

In fact, clouds were already gathering overhead and thunder rumbling in the distance. What little we could see of the river and the ocean had lost its azure bluish tinge and become the color of lead. We moved rapidly ahead. Fatigue had disappeared, pain had ceased. Soon we reached that dreaded place called the desert. There the scenery changed drastically. Emerging from a trail thick with verdure, shaded by vast boughs interlacing overhead like branches of an Italian arbor, we ran, as it were, into chaos.

As far as the eye could see stretched a kind of sandy waste, covered with stones shaped like the boulders thrown upon the shore at Dieppe and Havre by a stormy sea. These rocks, however, were from a foot to ten feet in diameter. Obviously an enormous river had rolled them there millions of years ago, then suddenly disappeared, absorbed by some upheaval. In the bed of this Mississippi not a flower, not a leaf, not a plant grew, nothing to indicate our trail except the trace, barely perceptible, left on the stones by parties that had gone before. The trip across this desert lasted an hour and a half. The weather grew more and more threatening, and no matter how quickly we moved, the guides kept urging us on.

There was no more singing, no more calling the friendly "Hal-lo-a," no more shooting stones from the sling. As for animal tracks, no one thought of such a thing; the passing of a serpent over stone is, according to a saying of Solomon, one of the three passages that leaves no trace. All in all, our fatigue was intense, and our anxiety extremely great. At length we crossed the desert and found ourselves in dense brush that appeared to be virgin undergrowth.

At the end of half an hour a guide approached my husband and said: "You were right in wishing to postpone this trip to another day, Monsieur; in a quarter of an hour the storm will be on us and if we wait until it is raining, it will be impossible to light our fire."

"And without fire?" asked my husband.

"Without fire, we shall perish of cold, for what falls as rain down below usually falls as snow up here."

"Well, we must light a fire."

Then, turning toward the men he said: "Stop here. This is where we must pass the night."

"Why pass the night here?" cried all the voices except that of Sir George, who appeared supremely indifferent as to whether he passed the night here or elsewhere.

All stopped and held consultation. We had just reached a place where it seemed as if one of the most terrific storms of Bourbon or the Antilles had recently passed. Within the space of a quarter of a league, the wind had stripped off leaves, overthrown the bushes as if they had been wheat, torn and uprooted trees. The scene of desolation was not unlike what Noah and his family must have witnessed when they ventured forth from the ark after the Deluge had created a second chaos.

In the meanwhile, as if in justification of our guide's foresight, the rain began to fall in large drops. Without further hesitation we were obliged to abandon the idea of resting and dining in the tents prepared for us at the summit of the mountain near the cascade, where our servants awaited us. Armfuls of brush that had piled up on top of an overturned tree were now collected to provide chips for the log, and an attempt was made to light some matches. Matches were abundant, but no good dry spot to ignite them so that they might start the fire could be found.

My husband conceived the idea of removing his waistcoat and striking a match on the inside of the cloth. As the match ignited, everyone held in readiness whatever paper could be discovered. Flaming papers and burning matches were then slid under the kindling. Fire and water fought together for a moment, but finally the fire conquered. Ribbons of smoke, a joyful crackling; and a shout of triumph from our lips announced victory.

From another tree trunk that had been overturned ten feet from the former a bench was made. Then long poles were cut and placed in the ground and two blankets stretched across them. As we had expected to sleep in the upper regions of the mountain, everyone had brought covering. Within a few seconds a kind of tent was improvised. With fire and a tent we could now with more tranquillity await the storm.

CHAPTER VI

RETREAT FROM MOSCOW

NO SOONER had our tent been prepared than the storm broke. First great drops of rain fell, then hail large as titmouse eggs, and, finally, flakes of snow. Simultaneously the wind became chilly, whistled, grew sharp and icy, and the temperature dropped, I am convinced, to five or six degrees below zero. We were under cover; we had a large fire and a tree that had been overturned for a seat. Among the men were two of indomitable spirit who had been in situations far worse than this. We began by making the best of our situation.

When the poet Scarron[1] was without a roast his wife told him a story. We now imitated Monsieur Scarron and listened to the tales told by these men. In the home of the poet Scarron only meat was missing, whereas with us supplies of every kind were lacking. And so, primarily to keep ourselves from feeling our hunger too keenly, we chatted, joked, told stories.

M. Truro, a lawyer of considerable wit, even invented a game— the game of convicts. Seven judges were appointed. The rest of the group were summoned before the tribunal; each one confessed his crimes and was condemned to some special punishment to conform with our situation; one was to sleep outside exposed to the storm; another was to be deprived of supper; another was to find firewood. This made us laugh, while the storm outside threatened to grow worse. I, alone, accused of folly for having followed this foolish expedition, and for being the only woman among twenty-two men, was acquitted, in view of the courage I had shown. But I confess that although the conscience of my judges acquitted me, mine pronounced me guilty.

We continued to play, however, until midnight. The game of "Judge" made two hours pass. By then, as the cold redoubled in intensity, gradually the gaiety, laughter, and jokes died out. Now and again a droll word would revive our drooping spirits, sparkling suddenly among our subdued voices like a slender tongue of flame in a fire three-quarters extinguished; then silence, except for a groan, which I could not restrain.

"What is the trouble?" asked three or four anxious voices simultaneously, among which I failed to recognize that of Sir George.

"One side seems to be entirely frozen. In fact I can no longer feel my left arm or leg."

The men, who were huddled together trying to keep warm now arose, collected some stones from under the snow, put the stones in the fire to warm them, then, when they were heated, placed the hot stones in their overcoats, covered me with them, and revived me to some extent with these improvised warming pans. Sir George offered his overcoat with the others, even, I might add, among the first. This did not prevent me from weeping with pain.

Then the men gathered around me trying to distract me by chatting. As for the fire, it was valuable only as a means of roasting me. The side turned toward the fire cooked, the other froze. Finally, I fell asleep. On toward five o'clock in the morning, the snow ceased to fall; by that time it was three or four feet deep. We decided to take advantage of what in nautical terms is known as a lull in the storm. I was awakened and as I felt quite numb, the suggestion was made that I be carried on a litter; I refused, saying a walk would prove beneficial. In fact, this was the only way of keeping warm. Everyone put on his own coat or overcoat and began to proceed on foot, first cutting long sticks to use in finding the road. I tried to follow, but my legs gave way. Assisted by two of the men, I was placed at the far end of the procession so that the trail could be broken by those ahead.

At the first step one leg fell into a hole, which would only consent to release me after extracting a portion of my epidermis. There was still another inconvenience from which those who went on ahead could not protect me; namely, my skirts touched the snow-covered bushes bordering each side of the path and as the result of this contact were constantly damp.

At the end of an hour's walk, I resembled a woman made of

sugar-candy; my garments were frozen and, in place of keeping me warm, made me cold. But our greatest anxiety was the desert. How could we cross it now that it was covered with three feet of snow when we had had such difficulty getting over it in dry weather?

Upon reaching the desert, we saw that the size of the stones made the road more visible under snow than it had been when bare. However, there remained the stones that slipped under foot. For some time my shoes had been in shreds and my stockings useless. The result was both favorable and unfavorable. My feet were frozen, but at the same time I could feel nothing. At last the desert was crossed. This was our Berezina.[2] With that behind us we felt secure, and our high spirits returned.

The hunter's instinct was again felt by the huntsmen. When they began to look for tracks, they discovered the snow literally embroidered with kangaroo footprints. Seeing them reminded me that I was extremely hungry. It was one o'clock in the afternoon and we had had no food since four o'clock the day before. Despite my aversion to kangaroo, I began to yearn for a roast leg of this substitute for hare, which had seemed so distasteful to me no longer ago than last evening. Now I understood the cannibalism of my good friends, the New Zealanders.

Finally, at two o'clock, we reached the tent that marked our first stop. We were not expected until six o'clock and as a result nothing was ready. The maître d'hôtel was profuse in his apologies. He had only cold meat. Can you fancy this makeshift for a woman who yearned for kangaroo? We fell upon it and avidly devoured the cold fare. We next began to look at one another. The fire had turned us black; we resembled chimney sweeps and coal carriers.

A fine fire was burning briskly; water for washing face, hands, and feet was soon heated. I made some sandals from napkins which I bound around my legs like Greek buskins or Catalonian espadrilles; we then proceeded on our way. Everything had frozen. On slopes too steep for the snow to cling, a polished surface slippery as a mirror had formed. The men slipped and fell like so many Capuchins with sandals, whereas my buskins held the frozen surface as if I had been roughshod. Now it was my turn to laugh at them.

Suddenly M. de Bellegarde, who was in the lead, stopped. "Wait," he called. "Here's a track that is unmistakable."

I approached with the others; the snow was striped by a long spiral.

"Oh," said the men, "a black snake has just passed this way."

At the words "black snake" I uttered a cry and clutched my skirt as if the viper were hiding in the folds of it. The black snake is the terror of Van Diemen's Land. It is a black reptile three feet long and an inch in diameter, and has a flat head dominated by two thick sacs under the eyes containing venom that is forced into the wound by a duct that leads through the teeth themselves. The pressure of the jaws serves to expel this venom, which penetrates deeply and instantaneously mixes with the blood. There is no known remedy for the bite of this atrocious creature. There is one curious thing about it, however, which is not based on proof: namely, that no matter at what hour the victim is wounded, he does not die until sunset. But at that moment death is inevitable; with the last rays of the day, the last sparks of life depart.

There is no instance known, according to rumor, where a native or a European, struck by a black snake, survived to the following day, unless bitten during the night; in the latter event his agony is longer, but invariably ends at the precise moment when the sun disappears from sight. Later we saw an example of the fatal and speedy effect produced by the bite of a black snake.

My husband and I were visiting Mr. William Moore of Hobart Town, when an extraordinary commotion was heard in the house. Mr. Moore rang to ascertain the cause of this noise and was told that the gardener's wife, who was gathering green beans in the garden, had been bitten by a black snake. We went out at once; the poor woman was just being brought in.

There was some hope for her; she had been struck in the heel and when she screamed her husband, who was grafting a tree not ten feet away, rushed over and with his pruning-knife immediately cleaned out the heel. A physician, who was called, bound the wound with cloths steeped in alkali and gave his patient alkaline water to drink.

The woman did not suffer much. But the numbness that began

with the wound gradually reached her heart. One-half hour before the sun set, her death agonies began, and when the last rays of day disappeared she gave a dying gasp. What is strange is that the snake is affected as much as its victim. Whatever wound it may have received, even if it has been cut to bits, the viper remains alive and moves until the sun disappears.

The one that wounded the gardener's wife had had its vertebral column broken by the victim's husband, then had been hung by the tail, and nailed to the wall. In that way there had been a kind of dissolution of continuity between vertebrae; and the weight of the head and the upper part of the body had lengthened the black snake by nearly a foot. And yet, notwithstanding this wound which should have brought death, life persisted; the reptile, like the woman, did not expire until evening. Both died at the same time. With such deadly powers, obviously the black snake is the terror of the colonists.

Thus the memory of Lady Franklin, wife of Sir John Franklin,[3] for several years governor of Van Diemen's Land, is blessed for the sole reason that she paid a bonus of ten shillings for the head of every black serpent brought to her. This reward was paid, not out of governmental funds, but from Lady Franklin's private purse. Sir John Franklin, governor of Van Diemen's Land, is the one who has since perished in the icy regions of the North Pole.

To return to our serpent. These men pretended they had seen it, but had been unable to overtake it. In extremely cold weather, snakes are not especially agile, and if the men had seen it, I am convinced they would have reached the reptile.

About eight o'clock that night, we finally reached the foot of the mountain. One hundred and fifty feet from the first slopes stood, as I have already said, the house of M. de Grave. We found him giving orders to five or six men armed with torches, who were about to start out in search of us. Having seen us pass, and not having seen us return, he was beginning to believe that some calamity had overtaken us; that we had been frozen, overcome by a tornado, or at least lost.

Of the eight or ten parties he had seen make the ascent since he had been living on Mt. Wellington, three had never returned.

Since his efforts were no longer necessary, he invited us to enter his house and wait for carriages, which he intended to have sent up for us from the city. Half an hour later the conveyances arrived.

In Hobart Town everyone separated to return to his own place of residence and change his clothes; we then arranged to meet at my house about eleven o'clock for supper. At that hour the entire party congregated in a commodious, warm, well-lighted salon whose two doors were opened at eleven o'clock to announce that "Madame was served." At my orders the maître d'hôtel of the Gaylor arranged to serve us an excellent supper. Its menu I left to his selection with the one recommendation, "No kangaroo." The party ended at four o'clock in the morning. What remained of the night did not seem like night.

Sir George, who should have paid me some compliments as our guest, managed to enter, dine, and depart without saying a word to me. This seemed like a wager, and I promised myself: "The first words he addresses to me will have to be extremely polite to make me overlook such rudeness."

CHAPTER VII

DOCTOR BLACKFORT

AS I REMARKED about Auckland, society in the islands of the Antipodes consists of three elements that are almost invariably the same: the employees of the government, the clergy, and the army. At Hobart Town, the governor, Sir Eardly Wilmot,[1] received frequently and had a large coterie of friends. Next in importance were the houses of the archbishop and the first secretary which were—perhaps I should not say more hospitable, for my idea of hospitality is not this constant feeling of restraint introduced into a salon under the form of etiquette—but more elegant.

After these two or three houses came that of the controller general, and two or three others where I knew I would be bored after being in those I have just mentioned. I do not include society in commercial and banking circles. It is impossible to give any idea of the enervating atmosphere in these aristocratic groups, with their somber gravity. This, however, is inevitable, for everyone is confronted with a convict population and is forced to set an example. Thus everyone must face boredom to prevent the others from finding life too entertaining. No one but an Englishman would show such devotion.

For my part, what I had seen had proved profoundly interesting; from the observations I had made I felt my time had not been wasted. Notwithstanding, I began to yearn for Auckland where I had my brave Maoris for diversion and good anthropologists to pinch my arm. I felt myself growing irritable, and knew that if my husband did not take me away within a short time from this stifling atmosphere, I should lose not only my looks, but also my health.

The capture and execution of three bushrangers, two wearing masks and a third carrying a gun while robbing farms, finally made me long to leave Hobart Town. There was something about the place that was extremely depressing. Robbery with masks, and robbery with guns in the case of colonial culprits, constitute a crime that is without appeal and punishable by death. Death is by hanging. That I deprived myself of this spectacle which undoubtedly would not have made me gayer can be readily understood.

The following day I happened to be in a certain house where, apropos of the death of these three wretches, a pathetic tale was told about Doctor Blackfort, a Protestant minister. This I shall now recount, for it will serve to illustrate my point that even in a government as admirably administered as that of Van Diemen's Land, there are, as everywhere, occasionally characters that escape the surveillance of their chiefs and are wholly unworthy of tasks with which they are entrusted. Here are two or three instances of this, which are, furthermore, possibly the only scandalous records of this character that are available.

The governor of Norfolk Island, the judge, and the doctor were involved. The two interlocutaries of the tale in question were, on one side, Doctor Blackfort and, on the other, a condemned man, John Cramner. For the anecdote to have any significance for our readers, it is necessary to explain who Doctor Blackfort was. I shall now describe him, for in view of the superb health enjoyed by this worthy minister, and the excellent care he takes of himself, I hope he will live forever and continue to make his eccentricities the delight of Hobart Town, much of whose gaiety would depart if God should call the worthy Doctor Blackfort to His fold.

Perhaps his name is not spelled exactly as I have written it, but I have my reasons for changing the orthography. In addition, the anecdotes I shall now recount, although new to France, are so well known in Hobart Town, that if I have used the name incorrectly, the first reader of these lines can readily rectify this error. Doctor Blackfort—every minister in the English church is called doctor— Doctor Blackfort at this period was a Protestant minister sixty years of age, fleshy, short, ruddy, well fed, who carried his head back and his stomach forward, and who minced along on short legs conspicuous by their thick calves, twisting his fingers over and over on his abdomen as he went.

His major preoccupation, and the road open to Satan if the reverend doctor were ever lost, was undoubtedly the table. His majordomo was the most important member of his household, and, like the laborer of Pierre Dupont [2] who was deeply in love with Jeanne, but who preferred that Jeanne should die rather than he should lose his beef, he would sooner part with his most intimate friends than his majordomo. And so Doctor Blackfort's majordomo was as well known in Hobart Town as the doctor himself.

The parishioners of the doctor who, on Sundays when the doctor preached at Church Hill, saw the majordomo slip into the church precisely at three o'clock, will attest to this fact. When he arrived a murmur was heard; everyone knew Doctor Blackfort's dinner was ready and the sermon would soon come to an end.

In fact, the majordomo does not need to say a single word, or make a single sign to his master; he merely comes and kneels piously in his place. At whatever point in his sermon the doctor may be, he understands one thing; namely, that God who is eternal can wait without any inconvenience, whereas dinner, which is a daily event, cannot wait without growing cold. And so the doctor pauses.

"My good friends," he says to his congregation, not unlike a novelist at the end of a chapter, "my good friends, this will be concluded the following Sunday."

Then he descends from the pulpit, takes his majordomo's elbow, and says: "Come, Tom, come," as he disappears at a brisk walk. Such is one of the men especially entrusted with holding service at the prison and in bringing lost souls into God's fold; he is an exception, however.

According to the story, there was a master cook, a veritable *cordon bleu*,[3] who excelled especially in making jellied calves' feet and who was about to be executed. Doctor Blackfort's majordomo, who was also an artist, had frequently attempted while his associate was practising his profession in the city, to obtain his secret from him, but the convict, who, being a Britisher of Great Britain, was unusually conceited, obstinately refused to part with it, and, when he had escaped, had taken it with him. In the meanwhile the majordomo lived in the hope that the fugitive would be captured and that his invaluable recipe would not be lost.

The hope of the majordomo was soon realized; the bushranger, having entered a farm wearing a mask, was condemned to death, and by a coincidence Doctor Blackfort was summoned to officiate during his last hours. As the latter was about to leave the prison he requested his majordomo to have his dinner ready at exactly four o'clock.

"Do you know the man whom you are to console, Reverend Doctor?" asked the majordomo.

"No," replied the latter with an indifference that proved rank was nothing in his eyes.

"What, you do not even know his name?"

"His name, it seems to me, is not a sin."

"No, but it is significant."

"What is he called?"

"John Cramner. Nothing more."

"John Cramner! Wait a minute, wait a minute," replied the doctor.

"Does the reverend doctor not recall that clever chef?"

"Certainly, the one who made such excellent jellied calves' feet?"

"Exactly."

"And who would never part with the recipe?"

"Never."

"Wait, wait," said the doctor, "I shall take the rascal out on a little road that is somewhat rough."

"Oh, sir," replied the majordomo, shaking his head, "I would not do that if I were in your place."

"What would you do, then?"

"I would attempt to win him over by kindness."

"And thus obtain his recipe?"

"Exactly, sir."

"Calm yourself, Tom; he will give it to me, or explain why."

And the doctor departed, saying to himself: "Doctor Blackfort, you are a simpleton if you cannot procure this recipe for jellied calves' feet."

Having reached the prison, he was taken down to the dungeon of the criminal. There he began an exhortation upon death such as only those who know Doctor Blackfort and have heard him preach can imagine. It was a lengthy series of banal sentences on human repentance and divine mercy, such as are kept in readiness by orators of vulgar minds to use on occasions of this character for souls hardened by habit, and uttered with half-closed eyes, with that shaking of the head characteristic of worthy men and with a swelling of the voice at the beginning of every phrase, terminating invariably in the same words uttered in the same tone as the rest of the discourse: "My dear brother, now do me the favor before you die to give me your recipe for jellied calves' feet."

The first time the condemned man heard these words he believed he had misunderstood. He turned toward the doctor. "If you please, Your Reverence?" he asked.

"My dear brother," replied Doctor Blackfort, "I believe I am not committing an indiscretion by begging you to give me, before you die, your recipe for making jellied calves' feet."

"Have you been sent to me by the government, sir, to prepare me for death, or to ask for this recipe?" asked the prisoner.

"Certainly to prepare you for death, my brother," replied the pastor.

"Well, then, do your duty as a minister; I am listening."

"Then I should like to remark, my very dear brother in God," responded the doctor, sanctimoniously closing his eyes, lowering his head, and clasping his thumbs together, "I should like to remark that I have come to administer the last sacraments of the Church."

"I hope," he continued, subduing his voice which he gradually lowered to a new intonation, "I hope, that I find you fully disposed to consider the extent of the crime you have committed toward God and man. But why are you so reluctant, my dear brother, to give me your recipe for jellied calves' feet? Remember clearly that when you are no more you will repent of having refused me, but it will be too late."

Then in the same voice Doctor Blackfort continued: "Your fault is great, my good brother, but it is written: 'I love the sinner who repents far more than the just man who has never sinned.' Provided that you repent, my good brother, you are then in a better position than the just, since you have committed a crime which he has not, and since you are expected merely to add to this crime the repentance that he cannot have, for what shall he repent who has not fallen? So you, my dear brother, are in the best position to win grace. That is why I, who console you in this way, I, who am retained to strengthen you, that is why I feel I am justified in asking you, as recompense for the trouble I have taken in your behalf, for this recipe which can no longer be of use to you since, in three days, you will be in heaven."

This exhortation lasted for three days. During these three days all the sentences of the doctor ended in this prayer, spoken with every gradation of persuasiveness and passion. But either because he was merely stubborn, or because he had promised to retain the secret of this famous recipe until he died, John Cramner steadfastly declined to satisfy the doctor's request, to the great disappointment of Tom who daily at four o'clock awaited his master on the threshold and when he came within sight called out: "Well, sir, did you secure it?"

"No," replied the doctor with a sigh, "but by God's grace, Tom, I will."

Then Tom would sigh in turn, while the doctor sat down at the table, sampling each dish with the tip of his tongue, as he remarked: "Ah, all this, Tom, all this is not worth the famous jellied calves' feet; but I hope that at the last moment he will relent."

"God will hear you, sir."

And the meal ends as mournfully as it began. Even after arriving at the scaffold, after the sentence was read, and after poor John had the noose around his neck the doctor made a final attempt. This time, however, the victim interrupted him.

"Mister sheriff," he said, "be good enough to remove the Reverend Doctor Blackfort, who prevents me from thinking of my welfare."

This time the doctor saw that there was no more hope, and withdrew with bowed head.

"Well, sir," cried Tom to his master as far as he could see him.

"Ah, the poor man," replied Doctor Blackfort, "God forgive him, but he died without final repentance."

The position occupied by the doctor among convicts was why he was usually consulted about all improvements introduced into prisons where they were confined, even regarding details of corporal punishment. When the old scaffold, furthermore, proved too narrow, a larger one was erected. One day Doctor Blackfort was invited to visit this new work of art. The doctor measured the scaffold with his usual dexterity, roughly measured the space reserved for each victim, and his work was done.

"Eight can be comfortably hanged," he said, "but nine will be inconvenient."

## Chapter VIII

## THE BASKET OF CHERRIES

THE restraint placed upon the society of Hobart Town and the constant necessity of posing before the convicts have already been mentioned. The placement of convicts with families has also been discussed, as well as the improvement in their morals by the good examples set before thm.

A tragic example was afforded by Mr. M——, one of the most substantial merchants in the city, an example inflicted, in the words of the Scriptures, on his own flesh. Mr. M—— lived near the falls, within a few steps of the factory, in other words, the penitentiary for women. There he had a magnificent house with a charming garden in which he raised flourishing specimens of all the fruit trees of Europe. Of all the inhabitants of Hobart Town, Mr. M—— alone had succeeded, after considerable effort, in raising and acclimating a cherry of the type that for some inexplicable reason is known to us as the English cherry.

Mr. M—— was a widower. The family consisted of himself and two sons, one whom, called William, was twelve years old, and the other aged eight, Tom; and three daughters, the eldest of whom was fifteen years old. The fourth unit of the family was an Irishman, the brother-in-law of Mr. M——. The entire domestic staff of the house, a staff totaling a dozen servants, belonged to the convict class. The gardener was a ticket-of-leave man, that is, he had become free by virtue of pledges given for good conduct; he was employed by his own choice at the house of Mr. M——.

It was during the latter part of the Australian summer that the cherries, anticipated by the entire family, who had been deprived of fruit in that particular year, promised at least to compensate for the light crop by their beauty. Finally it was decided that on the following day, after breakfast, the crop would be gathered. After breakfast Mr. M—— went out into the garden to inspect his cherries. During the night the tree had been entirely stripped of fruit; a theft had occurred. But who could have committed this theft? There were no strangers about; the dogs chained under a shed nearby had not bayed. Someone in the house must have been the culprit. Mr. M—— called his gardener.

"Céleri," he said to him, "look at the cherry tree."

"Yes," replies Céleri, "I have already seen it—early this morning."

"Not a cherry left?"

"Not one, sir."

"Evidently," said Mr. M——, "this has not been the work of thieves."

"No, sir. Someone has taken them."

"Someone has taken them! There is no doubt of it, good God, but who?"

Céleri rolled his eyes, but remained silent.

"Are you certain of your assistant?" asked Mr. M——.

"As I am of myself, sir."

"That is good! You may go, Céleri, and when you see the children, tell them I am waiting for them here."

The children who were day scholars were just leaving for school. I refer to the two boys; the girls had a governess. Both came.

"Willy," said the father, addressing the eldest of the two, "do you know who stole the cherries?"

"No, Father," the child replied.

"Do you suspect anyone?"

"Certainly," said the child, "it is Céleri, the gardener. I saw him under the tree this morning with a basket."

The gardener was there.

"You hear, Céleri," said Mr. M——, profoundly moved.

"Yes sir, I hear," replied Céleri coldly.

"And what reply do you make to this accusation?"

"God keep Master Willy from ever being in my shoes!"

"Céleri," cried Mr. M——. "Do you mean to imply that my son might be a criminal some day!"

"I said nothing, sir, I merely uttered a prayer to God."

"You are insolent, Céleri."

"Not intentionally, sir; by saying what I just said, I meant to be humble."

"That will do. You and your assistant will remain under arrest until someone can come from the penitentiary to search you."

Céleri bowed, and he and his assistant were locked by Mr. M—— in a room whose key he placed in his pocket.

"And now, Willy," said the father, "do you swear that it was not you who ate or stole the cherries?"

"No, Father," replied the child, "it was not I, it must have been Céleri."

"That will do; go to school and if you are reprimanded for being late, explain that it was not your fault, but mine."

An hour later, Céleri and his assistant were seized and placed in the penitentiary as criminals. The situation was serious; this meant either the privations of Norfolk Island, or the loss of their tickets-of-leave. Toward noon, Mr. M—— was called to the penitentiary to swear to the charge. He went, much preoccupied, but without the slightest doubt that his accusation was just.

Scarcely had he taken fifty steps in Campbell Street when he saw in a fruit stall a magnificent basket of cherries. Mr. M—— stopped abruptly. He believed he recognized his English fruit. If this were actually true, a much more simple way could be found to convict the thief. He entered the market, and asked the price of the cherries. The proprietress named a fabulous sum, some two pounds sterling.

"The devil," said Mr. M——, "that is fairly expensive, I should say."

"That's true, Sir, but what is rare is never dear."

"In fact," said Mr. M——, "I know only one garden in Hobart Town that has this superior fruit."

"That of Mr. M——."

"Exactly. But how do you happen to have his cherries?"

"Probably he prefers to sell them rather than eat them."

"And through whom does he sell them? His gardener?"

"No."

"What, no?"

"He has them sold by his children."

Mr. M—— turned pale as death.

"By his children!" he repeated. "Impossible. You must be mistaken."

"I am not mistaken. Two charming little boys. I had a visit from them at daybreak."

"And you are positive that these two children are the sons of Mr. M——?"

"They told me so, at any rate."

"Would you recognize them?"

"Perfectly."

"Ah well, wait for me; I shall return. For I am Mr. M——."

And Mr. M—— rushed out of the store, ran without stopping to the school, had his children called, took each one by the hand, and led them without saying a word, to the fruit market.

"Do you recognize them, Madame?" he said, pushing the two children into the shop.

"Certainly," replied the proprietress.

"You are the one, Willy, who sold the cherries to Madame?"

"Papa!"

"You are the one, Willy, who sold the cherries to Madame!" Mr. M—— repeated in a terrible voice.

The child was silent.

"Well, Madame," said Mr. M——, "the cherries are yours; you can sell them in any way you like and at whatever price you choose."

Then he took the two children by the hand.

"Come," he said. And he led them home and locked them in their room. Then he immediately went out to find the gardener and his assistant.

"My friends," he said, "I have suspected you unjustly. I offer you my most sincere apologies."

"Oh, sir!"

He extended his two hands to them.

"Forgive me," he said. "You especially, Céleri, for you were the one I especially insulted."

"With all my heart, sir; but what has happened?"

"Nothing. Now will you do me a favor?"

"Willingly, sir."

"Invite not only my friends but your friends, Céleri, to assemble here tomorrow morning in the greatest number possible.

"Sir."

"You understand?"

"Yes."

"Well, then, be on your way."

And he indicated with his hand that they were to depart. In the meanwhile his brother-in-law arrived.

"Well," he asked, "so you have freed the gardener and his assistant?"

"Yes," replied Mr. M——.

"They were innocent, then?"

"They were."

"Who were the culprits in this instance?"

"Willy and his brother."

"Willy and his brother?"

"Yes. Except that Willy alone was the instigator. Willy alone should be punished."

"You say that, but when the time for punishment comes, I know you will weaken."

"Not this time."

His brother-in-law smiled with an air of doubt.

"Furthermore," said Mr. M——, "you will be there, brother, and if I weaken, you may remind me."

And having clasped his brother's hand, Mr. M—— entered his home. He did not appear for dinner at four o'clock, nor in the evening at tea. Feeling anxious, his brother-in-law came and listened at the door. He heard him weeping and sobbing. He attempted to enter the room of Mr. M—— but the door was fastened on the inside.

"God help you," said the Irishman, for he realized that whatever had occurred that could make a father weep in this manner must be terrible.

By the following day the servants had fully executed the order that had been given them. At eight o'clock in the morning all the friends of Mr. M—— and a hundred acquaintances assembled in the garden around the stripped cherry tree, where they had been asked to gather. Everyone enquired what had happened and attempted to ascertain the object of the gathering.

Mr. M—— appeared, extremely pale. He greeted everyone, but without making any comments. Then a moment later the two children were brought in. The eldest walked ahead, weeping and frightened, not knowing what was about to happen, but trembling from head to foot. He wore only his summer trousers and a shirt. His brother followed fully clad; obviously he was merely to act as witness of what was to take place. But he was equally pale and trembling. The three sisters were standing with their governess on one side under a tree. The father had requested them to be there, too. Clad in little dresses of white muslin, with their charming faces pale as death, they had much the aspect of three statues. A mournful silence prevailed among all the bystanders.

"Gentlemen," said Mr. M——, "I have the honor to summon you here to assist at the execution of a robber and false accuser. This wretched child whom you see here has succeeded in making me commit an irreparable injustice against two men who were innocent."

Then he related the entire story, adding: "I believe this merits punishment that will be remembered throughout the entire life, both of the one who receives it, and of those who witness its application."

Turning toward the man who had brought the two children, he said: "Remove the shirt from the culprit, and tie him to this tree."

With a trembling hand the man took off little Willy's shirt and fastened him to the cherry tree. Then Mr. M——, raising his eyes to heaven, muttered: "God give me strength to punish my own child as I would a stranger!"

Drawing from under his overcoat a whip with several lashes modeled after those used to punish prisoners on Norfolk Island, amid the shivering but silent spectators he began to strike the child. Probably the father would have preferred to submit to the penalty rather than inflict it. His muscles and nerves were those of a man moved by grief, yet he was able to control and fortify himself against suffering while he struck a weak being who bent under each blow! Of all the spectators there was not one who was not weeping, yet not an arm was raised to deter him. Everyone counted the blows by the echo that each blow made in his heart.

During the first thirty-five blows the child cried. Then he was silent; he had fainted. Mr. M—— continued to strike. The child, according to his father's wish, was condemned to receive fifty blows of the lash. At the fortieth the Irishman stepped out of the circle and seized his brother-in-law by the arm. "Enough," he said, "enough!"

Mr. M—— turned questioning eyes to the circle that surrounded him.

"Enough," cried all the spectators.

"Have I done my duty as judge and father?" asked Mr. M——.

"Yes," replied all the voices.

"You will remember what you have just seen?"

"Always."

"Then leave, and report what I have done to whomever you may meet."

The spectators filed out one by one past Mr. M——, bowing to him with deep feeling. Then when the last had departed, he said to the Irishman, "Brother, send for a surgeon; the culprit has been punished, the child must receive care."

And he went and locked himself in his room. Today this child is one of the most honored citizens of Hobart Town. He relates this anecdote himself and when anyone doubts the severity of the punishment, he displays the scars that still form ridges on his back.

CHAPTER IX

THE BARRACK AND THE CASCADE

THE detention house for men, as I have already said, is called the penitentiary and that for women, the factory. The special names by which they are designated are the Barracks¹ and the Cascade. To add a final word of explanation, there are two factories for women, the factory for assignees, and the factory for punishment.

The factory for assignees, that is, the house for women who have left service and those who are in a position to enter service, is called Brickfield. The establishment where women go to pay the penalty imposed on them is called the Cascade. Here at the Cascade, in addition to the punishment of the tub which, as indicated, consists in washing the clothing of the prisoners, they are appointed to miscellaneous tasks. For these services they receive compensation stipulated by the government. They wash the residents' clothes. They make straw hats, the straw being sent out from Europe. They unravel old rope, whose hemp is to be used in making new rope. They make commercial linen, and linen to order, all for the profit of the government. Each supervisor has the privilege of selecting from the women of the Cascade the one who seems the most promising and training her for what in English is termed a "first hand."

Every branch of industry has its own group and own quarters, and every unit is set off from the adjoining group by having its special dormitory and separate recreation grounds. The women wear a uniform consisting of a white bonnet and blue skirt in summer and brown in winter. A Protestant pastor and a Catholic priest are attached to the establishment.

Every morning the women, upon rising, go to the chapel. On Sundays they attend all the services. In addition to the supervising matrons, who preside over the work, there are also women instructors. The latter have charge of the literary and moral instruction of the convicts, teach them to read and write, and give them advice as to conduct. Each quarter furnishes its daily contingent. Each individual receives instruction three times a week. A group of cooks has charge of feeding the entire group. The food is good and consists in the morning of a kind of broth called gruel; at two o'clock, a thick soup, beef, and potatoes; in the evening, bread and tea. When a woman has served her penal sentence in the Cascade, she is sent to Brickfield and becomes assignable. If, during her period of punishment she is guilty of misconduct, she is returned to the Cascade for a term determined by the authorities.

The dormitories and courts of the Cascade are immaculately clean. Each morning everything is washed and scrubbed, stone by stone; the visitor might think he was walking on marble. Assignable women, that is, those living at Brickfield, also have tasks to perform, but nothing more arduous than sewing. Like their sisters of the Cascade they, too, have women instructors.

The penitentiary for men has no subsidiary. Unlike the women, whose punishment is confinement, masculine convicts are sent to various stations on the island, where they are employed by the government in tunneling mountains, leveling roads, and constructing houses. They are divided into gangs or squads and placed under the surveillance of a guard. Whenever a new station is established, a chapel is immediately erected, then a large house with dormitory, refectory, etc.; so that the daily routine moves as smoothly as if the camp had been established for the past fifty years.

The conduct of each man is recorded, day by day, in a register kept by a guard; and the government never fails to encourage good conduct by favors. At the penitentiary male domestics can be procured just as female servants are available at Brickfield. However, a considerable distinction should be made between the social value of men and that of women.

The women, with comparatively few exceptions, are London courtesans of the lowest order. The men belong to all ranks of English society. There are deserters, political exiles, young men of good family who, in the flush of youth and heat of passion, committed crimes. Thus, to this land have been sent O'Briens and O'Meaghers, martyrs of Irish nationality. Many of the convicts are instructors in families; some are secretaries to the leading members of the government.

I have explained that at the time of my arrival at Hobart Town, Sir Eardly Wilmot was governor. He was extremely kind to me, and received me graciously, so in a certain sense I fulfill a duty in devoting a few lines to the death of this just man, of whom slander has made a martyr. It is trite to observe that Sir Eardly was a gentleman of the old school, since I have said that his name was Wilmot. He came out in 1844 to replace the famous Sir John Franklin. His wife, Lady Wilmot, remained in France, where she was supervising the education of her daughters. Sir Wilmot reached Hobart Town with his two sons. The eldest, Henry Wilmot, aide-de-camp to his father, was sent by him some time after his arrival at Van Diemen's Land to New Zealand to carry on a war against the Maoris; there he became a major, and there we met him. The youngest remained near his father.

Thus Sir Eardly Wilmot, far from his wife and daughters, was almost in the position of a bachelor. He was a man of haughty manners; he believed he was justified in leading a life of comparative freedom, provided he conscientiously fulfilled his duties as governor. As a matter of fact, he was extremely punctilious in all governmental matters. He did what no governor had done prior to that time: he mounted his horse and unescorted went to visit the various stations, appearing unexpectedly either during working hours or during mealtime. If it were the hour for work, he watched to see that the work was proportionate to the strength of the worker. If it were the dinner hour, he sampled the soup, the meat, the bread. If any of this was poor, the supervisor was immediately discharged.

No complaint was ever presented to Sir Eardly Wilmot without an investigation being made. No just request was ever made that was not granted. Among the unfortunate governors sent out to work with the convicts, there have been some just individuals. Sir Eardly Wilmot was far superior to them, for not only was he just, but he also had a sympathetic heart. Yet both in public and private life, Sir Eardly lacked that hypocritical austerity that is one of the basic virtues of a governor.

Sir Eardly Wilmot attended many parties, gave charming entertainments, and took long excursions with the ladies of the city without being aware of any impropriety or without a thought of evil. But this was more than adequate to afford grounds for the gossiping puritans to condemn him.

A formal accusation of debauchery and extortion was made against him in England, but he was too high-minded to know what was transpiring in the baser regions of mistrust and jealousy. He ignored the intrigues of office-seekers. One day one of his secretaries heard about the report and succeeded in procuring a copy of the denunciation. He came to Sir Eardly. The governor was standing in his library, reading. His secretary told him what had happened; this Sir Eardly declined to believe. The secretary showed him the document.

"Read it to me, sir," said the governor.

The accusation was so infamous that the governor rightfully should have ignored it. But he lacked courage. He turned pale as death, dropped his book, and placed his hand on his heart.

"In attacking my honor," he said, "they have broken my heart. They have killed me."

Nevertheless, he continued to fulfill his duties with the same zeal as before, but from that day on he felt that he had been, as he had said, mortally wounded. Fifteen days later he was confined to his bed. From then on he gradually grew weaker, with the insidious malady which the English refer to as a broken heart.

By this time the English government had acted on the denunciation and, without securing fuller information, appointed a new governor, Sir William Denison,[2] whom they sent out to Van Diemen's Land. He reached anchorage on the evening of Sir Eardly Wilmot's death; but, having learned aboard the ship on which he was traveling that his predecessor was in his death agonies, he refrained from firing the cannon or allowing any celebration.

Sir Eardly was no longer living in the governmental house for this had been made ready to receive Sir William; he was in a tiny cottage into which he had been moved to leave the large residence free for his successor.

The first visit paid by Sir William upon landing was to Sir Eardly. He found the latter in agony. The two men shook hands silently. Sir William left Sir Eardly with the words: "God be with you." The following day he passed away. The death of Sir Eardly Wilmot plunged the entire colony into mourning. For two days, in place of the lone bell that usually tolled for departed souls, every bell, not only in Hobart Town, but in every city in the colony, announced the demise of the former governor. Every ship at anchor reefed sail and lowered its flag as a sign of mourning. The entire army, to the last soldier, was commandeered to escort the body; all the convicts asked for and obtained leave to participate in the solemn obsequies.

The cortège was led by the new governor, who came on foot and followed immediately behind the hearse, and by the sons of Sir Eardly Wilmot, all the dignitaries, and all the officials of the island. Then came the inhabitants. For three days the shops and stores of Hobart Town were closed, as if for a public disaster.

Then an investigation was held, and the past conduct of Sir Eardly Wilmot surveyed, although in the minds of the public he was entirely innocent. This inquiry revealed one thing: namely, that Sir Eardly had never committed any fault but that of conducting himself like a great lord. The blame should be placed on the English government and not on his shoulders. Why send a Rochester to command a penitentiary of convicts?

CHAPTER X

THE SHEPHERD AND THE GOLD NUGGET

I WAS BEGINNING, as I have already said, to be bored with Hobart Town and to desire a change. So at the end of two months Mr. Giovanni told me that, in view of my entreaties, we would leave for Launceston and from there for Port Phillips. I confess that this news was extremely agreeable to me and the day for departure, left to my choice, was set for the following one. I was already beginning to have that zest for travel which has since made me, if not the most agreeable, at least the most adaptable traveling companion in the world.

We departed in one of those handsome and excellent English mail coaches that make ten miles an hour. Thus in ten hours we covered the hundred English miles [1] that separate Hobart Town from its rival, Launceston. Nothing could be more delightful than the route along which we traveled; the verdant country, dotted with charming cottages, recalled Normandy and England. I might add at this point that I had not seen Sir George since our excursion to Mt. Wellington; we left him at Hobart Town.

Launceston is the counterpart of Hobart Town, but lies on the sea rather than on the Derwent, and faces north rather than south. I have nothing further to say about Launceston than that it bored me to extinction after a few days and that, as there was nothing to detain us there, one pleasant morning we went aboard the *Shamrock,* a steamer plying between the ports of Port Phillips, Twofold Bay, and Sydney, and took our departure from Van Diemen's Land after remaining there three months.

Port Phillips is situated on the far side of Banks [2] Strait directly opposite Launceston in Australia. Large steamers, however, remain at Port Williams. Some strange caprice accounts for the development of Port Phillips where only small boats can land. To reach it, the banks of a river are followed—forgive my ignorance which, notwithstanding, I hope may prove one of the charms of the book—for I do not recall the name of this river. But what I do know is that these banks are merely a long series of slaughterhouses where sheep are killed; tanneries where their hides are prepared; and factories where their fat is prepared for the market. Here and there appear white mountains twenty-five, thirty, and forty feet high; these are the bones. These slaughterhouses, tanneries, fat, or rather tallow factories, these bones forming pyramids along the banks, give forth a pestilential odor that made me regard Port Phillips with horror even before arriving.

The commercial activity of England in fine wools, sheepskins, and Australian tallow, is well known. I have never seen herds like those that clip, as Virgil says, the hills and plains of Port Phillips. These immense solitary plains seem like vast seas where each sheep forms a wave. The various herds are in charge of free emigrants, Scotch, English, and Irish. At the time of our visit the port was only a mass of houses, but this mass was increasing daily. Out of it a city appeared to be rising. Wealth, abundance, future luxury, all could be sensed in the affluence that was apparent on every hand.

But since this was only mildly interesting to us, we might have remained only twenty-four hours at Port Phillips had we not been detained by curiosity aroused by a certain event that had just occurred. A few days before our arrival one of the keepers of these vast herds just indicated had appeared at the shop of Mr. B——, one of the leading goldsmiths of the city. The merchant knew at a glance that the man who had just entered his shop did not have the aspect of a purchaser. "What do you wish?" he asked.

The Irishman (it was an Irishman) drew from his pocket a shabby, ragged handkerchief, unrolled the handkerchief, and from its folds extracted a brilliant object the size of a loaf of bread.

"Look, Mister Jeweler," he said, "I want to know what this is."

B—— looked at the nugget encrusted with stones, turning it over and over.

"Where did you find this?" he asked.

"Down below, while watching my sheep. I saw something sparkling in the sun and I said to myself: 'The first time I go to the city, I must show this to some jeweler. I came to the city, your address was given me, and here I am. Has this any value whatsoever?"

The jeweler touched the nugget. It was pure gold.

"Well?" asked the shepherd.

"This has some value, indeed," replied the jeweler, "but not so great as you think."

"But at least it is worth something?"

"Yes."

"What is it worth?"

"How much do you expect?"

"How do you expect me to know? It is for you to say what you can conscientiously pay me for it."

"Well," said the jeweler, "here are four pounds sterling."

"But you should certainly add some money to buy shoes, hose, and one or two old shirts."

"No, provided I give you what is actually the value of your nugget. But wait. After all I will give you what you ask."

And calling his wife he told her to prepare a package from his own wearing apparel of the things the shepherd required and to give it to him. Then, while his wife was wrapping shoes, stockings, and shirts in a napkin, he inquired: "Are there many stones of this type in the place where the sheep graze?"

"I do not know," replied the shepherd. "I stumbled on this, picked it up, and brought it in to you. That is all."

"Well, if you find more, bring them in, too."

"I am certain to find them."

"And you will bring them to me?"

"Certainly, I will give you first choice."

Mrs. B—— entered with the package. The Irishman thanked the jeweler and left, convinced that he had been duped. He was not mistaken; the nugget contained four pounds of pure gold, exclusive of the stones, and being virgin gold it was of the highest quality.

By the evening of the day the incident occurred, all Port Phillips knew the story. Almost immediately the demon of speculation spread its wings over the city. The shepherd was found and sequestered; a joint stock company was organized to exploit the gold at Port Phillips. Finally, the directors of the society sought an interview with the Irishman. An effort was made to persuade the shepherd to lead the speculators to the place where the gold nugget had been found. At first the shepherd shook his head and stubbornly refused. But after a series of promises and threats his resistance was overcome. "Well, then," he said, "I will take you there."

Until time to depart the shepherd was placed in a room, well fed and well cared for, but out of sight. An expedition was organized with shovels, pickaxes, carts, horses, mills for sifting the dirt, etc. Finally the expedition led by the shepherd departed. The party consisted of all the shareholders who wished to assist personally in the first work and of almost the entire village population, who, more or less inadequately equipped for the trip, attached themselves to the procession. Some even left without provisions, relying on what they could find. This indeed was a universal fever, under a sun that roasted all. We watched the caravan pass. It consisted of two thousand persons.

"As a matter of fact," said my husband, "I am tempted to follow them and see, not the mine they will find, but what they will do if the shepherd is a liar."

"Do go," I replied.

And my husband departed. As the trip held no interest for a woman, I let him depart alone. At the end of only four days I received news of the party from the advance guard of disappointed men. For two days the shepherd had led the caravan under a sun of thirty-five degrees; then, having reached a mountain wholly composed of rock, he had stamped on the ground, hands in his pockets, whistling, and saying: "Here is where I found it."

Soon everyone began to dig, spade, and pick, uttering a cry of joy at each hope, a sigh of grief at each disappointment. The following day a search was made for the shepherd to ask him again whether this was the place the nugget that caused all this disturbance had been found. But the shepherd had disappeared. The shepherd had been carried off by a speculator.

A capitalist had said to him: "You are unwise to content yourself with one-tenth of the dividends of the company. Come with me to Sydney; we will purchase whatever is needed for our work, hire two or three men to whom we shall pay good wages; we can return by way of the interior; from Sydney to Port Phillips by land is six hundred English miles. No one will recognize us; we shall both work as miners and divide everything in half. In that way you will not be disturbed."

The proposal was accepted. Thus the disappearance of the shepherd was accounted for. No one knew anything about this arrangement. I alone was taken into the secret, the speculator being a friend of my husband. Let us briefly complete the history of the shepherd. The speculator hid him in the bottom of the hold of the *Shamrock* and paid the captain eight guineas to waive the usual formalities for receiving passengers on board.

Having reached Sydney, the speculator fulfilled his promise, feeding, looking after, and humoring his Hen with the Golden Eggs. There the necessary tools were purchased, including a wagon, a cart, all working implements, guns, to the amount of fifteen hundred pounds sterling. Four men were hired and promised, in addition to two crowns daily, an equal amount in dividends. The itinerary that was to be followed in the interior of the country was traced and the day of the departure arranged. But when the time came to leave, the shepherd could not be found. The speculator called him, searched for him, sent others to search for him, but in vain; he was never seen again. His disappearance remains a mystery to this day.

But interest had been aroused; engineers were sent out to conduct experiments at points comparatively remote from one another and ultimately, after three or four years, gold mines were discovered. Today they are being actively exploited. I might say, in passing, that the speculator who brought the shepherd to Sydney, half laughing at the adventure and half serious at the thought of the results, happened to be my husband!

I left Port Phillips not, this time, on the *Shamrock,* but on a poor schooner that picked up belated passengers and followed in the wake of the steamer. Our vessel touched at Twofold Bay where she remained in port twenty-four hours. As there was nothing to be seen at Twofold Bay, and as I had complained about it, the major-domo of the hotel where I was stopping suggested that I might like to see the son of one of the leading chieftains from the interior of Australia who had come to form an alliance with a chief nearer the coast. The young man and his companions were camping approximately an hour and a half from the city. Of course I accepted. I was, as usual, the only woman in the party.

Having waited for the heat to pass, we departed about two o'clock in the afternoon. The road skirted the bay which has the form of an immense horseshoe; the route was entrancing. The only blots on the landscape were the hideous islanders scattered along the shore, fishing, or collecting shells and polyp cast up by the tides on the sand. The natives of Australia and those of Van Diemen's Land, although different in origin to what is claimed, are the two most repulsive types of the human species I have ever seen: receding foreheads, large stomachs, thin legs; they even lack the characteristics of the monkey who would undoubtedly be humiliated if the scientists made a connecting link between him and these men. How different from my charming Maoris of Te Ika a Maui with their silk garments!

After traveling nearly an hour, we found ourselves on the outskirts of a vast forest with somber foliage. Here and there as at home the tracks of a stag appeared in the copse, trails the width and height of a man were visible; they were paths made by natives who came to fish in the bay. Following one of them, we plunged into the forest.

Another half hour passed; then, suddenly, we found ourselves in a vast glade; in the center of it stood seven or eight tents. Of these tents one was conspicuous by its crown of reeds. This belonged to the young chieftain and as soon as he saw us he rose and came toward us. On either side walked an old man. I, being a woman, was the recipient of the first compliment. That these savage races never lack the natural politeness which is not always found in civilized races, is quite remarkable.

He invited us to enter his tent. Like the others, it was a kind of gigantic beehive covered with banana leaves and was not distinguishable from its neighbors except that it was somewhat larger and adorned on top with a crown of marsh grass resembling our reeds.

Our majordomo explained that the two old men who accompanied the young prince were the counselors of the King, his father; their task was never to leave him and to watch over him night and day. Within the tent a mat was stretched on the ground; in the center of the mat, the place where the young man was accustomed to sit was indicated. On the right and left, places were marked for the two counselors.

The natives were engaged in weaving from native grasses, garlands with which to crown their young prince. The flower of this local plant bears a marked resemblance to our daisy, and looked well on the locks of the young man, black as a raven's wing. He was eighteen years old, and, by contrast to the abominable Alfuros [3] we encountered everywhere, seemed like an Indian god.

I presented him and his two companions with some pieces of

English money. They accepted these coins, in which they delight, with obvious pleasure, and by way of appreciation first placed them in their mouths; then prince and counselors gathered their gifts, called a native, and said a few words to him in their own language. The native appeared to be the crown jeweler; he had been ordered to pierce the pieces so they could be made into necklaces and ear-rings.

After half an hour spent in satisfying our curiosity, we expressed to the prince our desire to take leave of him. Then, in order to do the honors of the forest, he insisted on leading us back to it and in fact did conduct us to its outskirts. But there, just as if venturing into civilization were prohibited, the two old men, who never left his side, stopped him, each taking his arm. We took leave of one another. This was my initiation into savage life.

The following day we departed. From afar we saw outlined be-hind Sydney the chain of mountains whose color causes them to be called the Blue Mountains. Nothing is more spectacular than the approach to Sydney. Those who have seen both ports say that only Rio de Janeiro can be compared to it; usually, however, the preference is given to Sydney. On the left, upon entering, appear the public gardens known as the Domains; on the right charming villas, or rather, magnificent stone palaces. Upon nearing port we saw the thousand picturesque details of the splendid amphitheatres that make up the horizon of Sydney.

Although we were traveling on a simple little sailing vessel, we had the good fortune to disembark at the quay used by steamships. We found quarters at the imposing Royal Hotel on George Street, the same street on which stands the concert hall. I shall never for-get the appearance of this vast hotel with its bamboo balconies on every floor. From the one off our room we looked down the entire length of the magnificent street, which is three miles in extent.

Our ship having docked at one o'clock in the afternoon, we en-gaged a carriage for three o'clock, the hour at which the fashionable world of Sydney appears in handsome conveyances, an event for which I donned an appropriate costume. At Auckland, at Hobart Town, and at Port Phillips society is invariably the same—employees of the government, the clergy, the army. On the promenade and at the theatre the aristocracy is obliged to consort with a mixed caste. On the drive I saw an ex-convict who was now a millionaire and drove four horses. The pavement of King George was open to the world at large.

But this does not hold true in the salons; and so society is no more amusing or interesting at Sydney than at Port Phillips, Hobart Town, and Auckland. Everything is "proper"; this expression covers everything. But by way of compensation nature has been lavish! The promenade follows the sea; it is called Macquarie Road, and was laid out by the wife of the governor of that name. It leads to the public gardens called, as I have said, the Domains, and to immense lanes of trees though whose dome the sun vainly attempts to force its rays. They are fairy gardens, gardens sketched by the pen of an artist. One of these gardens—there are two of them—stretches along the sea; the other lies in the interior.

The sight of giant bamboo, Norfolk pines capable of sheltering three hundred persons, lemon, cocoanut, date, banana trees and, in the shade of this tropical growth, a flower that made me cry with joy as the periwinkle did Rousseau, belies description. It was my favorite flower, which I had not seen since leaving France—the violet! Not only one—thousands of violets. I looked at them mournfully. The effect the sight of these violets thriving five thousand miles from their native land, and condemned to die there, had on me was extraordinary. I carried some of these same violets back to France dried in the leaves of a book, side by side with some daisies gathered on the tomb of La Pérouse[4] at Botany Bay.

Upon our return we ordered our driver to stop at the French consulate for we had a letter for the consul, M. Pharamond. This and our cards were now left at his door. The following day as we were having tea, the consul was announced—I call him my countryman—for my husband, as I believe I have already mentioned, is Italian, of Greek ancestry. He had come not only to return our visit, but to place himself at our disposal. He had secured tickets for a concert and asked us to accompany him as his guests.

I regretted leaving my violets; M. Pharamond, however, assured me that the concert would be over in ample time to take another walk in the garden. I heard a duet of Bellini sung with such medi-

ocrity by an Alsatian *Pollio* and a provincial *Norma* that my mind
was straying to a thousand other things besides Bellini, when my
husband quickly nudged my elbow.

"Yes?" I said, returning from the Antipodes, or rather from
France.

"Wait a second before glancing toward our right, then in an
instant, look."

I followed his advice, and after five seconds turned my head. I
saw Sir George. He and the gentleman with whom he was watching the play had already been presented to M. Pharamond. They
had reached Sydney within the last five or six days.

"Well?" my husband enquired.

"Well?" I replied, "I hope I shall succeed at Sydney in hearing
the sound of his voice and that he will do me the honor of saying
something if only 'Good-day, Madame!' "

"He is too much in love with you," said my husband laughingly.

"What nonsense," I replied.

And I turned my head the other way. I could not resist, I must
confess, looking from time to time in his direction; but not once,
at least while I was glancing toward him, not once did he look my
way. At three o'clock the concert was over; M. Pharamond had an
engagement that prevented him from accompanying us home; however, he insisted on placing his carriage at our disposal. We accepted. But having reached the gardens, we sent the carriage back.
I am a fairly good walker, and wished to see the country at my
leisure, so it was agreed that we should return on foot.

The garden was as entrancing as the day before; the violets
seemed to have opened by the millions in my honor. I gathered an
enormous bouquet. Then we explored grottoes full of cool shade on
the shore of the sea, streams fringed with myosotis that resembled
from afar a bed of turquoise, and all my favorite flowers, as well
as many more. At five o'clock we took the road from the house to
the shores of the sea where I amused myself as the tide came in by
leaping from rock to rock, defying the waves as they approached.

The distance was greater than we had realized; the air, instead of
growing cooler, became warmer as evening approached. Instinctively
I told my husband to hasten. No sooner had we taken ten steps in

George Street than we heard a kind of alarm clock ring. Soon carriages came by, traveling at high speed; pedestrians appeared running as fast as their legs would carry them; shop doors slammed noisily. I anticipated a revolution.

"What is happening?" I asked a gentleman who was running after his hat, which a gust of wind had just carried away.

"It is going to blow a Brickfield," he replied, continuing to stretch his arm toward his hat that seemed animated by a desire to escape.

I looked at M. Giovanni.

"It is going to blow a Brickfield," I repeated, "Do you know what that means?"

"No, indeed, but since the others are running, we must run."

We ran. A woman passed near us, dragging her daughter and uttering cries as if the enemy had just entered through a gap.

"Madame, in the name of heaven," I asked, "what is the matter?"

"It is going to blow a Brickfield," she replied, making the sign of the cross, which indicated that she was a Catholic, but did not explain what a Brickfield was.

And all the fugitives called out, as they did for fires: "Brickfield! Brickfield! Brickfield!"

The malady, it appears, is contagious, for we began to run like the others toward our hotel calling: "Brickfield! Brickfield!"

We were soon enlightened. A hot wind, like one coming from the mouth of a furnace, struck our faces, accompanied by a tingling which would seem unbelievable if we had not seen the atmosphere turn a reddish color and felt that we were breathing brick dust in the air. Then we understood that the "Brickfield" was the simoon of Sydney. In an instant the coat, white collar, hair and face of my husband were the color of brick.

"My God," I cried, "am I as ugly as you?"

"As a matter of fact," replied my husband, "you can say farewell to your gown and hat."

For my robe, pearl gray in color, had turned a reddish-brown; my hat I could not see, for I was wearing it, but I had this satisfaction upon my return.

Aghast, we reached the hotel; we were red from head to foot.

The brick dust had penetrated wherever air could penetrate. "Baths, baths," we cried, falling on the sofa of our room. As I disrobed to plunge into the tub, I said good-by forever to my precious robe of pearl gray and my poor little hat. May God preserve you, dear readers, from a Brickfield.

CHAPTER XI

## SIR GEORGE SPEAKS TO ME

OUR LETTERS of recommendation gave us entrée into all the salons of Sydney, as we had been introduced into those of Auckland and Hobart Town. Everywhere the same restraint prevails; almost everywhere, with some few exceptions, the same ennui. The streets resemble Regent Street and the Strand; the salons are miniature replicas of those of Sir John Russell [1] and Lord Palmerston; [2] the same stifling atmosphere is invariably present. They are like clocks that are wound every four or five years and run a hundred years without stopping, or failing to indicate London time.

Life is regulated by custom and order, from offices that are even more orderly, if such a thing were possible, than those of England, to the functions and balls given by the English residents. Nothing is impromptu, improvised, spontaneous; everything is dull and correct, takes place on the proper day, hour, and moment, a mere shadow of joy, a mere spectre of pleasure, brought about by the somber and tragic method of a society that is bound by restrictions.

Every year at approximately the same season, the governor gives two balls. One of these balls occurs, so far as I can recall, during the first days of December. All distinguished foreigners are invited to this function. Naturally my husband received an invitation for himself and wife. This afforded me an opportunity to carry out my plan of going to a ball in a gown trimmed with real violets. Fortunately at Sydney, it was possible to procure any material that could be found in London. By a careful search, French dressmakers could even be located. Thus, with a French dressmaker and London material, an intelligent Frenchwoman, when she is the only Frenchwoman present, should succeed in being queen of the ball.

I ordered a gown of white corded velvet with flounces of magnificent lace that I had brought from France. I trimmed the dress myself, ten minutes before the ball, with garlands of violets. I also fastened two bunches of violets in my hair, and made an enormous bouquet to be carried.

The only jewels I wore were some fine pearl ornaments I had purchased at Batavia, consisting of a necklace, bracelet, and earrings, each pearl being separated from its neighbor by a small diamond; and I made my entrance into the ballroom with the confidence that is inspired in women by the feeling that their costume is simple, but at the same time in perfect taste.

The effect surpassed my expectations. As I was already known at Sydney as the French lady, when Monsieur and Madame Giovanni were announced, everyone turned. More than three thousand miles from Paris, I felt that I represented France, or, if you prefer, Frenchwomen. This indeed was a heavy responsibility, especially to represent those of today; for good taste is not always revealed in the costumes of my compatriots, especially those who wear elaborate bouquets of flowers, feather, ribbons, and laces, all on one unfortunate hat. Our national honor was saved; I was an immense success.

Immediately I was surrounded by every dancer in the room; the men congregated around us until I was almost suffocated and asked me for more quadrilles than I could have danced at three balls. I wrote down twelve or fifteen; then, since I believed that after fifteen quadrilles it would be time to depart, I closed my list. M. Giovanni, observing that I was receiving considerable attention, left me, as was his habit, to look after myself, and went on into the card room.

A quadrille was played, and I took my place with dancer number one. When I was engaged with my first partner, and before the second dance, I saw Sir George leaning almost opposite me against a console. Not once did I look at him in such a way that he could catch the gleam in my eyes. I cast only a few rapid glances in his direction and whenever I turned around he was always in the same position, not having moved during the entire quadrille. The dance over, my partner led me to my place. It was now the turn of dancer number two. He appeared at the first note of the orchestra. The quadrille commenced. Sir George still kept his back turned to the wall and leaned against the console. But he seemed very pale. Naturally I did not in any way connect this pallor with myself.

The quadrille ended, yet Sir George did not move. The orchestra began the prelude to a waltz. My waltzes, like my quadrilles, were engaged; my waltzing partner appeared. It was the French consul, M. Pharamond. I was overjoyed to dance with a fellow countryman, and never, perhaps, have I moved with more ease and—my God, I was about to say because there had never been any intimacy between me and M. Pharamond—with more abandon. He was an excellent waltzer of the type that takes as much pleasure in this kind of exercise as I myself; we did not stop once. In the circle we described my gown must have touched Sir George every time we passed him. He appeared to recoil, in so far as possible, to avoid this contact.

The music ceased. M. Pharamond took me to my place and asked if he might send me some refreshments from the buffet. I asked for a glass of lemonade. A servant brought me the glass on a silver plate. I had just taken it and was about to raise it to my lips when I saw Sir George detach himself from the wall and come directly toward me. I inferred that he was about to ask me to dance. I pretended not to see him and raised the glass to my lips. Soon, however, I felt him near me. Something like a magnetic current made me glance toward him; I felt a desire to laugh hysterically. By this time he was as pale as his collar, two tears trickled down his cheeks, yet his teeth seemed locked with rage. I lowered my eyes quickly.

"Madame," he said, in a tone of voice gentle yet firm, a voice such as I had never before heard vibrate in my ears, "I am driven to telling you that I cannot allow you to dance another quadrille this evening, and if you do so despite my plea, I give you my word of honor, I will blow my brains out under the balcony."

I should have liked to have been able to leave with a loud burst of laughter, but this was impossible; one of the tears I had watched roll down Sir George's cheeks had just fallen. I turned my eyes toward him; his agitated countenance left no doubt as to the sincerity of his threat. A strange shiver of fear seized me. I laid the glass of lemonade on the silver plate, rose, and in a tremble, without glancing back, rushed to the card room and, leaning over the back of my husband's chair said to him: "My dear, unfortunately we must leave now. I feel ill."

He looked at me in astonishment and saw that I was on the verge of fainting.

"Sir," he said to a gentleman, who was betting for him, "take my cards, I beg of you, and play for me, for when Madame Giovanni leaves a ball she must be extremely ill."

Leaving his stake, which was one-thirtieth of a louis, he placed his arm around me, and led me toward the cloak room. I secured my wrap, our carriage was called, and we returned to the hotel. There my heart overflowed and I began to weep. All this was attributed to nerves, and it was not until two or three years later that I told him what I asked his permission today to tell my readers, as a wholly natural thing for which I could in nowise be responsible.

The next day the player who had taken M. Giovanni's cards brought him two or three hundred louis; he had passed three or four times and had continued to place the same bet for the one whom he represented.

I did not see Sir George at Sydney again, but I did learn that he had left with his friend, Mr. Stewart, for a trip in the Blue Mountains. A month later we left Australia to return to Auckland and it was a matter of considerable relief and pleasure to depart. We passed three weeks at sea on an uncomfortable boat whose name has escaped me. I was overcome with joy to return to my port of Auckland with its fruit, vegetable, and fish markets, its women nursing dogs and pigs on the beach, my Maoris smoking, together with the beautiful native women with the capes of Scotch silk and bare legs, and my bric-à-brac shops.

My house on the tiny bay proved to be in excellent condition; everything had been cared for by my fine Zealanders. We luxuriated in the joy of being "at home," so pleasant to the traveler who has recently endured for a period of five or six months life in a furnished hotel and table d'hôte food. I was rid of the famous kangaroo stew; and I listened to the singing of my tui who seemed to celebrate my return by airing like a string of pearls his most brilliant trills. There was nothing, even to the baying of wild dogs, that I would not have taken pleasure in hearing when, as Shakespeare says, they bayed at the moon at night.

We had been back now at Te Ika a Maui for approximately one week when, while walking one evening on the veranda with my husband, we saw signals being hoisted with the Australian flag. This indicated that a ship was coming from Port Phillips, Victoria, or Sydney. At the same time we saw a brig maneuvering to enter the port. My husband began to laugh.

"What is it?" I asked.

"Will you make a bet with me?"

"What?"

"That Sir George is on that ship."

I blushed unconsciously and answered only by one of those exclamations that have no meaning. But I was vexed by this pursuit. The following day the *New Zealander* announced that a boat had just come in from Sydney and that among the passengers carried were Sir George and Mr. Stewart.

CHAPTER XII

AN EXCURSION

AT THE TIME of our return to Auckland, the aspect of the city had completely changed, for the struggle between the English and Maoris was already growing tense.[1] Two warships were stationed in the harbor, and a surrounding wall had been built to protect the white population in case the Maoris should prove the stronger.

For some time I had been teasing my husband to make an excursion into the interior of the country; but he believed that the time was not opportune, since the English and Maoris were waging a bitter war. But I, on the contrary, insisted, finding a new stimulus to my curiosity in the complication of events. My husband began by refusing outright, then discussed the matter, then finally yielded. "What woman desires," says an old French proverb, "God desires."

During my expeditions among the tents I had become acquainted with a Maori chief, an ally of the English. I had purchased some curiosities from him and had succeeded by means of small gifts, in winning his friendship. It was to his house, in his *pa* ² that I expected to go. I believe I have already explained that the villages of Oceania are called *pas*. Furthermore, I had taken a few elementary lessons in the Zealandian language from M. Forster, the Catholic priest, with the result that while I could not converse fluently I could at least ask a certain number of questions and understand the replies.

When our excursion was decided upon, I profited by the absence of M. Giovanni to have the man and his wife visit me. No sooner was the woman in my sleeping room, than curiosity overcame her and she began to touch everything. The husband gave her a thump on her head and forced her to desist; then he in turn began to finger our possessions. I went out to look for a bottle of aniseed cordial, first giving each of them a glass of Bordeaux. They began by touching it and making a grimace, probably because the beverage was not strong enough. They were about to empty the bottle when my husband entered and discovered me engaged in pouring out drinks. The woman was squatting on her heels; the husband was looking at my curiosities; both had their glasses in their hands.

"But wicked woman," he cried, half laughing, half angry, "do you wish to pay a fine of one hundred pounds sterling?"

"What for?"

"You certainly know there is a fine of one hundred pounds sterling for whoever gives a glass of brandy or rum to a Maori."

"Yes, but this is neither brandy nor rum; it is aniseed cordial, so we are not infringing on the regulations."

My husband lifted the bottle from my hands, took the glasses from the man and his wife, and placed them all in a cabinet. We then began to discuss our trip. However, we had considerable difficulty in making them understand. Fortunately, in the meanwhile, Doctor Aubry entered and acted as interpreter. The chief and his wife seemed willing to guide us to a leading *pa*. I think I have already explained that this is the name given to a Maori settlement.

Then began a new struggle to overcome M. Giovanni's caution; but as usual, prudence gave way to curiosity and, three or four days later, preparations for the journey having been completed, we departed, guided by the chief and followed by a certain number of Maoris. Soon we reached the outskirts of the forest, which began one or two miles outside of Auckland. Having reached this point, we followed a cross road; my husband carried his gun and fired at birds, while my chief pointed out springs of thermal water at certain intervals along the road.

At each spring there was a group of tents housing an entire family, father, mother, children; then around the tents a multitude of pigs, flocks of chickens, and swarms of dogs. The village which was our destination was situated on the east side, the side near the Bay of Islands, in a delightful location with the sea visible in the distance through groves of trees.

One or two cries uttered in a peculiar fashion announced our arrival, and soon everyone rushed out of his hut and came toward us with a haste that proved that the chief had prepared them for our coming in advance. The large family of our guide made us especially welcome. In an instant the words, *oui-oui,* repeated over and over, were heard from one end of the *pa* to the other. Undoubtedly we were expected with as much impatience as the prodigal child, for the fatted calf, in the form of a suckling pig, had been killed in honor of our arrival. At the same time the Maoris scattered right and left to seize and wring the neck of every animal on which they could lay their hands. For a moment there was a hideous concert of squealing pigs, howling dogs, and cackling hens, like a revolt in the Ark.

A moment later eight or ten Maoris returned, one carrying a pig, another two dogs, another seven or eight chickens. At the end of an hour we had a chicken pilau, dog stew, and pig á la clay. Everyone knows how to make pilau, everyone knows how to make stew, but perhaps my readers do not know how to prepare pig á la clay. This is the way the dish is concocted. The pig is killed, rolled in clay, and placed in a pit where it is cooked; then when it is done the clay is removed together with the skin, the stomach is taken out and, after the intestines have been removed, rolled in leaves, and served warm with salt and lemon. My husband found this manner of serving pig far superior to our European method.

However, I did not even sample it, but feasted instead on pumpkins and potatoes which were not on the whole very unpalatable. After dinner we began to prepare to make ourselves as comfortable as possible for the night; under a kind of shed our traveling hammocks, that had followed us on horseback, were hung. A large fire was built, and we lay down, fully dressed, of course. It was extremely foolish of me to be afraid, especially after the way we had just been received, but I am constituted that way; if I know there is danger ahead I go to meet it like a man, perhaps even more boldly and more imprudently than a man, but when actually confronted with it I realize that I am a woman, I attempt to moralize; but it is too late, and I cannot turn back.

This time there was, as usual, no opportunity to withdraw. I was in my hammock with no protection but my husband, whose gun was in the hands of the natives, who were examining it covetously. Such a weapon would have been a priceless treasure to the man who carried it. Furthermore, my husband set an example that I should have followed, for he slept soundly. I, for my part, made a pretense of sleeping, but kept my eyes on everything that was going on around me. Every movement seemed to have a hostile significance and God alone knew the reason for this activity on the part of the islanders, who did not sleep all night.

But the following morning I found out that the purpose of this universal insomnia was to protect us, and that the entire tribe had remained awake in our honor. A few moments before the sun rose I fell asleep; for the past two hours I had been listening to the charming concert of birds that always precedes the approach of dawn in New Zealand. My rest was of brief duration; I was aroused by my husband, who had slept soundly and had not doubted that I had done the same.

The chieftain was waiting to initiate us into the mysteries of the catacombs of his tribe. He led us ahead a hundred steps into a glade. There he stamped with his foot. We had arrived. Then he removed a stone covered with sod which disclosed the entrance to a subterranean passage. He invited us to descend.

"Certainly," said M. Giovanni, "that is not difficult."

"I can manage it," I cried, and in fact jumped down onto the first step of an underground stairway that led far down into the earth.

M. Giovanni, seeing me rush ahead, followed, shrugging his shoulders. As usual I had started off in a determined manner. We descended thirty steps and found ourselves in vast catacombs that had been excavated fifteen or twenty feet underground. The entire village could bury themselves in these rooms. Every village has its subterranean retreat like the one we had just visited; in case of invasion, if the tribe is too weak to repel the invaders, they disappear. Unless through treason, it is impossible for a European to locate the catacombs.[3] Then, should they be discovered, since each catacomb always has three or four exits, while the enemy is groping in the darkness, the village clan emerges from cover and shoots the assailants in the dark.

Once, in 1847, the English decided to surprise a large number of natives who had congregated in one of the most important *pas* of Te Ika a Maui; they surrounded the village and entered, sword in hand. The natives were at prayers. The latter, after a short defense, aware that they could not resist, escaped through their catacombs. However, although nearly locked, the last ones could not close the hole in time and the English discovered it. Twenty-five soldiers, led by an officer, descended, and never came back.[4] Such catastrophes in general are unknown; the English conceal them, and the Maoris have no newspapers.

This time it was my husband who was ill at ease; I, on the contrary, found much of interest as we retraced our steps. Ten minutes later we were back in the village. A Maori chieftain, a relation of our host was awaiting us; he had come to beg me to act as godmother for a child whom his wife was expecting at any moment. He lived at the Bay of Islands.

Of course I accepted without any hesitation. First of all, this offered an excuse for a new trip, then, not everyone can have a godson or daughter in New Zealand, and I always enjoy having what no one else has. We arranged a day to visit the Bay of Islands. I purchased a few curiosities, among them a bellows which could be played like an accordion, then we returned to Auckland. I was delighted with my bellows which were carved in an exquisite manner.

CHAPTER XIII

## THE BAY OF ISLANDS

OUR SOJOURN at Auckland was rendered extremely monotonous by the general preoccupation with war. Thus I awaited with considerable impatience the day set for our expedition to the Bay of Islands.[1] Finally it arrived. The preceding night I could not sleep for joy. I had persuaded M. Giovanni in place of traveling overland, which was a journey of several hours, to round Cape Oton,[2] a full day's trip. I had also persuaded him, after considerably greater difficulty, to travel in an Indian canoe. For some time I had been extremely eager to glide through the water in this kind of arrow. At dawn we took our places in our boat. This, like all canoes, was an immense tree trunk that had been chiseled out into the shape of an immense fish with a hollow back that swam with head and tail out of the water. Six rowers formed the fins of this enormous cetacean.

They were seated, as was their habit, in single file; painted the same color as the skiff, they seemed to form part of it. Two places had been reserved in the center for my husband and myself. Once in the canoe, obviously it was imperative to retain the center of gravity; the lightest movement to the right or left, and the boat would capsize. To the Maoris, furthermore, all of whom, both men and women, are excellent swimmers, this is not even an accident.

As far as Cape Oton the wind was against us; we progressed by the laborious use of the oar, keeping within half a mile offshore. But after Cape Oton had been doubled we had a stiff breeze. One of the rowers prepared a small mast, then removed his wrap out of which he made a sail. This left him with a mere loincloth around his waist, in other words, his *tapa*. Thus we glided along, skimming the waves as rapidly as the gulls that flew on all sides.

It was in this same Bay of Islands which, on toward five o'clock in the evening, we entered under full sail, that Captain Marion Du Fresne and part of his crew were assassinated and devoured by the natives.[3] This occurred on June 12, 1772, and the memory of it is still so fresh in the land that when a French ship comes into the bay the natives ask if it has come to avenge the death of Captain *oui-oui,* massacred by their ancestors.

At the time we reached the Bay of Islands, the English village was completely demolished with the exception of the house of Monseigneur, the Archbishop of Pontvilliers. He owed this favor to the veneration the natives had for him. Three times the English occupied the village and three times the great chieftain Eki Eki [4] descended from the mountains and with his own hand tore down the British flag.[5] The Bay of Treachery had become the Bay of War.[6]

We went into the tent of the father of the child for whom I was to act as godmother and who was called Pouka Pouka. Madame Pouka Pouka had given birth that very morning to a daughter. Since the Catholic church had been destroyed when the village was burned, the ceremony took place in the dining room of Monseigneur, the archbishop, which had been converted into a chapel. I bestowed on my godchild the names of Louise Henriette Elaine, then gave her an Irish nurse. I had my reasons for doing this; I wished to take the infant to France. I consulted my husband about it and won his approval; then the parents, who offered a little prayer and finally in turn gave their consent.

I believed that I was about to have my tiny New Zealander when suddenly one morning the parents arrived in distress saying the child had disappeared. An investigation was made. Relatives from the interior had learned that Pouka Pouka intended to give her daughter to a godmother *oui-oui* who would take her to Europe. Reluctant to have her commit this crime of high treason against their tribe, they removed the child. This happened a month after my return to Auckland.

I remained only three days at the Bay of Islands. At the end of this period I went aboard my canoe and sailed toward the small bay which we entered without accident the following night.

# VOLUME II

## Chapter I

## SIR GEORGE AGAIN

THE day after my return I went strolling by myself, as was my custom, visiting the tents of my Maori friends, who, every time I appeared, if only after an absence of three days, welcomed me joyously. Running in front of me and behind me came a procession of babies, whose cries of welcome were not wholly disinterested, since I seldom left without giving them some small presents; either silver, or some little token. Suddenly I saw approaching from a distance two gentlemen whom I recognized, one as Mr. Stewart, the other as Sir George. I did not believe it would be necessary to change my route because of them, and so our trails crossed. As they passed, these gentlemen spoke to me and I replied by a slight movement of my head. Naturally I was discreet enough not to turn around, but no sooner had I taken twenty steps than I heard hasty steps behind me. I considered it wise neither to hasten nor slacken my pace, and continued on my way.

Suddenly I felt someone seize my arm and clasp it violently. I turned around to see who could be acting in this familiar manner. It proved to be Sir George. His eyes were haggard, he was as pale as death, his teeth were chattering.

"Madame," he said in a petulant and trembling voice, "it seems to me that the least you can do is to answer when anyone speaks to you."

"I replied by an inclination of the head, Monsieur; I cannot stop in the middle of the road and make you a curtsy."

"I say you did not notice me, Madame," replied Sir George in exasperation, "see that this does not occur again, for, if this takes place once more it may be I who will kill you, but the fault will be yours."

"Ah, Monsieur," I replied, "how monotonous your conversation is. This is the second time you have spoken to me and your subject is always the same!" Disengaging my arm from his hand, with a sudden movement I turned my back on him and resumed my stroll. But I could feel that he was remaining just where I had left him and was watching me from a distance. He did not take a step toward me. Where the road made a bend, I glanced back; the curve in the road hid me from Sir George. I was now free from further embarrassment, at least for the time being.

The following day my husband and I had tea with Lord Grey, now governor at the Cape. Lord Grey was a charming man, an aristocrat to his finger tips. Unfortunately he had to pose, as the governor of Hobart Town poses, as the governor of Sydney poses. Consequently, his salon was as tiresome as the other salons I had already visited. Our only pleasure was during the moments we were able to chat with him.

Toward ten o'clock Sir George and his inseparable friend, Mr. Stewart, entered. I felt myself blush up to my ears. I had said nothing to my husband about what had passed that evening, and I trembled, expecting Sir George to indulge in some new eccentricity which, if it should take place before my husband, could not fail to have a tragic result, in view of M. Giovanni's impetuous nature. However, Sir George did not approach me, did not greet me, did not address a word to me. In the conversation which soon became general, I joined; he avoided making any remarks to which I might feel called on to reply. I confess that I could not understand the conduct of this gentleman. I attributed his whims, amorous or choleric, to mental irresponsibility, and even today I am unable actually to find any other reason for his actions.

The evening passed in this manner. As I was about to leave, he came straight to me; I could feel his presence just as I felt it on the road. I did not look in his direction; I waited.

"Madame," he said, "will you forgive a poor fool who is powerless to control his feelings, and the extremely strange way in which he has conducted himself toward you? I am more unhappy than I can say, and I am especially unhappy at the thought of having displeased you to such an extent that I can never regain your good graces." Then, without waiting for me to reply, he left. Outwardly he had all the air of merely speaking to me casually; I alone heard the words he had just uttered.

Immediately after Sir George had left and just as my husband and I were about to take leave of the governor, Major Wilmot was announced. He was, as I have said, the son of Sir Eardly Wilmot, whose death I described some time ago. Like his father he was a true gentleman; we knew him and so I turned, with the smiling face with which a sympathetic friend is welcomed, toward the door through which he was entering. He appeared behind the servant who announced him. As he entered, a cry went up in Lord Grey's salon. Major Wilmot was so white that he seemed like a corpse rising from his tomb.

He had just received a terrific shock. The previous evening during a skirmish with the New Zealanders, his best friend, Captain Williamson, had been taken prisoner. Although thoroughly familiar with the unspeakable habits of the savages with whom he had to deal, Major Wilmot had, throughout the first day, a certain amount of hope. A Maori had been sent to the enemy camp to offer a ransom for the prisoner. He had just received his answer. The reply was a piece of human flesh that had been removed from the body of his unfortunate friend. The cannibals had eaten the balance. The natives of the island, by the way, eat only prisoners of war.[1]

For some time my sojourn at Auckland had been wearisome. War prevented excursions into the interior; and those who had friends in the army lived in constant fear of receiving gifts of the kind just sent to Major Wilmot—which was not a happy prospect.

So I finally requested M. Giovanni to shorten our sojourn at Auckland. My husband had nothing more to detain him at this place and was invariably so kind that he never refused any of my requests. He consented to our departure and urged me to begin to make final preparations. However, he did express a desire to participate before our departure in a great fête that the tribe of Eki Eki was about to give in honor of the tribe of Moa Moa.[2] Of course, I would enjoy nothing more.

CHAPTER II

EKI EKI

EKI EKI is the great chieftain who, during the years 1850 and
1851, headed the native war against the English. The place
where this fête was to be held was on the other side of the chain
of mountains that divided the island throughout its entire length,
and promised to be one of the most extraordinary celebrations of
its kind ever given. Enough food had been provided to feed forty
thousand persons for three days. Supplies for these three days included sweet potatoes, roasted pumpkins, rice, maize, roast pig,
small dogs, fowl, and various kinds of meat. Each of these delicacies
had to be served separately from a canoe, which was thus used as a
dish.

This was the great fête in which all English officials and Europeans in Auckland participated. The natives departed to a man,
clothed in their finest garments; the village gave up its living, so to
speak, as the tomb on the day of judgment will give up its dead.
The trip was the same one I had taken when I was to become a
godmother. This time, however, we did not make the voyage in a
pirogue, but in a European canoe. A place had been offered us on
the government ship that was carrying Sir George Grey to the Bay
of Islands, but I had declined, preferring to go in my canoe and
return on the warship. I must confess that few sights are more
inspiring than the view of the Bay of Islands covered with a large
part of the population of New Zealand. The natives were clothed
either in their straw matting and *tapa* cloths, or European coats and
no breeches; others wore breeches and no coats. Some, adorned with
blankets and cravats tied around their necks, walked as stiffly as
members of the House of Lords on their way to Parliament;
others had as their sole costume a small belt the width of four
fingers, and a large straw ornament standing upright in the hair.
Mingling with the crowd were the women with their large wraps
of gaudy colors knotted at the neck and their magnificent hair
hanging thick and glossy over their shoulders. The entire crowd
which was engaged in drinking, smoking, strolling, making them-

selves conspicuous, blinking their eyes at the Europeans and, to use a purely French expression, parading in the "Longchamps"[1] manner, presented an unique spectacle, the most curious I have ever seen.

Two English warships arrived under the pretext of participating in the fête, but in reality to watch it, for it was not without some trepidation that Sir George Grey[2] and General Pitt,[3] lieutenant-governor, saw this large group of natives congregate. However, orders had been issued not to disturb this gathering in any way. On the contrary, from the ships, which had all flags flying as if for a national fête and their entire bands out on deck, resounded such airs as "God Save the King" and "Rule Britannia." Furthermore, the two ships were so near shore that the natives heard every note of the English music.

Just when this music had put everyone in high spirits, our canoe arrived. I did not lose any time; as soon as I stepped ashore I glided out among a circle of dancers composed of two or three Europeans and a dozen natives. I glanced around, looking for my husband, who following my example had succeeded in finding a place among a dozen beautiful Maoris, with whom he was performing the primitive dance called the *"Pont d'Avignon"*[4] or *"Latour prends garde."*[5]

The leading chieftain Eki Eki, the man who caused the English so much trouble, was not at the fête, but was watching it together with an old friend and his wife from a lofty mountain. This old friend was the great warrior's one minister; his wife was his solitary aide-de-camp.

When the battle was about to start, Eki Eki placed his clothes on the ground and nude, with no other insignia of command than a plume placed in his hair, marched on the English. His wife did not leave him and since he fought with two guns, she loaded one while he fired with the other. Now all three, great chief, friend, and wife were there on the mountain.

The governor, Sir George Grey, having learned that Eki Eki was present, sent an aid-de-camp up to invite him to come down to the bay and honor the fête with his presence. Eki Eki, however, shook his head; he had no confidence in the invitation and remembered the last surprise of the English.

"Tell the governor," he replied proudly, "that he can come to his master if he wishes to speak to me."

When M. Giovanni and I had danced until we were weary, we sat down; I at the table of Pouka Pouka, the great chief for whose daughter I had acted as godmother, while M. Giovanni, somewhat more informally, rested on the grass with the dancers, who brought him large quantities of European food served in the Asiatic manner. From my table I could see him among his harem, and each time that our eyes met, he made signs indicating that he was finding considerable amusement. After dinner I begged Pouka Pouka to present me to his friends, the other chiefs, which he did immediately, adopting for my presentation this formula: *"Ma wahine, oui-oui."*

In other words, "A white woman, yes, yes."

And so I had the honor of rubbing noses with two or three of the most celebrated chiefs, which made me regret having insisted on this presentation. Following our example, several other Europeans dined and danced, but I doubt if any of them enjoyed themselves as much as we did.

To enable the party to end as well as it had begun, one of the warships sent us a canoe which the Maoris made every possible effort to prevent us from entering. My husband especially, so far as I could see, ran the risk of being pulled to pieces by the beautiful Kanaka women who crowded around him on all sides.

My preparations to depart did not take long, for I merely had to leave some cards in the village. As regards my good Maoris, I fully expected to say good-bye to them in person. Perhaps some day they might have betrayed me and killed and roasted me as they did Captain Marion (Du Fresne),[6] but what I do know is that they made innumerable protestations of affection when they departed. What proved most difficult to carry away was our collection of birds and miscellaneous curiosities. With my two hats and my three or four dresses, I could have toured the world.

We booked passage on the *Stevens,* a delightful little brig of 1,200 tons, that was making a tour of exploration throughout the Society

Islands. After sending aboard the usual furniture for our cabin, that is, my piano, my two Voltaire armchairs, and an excellent carpet, we embarked.

Toward evening anchor was raised, and for the second and last time we departed from New Zealand. The weather was foul. I did what I usually did under such circumstances—I retired. For five days the sea remained choppy, and we proceeded under a head wind. On the fifth day about two o'clock the wind veered and became oblique; the sea soon grew calm and the movement of the brig ceased to be troublesome.

There was soon considerable improvement in my condition, which for four days had been deplorable. But the other passengers as well had paid their toll to the sea, among the first being M. Giovanni. However, about eight o'clock that night, he was so insistent that I decided to put on a robe and go down to the salon for tea. As I entered the room—I was leaning on the arm of M. Giovanni—I felt him clutch my hand.

"What is it?" I asked.

"Look at the end of the table," he replied.

I looked and saw Sir George buttering some bread, exactly in the manner of Werther's Lotte.[7] Sir George, who, ill like myself and quite humiliated at having been sick, had just left his cabin for the first time. I confess that I may possibly have had a certain tinge of feminine vanity. Could I, truthfully believe indeed, that it was on my account that Sir George had embarked on the *Stevens,* and that merely to see me he had made a trip among the Society Islands?

You ask, "So you love him, then?"

I am certain there is not a woman who would not have asked this question. But is it necessary to love a man to desire to have that man shower you with certain attentions and to be humiliated if he ceases to notice you?

CHAPTER III

TAHITI

I HAD NOT seen my traveling companions until that time. We
carried twenty-five or twenty-six passengers in all; some fourteen or fifteen men, and eleven women. Several were traveling on
business. Others, like ourselves, were tourists. All were English except my husband and myself; he was Italian and I was the only
French citizen on board. The fact that I was a Frenchwoman, and
especially my French traits, won me universal popularity.

As soon as I had conquered my seasickness, I found myself on
the following day as much at home aboard the *Stevens* as I had
been on the ship that brought me from Mauritius to Auckland.
Having had tea, the beauty of the night, as I have observed in the
preceding chapter, lured us up on deck. There Sir George approached us and, after a respectful salutation, asked me how I felt.
Apparently he was growing more and more loquacious.

I was leaning on the arm of my husband, who assumed the responsibility of telling Sir George that until that time I had been
quite miserable, but that he hoped, as did I, that my illness would
not return during the remainder of the voyage. Sir George, too,
had suffered considerably, and when I first saw him in the salon
buttering bread, he, too, had left his cabin for the first time. Aware
that I was not taking part in the conversation, he bowed and departed.

From then on, as I have said, I resumed my normal life on ship-
board; that is, at six o'clock in the morning, after having thrown
three or four buckets of salt water over my body, I donned my
little white dressing-gown, always as fresh as if it had just left the
hands of the ironer, and, with head and arms bare, went up on deck,
teaching the sailors to sing while they pumped; listening to their
fantastic tales, or inventing some myself; and revolutionizing the
cuisine of the cook, who only knew how to roast meat and boil
fish, by going down into the galley where I introduced fricasseed
chicken, salmi of duck, and omelette. This started considerable
gossip among the ladies, who maliciously excused me to the men,

who did not malign me, by saying: "What do you expect? She is French!"

Yes, fortunately, dear ladies, I am French, which meant that I was always singing and never bored; that between music and cooking, between reading and strolling on deck, between chatting in the salon and chatting in the forecastle, the days, which seemed long and tedious for everyone else, passed quickly and pleasantly for me.

Sir George, however, made no further attempt to speak to me; his dumbness had returned. He even made a definite point of not coming near me. The dinner hour brought about a new revolution. The ladies, pretending to be fatigued by the sea, came to the table in their morning costumes. On the contrary, after the first day, I put on my evening gown, semi-formal and slightly décolleté, with short sleeves because of the extreme heat. Another scandal! Was I the mistress of the house to set the standards for the other passengers? At the end of eight days, however, there was not one single woman who failed to come down to dinner not only properly dressed, but even in her most flattering costume.

Observe, gentle reader, that these minor feminine disagreements at sea where distractions are so rare, always amuse the masculine onlookers to a marked extent, and even Sir George himself, despite his Britannic gloom, could not refrain upon two occasions from bursts of laughter. The contagion spread even to the captain, who was now obliged to wash before dinner. Once when he came to the table in his shirt sleeves I rose, returned to my cabin, and requested that I be served there. The captain asked the reason for my disappearance from the table, and I sent word that when I wished to dine with men in shirt sleeves, I would not bother to come down to the salon, but would remain aft with the sailors. Mr. Smith learned his lesson so well that he decided from then on to put on his coat before coming to the table.

One day I had an inspiration: namely, to have my piano brought from my cabin to the salon. After tea I began to play a quadrille, and ten minutes later a general ball was being held aboard the *Stevens*. And so the days passed until one day there resounded the cry of "Land." From Auckland to Tahiti not a rock had been seen. At the cry of "Land" everyone came up on deck. Off on the horizon appeared the peak of Orohena [1]—a blue mass silhouetted against the azure sky. As we approached the mass took shape; the lower areas of the mountain came into view and the land became a ruddy yellow, like ochre mixed with a small amount of bistre. Then great dark streaks were distinguishable in the mountains. These were the openings of valleys.

Finally, as we neared shore, the verdure itself seemed to descend the slopes and unfold at the foot of the mountain by the edge of the sea. Twelve miles out at sea the perfume of oranges, pandanus,[2] and gardenias [3] was wafted over to us. It was the breath of that terrestrial paradise called Tahiti. As objects became more distinguishable, verdant islets appeared to detach themselves and stand out from the shore. These proved to be capes shaded by cocoanut and pandanus trees whose gigantic flowers, an exquisite yellow-gold in color, dropped like an artillery bombardment.

The island, with the exception of some narrow passes, is surrounded by reefs over which the sea breaks. A mile or so from these reefs an Indian pilot accosted us. He was naked with the exception of his *paser*,[4] a piece of vari-colored cloth which the Tahitians knot around their bodies.

Guided by this pilot, the *Stevens* moved boldly through one of these openings and, having passed the line of reefs, soon found herself in a sea calm as a lake. Kanaka skiffs came out to meet us. At the end of a two months' voyage, everyone was eager to go ashore, especially since this land had been described as a veritable Eden, by those who had already visited it. And so, with unusual alacrity we descended into the skiffs. These are built, like those of New Zealand, out of a single tree trunk, but are infinitely more picturesque. They are flat at the bow and stern, and are handled by a lone man stationed in the rear end, who propels the canoe by a paddle.

We alighted on the beach. Approximately four paces from the landing place lies Papeete. The village of Papeete [5] consists of a circular group, not of houses, but primarily of huts. What few houses have been erected have been built by Frenchmen. These huts, the habitations of the Tahitians, which are much like bird cages, are of ironwood; [6] they are long, low, rounded on the two ends, and covered by pandanus leaves arranged like tiles. They resemble immense trellises similar to those used on the walls of our gardens to coax the native vines and convolvulus to climb.

The inner roof is formed of exposed rafters weakly supported by two stakes placed at the point where at each extremity the roof begins to slant. In the houses of the wealthy these rafters are covered with mats done in red and black designs. In addition to their decorative features, they have the advantage of preserving the rafters from a kind of insect that infects them.

In appearance Papeete is both unsophisticated and charming; a land of white huts, bursting with song and laughter, shaded by gardens filled with cocoanut, guava, orange, citron, and pandanus trees.

The stranger entering the village finds shade, fruit, and perfume, in addition to pleasure, that invisible flower whose fragrance, furthermore, is invariably inhaled throughout the island. And what of the tree on which blooms the scented flower, that is, the Tahitian woman?

Woman in Tahiti is wholly absorbed with love. Her rôle is preordained; she has been created beautiful and she loves; that is her mission on earth. However, her type should be described, for it is essential first of all to become accustomed to her, before her charm is finally disclosed.

The Tahitian woman—one is typical of all—is small, round, copper-colored, and admirably proportioned; she blushes readily and obviously, a natural tint that shows through the copper of her skin, when pleased. Her hair is long, abundant, and somewhat coarse; some women, although these are in the minority, have chestnut hair with yellow ends. Her lashes are long and black, with eyebrows arched, eyes well spaced, and nostrils, like Indian nostrils, wide and keen to scent danger, pleasure, and love. The cheek bones of the native women project; the nose is somewhat flattened; the lips are defined by a kind of line. The teeth are white as pearls; the hands small and charming; but the feet which are invariably bare, are slightly turned in and deformed from walking.

The costume of all Tahitian women consists of a kind of cloth made up of four squares placed end to end; it is wrapped around the hips, and covered by a long straight garment hung from the neck. Behind the lobes of the ears, where the Maoris and New Zealanders usually carry pipes and tobacco, Tahitian women carry flowers, various kinds of wild roses,[7] gardenias, and a small green plant that they bring down from the mountains. As if aware that they themselves are merely living flowers, their deepest sympathy is for their sisters, the inanimate flowers; their coiffures like those of the ancient woodland nymphs are crowned by the same flowers they wear over their ears, that is, assorted roses and gardenias. They are born on flowers and brought up in the midst of flowers.

One day, however, they made the mistake of abandoning this charming coiffure, as the result of a speculation made by a man whose name has since had an unpleasant amount of notoriety in France. The missionary Pritchard[8] had had—where I do not know— an opportunity to purchase what is called in commercial phraseology a line of hats, which were hideous imitations of the type known as Mary Stuart. Whoever created such monstrosities, He alone knows. Then Pritchard preached a long sermon on the indecency of women coming to listen to prayers with flowers in their hair and ears, and he announced that henceforth God would look with favor only on those who wore his hats.

The shipment was placed on sale and immediately purchased. So long as the hats lasted, the Tahitian women were grotesque. Fortunately, they aroused so much comment, and the women agreed so universally among themselves that such a headdress was, if not hideous, at least ridiculous, that the style went out of vogue, and, at the risk of appearing unseemly in the eyes of the Lord or of not being recognized at all, they returned to their native coiffure.

But the memory of this headdress has remained even to our day and will continue to remain for some time to come; out of it an era emerged like the Mohammedan hegira. That era extended from 1840 to 1844, and is called the Age of the Pritchard Hat. The famous missionary made two or three thousand dollars by this pious change introduced into Tahitian modes; he asked nothing more.

## CHAPTER IV

## THE DAY OF A TAHITIAN WOMAN

THE TAHITIAN woman rises with the sun, that is, at six o'clock in the morning. In Tahiti the day has just twelve hours. The sun rises at six o'clock in the morning and sets at six o'clock in the evening. At these two times of the day it is possible to set a watch without fear of inaccuracy. In fact, a watch is unnecessary, God having given everyone the large timepiece called the sun. So at six o'clock in the morning the Tahitian woman rises with the sun. Upon awakening, she runs to the river, wrapped in the garment in which she slept. Having reached the edge of the stream where there is rarely more than a foot and a half or two feet of water, she removes her wrap and crouches on her heels; she then unfastens her hair, letting it fall like a veil, and through every pore of her skin finds a voluptuous delight in the invigorating freshness of the water. As all the women have this same habit, they congregate in the river between six and eight o'clock in the morning. This river is their club where they chat, or rather gossip—the only word that can describe their incessant chatter. They might be termed a flock of fresh water birds who warble in emulation of one another.

At eight o'clock the aquatic séance terminates; each woman has exhausted what she had to say, and is refreshed for a few hours; her appetite has returned, and she goes back to her house. The Tahitian woman in her food instincts is a true child of nature; like the Arab she eats heartily if there is much to eat; little if there is little. Her breakfast, frugal or abundant, is suspended near her hut from the branch of a tree in a basket. Usually the basket contains figs, a slice of breadfruit, and a piece of fish cooked in ashes, like the suckling pigs of the New Zealander, and wrapped in the leaves in which it was grilled. She begins with the fish, which she dips in a bowl of salt water and then drains before eating, just as we handle green walnuts. Finally she nibbles the fish; after the fish she has dessert, accompanying it with two or three glasses of excellent water brought from a neighboring spring. In this manner she breakfasts. When she has finished—the act of eating usually takes place inside her hut—she takes her mat, the small pillow on which she rests her head, and her Bible.

Then, carrying this load, she goes out, selects some tree—guava, cocoanut, pandanus, or orange—places her mat in the shade, lays her cushion at the tip of the mat, lies down on the mat, rests her elbow on the pillow, her head on her hand, with the other hand holding the Bible, and reads. Either from lack of interest in a tale that is always the same, or from drowsiness, gradually her head droops on its support, the Bible falls from her hand, her head seeks the pillow in anticipation of what might occur, the eyes close, and the reader falls asleep. Thus she rests for two or three hours, moving but slightly from the position taken for sleeping, or assumed when sleeping.

At noon or one o'clock she awakes. Still drowsy she runs again to the river. This time she wears her dressing-gown and her *paser;* as in the morning she quickly drops all her garments and kneels among her companions. Then the chatter begins again, but less rapidly than in the morning; it is warm and everyone is tired, even of talking. After one or two hours of bathing, she returns to her hut; but since the road burns the soles of her feet, she now walks on the grass and flowers which adorn both sides of the road. Returning home about two o'clock, she arranges her costume, braids her hair, places fresh flowers behind her ears, and goes out to pay visits in the village.

To whom? To the officers! The officers stroll, or smoke at their windows.

The Tahitian woman is fond of little drinks, cigars, and pieces of sugar. If she desires a little drink, she stops near the officer from whom she expects this gift, gives him her brightest smile and says: *"Ma namou iti"* [1]—a little brandy for me.

If a piece of sugar, the smile remains the same; the phrase alone varies. *"Ma tiota iti"* [2]—says the collector. This means: a little piece of sugar for me.

If she has an urge to smoke a cigar, the same smile, but a slight change in the formula. *"Ma ava ava iti,"* she says—a little smoke for me.

The officer gives her his cigar, the woman takes two rapid puffs which she soon exhales, then a third, which she makes as long as possible.

Thereupon, she coquettishly salutes the officer, returns him his cigar, and departs, her head turned back, making rings with the smoke which she throws vertically in the air. All this is accompanied by little flirtations full of grace. She then returns home by the longest route; it is four o'clock, the officers are about to dine at Marius's or Bremont's.

She has procured a supply of flowers in the officers' garden; she has two hours before her; it is now time for her, too, to dine and arrange her crown. The crown arranged, she dons her finest robe, a silk robe if she has one, then listens to see whether she can hear music in the government garden. At the first sound of the brass instruments, the Tahitian woman leaves her hut and walks toward the garden. She meets a friend and takes her by the little finger; thus they arrive, two by two, holding themselves like recruits on parade. Having entered the government garden, they squat on their heels, retaining with admirable equilibrium their balance during long hours.

Their numbers are soon so great, and they are crowded so closely together, that a pin thrown in the air would not find room to alight on the ground, and a variegated carpet appears to extend completely over the government court. At first immobile, and apparently interested only in listening to the music, they finally end by gradually moving heads, arms, then the whole body in unison. All this time, at least ostensibly, they do not appear to dance, but retire into remote corners where they can be seen keeping time while the carpet moves at the corners like a wave.

The officers promenade in the small openings that the Tahitians save for this purpose much as gallants strolling through the Tuileries, the Champs Élysées, or Gand Boulevard pass between the interstices of chairs. They speak a few words of Tahitian to their acquaintances; needless to say the Frenchman speaks Tahitian as he speaks all other languages, that is, badly. And fortunately, it should be added, the Tahitians do not speak French. They know only two phrases in our language, which they speak with a charming accent, suitable for a language entirely of vowels.

Here is the first phrase: *"Farani, allé tiné, il e tatra."*

But is this French?

Certainly; only it is Tahitian French. This actually means: Frenchmen, come to dinner; it is four o'clock.

Here is the second: *"Tantinet fanata tatou!"*

Do you understand? No.

"Sentinel, be on your guard!"

But why "Sentinel be on your guard"?

Because of the fact that when we were at war with the natives the sentinels, according to their custom, called from time to time to one another: "Sentinel, be on your guard!"

Remembering this nocturnal cry that attracted them, they repeat it without knowing what it means. About seven o'clock the music ceases. Then the Tahitians return to the shore. As they had rested for an hour, they now promenade in groups, the connoisseurs finding in the movement of their hips a rest from the governmental music.

They stop before verandas where officers are smoking and sipping their coffee. Then the *ma namou iti,* the *ma tiota iti,* and the *ma ava ava iti* begin once more. Each one has her small glass, eats her piece of sugar, smokes three puffs from her tiny cigar. Then, this triple gourmandizing satisfied, they remain and crouch as usual on their heels, attempting to play on their eminently French instruments variations of the music they have just heard. In this way a blissful hour is spent. It is the intoxicating moment of the day. The trade winds cease; the land breeze rises, bringing the aromatic perfume of the mountains; the sea is calm; the sun sets behind the island of Moorea, filling the west with fire, against which stands out in silhouette the blue mass of the mountains. Finally, taps, played by the bands on the ships at anchor, is heard from afar in the harbor. The final signal of retreat will be a cannon shot. But an instant before this cannon shot resounds, the entire group of Tahitian women, like a flock of vari-colored birds with flapping wings, disappears.

The cannon shot is the warning that they must keep off the

streets. The day of the Tahitian woman is now over and night begins. The majority of these charming doves enter a foreign dovecote. Everywhere the officers hold soirées. They play cards and a Tahitian game that resembles beggar-my-neighbor. The French, invariably gallant, have carried politeness to the extreme. They have learned this game as they have learned the language, at the same time and by the same method.

The soldiers who do not play, chat together; and, with those who do not care to play longer, talk of friends who are absent on expeditions in the island, or who have left permanently to return to the sterile land, as they call our France, la belle France.

The conversation runs as follows: Do you recall such and such a man, the first day we saw him on the river? *Avoi!* What would he say if he were here! He spoke Tahitian so well! *Avoi.* We shall never see him again! He is dead, *avoi!* He is married, *avoi, avoi!* Then they weep, repeating *avoi, avoi,* until the hour to depart arrives, when they take their leave.

Some, perhaps, do not depart. If they remain, they do not pass their time in idleness! There is no infringement of the regulations if they do not leave until day dawns. If anyone leaves, the officer must escort his departing guest or one who is entering, in order to protect the beautiful belated Tahitians from the sentinels.

At six o'clock in the morning, another day like the previous one commences; the next day is the same, and thus the hours pass indefinitely between bathing, flowers, music, gambling, love.

CHAPTER V

TAHITIAN MORALS

HOW WEEKDAYS are passed has just been described; life on Sundays which brings a change in daily habits will now be discussed. On the Sabbath the Tahitian sleeps all day and refrains from eating warm food. This, in conformity with the English custom, is a day of rest. The English have a law against making fires on Sunday for anything but tea. And since the Tahitians have never been able to accustom themselves to tea, everything is cooked a day in advance and eaten cold. All manual labor, including cooking, falls on the men; the sole task performed by women consists in making their own robes.

Unfortunately, they cannot dispense with the work of bringing their children into the world; otherwise they would force this labor on their husbands. As soon as the infant is born, however, it is left to its own resources on the grass. When an infant or child weeps in Tahiti, it is certain to be a European. I never heard a native child sob or cry. As soon as it is able to crawl, it is placed on the shore of the sea in a small hole in the sand made in such a way that the water comes up to its waist. The infant, who is warm, seeks coolness, gradually approaches the water, and one fine day ends by swimming like a duck.

In Tahiti the child learns to swim as he learns to walk, alone, without an instructor and without leading strings just as, six or eight years later, he makes love. Merely to watch Tahitians swim in these limpid blue waters, waters that are so calm that it is possible to see, thirty or forty feet under the water, the marvelous submarine growth that has gradually built up reefs of coral surrounding the island, is a delight. Imagine sponges of madrepore, where each hole is a dark and gaping abyss in which fishes of all kinds and colors— blue, yellow, red, and gold—are seen to swarm. Then, amid all this, without a thought of the abyss, rocks or sharks that pass from time to time with the rapidity of arrows in the pursuit of other fishes, the Tahitian woman plunges without other covering than her long hair into the water that seems with its clarity rather like dense air; she swims ahead, comes back, rolls over, completely at home in the sea. Occasionally she comes up to the surface to breathe, pitting her speed against the fishes that glisten like humid lights.

This constant contact with the water is what makes them so seductive to Europeans, and despite the abominable native or exotic pomades they use, they never have any trace of an unpleasant odor. They embody the fable of the nymphs of Amphitrite [1] following in the wake of their queen. Possibly those sirens might excel the Tahitians in singing, but they could scarcely surpass them in swimming. In the art of love, the Tahitian women have outdistanced all goddesses.

Bougainville [2] was the third traveller to visit Tahiti; the first was Quiros,[3] the second Wallis.[4] Bougainville named the land Nouvelle Cythère, a name that seemed to have brought in its wake misfortune. Ever since the natives of Tahiti welcomed Europeans, the population has diminished by three-fourths.

I saw a young Tahitian girl, scarcely fifteen years old, die.[5] Her name was Maïotei, and she faced death with a resignation bordering on indifference. I entered her hut one morning. With me was a Tahitian interpreter.

"Well, Maïotei," I said, "are you better?"

She smiled. "Yes," she replied, "by evening, I shall be dead."

In fact by evening she had ceased to live. The following day I returned. She was stretched out fully dressed on the mat and covered with flowers; relatives wearing *tapas* on their heads surrounded her. Every native man or woman who passed came and placed an armful of flowers on the child; then he or she knelt, covered the head with the *tapa,* gave a few sobs, and, sympathy having been extended, departed. The following day the parents of Maïotei carried her outside of Papeete. I enquired where the father and mother intended to inter their daughter. No one but they themselves know, was the reply I received to this question.

Tahitians, as a matter of fact, hide their dead, carrying them to remote and inaccessible places, and only relatives can ever find the tomb of the one they love. But tragedy is soon forgotten at Tahiti; life is easy, the air pure, the flowers abundant and perfumed. Why should the living brood over the memory of the dead? The mother thinks occasionally of her daughter; she remembers her when no one else misses her. For a mother always remembers her child.

The women are not jealous of their foreign lovers and cannot understand why the latter have such strong feelings in the matter. It is all so simple! The Tahitian who observes any irregular conduct on the part of his daughter, wife, or sister, would not think of being jealous. A young French painter, who had been in Tahiti for five years and who was still living with a young Tahitian woman, told me that he had endless difficulty preventing her from telling him about her many infidelities.

In 1845, word came from France that threatened to overthrow

these customs. The government proposed, if irregularities continued on such a scale, to force every woman whose conduct was a public scandal to wear a yellow robe. A period of fifteen days, that is, two Sundays, was allowed to elapse so that every woman might enter the path of virtue. After the expiration of this period, then watch for the yellow robes! The Tahitian women made a secret agreement and the following Sunday left their homes all wearing yellow robes. Every shade was represented, from jonquil yellow to a pale straw color. Being wise women, they had taken the matter into their own hands.

These irregularities do not prevent marriages—marriages between the natives, marriages between natives and foreigners. And nothing is simpler than a Tahitian marriage. They meet, please one another, love, announce the fact, and decide to live together. The woman now brings her chest into the house of her fiancé; the fiancé adds some small gifts to the property of his mate, and they are married. After marriage, they deceive one another, find it out, and forgive, but finally grow too indifferent to forgive. That day they disagree. The woman removes her chest and takes it elsewhere. The divorce is announced.

Frequently, this is accomplished in a more spectacular manner. During my visit to Tahiti, a young woman named Marietta listened to the solicitations of an Englishman and, contrary to all customs of the islanders, agreed to follow him to Europe. That same evening from afar, a woman was seen swimming toward the port. It was Marietta. Her Englishman, soon repenting that he had taken her, and aware of the disagreements this fantastic situation might cause, had decided that the course of wisdom was to throw her into the sea. Fortunately the ship was only fifteen miles away from Tahiti. Marietta swam home.

CHAPTER VI

THE INTERIOR

WE STOPPED at the Hôtel de France, run by Victor. Had Cook [1] and Bougainville, when they landed for the first time on the shore of Papeete, been able to foresee that some day there would be a Hôtel de France, run by a Frenchman named Victor, they would, indeed, have been astonished. Our accomodations consisted of a large sitting room with a sleeping chamber adjoining. But once ashore, it is not my custom to lounge in the comfortable rooms of a hotel. The day after my arrival, I saw everything there was to see in Papeete, so the next day I began my excursions. There was no way to travel except on foot. For several kilometers the route was over magnificent roads, naturally macadamized, which seemed made for easy traveling. They terminated, however, in native trails that disappeared in the mountains, where the traveler would have been obliged to alight, not only from a carriage, provided he had a carriage, but from a mount, provided a donkey was procurable.

These preliminary excursions aroused a keen desire to undertake a trip of some length. First I hoped to climb to the summit of Orohena but was told that only one person, an Englishman, had reached it. Englishmen, as we all know, climb where no one else can. Some day we shall probably read an account of the journey of an Englishman who succeeded in reaching the moon!

I was extremely eager to accomplish as much as the Englishman; but either because my husband had passed the word around, or because there was actually some danger of losing my life, I could not find a guide. I was forced to content myself with crossing the island and visiting the lake which is in the center of the mountains. After considerable urging, I persuaded M. Giovanni to accompany me. M. Giovanni could never understand, when he was stretched out on a comfortable divan with an excellent Havana cigar in his mouth and a cup of tea or coffee nearby, why anyone could think of leaving such comforts to go out and expose himself to the heat or cold and sleep on a mat in the mountains. Notwithstanding, since M. Giovanni was invariably accommodating, he always ended by acceding to my desires, even if these desires were wholly distasteful to him.

And so one fine morning we left Papeete with a native guide to cross the entire length of Tahiti. Tahiti has less than a score of miles of actual road, and because of the difficulties encountered the journey required seven or eight days.

No more Voltaire armchairs and comfortable soft carpets! A mat, and two or three changes of clothing each, comprised our entire luggage. M. Giovanni took his double-barreled gun, his inseparable and faithful companion on all journeys. The first stages of the trip were like walking in a garden; and what a garden! Gracious Lord, admit me into such a paradise and I will ask nothing more for eternity!

The roads, or rather great paths, that appeared to be graveled with fine sand, were ten feet broad and roofed with verdure so thick that the sun's rays failed to penetrate. For a ceiling there were bananas, cocoanuts, guavas, papayas, and the ironwood tree with its red wood and feathery branches that seemed like a huge asparagus plant run to seed; with, here and there, orange, lemon, and pandanus flowers—a trip through a fairyland that should rightfully be called the isle of perfumes. This is characteristic of the land not far from the seacoast; but upon entering the valley and reaching virgin vegetation, the difference is striking. Here were found bindweeds as in America, bamboos as in India, and the mappa [2] which bears a fruit similar to our chestnut, but tougher. The road soon terminated in a footpath, and the path in a sheer ascent.

We now entered a dense labyrinth of branches interlaced with the trunks of overturned trees through which we penetrated only with difficulty. When we thought we were walking on the ground, we discovered that we were on top of a mass of undergrowth from which we feared to descend. And when we thought we were walking on a solid tree, mistaking the parasitical plants that enveloped it for leaves, the weight of our bodies would cause this old stump, weathered by the elements and rotted by dampness, to crash, crumble, and fall, carrying us with it. Yet all this happened without personal injury; in Tahiti the abysses appear to be padded.

At one time these valleys were inhabited, and traces of the habitations are still found, but now they are all deserted. Fevers—for thus Tahitians designate the scourage that decimates them—have carried off three-fourths of the population. An old man told me that they were introduced by a black bird, that he had seen this bird, and that when the harbinger of death vanished from the island, it left in its wake a long trail of fire. This old man was nearly one hundred years old; he recalled having seen Cook, whom he called *tou-tou*.

Conversation between us and our guide languished; we succeeded in exchanging only a few words because of the limitations of our vocabulary. We knew enough to make our questions clear to him and he also understood us perfectly; but we failed completely to understand what he replied.

Evenings, when we were worn out, we searched for a piece of ground that suited us; we then indicated by signs or by our meager vocabulary: "We wish to remain here."

The native understood us, made a sign of acquiescence, and disappeared. At the end of five minutes he returned with an armful of banana leaves and a bundle of bamboo. In three-quarters of an hour, our hut was built. He attempted to make a fire. Phosphorescent brick, safety matches, and even flint are wholly unknown, or rather completely ignored by the natives. Fires are started in the following manner. I had often heard of the method of making them by rubbing two sticks of wood together, but I had never seen the least spark produced by this procedure. So I watched this operation with the greatest attention.

Our guide took two bits of ibiseus.[3] One was flat as a razor strap; the other was pointed like a stake ready to be placed in the ground. With the aid of the pointed stick he made a groove in the flat piece and, rubbing always in the same place, pressed down on it. First, at the tip of the groove, appeared a reddish spark. Next the red gradually became black. Then it smoked, and in the center of the groove glowed a small red flame. This was the fire.

The spark was then enclosed, ready to ignite and still feeble as the day it was born, in a bundle of dry moss. The guide now waved his arms like a windmill, constantly accelerating the movement. For a time the bundle smoldered, finally bursting into flames. The moss was placed on a fagot prepared in advance. Our fire was prepared! To procure food was an equally simple matter. The native disappeared again, returning with fruit from the breadfruit tree, a wild banana, an eel—caught where or how I do not know—and some fresh-water prawns as long as smelts.

Meanwhile, we prepared a New Zealand oven in the ground and at the end of an hour our dinner, cooked in banana leaves in place of a pot, was served to us on these same leaves instead of porcelain plates. Occasionally, my husband brought down a wild hen which he had us roast.

When evening arrived, the native disappeared again and returned with an armful of fragrant leaves which he placed on the ground. This was our couch for the night. The third day, after an interminable series of ascents and descents, and after an especially hard climb we found ourselves at the summit of sheer, cliff-like rocks that dominated the lake. The water below shone like a sapphire at the bottom of a gigantic well. The ascent had been difficult; at first glance, the descent seemed impossible. The vertical walls, that appeared to be of volcanic formation, offered by way of support to our hands and feet projections only two or three inches wide. The situation was extremely perilous.

The native was preparing to guide us over this dangerous route when we made him understand that such a route was impracticable; we had difficulty in impressing on him the fact that one man could not necessarily go where another man had gone. Finally we insisted, and he took the trouble thoroughly to inspect the cliffs. After considerable search a path was discovered; this path was a foot and sometimes a foot and a half wide. Compared with the trail he had recommended, this seemed a regal route.

After an hour's work, during which hands were required as much as feet, we found ourselves, not on the edge of the lake, but near a wide beach. At this point the shore was fairly extensive; it was covered with sugar cane, smaller than that grown in the Antilles, and also sweeter, far more tender, and more delicious. We laid in a supply for the rest of the journey. The cane afforded us considerable amusement; when broken and sucked like barley sugar it makes a delicious sweet.

But our troubles were not yet over. We had hoped to cross the lake but, as can be readily understood, there were no means of transportation. The guide left us. An instant later, not far behind, we heard the sound of a heavy body falling. We turned around. It proved to be the trunk of a banana tree that had crashed not fifty feet away. Then came a second thud, then a third, followed by fifteen or twenty more loud noises. We now realized that this must be our raft that was descending, by leaps and bounds, over the cliff. We were not mistaken. With the aid of some sharp sticks the Kanaka, in less than two hours, had constructed our raft, twelve feet long by eight wide.

The center of this raft was provided with a kind of buttress on which we sat astride; the native placed himself at the end, began to paddle, and we left the shore. An hour later we reached the opposite bank in safety. From the far shore we caught a glimpse of the sea through the trees. That same day we attempted to cross the island in its entire length. We then took a canoe and returned by water, doubling the southeast point of Tahiti, which was another voyage of three days' duration. Every night we drew the canoe up on the shore and slept at some village. Before disembarking at Papeete, we made a short visit aboard the French warship. Inasmuch as we were fellow countrymen, the French officers would not allow us to leave until refreshments had been served. Then the captain offered to present us to Queen Pomaré.[4]

Queen Pomaré, well known among us by virtue of the choreographic fame of her namesake, who was the illustrious friend of Mogador, the popular partner of M. Brididi, is the third heiress of that name. Pomaré I, who was born in 1762 and died in 1803 (1805), was called by her uncle to the succession of the Tahitian throne, which the latter had usurped. Having waged a long war against the insurgents, he finally subjected them with the aid of English arms. In 1797, he received the English missionaries on his island.[5] His first name was Otou; he was surnamed Pomaré, in other words, he who coughs in the night, for it seems that the illustrious founder of the dynasty of Pomaré was afflicted with an obstinate case of catarrh.

His son, Pomaré II, who was born about 1780 and died in 1821,[6] followed in the paternal footsteps, gained English support, reigned during an age of civil disorders, was forced to leave the island, was converted to Christianity in 1817, and, in 1819, baptized. That same year he gave a kind of charter to his people. It is his daughter who now reigns. She has changed her name, or rather her surname, three or four times. Once, during an inundation, she was on the point of perishing like Moses, when the man who was carrying her cradle, afraid to brave the waters with her, hung her from the limb of a tree. From this episode she derived the name of Vairaa Tou, meaning suspended from the branch of a tree, the tree from which she was hung having been an ironwood tree.

And when, following her exile in 1842, she returned in 1847 and was observed shedding tears over the condition in which she found her kingdom, this people, among whom names are vital and whose language is rich in imagery, called her Arii Tahi Moi; in other words, the Queen who weeps over Evil.

For a time there was grave danger that the Pomaré line would become extinct and everywhere the remark was made openly that if the Queen did not provide an heir or an heiress for the throne, it was not her fault, but that of her husband, Tapoa. The Queen, who was also convinced of this, bowed to the wishes of her subjects, repudiated Tapoa and married Arrisfaiti, the King who Ordains. The King who Ordains has revealed himself worthy of the important mission entrusted to him; in five years the dynastic line was strengthened by five princes and princesses. Unfortunately, the age of the Queen now prevents the line from being further extended.

Queen Pomaré is preparing at the present time to make a trip to France; the latest news received from Tahiti reports that she will honor the next Exposition with her presence.

## CHAPTER VII

THE REAPPEARANCE OF SIR GEORGE

OUR VISIT to the Queen was arranged for the following day. The august princess to whom we were about to pay homage had returned to her native land only a few months before. Having solicited, in 1842, the protection of France, one fine morning she took refuge on an English boat.[1] At length, finding the European attitude tyrannical, she returned to her kingdom, to the profound joy of the Tahitians. In honor of her return elaborate celebrations took place; a throne was erected on her veranda, and every district in the island sent a delegation to congratulate her and offer presents. These gifts consisted of fruits, materials, and silver. The King, Louis Philippe, sent as his contribution his usual present—some exquisite Sèvres vases. I saw them lying broken in a corner of the royal palace; the children were playing quoits with the pieces. Queen Pomaré, unaware of their value, had taken no more care of these vases than if they had been ordinary jugs.

Seated in her armchair, she received the delegations, while French music played the national air of the country, for Tahiti, too, has its national air, "Transform me, Brahma!" Queen Pomaré, observing that the English had their "God Save the King," and the French their "Marseillaise," desired, like a true queen, to have her own national air, so had selected from the "Lampe Merveilleuse" the air in which these words occur: "Transform me, Brahma!"

This refrain was adequate for her purpose and as it has no political significance it is probable that, if revolutions come, it will continue to remain the Tahitian national air.

The Queen, on this solemn occasion, was clothed in an abbreviated robe of Kanaka yellow. Her orator stood nearby, for in their primitive naïveté, the kings of Tahiti do not personally deliver the speeches prepared for them; they have an eloquent orator who discourses in their behalf. Around the Queen stood her maids of honor. Preceded by men and women dancing, each deputation approached the Queen; then came the women bearing gifts. They wore a kind of *poncho*[2] made from the bark of the breadfruit tree that was painted yellow and purple with *cuscumma*[3] and *mico juice*.[4] They were literally covered with flowers—the festive attire of the Tahitians. First they cast flowers at the feet of their Queen, next their *ponchos;* then they fell on their knees, weeping with bowed heads, and placing silver in the creases of her robe.

In the meantime, the orator spoke. The men followed, carrying fruits, pigs, chicken, in fact every kind of product of the island. In the evening there were fêtes and dances, while everyone grew intoxicated from drinking orange brandy. This, then, was the beloved Queen by whom we were about to be received, being taken to her home by officers of the French fleet.

We arrived. The Queen lived in a charming one-story house entirely surrounded by gardens, with mats on the floor and walls frescoed and painted to resemble marble. She was waiting for us in her salon, with ten or twelve maids of honor, a kind of flying squadron in the manner of that of Catherine de Medici, who had been selected from among the most noble and the most beautiful Tahitians of the island. I believe, however, that in Tahiti nobility is still synonymous with beauty. Beauty in these daughters of nature consists, as among our own handsome women, in a graceful and slender carriage, slim hips, long black hair and large, well-formed eyes, shaped like almonds. The eyes of these beautiful women of honor, either by natural endowment or deliberate intention, are unbelievably gentle. The nose is less flat than that usually found in the majority of the Kanaka race.

The Queen, aware that I was a white woman and, furthermore, a Frenchwoman, rose, came toward me, and spoke to me intimately. "You are a Frenchwoman?" she asked.

"Yes, Your Majesty."

"From Paris?"

"No, from a suburb; I was born at a small village called Auteuil."

"Where have you come from?"

"From New Zealand."

"Then you have seen the Maoris?"

"I lived among them; they were my friends."

"Ah! They are a fine race, a race of warriors! Did you know Eki Eki?"

"I have dined at his table."

"A great man, a great chief, a great warrior. Eki Eki, the Napoleon of New Zealand!" Then she asked me many details about the war, listening to me eagerly and revealing her sympathy for New Zealand. Soon she ordered refreshments. These refreshments consisted of pineapple juice, mixed with Madeira and sweetened water. Then, expressing her great friendship for the French, she invited me to come again.

Two or three days later I returned. She invited me to stay and dine with her, so I accepted. Dinner was served in the French manner. While we were dining, a French ship was announced. She proved to be a whaler. But while coming to fish for whales in the Pacific Ocean, she had had the idea of taking on a load of women's hats. Of course, these were hats that the shops of Nantes, Brest, Rochefort and Lorient had been unable to sell for the past three years. On a preceding voyage, her owner had heard rumors of the successful sales the good Mr. Pritchard made in hats, á la Mary Stuart, and the idea had occurred to him to do likewise. But hats, as far as he was concerned, were of the type of *bibis*. Having first paid homage and presented the Queen with three or four of his most beautiful hats, he next asked permission to place what remained on sale.

The Queen acceded to his request; she not only granted it, but even announced that she would take pleasure in seeing the ladies of the island adopt this type of headdress. Then, turning to me, she was kind enough to say that, although I had said nothing, yet it was because of my beautiful eyes that she had accorded the favor that had just been bestowed on my fellow countryman of the whaler.

The following day an assortment of *bibis* in red, blue, and white was offered for sale. The colors were patriotic, but quite ugly. The Queen's desire had been made known, and so the women bought these ugly hats to honor her court. The cheapest were sold at from thirty to forty francs. The captain stood aside, laughing at his good idea and holding his sides; the following day three hundred *bibis* of all kinds adorned the islanders.

While returning from dining with the Queen I thought I saw in the window of the Hôtel Victor a familiar head. At the same time my husband waved his arm at me. "Look over there," he said.

"Yes."

"Do you recognize anyone?"

"Yes."

The familiar head was that of Sir George, who had followed us, and who had just arrived with his friend, Stewart. My nightmare had returned. This time, however, the situation was more unpleasant. Not only did he refuse to greet me, but whenever he met me alone, he stopped, sneered, and uttered some rude remark. The poor chap had finally succeeded in thoroughly disliking me. At the end of eight days, he and his friend were the lions of Tahiti. They had quite a harem of Tahitian women, among whom they lived like pashas. This occupation distracted their attention from us and gave me more freedom of action. I continued my excursions and observations.

The French conceived the idea of planting vineyards in the island, teaching the Tahitians that the vine bore wine, that is to say, produced the liquor that they enjoyed so much and knew so well when they saw it in its glass container sealed with red wax. To set out the first cuttings of vines, they selected the garden of one of the richest inhabitants of the island, which was suitably placed, and explained to the owner the importance of the experiment, which he was permitted to watch. But they neglected to explain the different processes the grape went through before it was ready to be placed in the bottle. The result was that when vintage time arrived, the owner was in despair when he did not see bottles already sealed hanging on the vines. In his garden were also several vines of gourds and he failed to understand why these two plants did not bear the slightest resemblance to one another upon reaching maturity.

The Tahitians believe in ghosts, which they call Toupapao; fear of them often make men and women rush in terror into their huts, as if they had seen the shadow of their parents or their dead friends. During my sojourn at Papeete, a Tahitian, an extremely brave man, nearly died from fright caused by such an imaginary apparition.

A young painter named M. Charles Giraud, the person who acted as interpreter at the deathbed of poor Maïotei, had been here for four years. He lived with a Tahitian girl called Metua; his brother-in-law, to whom he was devoted, was one of the insurgents. Frequently, when weary of his brush and palette, he would take his cartridge box and gun and make a short journey. Now during the skirmish at Punani, a medical student named Porret, whom he resembled to a striking degree, was killed. Having seen the body of young Porret among the dead, Metua's brother mistook it for that of M. Charles Giraud. When the insurgents were about to throw the body of the Frenchman from a high cliff into a kind of abyss destined to serve as his tomb, the Tahitian approached and, placing his hand on Porret's body, which he mistook for the corpse of his brother-in-law said: "This man is looking at me; he is taboo; [5] I must have charge of burying him."

The body was entrusted to him; he immediately went down into the valley and piously buried it. This solemn office having been accomplished, he removed the dead man's sword and a ring he wore on his finger. The sword was taken to the government; the ring carried to his sister.

During the war it was not unusual to see a rebel, yielding to some feeling of piety, enter the city without demanding safe conduct, and surrender himself into the hands of the insurgents. The French invariably respected the motive that inspired the native to such conduct and allowed him freedom to return to his own people.

When Metua's brother entered Papeete about dusk, one of the first sights he saw was M. Charles Giraud coming toward him. Yet he had seen him lying dead and had buried him that same morning. For an instant he was paralyzed with terror, then cried: "Toupapao! Toupapao!" Then, as M. Charles Giraud continued to advance, he fled. When he began to run, the young painter, who had recognized his brother-in-law, began to run after him. That this belief in a phantom not only appearing before him, but even pursuing him, inspired fresh terror in the poor wretch, can be readily understood. Fortunately, his fear was so great that his strength failed; M. Charles Giraud succeeded in joining him, and convinced him that he was actually alive. This brave warrior had fled before what he believed was a ghost and had been almost out of his mind when he saw this apparition pursue him.

The men have an innate and native sense of chivalry. One of the chiefs who fought Fantahuha, that is, on the far end of the island where he made his stand during the revolution, was captured by another chief who served in our ranks, Tareiri, who will come up for discussion again. Led aboard one of our ships the prisoner, who was fairly important, was kept under surveillance by two sailors. However, one day when the latter had their backs turned, the Tahitian jumped on a gun-carriage and from there escaped into the sea. At the cry of alarm raised by the two guards, the men on deck ran for their muskets and opened fire on the prisoner. But he was already far away. Then, at the sound of firing, the guards on shore appeared. The fugitive decided on his course, and passed through the line of his pursuers. Then, leaping forward, he sped into the forest, and in a few moments was out of danger. But soon, by making a detour where no one paid the slightest attention to him, because of the resemblance between one native and another, he emerged on another road and went directly to the government. The tale of his escape was already known.

"I am such and such a person," he said. "I am the man who just escaped from the warship. If, while I was prisoner, I had offered to rally to your support you would have said: 'He is afraid.' I am free, and have come to tell you of my own accord I wish to be a Frenchman; will you accept my services?" Of course his services were accepted.

Tareiri, about whom I promised to say a few words, Tareiri—to digress a moment from the prisoner whose history has just been told—was a handsome young man twenty-five or twenty-six years old when he joined us and served in the French ranks, after having been chief of the district of Haapapé. In one of their raids against us, an attack in which the French triumphed and remained in control of the corpse-strewn battlefield, Tareiri lost his brother.

The body of this brother lay almost in the center of our camp. How could he slip through, how could he crouch, how, finally, could he make himself invisible? Yet he succeeded in finding his brother's body and removing it through the line of our sentinels and between the fires where the soldiers were cooking their suppers—how, no one knew. As a member of the French ranks, he became one of our bravest allies. In the battle of Fantahuha, where fighting took place from cocoanut tree to cocoanut tree, he served on our side. This combat was in the nature of a duel on a grand scale. Our ally was especially attracted by a certain native chieftain. The latter opened fire ten paces away, but missed him. So great was his dexterity, that Tareiri could invariably in turn fire on and kill an adversary. However, he flung down his gun, which was loaded, jumped on his adversary, took a firm grip, rolled him over on the ground, and took him prisoner. It was the Indian whose flight was described a short time ago. Tareiri was decorated by the Légion d'honneur; he was also asked to come to France and see Paris. He accepted.

My readers may recall having seen some seven or eight years ago an elegant young man with a somewhat bronzed complexion, beautiful hair glistening like the wing of a raven, a cross in his buttonhole, fashionably attired, with lorgnette in hand, on Gand Boulevard and the broad Avenue des Tuileries. This was Tahitian Tareiri, who was not only civilized, but a Frenchman. He was introduced to King Louis Philippe. An officer of the expedition, who spoke Tahitian, served to introduce him and act as interpreter.

"Ask him," said the King, "what has impressed him most deeply in France?" The officer interpreted the question to Tareiri.

"The cordial welcome I have received from the French people and the gracious favor accorded me by the King," replied the Tahitian.

A courtier could not have uttered a more gracious reply. Tareiri has since returned to Tahiti where he gradually resumed the costume and customs of the country and where he speaks of his voyage to Paris as if it were a dream.

I shall now turn to the subject of Tahitian fêtes. Frequently an *upaupa,* or fête, is organized. A rendezvous is arranged for some charming spot where all three luxuries of native life—shade, water, and grass—are available. The women sally forth in their finest robes, the men in their best coats—and all, men as well as women, reach the place designated covered with gardenia flowers and divine roses. The honors of the greensward fall to the women of the nearest village. The scene is one of the most beautiful imaginable; like sisters all are adorned in the same manner, and are so covered with flowers and leaves that they resemble island nymphs or dryads. The men, on the other hand, having prepared pigs, chickens, and bananas, are occupied with the feast.

Ovens are dug in the ground and heated. Orange brandy has been in the process of preparation for three days. Toward noon, that is, upon arrival, they eat; as they eat, they drink water, but after the repast *namou* is consumed. *Namou* is orange brandy; it is also known as *kava*. When they have become intoxicated, dancing begins. Then twenty beautiful girls, dressed exactly alike, resting on their heels, form a single line and chant a monotonous air which is not without a suggestion of passion. Behind them, men play the flute through the nose, holding one nostril to make the tone stronger. Other men, clapping their hands, imitate a squeaking pig.

A young girl detaches herself from one end of the line, as a link is removed from a chain, a pearl from a rosary. Those who remain squat on their heels; the men, who stand behind them, furnish both orchestra and background. Some beat time on the trunk of a cocoanut tree. Out in front of the line the dancer now takes a step, and rises on the same foot, with hand stretched before her. Then she turns, rises on the other foot, and extends the other hand. The hands twitch with a kind of nervous movement that makes them reflect light. In times past, to accentuate these reflections, the hands were tattooed. When the first dancer has completed a few measures, another leaves the opposite end and also pirouettes. The others follow in turn. The one who makes the most expressive gestures and achieves the highest type of native grace in accordance with native standards, is, according to their primitive tastes, the one with the most wanton appeal.

Gradually, all the beads of the rosary are told and the ballet becomes general. Thereupon, cries like those raised by the bacchantes on Mt. Rif, the bacchantes on Mt. Cithaeron, resound. In a civilized land, at this already belated moment, the curtain would fall. But in Tahiti the curtain never falls, the act goes on until it is finished, until the actors disappear. The denouement is called *Etanu*

*Terneia.* Tahitians have another dance, in fact two more dances, but no attempt will be made even to discuss the third. The second, however, will be briefly mentioned. This dance is called Fishing for Whales. Frequently employed as sailors aboard whaling vessels, the Tahitians often assisted at the capture of whales. It is this act that, with their usual naïveté, they portray. Ten women represent a canoe being pursued by a monster. The movement of their hands simulates the movement of oars; the undulations of their body, the undulation of the sea. The principal actor stands at the helm, stick in hand, ready to harpoon the whale after it appears. Another man is stationed at the top of a tree representing a mast. In his hand he holds a bamboo spyglass. This is the lookout charged with signaling when he sights a blower.

The whale appears. He is a man who spouts water through his mouth and nose, accomplishing this act with the assistance of a gourd full of liquid. The canoe begins to pursue the monster who attempts to escape, making turns and detours which display the versatility of the actresses who take the part of the canoe. From time to time the whale returns, then, blowing vigorously, throws water on the rowers of the boat and the leading actor. The principal character, the rowers, and the whale, now prepare for the final struggle, which it is impossible clearly to portray.

In a preceding chapter a description was given of how gentle and easy death is in Tahiti. Equally simple and tranquil is birth. A woman in labor suffers less than an hour and is aided by two or three friends. Having given birth, she goes to the sea, supported by her friends, swims ten minutes with their assistance, and, still leaning on them returns to her hut. That is all. The following morning she continues about her work.

## CHAPTER VIII

## THE MARQUESAS. STATION AT THE ISLE OF PINES. BELADA. MONSEIGNEUR DE DOUARE. THE ALCMENE. MASSACRE OF M. DE VARENNES AND HIS COMPANIONS

WHEN LIFE at Tahiti began to bore us, my husband suggested a trip to the Marquesas Islands. Of course I acquiesced, for the presence and rudeness of Sir George had become intolerable. We left on a small brig that makes the trip from the dangerous archipelago that extends from Kemin [1] Island to Nuka Hiva. The trip had no extraordinary features. The Marquesas, as is commonly known, were discovered in 1595 by the Spanish navigator, Mendaña,[2] and named Marquesas in honor of the Marquis de Mendoza, Viceroy of Peru. On March 7, 1774, Cook also landed on the island.[3]

Upon our arrival at Nuka Hiva we were impressed by the barrenness of the coast. I do not recall ever having seen more desolate or more sombre cliffs. A passage that appeared to resemble Dante's infernal region provided an entrance into the bay. No sooner did we enter the bay than the scene changed. The water, tranquil and blue and surrounded on all sides by verdant valleys, was like a sapphire set in emeralds. Apart from its almost invisible communication with the sea, this bay has much the aspect of a lake into which appeared to empty all the streams of the island. The bay is surrounded by huts; on a small promontory rises a fort built by the French.

The inhabitants of this bay were at war with Taipi-Kai-Kai. They are all cannibals and eat one another whenever and wherever possible. The men, in order to give themselves a more striking appearance, are tattooed from head to foot. Not so much as the thickness of an eyelash is left unpainted. Usually the most attractive designs are reserved for the shoulders and shoulder blades. Some bodies appeared to have been dipped in a vat of Prussian blue liquid. The majority of faces are diagonally striped by a line some three inches wide representing either a bar, a band, or the face of an escutcheon. Often these designs are highly colored.

Tattooing is done with the aid of a small rake of whales' teeth. The rake is dipped in a walnut shell, and applied on the spot to be tattooed, then struck with a small hammer. This operation draws blood and must be extremely painful.

A chief named Pacoco, with whom we made a trip into the interior of the country, told me the following tale. He said that prisoners are not eaten for pleasure—Pacoco defended himself strongly from the sin of gourmandizing—but for revenge. The custom is followed of striking the victim with a tomahawk, slitting him open with a knife, and removing the intestines; then the chief whose nail on his index finger is extremely long and sharp, plunges this nail into the ball of the eye, removes it with a circular movement and swallows it much as a singer, who favors his voice, swallows a fresh egg. With a blow of his hatchet, he now severs the phalanxes from the hands and while the body is cooking, sucks and gnaws the fingers as if they were hors-d'oeuvres. At such celebrations, fêtes and dances take place.

Whoever has seen one Polynesian island has seen them all. The men are entirely naked, except for a small piece of cloth used as a girdle. They wear a headdress of cock feathers held together by bands, not unlike those on the plush hats worn by the grenadiers of the guard. Among them often appear feathers made from stalks of straw. Around their necks hang necklaces of shells and red berries. The chiefs own pieces of red material which they place on their backs and tie together in front. The women, who indulge in the most unbridled license, are adorned with a large piece of cloth similar to that worn by the Tahitians under their wraps; they bedeck themselves in this material which is then wound several times around the body and which is further adorned by an enormous knot on the back.

We remained only a short time at the Marquesas Islands. The natives were engaged in tribal wars that made journeys on shore difficult. In fact, they had recently captured, roasted, and eaten an Englishman living on Dominica. Returning to Tahiti, we remained there six months longer, then left for New Caledonia. En route we were obliged to stop, and put in at the Isle of Pines. A mast had been cracked, and threatened to fall at the first storm. Since the natives are crass cannibals,[4] no one went ashore except in a well-armed canoe. My husband made two such trips, but would not allow me to accompany him.

We were visited aboard ship by Monseigneur de Douare. All our missions—unlike those of the English in this part of the world who are far too much occupied in speculative ventures—are the homes of martyrs. These poor priests are first robbed, then, one by one, little by little, they are assassinated and devoured. Monseigneur de Douare alone escaped. His entire fortune, estimated at thirty thousand pounds, had been used to extend the Faith. Three years ago he, too, so I was told, was killed, roasted, and eaten. At that time he was dividing his time between the Isle of Pines and New Caledonia.

Having exchanged our cracked mast for a new mast, we were soon under way once more, arriving, shortly before the month of December, at the port of Balade. New Caledonia[5] was discovered by Captain Cook on September third at eight o'clock in the morning; by five o'clock that evening he was less than two miles away. Monsieur de Bougainville,[6] who followed the same route taken by Captain Cook several years earlier, said that in passing through these regions he found an absolutely tranquil sea, and that several fragments of fruits and wood floating by near his vessel, convinced him that undiscovered land must lie in the direction from which the wood came.

Anchor was dropped on a floor of shifting coral. In some mysterious manner, a sailor secured a magnificent branch of coral, which I purchased. This fine specimen, with its many branches, was burned in one of the three or four fires that claimed us as victims in California. I was occupied in admiring my coral branch when one of the Brothers from the Mission came aboard. The captain questioned him about the advisability of landing, for he had intended to take on a load of sandalwood and some provisions. The good priest did everything in his power to prevent this, pointing out that such an attempt was not only extremely dangerous, but almost impossible, with the few men he had aboard. This was a matter of profound regret to the captain, for the country abounded in sweet potatoes and maize that grew out on the lush plains, and along the banks of broad rivers, some of which are navigable. The following day the natives came aboard bringing, in canoes far less beautiful than those of New Zealand, sweet potatoes, pigs, poultry, maize, and nuts.

For five weeks we remained here at anchor. During this period my husband went ashore twice, and returned, fortunately, without a mishap. One morning a warship flying a tricolored flag was sighted. She proved to be the frigate *Alcmène*. We had already heard of the terrible event that had occurred on the banks of Sequeba Island,[7] where the young and unfortunate De Varennes and his companions were murdered. One of the eye witnesses of this tragedy now told us the hideous details as follows. For greater accuracy, we shall let him tell the story:

"The frigate left Tahiti on April 20, 1850. Our mission was to visit most of the Tuamotu Islands, the Navigator Islands, Wallis, Aneiteum, the Isle of Pines, and especially New Caledonia. Our absence from the station of Tahiti was not supposed to be prolonged beyond four or five months, but due to circumstances beyond our control, we found ourselves, after an absence of ten months, still far from Tahiti.

"Our first visit to the islands of Tuamotu,[8] Wallis, and Aneiteum[9] met with signal success. We lost only one man at the Navigator Islands. At the port of Aneiteum the difficult part of our navigation began, for the frigate had set her course constantly between the reefs.

"Upon arriving at the Isle of Pines, we found the Mission already established and the priest at work. Monseigneur de Douare was in charge of this dangerous post. Two more priests and three monks lived on the Isle of Pines but outside the station. All had just escaped death by fleeing from New Caledonia and taking refuge aboard a small English vessel that happened to be passing within range of their dwellings; they had already been robbed of their supplies and stripped of their clothing, and, several days later, probably would have been served roasted for the great annual festival that takes place at harvest time. But God watched over them; for the present at least they are safe. Unfortunately this delay is at best temporary; Monseigneur de Douare insists on establishing a mission in New Caledonia and will make any sacrifice, even that of life itself, to achieve that goal.

"M. le comte d'Harcourt, in command of the *Alcmène*, learned of this from the lips of the missionaries themselves; he was authorized by the governor of Tahiti to protect fully all outlying French Missions that might be in danger. So he decided to remain for some time at the islands. But when supplies began to dwindle alarmingly, the commander decided, after a conference with Monseigneur de Douare, to take his ship to Sydney for repairs and provisions, and to replace the various objects that were missing, as well as to refresh and rest the crew, who were showing signs of weariness.

"We accordingly returned to Sydney and after a sojourn of two months, left to return to the Isle of Pines, reaching the latter port in September, 1850. We remained only one month on the island but during this time we experienced considerable difficulty holding the savages in check.

"Having been assured upon leaving that for the time being the Mission was safe, we set a course for New Caledonia, some twenty leagues beyond the Isle of Pines. New Caledonia is about eight leagues in length from north to south and fifteen in width. Its population is estimated approximately at sixty thousand. For the most part the inhabitants are a robust and sturdy people. The high mountains, large rivers, fine cascades, rich pastures, and thick forests of this favored land afford them endless advantages.

"The commander decided to make a tour of this group of islands with the purpose of checking the hydrography of the different ports. This was a dangerous task, one involving constant navigation between reefs. Furthermore, it was fatiguing, for the ship was forced to anchor every evening and weigh anchor again in the morning.

"Our first port was Huailu; it was here later that we were to suffer the loss of our beloved comrades. Upon our arrival at Balade, the commander's canoe was dispatched to search for a pass through the reefs. This canoe, which was to serve as guide for the sloop of war, was manned by an officer, M. de Varennes, who was in command of the craft, a subordinate, M. Saint Phale, a second mate called Perrot, eleven Frenchmen, an Englishman, and a Kanaka pilot, that is, one of the natives. This completed the party; in all, sixteen persons. They had supplies and ammunition to last eight days. They also had orders not to touch at the island except in the event of some emergency.

"By the end of three days the canoe had made the rounds and discovered the pass for which it was searching. The only task left for the officer was to make a plan of the islands in the vicinity of Caledonia and conduct a search for the corvette. On the evening of the third day, having approached fairly near the islands with their boat, our companions anchored, intending to pass the night off Sequeba Island. The natives saw them, and large numbers of them assembled every night on this latter island. The following morning, since the canoe had need of water, and since M. de Varennes believed he could rely on the friendship of the natives, who invited him by signs and by displaying handfuls of cocoanuts and fruits to come ashore, the canoe landed.

"The natives received our men hospitably, and only a few moments elapsed until, according to a custom followed in the Polynesian Islands, each one had his *joyau,* or friend. Upon landing, our countrymen prepared coffee, enjoyed a tranquil breakfast, and then began to load on what water was required by the canoe. This accomplished, the officer gave the command to put off from shore. What suddenly drew the attention of the unfortunate De Varennes and apparently made him decide to hasten his departure, was the large number of natives who had congregated on the small island, and the fear of a surprise attack. This fear made him give the order to embark with more rapidity than was politic.

"The entire crew were already in the canoe; M. de Varennes was alone on land and, occupied in raising the lower part of his trousers before climbing into the boat, had his head down. At that instant a native approached and gave him a treacherous blow with a club that caused him to lose his balance. M. de Varennes fell face downward into the sea. Then, for the first time, the men in the party realized that all the natives who surrounded the canoe were armed, some with hatchets, others with tomahawks. Prior to that time no signs of hostility had been apparent; the Indians

appeared to be satisfied with the promise made by the Frenchmen
to return soon.

"When they saw their officer, attacked by the natives, fall over
into the sea, members of the crew leaped into the water and attempted to seize his body and place it in the canoe. They were
somewhat less perturbed when they saw that M. de Varennes was
not actually dead, but showed signs of life; but as they raised him
in their arms, a Kanaka seized him by the hair and with a blow
from his hatchet split open his head. Death was instantaneous.

"The second mate, the brave Perrot, aware that they had been
trapped, decided at least to sell his life as dearly as possible. He
turned and with the rapidity of lightning, grasped and at the same
time wrested the bloody hatchet from the hands of the Kanaka,
and with a furious blow split open his face from his forehead down
to his teeth. But he had barely time to realize that he had avenged
his officer before he, too, died, struck down by a tomahawk.

"The natives now fell on the sailors, massacring twelve men on
the spot. Three of the sailors flung themselves into the sea, but
were captured that same evening by the Kanakas, and undoubtedly met the same fate. Our men were also forced, in addition to
all this, to witness a hideous spectacle. The murderers, having
robbed their victims, stripped some of them, killed them on the
shore, disemboweled them, and prepared to roast them. The work
of the women then began, for a certain group fulfill the rôle of
cooks in these shocking feasts. Wrapping the mutilated bodies in
cocoanut and banana leaves, they lit the fire, heated the stones
that serve for grills, and on these stones placed the bodies of our
miserable comrades. The three sailors who had escaped death and
whom death awaited were there and forced to assist, to the joy of
these wretches who danced around the fire.

"We, aboard the corvette, knew nothing of what was happening
on land; but not having had any news from our poor comrades,
the commander began to feel anxious and decided to send a second
party in search of the first. Like them, this group was heavily
armed and in charge of an officer. A missionary named Brother
Jean who knew the native language was sent with this new expedition.

"The canoe set out, and the fourth day after its departure returned, bringing in tow the commander's canoe with the three men who had escaped the general massacre aboard. We owed their safe return to the devotion of Brother Jean who, alone, unarmed, and carrying his rosary, went ashore to rescue them. What now remained to be done was to avenge the dead; the commander made all preparations for this purpose.

"We left the port of Balade, and anchored that same evening near Balabac Island. Several hours later we departed for Massacre Island. Having sighted it, we observed extraordinary activity on the part of the canoes, which were passing from island to island. The appearance of the sloop of war had disclosed our intention.

"At two o'clock in the afternoon we anchored before Taal Island; an hour later the landing party went ashore led by the commander in person. Under our deadly aim hundreds of savages fell. Our men now opened fire on their canoes, destroyed whole villages, and burned all their plantations. The commander then gave the signal to reembark and steer toward the other island. The order was followed and the experiences of Taal repeated.

"The corvette thereupon returned to Mission Island—also known as the Isle of Pines—to carry the good priests to safety; Monseigneur de Douare, however, refused to leave, declaring that he intended to remain in the hope of redeeming this race of cannibals."

We arrived only a few days after these events occurred. Our ship had made the voyage primarily because of an arrangement between my husband and the captain, who desired to ascertain whether it were possible to open up a traffic in sandalwood in New Caledonia. Having recognized the impossibility of attempting to establish intercourse with these ferocious natives, our ship had returned to the Isle of Pines and put in to take on a load of gourds and tropical fruits.

One morning—all this took place in December, 1850—one morning we sighted the corvette *Alcmène* anchored a few hundred fathoms from us; she bore every indication of being in mourning. Several officers came to visit us; they had crape on their arms, and each sailor in his own peculiar manner gave some indication of grief. My husband and I soon went aboard the *Alcmène*, where

M. le comte d'Harcourt did the honors. A head officer there made me a present, in honor of the fact that we came from the same land, of a copy of a hydrographical sketch that had just been completed and was to be sent to the Ministère de la marine. To it were affixed portraits of two of the leading chieftains who had directed the massacre; these portraits had been made by one of the three prisoners. One represenetd a Kanaka with his *tapa* on his head, a tomahawk in hand, a row of red beads around his forehead, and a scarlet cover on his back. This was the chief who killed M. de Varennes, and whom the second master, Perrot, in turn killed. The other was that of the second chief who participated in the massacre and who mutilated the bodies of our unfortunate compatriots. The latter belonged to the island of Balabac, the most dangerous of all islands in the Archipelago. He attempted to escape by swimming. Recognized while escaping by one of the three prisoners and pointed out to his comrades, he was captured after a bitter pursuit and brought aboard the corvette, where the sailors seized and shot him. It was during the short time when, impassive and awaiting death, he was sitting at the foot of the mainmast, that the naturalist on board sketched his portrait. Three days later we set sail to return to Tahiti.

## Chapter IX

## A NEW VENTURE. INTEREST OF THE TAHITIANS IN POMADE. DEPARTURE FOR CALIFORNIA

WE returned to Tahiti, convinced, as I believe I have already said, that there were no business opportunities at the Isle of Pines and New Caledonia except in the marketing of produce, and I felt as at the moment when the good Maori of New Zealand pinched my arm when he said *makai,* that my avocation did not lie in that direction.

At the end of a six months' sojourn at Tahiti, the occasion for which we had been waiting arrived. A ship carrying a cargo of sweet potatoes, apples, onions, preserves, and syrups, entered the port of Papeete. The captain had been unable to sell his merchandise as he expected. My husband had an inspiration and bargained for the entire shipment for twelve or fifteen thousand francs. Then he came to tell me that, if I were willing, we would leave immediately for California.

For two years the whole world had been talking of the land of gold; my dream had been to visit it. So I accepted joyfully. I did not especially enjoy Tahiti where I saw few persons except Queen Pomaré, an enjoyable acquaintance, but one whose friendship was inadequate to fill twelve hours of the day. My investigations had been completed and, in addition to what I have already recounted, I had discovered only one additional fact—the obsession of Tahitian women for pomade. This they use upon all occasions much as Belleau's Amphitryon used nutmeg. When traveling, the bundle for which they show the most concern is their pot of pomade. Their husband, lover, or brother, carries it on the end of his stick; lacking husband, lover, or brother, these beautiful, lazy creatures carry it themselves.

The young painter whom I have already mentioned, M. Charles Giraud, told me that, during a recent raid in which he took part, a poor woman was taken prisoner. Of all the personal effects in her hut, she was interested merely in carrying away two pots of pomade. She attached these two pots of pomade to the end of a pole, much as Saint Roch attached his gourd. But the string by which they were suspended from the end of the pole allowed them to swing too freely; the two pots, as they balanced, collided and broke. With tears falling, the poor Tahitian woman knelt down and cried over her jars of pomade; this woman who had not wept for far more serious calamities. Then she gathered the remains down to the last bit in her hands, in the meanwhile beating not only her hair, but her whole body with her hands. She had lost cosmetics that should have lasted three months, but she traveled under the fiery sun, proud, glistening, and perfumed. The only complaint of the Tahitian women against French perfumers—French perfumers are usually whalers—is the deceptive thickness of the French pots in which these honest traders place their merchandise.

But to return to ourselves and our speculation. Now that he owned a cargo of sweet potatoes, apples, onions, syrups, and preserves, M. Giovanni arranged a price for the transportation of our merchandise and ourselves with Mr. Huggins, captain of a magnificent three-masted merchantman, *Baretto Junior,*[1] a ship of 2500 tons, which was about to depart for California. As we were the most important passengers on the aforesaid three-master, we were able to secure the best accommodations. These quarters consisted of a magnificent cabin with two windows, that held a large bed, my two armchairs, my carpet, my piano, and a complete set of furniture for California. Then, for a library, the *Dernier Jour d'un Condamné* and *Monte Cristo.*

The passengers were numerous, but all were acquainted with one another. We had met at Tahiti, and again at New Zealand, caught a glimpse of one another at Hobart Town, at Port Phillips, or at Sydney. It is odd how, in countries widely separated from one another by sea voyages lasting a month or six weeks, travelers constantly meet.

There was only one other woman on board, Madame Barry and her daughter, a charming child six or seven years old, who was still far too young to pass for a woman. Our ship carried a total list of thirty passengers. We were welcomed, upon coming aboard, not only by Captain Huggins, but by his brother. They were charming young men, polished and courteous as only Englishmen can be when they so desire. Having reached the ship, we found that dinner was being served. The sea being calm and the breeze favorable, the ship got under way. Everyone ate with a good appetite.

During desert, after champagne had gone the rounds, the passengers grew extremely self-confident, scoffing at the thought of *mal de mer* and defying rolling, pitching, head winds, or even tempests, to upset them. All went well until evening. But during the night one of those sharp squalls often encountered in this ocean known, for some mysterious reason, as the Pacific, blew up and the ship began to dance to the glimmer of lightning and the music of wind and thunder. Everyone hoped that when day dawned the wind would fall. But the wind redoubled. A wave inundated the galley and would have carried off the cook, if he had not hung on by a rope.

Despite the defiant attitude revealed the previous evening toward squalls, only three persons appeared at the table. Twenty-seven others remained in bed. The galley had been demolished; there was no way to make a fire. And so neither bouillon nor tea was served. Furthermore, the cook took advantage of the fact that he had no kitchen, to be seasick. Although the captain spent a large part of his time on the bridge, yet he assumed charge of the invalids as well. Since there was no tea and bouillon, he took a bottle of champagne in one hand and a glass in the other and went from cabin to cabin offering this foaming diet to the invalids while his brother served as a kind of hospital assistant. On the second day not a single person appeared at the table. We could hear the captain and his brother laughing, for the good men were clumsy nurses.

At four o'clock that morning, as my husband cried with every ounce of strength he could muster: "Take me and throw me into the sea!" a sharp squall broke one of our windows, just as if the sea were attempting to force its way in, and blew heavy gusts into our cabin. Simultaneously, a terrific crash was heard, accompanied by the noise of something breaking. The mainmast had snapped like a match and fallen on the deck. Two or three groans, like the wail of the spirit of the waters, came through the air. It was the cry of two or three sailors who had been wounded by the falling mast.

The deck presented a curious spectacle. The strongest sailors crawled around on all fours or leaned on any object that could serve as a prop. The ship appeared about to founder at any moment, and what little sail was carried was rent and torn to shreds by the storm. This situation lasted three days. During the storm, the captain guided his ship with rare skill, and with admirable devotion cared for his invalids. Throughout these three days he did not sleep and scarcely ate! At the end of that time the wind died down and the sea gradually grew calm. Finally, at the dinner hour, several invalids whose appetite had returned, dragged themselves to the table. The table, however, felt the loss of the kitchen, for as yet stoves had not been set up. And so the diners were obliged to content themselves with preserved meat, vegetables, and fish.

Every member of the crew was incapacitated; the second officer had cut his thumb with a hatchet; Madame Barry did nothing but groan; but the child, who remained in bed drinking a small portion of champagne which the captain had brought her, had not uttered a single complaint. During these three days, one or two glasses of champagne was all I could take. My husband, incidentally, uttered cries of dismay whenever anyone suggested he should take some nourishment. It was seventy-two hours before the kitchen was reorganized and the cook's strength returned. Gradually the guests revived, but fifteen days passed before the majority could take their places and the entire thirty diners assemble.

As the late comers drifted in, they were mildly teased in proportion to their tardiness. Soon our intimacy, that had not had time to assert itself, inasmuch as we had spent only five or six hours together, began to develop aboard ship. A sharp, but favorable wind continued to blow. Everyone still suffered to some extent, but all felt that we were making good time, and that gave us courage. As soon as I was able to stand on my feet, the captain came to me and gave me a bunch of keys that opened certain lockers where I could find all sorts of choice supplies which he amiably placed at my disposal, so that I might in turn dispense them to my traveling companions.

"Here are the keys of the supply room," he said to me, "you have permission to dispose of them, but only on the express condition that you will see that we live well."

I cannot say whether the captain gained weight on our diet, but I do know that he did not economize on us. There was a maître d'hôtel aboard. This maître d'hôtel had orders to follow the list of extras I gave him. Our provisions, furthermore, were excellent. We had sheep and pigs in pens, hens and roosters in profusion in cages, and fresh eggs in abundance. As I was up and about the second day after the storm, I gathered the eggs and distributed them to the invalids.

In addition there were two cows that gave milk for coffee and tea. At eleven o'clock breakfast was served. It consisted of fish, chops, cold meats, and eggs with various sauces. We remained at the table an hour sipping tea or coffee, and listening to the captain's stories. In addition to the fact that he had, as I have said, a gentlemanly appearance, the captain was a man of considerable wit. He was a delightful raconteur. Being an Englishman, to him all Americans were Yankees. His travels had often led him to San Francisco, and, thanks to his tales, possibly somewhat exaggerated, but always fundamentally true, we knew California before we actually landed as well as I knew it after a sojourn of two years. At three o'clock in the afternoon, the captain gave the signal that luncheon was ready. This consisted of cakes, fresh butter, cheeses, port, and champagne.

From four to six o'clock, everyone lounged. Prizes were offered for those who would invent exercises that would induce hunger by six o'clock. At six o'clock everyone came to the table, remaining there until eight, then went up on deck, smoked for an hour, and made up tables to play vingt-et-un. The thing that invariably happens when friends play vingt-et-un occurred. The game begins quietly. Each player draws a small coin from his pocket, agrees not to exceed the maximum of a dollar, and ends by placing one hundred dollars on one bet. And this, furthermore, was not in California!

Drinks, including several kinds of wines, were passed by servants as we played. At midnight there was a cold supper, accompanied by Welsh rabbit. The French reader probably does not know what a Welsh rabbit is, and what the name signifies. I myself do not know what the name means, but I can explain what it is. Slices of bread are cut and toasted before a large fire, buttered and placed on a plate, which is carefully kept hot. Then in a small silver casserole are placed equal amounts of butter and Chester cheese, according to the quantity desired, a glass or two of stout; some allspice, salt, and pepper are added and all is placed over the fire. Then, when it is thoroughly mixed, it is poured over the toasted squares, and served hot.

From time to time I myself invented new dishes. Inasmuch as our two cooks were English, every time a French dish appeared on the table, everyone knew it was my creation and celebrated, except Madame Barry who found nothing good, because everything was exceptional and too unusual for her taste. She was always bored, found nothing to occupy her time, and amused herself by teaching her small daughter who, having been extremely well brought up to the age of nine years by her aunt, understood none of the coarse manners of her mother, and expressed with infantile frankness her amazement.

I, too, spent considerable time with this child, whom I deeply loved. I was on deck by six o'clock in the morning listening to the sailors' stories and teaching them my song called "la Pompe"; at nine o'clock I went down to my cabin to give my small pupil, Madame Barry's daughter, lessons in writing and music. When I was satisfied with her, I rewarded her by giving her permission to take a bath in the room adjoining my cabin. She would then go, joyous and fresh as a rose, to share her happiness with her mother. The mother never envied this bouyancy to the point of asking for herself the same favor that I accorded her daughter.

Madame Barry had one other diversion. That was to make the poor child take medicine every four or five days. This medicine was extremely distasteful to her. She could be heard crying, and everyone knew what it meant. Madame Barry was a kind of rich peasant, who had brought a certain amount of money to her husband as a dowry. Having come to New Zealand, her husband had established a business as wine merchant, in which he had been very successful. When word came of the discovery of gold in California, they decided to change the seat of their commercial activities. The husband left in advance for San Francisco, where his business was even more successful than it had been in New Zealand; his wife was now on her way to join him.

With the fine weather and long evenings on deck, we decided to read aloud. My husband had a kind of Pandora's box in which on special occasions I rummaged. Aware that no one else had any books, I reached my hand toward the aforesaid box, plunged it in twice, and drew out the two books I have already mentioned, that is, *Monte Cristo,* and the *Dernier Jour d'un Condamné. Monte Cristo* was in English. We decided to begin with this. Each evening everyone assembled on deck, stretching out on blankets and all the cushions that could be found on the boat. Everyone reclined in order to listen with greater ease under the blue canopy of a magnificent sky lavishly embroidered with gold stars; I read by the flicker of the night lamp in the binnacle, whose light was reflected over my book.

The reading lasted eight evenings. Each time I began, I attempted to read only three or four chapters; but when I stopped my listeners would call "Go on, go on," so I continued and this tale that should have lasted throughout the entire trip was completed in a week. We next read the *Dernier Jour d'un Condamné*.

At the end of three weeks the storms began again. The ship was full of water and it was necessary, as in our voyage from Mauritius to Auckland, to man the pump vigorously. This was where the song I had taught the sailors revealed its worth. I, and five or six other passengers, kept our health. The captain had charge of his hospital, and I went from bed to bed offering tea, bouillon, or champagne.

Finally, we began to talk of our arrival in the near future in San Francisco. The ship was traveling at good speed, making approximately fourteen knots an hour. One morning the captain told us that before the day was over we would sight land. At five o'clock in the evening, the captain's promise was realized. The following day we entered the bay, but the fog was so dense that we could not see the bowsprit of the ship. However, the weather finally cleared, and on toward five o'clock in the afternoon, just as anchor was about to be lowered, the fog vanished completely and we could see the magnificent panorama that extended before us. This was in February, 1851.

Never, on any of my travels, have I seen the numbers of boats that appeared in the port of San Francisco. As many as six hundred could be counted! It was like being in an immense forest devoid of leaves. The movement that took place in this bay was considerable, and the port of London is the only one that presents a spectacle to compare with it. Furthermore, on all sides only gold was seen, only the sound of gold was heard. This, indeed, was the bay of El Dorado. A certain amount of anxiety was felt about our cargo, for it was extremely perishable, and the various storms we had encountered had not served to allay these fears.

Every onion and apple, however, was wrapped like an orange in paper. Everything proved to be in excellent condition. We arrived with one hundred tons of merchandise.²

CHAPTER X

ARRIVAL AT THE BAY. APPEARANCE OF SAN FRAN-CISCO. WHAT OUR FREIGHT AND TRANSPORTATION COST. EL DORADO. MADAME BARRY. TRIP ASHORE. AN AFFLUENT CALIFORNIAN

THE first thing sighted upon entering the bay of San Francisco is Telegraph Hill.¹ This is actually a small hill the height of Montmartre. From its crest, swathed in green, rise a windmill and the telegraph for which it is named. Whenever a new fire destroys San Francisco, everyone takes whatever he can save, including himself, to Telegraph Hill, which, as indicated, derives its name from the structure on its peak. The hill is covered with small wooden houses that seem like chicken coops piled not on top of one another but beside one another. Not a single tree shades the houses. As the ship advances up the bay, on the left the lands of Contra Costa and San Antonio come into view.² Finally San Francisco is sighted, and before the eye unfolds a vast conglomeration of houses built of wood and iron.

However, once on land—observe that I am speaking now of the time of our arrival, that is, at the beginning of 1851—the city seems to be laid out in an orderly manner. The houses are placed in a line and the only real criticism that can be made of the streets is that they terminate in a mound of sand that, incidentally, recedes each time a new house is built on the same row.

Having reached the end of our route, we dropped anchor. We were now about to ascertain whether all the marvelous tales we had heard about California were actually true, and whether the heavy expense we had incurred in transporting ourselves and our cargo to San Francisco would be justified. Some idea of the amount of these expenses will now be given. We had paid for our passage in the *Baretto Junior* fifteen hundred dollars, an exorbitant price because we were bound for El Dorado. In addition, for our apples, onions, sweet potatoes, and preserves, another nine thousand was added, making more than ten thousand dollars. This speculation, I must confess, I had believed would be justified. The cargo cost us some three thousand dollars, that is, less than one-third of the transportation charges, for the captain from whom my husband had purchased it had sold it at a loss. There was, furthermore, something terrifying in the idea of having invested, for the first time, thirteen thousand dollars in sweet potatoes, apples, and onions.

No sooner had we dropped anchor than, as at the ports of Tahiti and the Marquesas, we were surrounded by a flock of small boats. The latter, however, were not manned by savages garbed in their typical native costume and speaking only one language, but were in charge of civilized and highly active men who offered their wares in a variety of languages, among which, to the profound satisfaction of my lazy ears, the French language predominated.

The wares offered proved to be milk at one dollar the pint, and oranges and apples at twenty-five cents each. On all sides rose the shout: "Porters, cheap porters, five dollars to carry a carpet bag; ten dollars for a bag and a trunk!" But with it all what attracts is the sight of gold, the sound of gold; this is the goal of the merchant with his milk, apples, and oranges; the goal of the porter who, to make change, takes out a handful of gold and searches a long time among that gold to find a paltry fifty-cent piece. From the moment the ship enters the Bay, the true character of San Francisco is strikingly obvious; here, indeed, is the land of El Dorado.

But what especially delighted my husband and myself was the sight of these apples, much inferior to our own, selling for twenty-five cents apiece. If we could sell our sweet potatoes and our onions on the basis of the price of these apples, our cargo would be worth almost half a million dollars. Upon arriving in the Bay, the captain, however, warned us against the activities of the agents who boarded vessels and, before merchants knew local conditions, made arrangements to handle their merchandise. As a matter of fact, a crowd of these speculators descended on the *Baretto Junior*. One of them, reputed to be among the wealthiest produce merchants in San

Francisco, attached himself to my husband. Suddenly I heard him cry out: "Why my dear sir, your fortune is made."

Naturally, I approached with a certain alacrity. M. Giovanni had just told this Californian of what our cargo consisted, and the latter had not concealed the fact that the city did not have on hand at this time any of the produce that made up the cargo of the *Baretto Junior.* Moreover, before the meeting terminated, the speculator offered my husband, free of all customs' duties and other charges, two American *reals*[3] for each apple and onion. In other words, a valuation was placed on these fruits and vegetables of twenty-five cents each. He also offered twelve cents for each sweet potato. We had seventy tons of apples and onions, and thirty tons of sweet potatoes.

Thus, M. Giovanni could land with his hands in his pockets and be a gentleman of leisure; he had several hundred thousand dollars of his own. He was about to accept and I was persuading him to the best of my ability to do so, when Captain Huggins touched him on the arm. M. Giovanni turned. "Don't allow yourself to be outwitted," the captain said to him.

"The deuce, almost half a million," said M. Giovanni, "what a calamity!"

"Never mind, if he offers you that amount for your load here at anchor, it is because it must be worth four, or at least three million, on land."

There was a certain amount of logic in this comment.

"Well," said M. Giovanni to the speculator, "I will consider your proposal."

The speculator bowed, and went off whistling.

What interested me primarily was the indifference of this speculator. He had just offered M. Giovanni a fortune for his produce; the latter had refused, and the former had gone away whistling, without concerning himself more over a lost sale, than if it had involved a bunch of radishes.

In the meanwhile Mr. Barry,[4] who knew his wife was aboard the *Baretto,* arrived. After embracing Mrs. Barry and his daughter, he hung chains of gold around their necks, placed some rings on their fingers, presented them with some watches and chains and gave a *slug*[5] to the child. The *slug,* which I saw for the first time, is an octagonal piece of gold worth fifty dollars which is coined in San Francisco. Thus nothing but gold is seen everywhere, always gold.

Mr. Barry was superior to his wife. Although we had never seen one another before, yet from our former connections we felt like old acquaintances. He invited us to stop for a time at his house. We accepted and went ashore. Half of San Francisco had been burned, and was still smoking.[6] Except for the smoke, the fire appeared to have been quite forgotten. Rebuilding was progressing at full speed on the still warm ashes.

We arrived at the home of Mr. Barry. He was living on Dupont Street and had not suffered any damage, for the fire had not extended that far. He was a wholesale wine merchant and conducted along these particular lines one of the most extensive businesses in San Francisco. What impressed us upon arriving at his house was the absence of the most basic necessities. Obviously, men came here to earn, not spend, gold. Mr. Barry invited us to dinner. We accepted. Some kegs were brought in on which planks were placed. This was the table. Over them was placed a cloth or sheet. This completed the preparations. Beefsteaks were now procured from a restaurant. Mrs. Barry, who had been such a little lady aboard the ship, who had arrived punctually at the dinner hour, who had toyed with her fork over two or three morsels on her plate before selecting one, was forced to take off her cashmere robe, and attempt to find some knives and forks.

"Apparently," she said to her husband, "you were not planning to dine at home today, Mr. Barry?"

"Certainly, my dear."

"But why did the cook not prepare dinner?"

"Because there is no cook."

"Then the maid should at least have set the table."

"There is no maid. The deuce! We are extremely fortunate if we have clerks."

"Good heavens, then how do you live?"

"My dear lady, we manage somehow. When we are hungry, we endeavor to eat, but no one has time to arrange in advance for dinner." Finally a clerk arrived with bread purchased at the baker's, and four beefsteaks procured at a restaurant.

From the moment I entered the house, I had felt fleas climbing up my legs. No sooner were we seated before the planks than, just as if someone had called them, rats began to appear on all sides. They ran between our feet and frisked around under the table like so many cats. No matter! The Californians have no interest in such trifles; they have other things to attend to; they must find gold.

Conditions were even worse when the time came to retire. The beds were nothing but large packing boxes that had been inverted and a mattress placed in the bottom. Our hosts even sent out to buy covers and sheets. Mr. Barry, upon making his evening rounds, came to wish me good-night and found me weeping in my coffin; my husband, however, was already asleep in his.

"What is the matter with you?" he asked, "are you ill?"

"Alas! No, I am merely sad, nothing more."

"Why?"

"Can't you imagine?"

I made a gesture indicating the supreme distress into which the absence of the most elementary comforts plunged me.

"Oh, yes," he said, "I understand; but be calm, you will adapt yourself."

"So this, then, is life in California," I cried.

"No one comes here to live, my good friend," replied Mr. Barry, "everyone is here to make a fortune as rapidly as possible and to leave and be comfortable elsewhere. So try and sleep, do not let the noises you will hear after five o'clock in the morning disturb you."

## Chapter XI

## THE BELLA UNION. THE LYNCH LAW

OBVIOUSLY IT would be impossible to remain with Mr. Barry; not only were we extremely uncomfortable, but we were also inconveniencing him to a considerable extent. As already indicated, the houses lacked at this time the most elementary conveniences, and despite the fact that all kitchen and domestic equipment was exceedingly cheap, there were no women to use them. As a matter of fact, French, English, or Chinese porcelain sold at fifty per cent under the market prices asked in Paris, London, or Canton, yet entire hampers of plates, dishes, tureens, and cups were abandoned at the doors of stores; vehicles, touching the houses, broke them as they passed. No one cared to purchase them because of the fire.

In the morning, we went out to find a hotel,[1] which asked us, for single lodgings, two hundred and fifty dollars a month, that is, somewhat under fifteen hundred francs. We were finally obliged to make arrangements with a cheaper place that furnished both meals and room for the more moderate price of ten dollars daily, that is, three hundred dollars a month.

We had disembarked Saturday about two o'clock. I neglected to add that that same evening Mr. Barry and some friends took my husband out to show him the sights of the city. As these gentlemen had only a limited amount of time to spend, they began by visiting the most spectacular place in the city, the gambling house called the Bella Union,[2] situated on the Plaza. This establishment, one of the first to be founded, even today is the most ostentatious in all San Francisco. In its two main rooms there are nearly two hundred gambling tables with their bankers, croupiers, and assistants. The assistants were decoy women: they wore lavish costumes of velvet, and many diamonds. Although the youngest was not under thirty-five or forty years years of age, yet these so-called ladies were an innovation in a country where the ratio of women to men was one in five hundred. The gambling games played at these tables were roulette, trente-y-quarente, monte,[3] faro, vingt-et-un, and lansquenet. At every table a Frenchman acted as croupier; they were invariably selected for this honor, for the Americans considered them the most trustworthy of all immigrants who flocked to San Francisco. Each table consisted of a croupier, two bankers, and a raker. The price was thirty, forty, and even fifty dollars an evening for a table. The stakes were either gold dust, specimens of ore, or gold coin. Gamblers usually carried gold nuggets of dust in their belts from which hung, caught by some carbine swivels, either a brace of pistols, or a single revolver with seven chambers. Gambling was conducted, as in the thieves' den in Gil Blas,[4] with one hand on the wallet, the other on the gun.

A pair of scales stood on each table. The player first placed his gold in one of the balance plates, which then sank. If he lost, the banker took the gold; if he won, the banker turned into the scales a weight equal to what had been staked. An orchestra added a festive touch. This consisted of a piano, a violin, and a harp. The three performers were placed in one corner on a stage; they cost the proprietor of the establishment three hundred dollars an evening. After each round, the table was covered with gold. M. Giovanni observed that the amount wagered on a single game of trente-y-quarente was often one hundred thousand dollars, that is, some five hundred thousand francs.

Tables could be had only with considerable difficulty. The main room was not only the rendezvous of the players, but even of bankers and merchants, who used this house as a kind of exchange. In those days San Francisco had neither clubs, circles, nor societies. Now that all these organizations exist, no one except players ever goes to such places as the Bella Union, if he values his good reputation. The owners of this gambling house were Messrs. Ross and Sullivan.[5] They had no silent partners; all the money invested was their own. In the evening, after the gambling was over, each banker counted the receipts at his own table, placed the funds in sacks, listed the money, gold dust, or specimens in his little book, and carried the sacks to the strong box.

The two proprietors, Messrs. Ross and Sullivan, constantly circulated through the rooms. Both were young, elegant, and handsome. Mr. Sullivan, in particular, resembled a fashion plate. Occasionally, when a croupier wished to leave his seat, he made a sign to one of these gentlemen; Mr. Ross or Mr. Sullivan then sat down at the table and kept tally in person. The croupier returned, took his seat, and the proprietor who had been keeping score then resumed his stroll.

Gambling began at six o'clock; at the same time the strong box that had remained open until each banker had time to locate his own bag was closed. What was especially remarkable was the fact that no one watched to see that every banker took only his own sack, and did not make a mistake and take the wrong coin. No one kept check on these men. Entire confidence was placed in them, and at no time did any difficulty result from such trust!

A man might easily have escaped with a bag holding one hundred thousand dollars; however, gold was so cheap that such things never happened. A check of the gold was made only on Saturdays. Each Saturday the capital was set aside, and the profits that had been made during the week were turned over to the proprietors. Every evening all employees were paid, even the *paillasses,* or clowns. This was the name given the housemen, that is, the men who made a pretense of playing and who actually gambled only with house money. These decoy men received from five to six dollars an evening. Like the bankers and croupiers, most of them were Frenchmen. Every evening supper was served before the games began; only champagne then worth seven dollars a bottle was drunk. The supper cost about one hundred dollars. Messrs. Ross and Sullivan issued the invitations as they strolled about the room.

At the moment when M. Giovanni, with a curiosity that can be readily understood, was examining these many tables that appeared to be surrounded by bandits, where the players were usually garbed in linen trousers, woolen shirts of blue, red, or yellow, and armed with pistols, revolvers, knives—at the very moment when these gentlemen, as I was saying, were watching these sights and smoking their cigars, an uproar was heard in the anteroom. Mr. Sullivan rushed to the scene of the disturbance. He was an extremely brave man, one who never hesitated to throw himself among the quarrelers no matter how excited they might be, and to talk to them in low tones and with a calm air, with the result that usually at his voice or gesture the altercation ceased.

This time, however, he arrived too late. A dispute had just taken place in a low voice. The men involved, having decided to settle the argument with a pistol duel, found it simpler, to avoid losing time, to place themselves in the center of the room, twenty paces apart, revolvers in hand, and fire seven shots at one another. That some of their shots might strike the bystanders did not in the least disturb the combatants. Two or three were fired before Mr. Sullivan, aided by several volunteers, succeeded in disarming the trouble makers. A cry, however, had been raised at one of the tables. Mr. Otto, the banker, had received a bullet in his foot, and was being carried out; but no one thought of stopping the two duelists, who were American miners. By this time M. Giovanni and Mr. Barry had seen everything there was to see, for this type of skirmish was not extraordinary. They now returned to the house and as they described the entire affair, there was a noticeable contrast between the astonishment of the former and the tranquillity of the latter.

The following day, which was Sunday, while the gentlemen were smoking in a small back room, and while Madame Barry, the child, and I, having raised the blinds, were looking through the window of the store, suddenly a crowd of men was seen running, gesticulating, and uttering loud cries.

Through them a carriage passed with the noise and rapidity of thunder. A mob, larger and more excited than the one we had first seen, followed the carriage. The situation, to be clearly understood, requires a word of explanation. At that time, when San Francisco was not yet governed by an adequate code of laws, a Vigilance Committee [6] had been established consisting of honest men from all over the country who were delegated by their countrymen to administer justice when the need arose. This committee formulated what was known as the Lynch Law. The first man to participate in this method of meting out justice was probably called Lynch. To administer justice without legal authority was thus called acting under the Lynch Law, that is, applying Lynch's law.

Now the Vigilance Committee had arrested several men accused of complicity in starting the last fire. They were convicts from Sydney, [7] belonging to a class known as "Sydney ducks." The past record of these two men was far from favorable; having been transported from the metropolis of London to Sydney, they escaped from the place to which they were deported and were wanted by the authorities of the former city. The committee, after considerable difficulty, procured their release, by guaranteeing that justice would be done.

Suddenly rumors, which the committee regarded as authoritative, circulated to the effect that in return for information furnished by the two culprits, the law might possibly set them free. When these rumors were repeated time and again, the Vigilance Committee decided to take definite steps.

At eleven o'clock in the morning, several members of the group entered a carriage and reached the prison as prayers were being held; the doors were thrown open; they entered the chapel, seized the two men, compelled them to enter the carriage, and drove them at full speed to the place of execution. The carriage that carried them was the one that had just passed. Upon hearing the crowd running and shouting, and at our own urgent request, our men rushed out of the house and followed the crowd. The conveyance stopped on Montgomery Street before a house, in front of which hung some pulleys used to hoist merchandise into lofts, where on the first floor the Vigilance Committee had assembled to discuss the matter.

The two men were pulled from the carriage by brute force and carried into the building. There they found themselves in the presence of judges who had already pronounced judgment. They were condemned to capital punishment and given five minutes to prepare to die. At the end of that time, the cord of the pulley was drawn inside the room. A double slipknot was prepared, and then passed around the necks of these two prisoners. At a given signal, six men holding the other end of the rope pulled with full strength and soon swung the two condemned men dangling from the end of the rope out into the street. At the end of five minutes justice had functioned. The culprits ceased to exist. After the two men had been hanged every bell in the city tolled in their honor. This was the first execution ever held on a Sunday [8] in San Francisco, and was, I believe, the last.

On Monday our trunks were moved to our new lodgings and while our goods were waiting their turn to pass through the customs, we began to explore San Francisco.

CHAPTER XII

## THE AMERICANS

WHAT INTERESTED us especially on our first tour of inspection was the activity on the streets, some of which were already paved with planks, while others were still muddy.

Since 1848, a time when no one dared venture forth without waterproof boots and when such boots, that came halfway to the knee, cost fifty dollars a pair, tremendous progress had been made. To give some indication of what these streets, a kind of moving morass where the pedestrian might founder, were like, we were told by one of our friends that in 1849, when he stopped to chat for a moment with his friends at Washington Place, a rumor reached them that a brig had just dropped anchor, bringing twenty-five Mexican women. These immigrants were in much the same situation as the Romans, the evening before they carried off the Sabines.

Having learned of the arrival of these twenty-five women, Mr. Betty [1] and his friends ran as fast as their legs could carry them in order to reach the port before all of them had been seized; but unfortunately, three of the four men neglected to make the usual detour, and sank in mire up to their knees. The more effort they made to extricate themselves, the deeper they sank. Only one, who realized that upon certain occasions the curved line is the shortest in the end, reached port; however, he was too late. The Mexican women had already been taken.

Meanwhile, the three unfortunate men who were bemired cried for aid, and it required the combined efforts of an engineer of bridges and highways and a mechanical apparatus to extricate them from their dilemma.

At one time the sea came up as far as where the center of the city now stands. San Francisco has shifted its location repeatedly. The huge mounds of sand, in which the majority of streets originally terminated, have already been mentioned. As fast as new houses were built, the mountains of sand were replaced by these dwellings. Moreover, as the city spread toward the bay, these sand mounds were forced into the sea which, incidentally, was filled with countless ships riding at anchor, which had been deserted by their crews.

Ships came in in incalculable numbers. Not a single cargo, however, could be marketed. The crews deserted, went ashore, and immediately headed for the placers. The captain remained aboard and, recognizing the impossibility of manning his ship, cut down the masts; the ship thus became a pontoon, and was converted ultimately into a store; the merchandise with which the ship was loaded was gradually transferred ashore. Either the captain built or had someone build a smaller boat for him, and after the hull of the old ship became useless, it was sunk.

The Americans purchased for insignificant sums what were known as water lots; they were soon filled in and became land lots. Thus by the end of six weeks, an entire new quarter would rise; by the end of six months, a city that was entirely inhabited extended toward the Contra Costa. In this was apparent not the hand of God, but that of the indefatigable and adventuresome Americans to whom obstacles did not exist and who overcame stupendous difficulties in the course of his rapid progress.

One section of San Francisco, on the other hand, expanded inland. Beyond the city, land had no value. To become owner of whatever amount was desired—this, however, held true only in the early days of California—a hut was built; around this domain a boundary line was drawn, in the same manner that Romulus defined the city of Rome; a small tax was paid to the government, and ownership was established. This was what was known as squatter's rights, rights which gave rise to so many disagreements.

What was especially noticeable in the varied activity of the streets, in the crowds that pressed, elbowing and jostling one another, was the almost total absence of women. The few that lived in San Francisco wisely kept within doors. For an honest woman to go out alone was unsafe—provided a woman who went out alone could be considered an honest woman.

On every hand, as far as the eye could see, the woolen shirts of the miners were visible. From time to time among this worker's uniform, a black coat would appear, but this was a rare occurrence. A large number of carts, some drawn by horses, others by hand, were in evidence, but no cabs. Only two or three of the latter were available in San Francisco and they cost fifty dollars a day.

Movement in the streets, already somewhat congested in view of the large number of passers-by, who walked rapidly like men not out for pleasure but actively engaged in business, was hampered by piles of miscellaneous merchandise from every land, merchandise of varied value, which was piled before stores already full to their doors and even to their windows. Lines of people stood in front of clothing, tool, and supply houses; but shops dealing in luxuries that have since made such large fortunes were neglected, and did not forecast our beautiful bazaars which, with their elaborately-gowned shopgirls, clerks in black clothes, and carpets extending into the street, now openly solicit the trade of the pedestrian. I refer to the firms of Kandler, Guérin, and Pommier.[2]

Amid all this chaos, or rather this genesis, stone houses were occasionally constructed. The majority of the stones arrived cut and ready to use from China, and came from buildings that had been demolished. While there was excellent stone in the vicinity of San Francisco, yet everyone preferred to pan gold rather than work in the quarries.

The finest and most important buildings of this character were those occupied by the firms of Argenti,[3] Burgoyne,[4] and Davidson,[5] and, lastly, the El Dorado,[6] which was erected in the early days of San Francisco and which, despite all the disasters, remained like a ghost out of the past, still standing after each fire. There were, in addition, houses of cast iron, believed to be indestructible. But after the first fire they were found to be as twisted as a man with gout, or the damned and, like the bull of Phalaris, they had consumed their inhabitants. As yet, there were neither street lamps nor gas; in the evenings the lights from the shops lit the streets.

Churches consisted of a Catholic church and a Protestant chapel.[7] The Catholic church was located on Jackson Street; fire had never traveled that far.

Among theatres was the French playhouse called the Adelphi,[8] which had never been burned, and one or two small American theatres.[9] There was also the post office, an amazing establishment, probably the busiest post office in any part of the world.[10] Fortunate, indeed, would be the theatre in Paris or London that could attract for evening performances a queue like that stationed daily before the door of the post office in San Francisco.

Recreations were gambling, the theatre, and sacred and profane concerts. Only a few of the gambling houses, however, made fortunes. Hertz's [11] gambling is a typical instance of a failure. Hertz arrived in San Francisco with funds and, notwithstanding his immense talent, I believe that the amount of French money he lost in San Francisco greatly exceeded the amount of California gold he carried back to France.

At this time, the proportion of women to men, I believe, was less than one in five hundred. When going out in the evenings with our husbands, we were fully aware that however well armed, we could seldom stroll along without being surrounded and stared at in a manner that would be quite disagreeable anywhere but in California, but entirely excusable there, at the time to which I refer. I shall recount in due time an ugly affair of which I, quite innocently, was the cause.

We arrived, as I have said, early in the year; the weather was bitterly cold. Not a single house had a chimney. The gold fever took the place of fire. Moreover, the climate of San Francisco is miserable, changing three times a day. Every night, that is from midnight until three o'clock in the morning, a mist falls which could in reality pass for rain. In the morning the dew ceases to fall, but the humidity and mist persist. At eleven o'clock intense heat sets in. In the afternoon a strong wind, carrying blinding clouds of dust, sweeps down off the mountains; this blows from two to six o'clock. Then comes an icy cold that lasts until eight or nine o'clock. From nine o'clock to two o'clock in the morning, bewitching night.

There is one particular place in San Francisco, moreover, where such a strong wind invariably blows that no man's hat, however well secured, or woman's hat, however well tied, can withstand it. This point is at the intersection of Kearny and Washington streets near the El Dorado; the place is known as Cape Horn.

Now what, in this conglomeration of peoples, are the characteristics of each? The leading nationalities that flocked from all over the world to California were: the American, the French, the Chinese, the Mexicans, and the Irish. Then, forming a kind of distinct category, came the Germans, the Italians, and a few Englishmen. But in all fairness it would be unjust, under these circumstances, to generalize about nations from the types thus represented. Most conspicuous of all were the Americans.

CHAPTER XIII

MORE AMERICANS

THE AMERICANS provided the backbone of the country. The land was their own. Here they felt at home; and here they were constantly in evidence regulating questions of law. In number they exceeded all other nationalities who flocked to the mines. Being able workers, labor, no matter how arduous, never disturbed them. They surpassed every other race in extracting gold. In the city they controlled all commerce of any importance. They were bankers, agents, gold merchants, powder merchants, and even monopolized the trade of barber! They owned all the steamers that plied in and out of the bay, all railroads, all means of rapid locomotion.

The proverb, "Time is Money," is typically American. An American seldom remains idle. He prefers to destroy something, rather than remain unoccupied and is constantly engaged in some kind of manual task. He is wholly without intellectual resources.

Typical of this need for activity is an anecdote which, I recall, often made me laugh and which frequently afforded the Americans themselves considerable amusement. One day an American reached London, entered a hotel, and requested dinner. By chance this request was addressed to the only American waiter in the hotel. The latter at once recognized a countryman. "Immediately!" the waiter replied.

But to serve dinner immediately requires, after all, at least a quarter of an hour. The latter, after requesting the head cook not to delay, looked around and soon located a small stick. He carried this stick to the American without saying a word. The American thanked him curtly with a nod of his head, drew from his pocket a small knife, and began to whittle the stick into a thousand pieces.

The waiter had thus saved the backs of the armchairs. At the end of twenty minutes, dinner was announced. The American was not impatient; he had been occupied. However, the room had to be put in order, for it was full of shavings.

The American is never separated from his little knife; his knife is his most intimate friend. But I cannot refrain from reproaching him openly for the unpleasant manner in which, when he has nothing to whittle or cut, he uses it for a toothpick. The way he handles the knife indicates whether he is contented or in a bad humor; whether the business in which he is engaged is on the road to disaster or success. The American who cuts from the outside in is in a good mood, and has made a good deal; the man who cuts toward the outside is in a bad mood and his business is not flourishing.

This was explained to me by an American, a man of high spirits and dignity, as we sat side by side on the deck of the *L. Stevens* where he was occupied in cutting the leather thong of his boot, not daring, in spite of his obvious desire, to attempt to whittle the top of his armchair, or the ship's railing.

First and foremost, the American is courageous and a good worker. He undertakes vast enterprises in the following manner. A forest ripe for exploitation is discovered. A group of Americans is organized. They start out, arrive, cut down the forest. Then the place is cleared. The trees having been felled, there remain three main avenues which usually provide the American with an outlet for his energy; a newspaper can be established, a steamship constructed, or a railroad laid out.

New enterprises are being constantly established and to this activity is due the development of California.

There are at New York—and New York is typical of many American cities—there are at New York, for example, three steamers that leave for a certain destination. The first makes the trip in one day; the second makes the trip in two days; the third makes the trip in three days. The one taking one day omits one trip after every three voyages. The one spending two days on the way omits every seventh voyage. The one requiring three days omits every thirtieth voyage. Two out of every three Americans will take the boat that lays off after three voyages. The American who travels *on business*, does not know danger. To him *Time is Money*.

The Americans, at least in San Francisco, were notorious as oppressors; I know little about them otherwise. Here is a typical instance of it. One night our consul, M. Dillon,[1] was suddenly aroused by a Frenchman who had arrived on one of the Sacramento steamers. M. Dillon asked the Frenchman to come into his room, where the latter told him the following story. Two Frenchmen, father and son, one old and the other young, were extracting gold near the road on one of the plateaus, up in the mountains. This claim was approximately a two days' journey from San Francisco. They were disturbing no one, and no one had disturbed them.

One fine day the location they had chosen attracted the interest of two American miners. The latter notified the two Frenchmen to leave. The father refused. The Americans then threatened to use force. The father replied that he would resist. He was captured, carried away and, as he resisted, as he had sworn he would do, he was stripped and whipped by the two men, while four more men held his son, who was forced to look on while corporal punishment was inflicted on his father.

"Now," the two Americans said to the old man when the dastardly act was over, "will you abandon it of your own free will?"

"No."

"Then it is your son's turn."

And so the son, in turn, was maltreated before the eyes of his father. Finally they were removed by sheer force; the men also threatened to fire on them like dogs if they were audacious enough to return. The two Frenchmen took refuge in a cabin, some miles away, where they were hospitably received. The owner of this cabin, a Frenchman like our host, indignant at the treatment given his two compatriots, was the man who had come to demand justice.

Ringing a bell, M. Dillon asked for his clothes and riding boots. He now went to the mayor, Mr. Brenham[2] and asked for two judges, who would be authorized to handle the matter. These were immediately supplied. M. Dillon who, incidentally, is highly esteemed, merits all the confidence accorded him.

He departed on the first steamer, then left the ship and, led by his guides, traveled overland. On the second day he reached the cabin where the two Frenchmen had taken refuge. Meanwhile, the two Frenchmen had remained inside the cabin around which had assembled a mob of some fifty Americans. He made his way through the crowd which pressed around him, and, accompanied by his judges, placed himself in the center of the mob, then addressed the men in English. M. Dillon, incidentally, spoke excellent English.

"My brave boys," he said, "since the birth of California in 1848 we have made, and are still making, considerable progress toward civilization. How, then, is it possible, in the face of the tremendous strides we are making, that in 1851 scenes as barbarous as those that have just occurred can still take place? You may rest assured that, for my part, loyal to my duty as French consul, and obedient to the feelings of justice and humanity that are in the heart of every honest man, I can never suffer a Frenchman to be maltreated by Americans or men of other nations any more than, in so far as it is within my power to prevent it, I would allow an American to be molested by a Frenchman. My unfortunate compatriots have already suffered more than their share as you know, since, to the misfortune of every man present, there is no authority in California but that of force. Today, however, this law will not hold. I have other support, as the presence of these gentlemen here with me will attest. Come, my brave lads, you are honest men; help us bring these two bandits to justice."

While uttering these final words, M. Dillon noticed three or four Americans whose faces pleased him. He went over to them and, placing his hand in turn on their shoulders, said: "You, you and you, go and bring me the two culprits."

The Americans thus indicated bowed, departed, and within an hour the two culprits were in the hands of the judges. Led to San Francisco where they were imprisoned, the two guilty men were tried and condemned, although sentence was passed by American judges. Let me say a few more words about the character of these people who are so independent.

An American never refuses a day's work, no matter what the price. If unable to obtain five dollars for the day, he will take four, three, two, even one. A Frenchman, on the contrary, refuses to work unless arrangements are made to pay him current wages. The Frenchman thus runs the risk of not dining one day out of three, whereas the American dines, poorly perhaps, but yet he dines. I have seen episodes of this character repeated time and again. I recall one occasion when a Frenchman asked M. Giovanni, who preferred to employ any other nationality rather than my poor compatriots for work, asked: "How much do you pay a day? Five dollars?"

"Three dollars is all I can offer."

"Four, if you please," replied the Frenchman.

"No, three; take it or leave it."

The Frenchman turned his back and departed, muttering impertinent remarks about M. Giovanni. Soon an American appeared and asked: "Have you any work to give me, patron?"

"Yes."

"So much the better."

"How much a day?"

"Whatever you wish."

"No, set the price yourself."

"You are reasonable; you know what a man receives a day."

"Three dollars; is that satisfactory?"

"That will do, if that is your price."

And the American started work and, for three dollars, accomplished twice the amount of work a Frenchman would have done for five.

Usually, irrespective of the country, the poorest workers encountered are the men from our own native land. Among outstanding antipathies of the American is his dislike of the negro, or mulatto. M. Giovanni watched with his own eyes the scene I shall now recount. He was nearly prostrated with laughter and his sides literally shook with mirth. He was crossing Washington Square. Among activities centering around the square is that of bootblack. This occupation is usually in the hands of Frenchmen. A mulatto placed his foot on the box of a French bootblack. The latter was not disturbed by his client's color; he took his brush, and rubbed. An American, passing by, stopped before the group as if he could not believe what he saw. Then, convinced that he was not mistaken, he showered heavy blows on the mulatto.

"See here," he said, "this is for having had the impudence to allow yourself to be shined by a white man, wretch!"

Having beaten the negro, he then turned on the white man. "And this," he said, "is for having been coward enough to black a negro's boots. In no country but California would the sight of a white man engaged in such a task be tolerated!"

The American is extremely punctilious about religious observances and matters pertaining to women. The comparatively slight success of Lola Montez [3] in America arose from the belief that she was obviously attempting to exploit the memory of her ill-fated adventures. Brazenness of this character offends the American taste.

In its infancy, San Francisco was a kind of Gomorrah. However, after American authority began to function through the efforts of Mr. Garrison, [4] San Francisco began to resemble other cities, and if its morals were compared with those of present-day Paris or London, the advantage would remain with the former.

Money is the ruling passion of Americans. The favorite proverb, as indicated, is: "Time is Money!" Their real religion, it might be added, is The Almighty Dollar. An anecdote—I might cite hundreds—will prove to what an extent they persevere and how they invariably reach the goal for which they start.

After remaining six years in California, an American, a worker at the mines, succeeded in saving three thousand dollars. This amount was comparatively slight for so many years' work. It was the total amount he had set as the minimum. The sum amassed, he returned to San Francisco, having decided to leave California and take this small fortune to his wife and children, to whom, in addition to the amount he had saved, he had been remitting at regular intervals a small allowance.

The steamer he was to take did not leave until the following day. That evening, not knowing what to do, he entered a gambling house. It was not the first time, but he had never played. He approached a table, mechanically watched the game for a while, then appeared suddenly to be struck with an idea that to him seemed so terrible that his face became sufficiently distorted to attract the attention of everyone nearby.

Detaching the belt in which he carried his little fortune acquired with so much difficulty, he placed it on the scales saying: "Home, or the mines again!" He placed his bet on the red.

The banker spun the wheel and, during the twenty seconds that it revolved, the most seasoned gamblers were terrified at the way the American watched this ball on which his life seemed to depend. He was a man of forty-five, with strongly-defined features, and a black beard and hair. The ball stopped on the red; the American had won.

He uttered a cry that seemed as much a groan of grief as a shriek of joy. "Three thousand dollars," he shouted like a crazy man, "Three thousand dollars!"

Carelessly the banker counted out three thousand dollars. The American placed them in his belt and left the room. He entered his hotel, requested the key to his room, and locked his door. The following day, as no one had seen him appear, the door was forced. He was found dead, with his money bag clutched to his breast. His hair and beard had turned white!

# VOLUME III

## CHAPTER I

## THE FRENCH

SECOND IN importance, both in number and influence, to the Americans came the French; although less numerous than the Americans, the French outnumbered all other nationalities. The latter, generally speaking, arrived without funds, bringing as their sole asset to acquire a fortune, gaiety and adaptiveness. The men who were the most successful were those who had a profession. Few made good miners. Invariably, when attempting to mine, they worked in groups of twenty or thirty, dined together, sang Béranger's [1] songs at dessert, swore that no matter what happened they would never leave one another, formed a society, and bravely set forth full of hope and enthusiasm for the mines, with visions of pockets bursting with gold. Many Frenchmen reached the placers, not knowing a word of English; when they learned a single word, which they used upon all occasions, they believed they had mastered the English language.

Whenever a Frenchman started work, he would dig here and there, but never thoroughly test a location. Often he would abandon a claim just before gold was struck, then quarrel with the Americans who, having taken over his claim and found rich gravel six inches below where he had stopped work, laughed at him. Not understanding what these Americans were saying and unable to speak fluent English, his only method of reply was to pull out his revolver. Pistol shots had a universal meaning, known to Frenchmen and Americans, far more eloquent than words. In the gold fields men shot to kill. Characteristic of French pioneers was the readiness with which they became discouraged at the crudeness of life and left the mines.

Frenchmen disliked the American pancake, called the flapjack,[2] or Jacques' mouthful. If their group numbered twelve, one would be sent out to hunt, and another would be appointed cook; in this way they deprived themselves of two able-bodied men. Although Frenchmen occasionally succeeded at the mines, yet this occurred only in exceptional instances. The Americans have invariably proved far more competent in this type of work.

Their incessant, most bitter, and deadliest enemy was the Irish-American. The term Irish-American is used because many naturalized Irishmen, many of whom are malicious scoundrels, reside in America. The Irish of California were no better than those in any other part of the country. Yet I should like to make the general remark that it is unwise to judge an entire race solely on the manners and conduct of a few individuals.

Not long after our arrival, that is, during the year 1851, two Frenchmen were living at one of the placers at Downieville in the Sierra Madre, a mining center located 120 miles from San Francisco, which has since produced an immense amount of wealth. The two Frenchmen felt ill at ease among the Irish and Americans, but the example, especially of the latter, revived their courage. These men had a claim, as a hole dug for the purpose of finding gold is called—I had completely forgotten about it at the time, but I recall it now—these men had a claim that gave promise of being an excellent producer and which was on the verge of fulfilling its promise.

The Frenchmen, furthermore, were quietly exploiting their claim and apparently living on a cordial footing with their Irish neighbors, wholly ignorant of the fact that their holding was coveted by them. One morning the cabin of the two Frenchmen was rudely entered, the men were forcibly removed from their shack and, amid cries and threats which they failed to understand, dragged before a kind of court composed of Irishmen and Americans. There an American who spoke a few words of French explained to them that they were accused by the two Irishmen of having entered their cabin at night and stolen their gold dust.

The two poor men who had been accused defended themselves with righteous indignation, protesting and swearing they were innocent; but no one understood them, or rather no one cared to understand them. All the Irishmen sided with their compatriots, banded together against the accused men, passed a rope around their necks, and prepared to hang them from two trees, carrying out the Lynch Law. Just before raising them off the ground, however, they insisted that the two Frenchmen swear to the robbery, respite being promised in return for a full confession. The accused replied that they could not swear to a crime of which they were innocent; they were ready to die, but would die protesting before God and man that they had not stolen the gold dust.

Then the ropes were pulled. The two unfortunate men were jerked off the ground, but after a few seconds their executioners allowed them to drop, shouting to them to confess. They could not confess, they replied, to a crime they had not committed and nothing would force them to lie. So they were hoisted again. This time, when death seemed imminent, suddenly a loud cry was heard on the road. Everyone turned. The sound that had been heard came from the lips of an American woman who was running with hair disheveled and in chemise and petticoat, crying: "Stop! They are innocent! In the name of heaven, stop!"

She then recounted, with all the volubility and strength of righteous indignation, that she had overheard one of the Irishmen plotting with his companion at the miners' boardinghouse to accuse the two Frenchmen of robbery. She swore on her life that she was telling the truth—that the two Frenchmen were not guilty.

"Let them go," said the Irishman, "but you will have to pay for the crime."

The executioners now removed the rope from the necks of the accused and, winding it around that of the poor woman, hanged her. At this terrible spectacle one of the two Frenchmen began to laugh hysterically. He had gone crazy. The other had become, on the contrary, wild-eyed and staring. Terror had made him an idiot. The two men were taken to San Francisco, where M. Dillon arranged to send the lunatic to a private asylum in Stockton. Insanity, incidentally, is not uncommon in California. The idiot he took into his own home where, after considerable care, he succeeded in restoring him to normalcy. I do not know whether the assassins were ever punished.

Let us now return to French activities in San Francisco. The immigrants of our country had to face a difficult situation. The poor devils arrived on a certain boat; the boat, no matter what its type, left them, as it were, at sea; that is, instead of landing them to face work, it landed them to face play, the lust for gold, luxury, the lure of fortune, women, and finally all the wiles of Satan.

Almost invariably gambling ensnared them. Many succeeded in this precarious profession and survived; however, the majority lost what little they possessed and took positions that, although respectable, injured their future. After losing everything the immigrant, in place of making good resolutions and finding honest work, usually went to San Francisco, deciding never to leave except as a final measure.

After the Americans, the first immigrants to form groups were the Frenchmen. Those who had escaped the danger just indicated—during the early days in California this was less serious—soon became gardeners, fishermen, hunters, commission merchants, porters, fruit dealers, nurserymen, small shopkeepers, croupiers in gambling houses, greengrocers, and strawberry merchants. Near Mission San José, Mission Dolores, and the Presidio stretch plains red with strawberries and covered with various wild greens which in the civilized world provide trade for greengrocers, such as valerianella, rampion, dandelion, and a kind of watercress that flourishes under large oaks and is edible only after it develops and abandons to the wind a small white flower, indicating the decay of the plant. This type of commercial activity was exploited with remarkable success until 1852, the year when the civilized salad known as lettuce, chicory, and romaine, replaced wild salad. We ourselves watched the building up of a fortune based on these greens.

M. D———, a former notary, an extremely courageous and worthy man, now some fifty years of age, arrived, lost all his money as does everyone, allowed himself to be influenced by bad example, attempted to earn money in various ways, became associated with a woman, and was abandoned by this woman who carried off their combined capital. Then he made a firm resolution, disappeared completely from the society that he usually frequented, and, one fine morning when everyone was asking what had become of him, was found selling herbs—a salad merchant. For two years he came, night and morning, with his basket full of assorted greens. At the end of two years he had in this way amassed more than twenty thousand dollars.

For California there has been coined the proverb: "There are no foolish tasks; there are only foolish men." During this period, except for those used for slaughtering meat, which were controlled by the Americans, all markets were in the hands of Frenchmen. After 1849, they were filled with many varieties of fine game which, on the whole, was comparatively cheap. Two partridges sold for one dollar as did two ducks; deer was fifty cents a pound and bear meat the same price. Hare, which was procured in the interior was, however, extremely expensive, selling for six or seven dollars; but hare, if necessary, could be omitted from the menu. Butchered meat was worth one dollar a pound. To what price the first chickens soared is not known.

Turkey was a luxury. In 1850 the price was sixty dollars; by 1853 it still brought from twenty to twenty-five. As regards turkey, I shall repeat what I have just said apropos of hare: it is possible to live without fowl when excellent game and all the fish found in Europe are abundant. Salmon was especially excellent. In the early days our Frenchmen who had the wise idea of becoming gardeners literally swam in gold. One cabbage was worth three dollars; a lettuce, two dollars. Radishes were sold by the half dozen, just as cherries are purchased in the month of May. When potherbs were available, they were usually proudly hawked from the basket.

A few eggs could be had in the markets, but they were considered luxuries available only to millionaires. They brought ten dollars a dozen; at this price, however, they were guaranteed to be fresh. By 1853 the price had dropped to four. Flowers were also available in the markets. A rosebud sold for one dollar; all fashionable young men wore rosebuds in their buttonholes. The smallest bouquet cost from four to five dollars.

There were a few French doctors in the city, but they were usually idle. Everyone was so busy in San Francisco that there was no time to be ill. Most of the doctors were highway robbers. During this period Doctor Oleivéra,[3] a reputable physician, and two or three of his associates, amassed immense fortunes, but the others made almost nothing.

These estimable Frenchmen had the best chance to succeed when the *lingotiers,* or gold seekers, arrived. In California *lingotier* is the term applied to those who arrive drawn by the lure of gold.

A portion of the receipts of a famous lottery,[4] it will be recalled, was appropriated to transport French emigrants into California. Then chaos broke loose, completely revolutionizing basic conditions on the coast. Our good consul, M. Dillon, was confronted with the difficult task of looking after all newcomers from France whom he attempted to send at once to the placers. As a matter of fact, M. Dillon even engaged accommodations for them in advance on the steamers that went up the Sacramento, and often paid their expenses in cheap boardinghouses. He received them upon their arrival and saw them off when they departed. He broke up their noisy meetings, dispersed their riots. What the French population owes M. Dillon will never be known.

He alone can tell how many times—he who perhaps was the only resident of San Francisco who never went armed—he alone can tell how many times when returning to the consulate after dark he was stopped by the threatening voice of a robber, or the humble appeal of misery. One evening two men barred the road. M. Dillon stopped.

"Monsieur Dillon?"

"Yes."

"Don't be afraid."

"Do I look like a man who is afraid?"

"Be good enough to come with us."

"Proceed."

The two men, with M. Dillon following them, walked on ahead through a narrow, little-traveled street, and went into a house that had the aspect of a robbers' den, for it ended in a kind of cave. There on a mattress without clothes and food lay a woman who had recently given birth to an infant.

"What is this?" he asked.

"A mother and child who commend themselves to your mercy, Monsieur Dillon."

"Why is such misery allowed to exist in San Francisco without someone letting me know?"

"We might have told you, Monsieur, but you would not have believed us. We wanted you to see it with your own eyes."

"That's right; here is fifty dollars for the mother. I will send Madame Dillon to you tomorrow to find out what the child needs."

Then M. Dillon returned to the consulate, escorted by the two men who accompanied him not so much to see that he arrived safely this time, as to kiss his hands once more.

## CHAPTER II

## JOHN. THE BEAUTIFUL CARLOTTA

AMERICANS REFER indiscriminately to all Chinese as John. The Americans have considerable difficulty pronouncing Chinese names; the time spent attempting to pronounce them is time lost, and no one knows the value of time as does an American. So they decided that every Chinese, most of whom are industrious, sober, and patient, should be called John. In the early days in California, Chinese junks plied between the great northern ocean and the great equinoctial ocean, crossed Micronesia,[1] and landed at San Francisco. Whatever the Chinese immigrants needed was brought with them—meat, dried in strips, smoked fish, tea, rice—the only money they spent here went for shoes, the purchase of working equipment, and rent.

Upon reaching California, the Chinese flocked to the mines like so many crows. Scattering over old claims abandoned by the French and Americans, they dug industriously, making one or two dollars daily. Satisfied with small but steady profits, before long they collected a large amount of gold.

John Chinaman resembles an ant. Like it, he is industrious and quiet, never mingling nor associating with other races. Upon reaching the land where he aspires to settle, he begins immediately to study the language of the country; he learns it quickly, speaks it with a frightful accent, but succeeds finally in speaking it. A cup of tea and chopsticks for eating rice complete his entire kitchen equipment.

Those who do not scatter to the placers become restaurant owners and cooks. They have been accused of forcing their dogs to eat rats; but perhaps the rat is as vilified in California as the cat is in France. I recall a warrant having been served on a certain boarding-house keeper in France, and upon this occasion it was claimed that if the judges who condemned the man had ever eaten cats, they would never care to eat anything else.

When the French arrived and, profiting by their European reputation as cooks, entered into competition with the Chinese, the latter became laundrymen. And this is what they are, and incidentally at extremely moderate prices, even today. No sooner do they lease a house than they fortify it with heavy timbers, which at once gives their place the aspect of a pagoda. As soon as they begin to settle on a street, everyone else is forced to move out, because of the high prices they pay for gambling and licensed houses.[2] The Chinese are inveterate gamblers; they play an extremely simple game, even and odd.

Like the French gambling houses, their resorts feature music. However, this music is Chinese, in other words, the most hideous music imaginable, for it is produced by a triangle and a large kettle. In imitation of the American and French gambling houses they have women for rakers; but these Chinese women are hideous. Both Dupont and Sacramento streets are entirely devoted to the two activities just indicated.

The Chinese have theatres, bazaars, and pagodas. The pagoda and theatre are closely associated. At the theatre they reveal amazing dexterity, especially in juggling, much as the Parisians excel in throwing knives. There is one particular Chinese bazaar in San Francisco that surpasses any of our most beautiful Parisian stores, where merchandise is extremely cheap.

An American named Duncan,[3] who began by acting as agent for Chinese merchants, is proprietor of this amazing place. His bazaar has magnificent display cases and a floor invariably damp so that dust will not cling to objects. Notwithstanding, his clerks are never seen without a feather duster in hand. To watch strangers arriving at this fine bazaar, courteously escorted by elegantly-clad Chinese merchants and a servant to act as interpreter, is a delightful and unusual experience.

When a Chinese has saved an amount planned for in advance, he leaves the country, never risking his savings in any kind of speculation. The notorious obscenity of the Chinese and the scandalous lives led by their women in San Francisco, have caused certain regulations comparable to those that Italy and Spain still make for the Jews, to be passed in their behalf. A certain quarter of the city has been reserved for them. They have their own ghetto. However, during the great celebration which they hold annually they are allowed to roam throughout the city; so long as it continues they shake San Francisco to its very depths. By day and night artificial fires glow; firecrackers burst on all sides under the feet of the passer-by; the skies are ablaze with rockets such as only Chinese can make. Inasmuch as they have handled powder for two thousand years, they are the foremost firework-makers in the world.

While the fête lasts, many Chinese move about the city on hired horses which are forced to follow behind the main procession only after considerable urging. Cues flapping, they ride their horses like awkward sailors. During the celebration they offer sacrifices of goats and ride out to visit the graves of their ancestors in the Chinese cemetery. Jovial Chinese are so rarely seen that their unusual gaiety at this time infects the entire city.

Next to the Chinese, the French, and the Americans, the Mexicans form the largest part of the population. Their wealth comes from land. Usually they do not engage in commercial activities, but live like veritable hidalgos. The Italians compete with the French in petty commerce. Persevering, sober, and not addicted to gambling, no occupation is too humble for them; they have, on the whole, the finest small shops in San Francisco, yet six of the largest Italian merchants began by peddling potatoes on the streets.

Speaking of Italy, the history of a famous Italian woman who lived at this time in San Francisco, comes to mind. Let us call her, if you like, Carlotta. In these days she was twenty-five years old with all the beauty of an Arlésien, a Roman, or a Greek. Her eyes and hair belied description. When she arrived from Naples with her husband, neither one of them had any idea of how to go about making a fortune. Their one purpose was to acquire wealth by honest means. But their friends jeered at their provincial scruples. Honesty, according to them, was merely relative. What is immoral at Geneva is moral at Paris, they maintained. What is immoral at Paris is moral at Florence. What is immoral at Florence is moral at San Francisco.

Finally M. —— —the wife has been called Carlotta, what shall the husband be named?—finally M. Balbi—suppose the husband is called Balbi—was persuaded that by acting as a banker at faro and placing his wife at the gambling table, he would soon acquire a fortune, and, since he did not cheat, an honest fortune. In San Francisco, as already observed, aristocratic callings did not exist. The proposal was taken under consideration by M. Balbi, Carlotta, and a friend of the house, the lady's cicisbeo, but, a rare and almost unknown thing, an honorable cicisbeo subsequently referred to as Chevalier Cellani.

Accordingly these three persons—Chevalier Cellani, M. Balbi, and Madame Carlotta—held a conference. Should M. Balbi be a faro banker, should the beautiful Carlotta be raker, should Chevalier Cellani become the associate, or rather the supporter of the association? Despite some objections raised by the fair Carlotta, the questions were decided in the affirmative.

The method of procuring a faro table in San Francisco is extremely simple. A large café is entered, and the proprietor of the house addressed.

"Monsieur," the stranger says to him, "I should like to manage a gambling table in your house."

If the stranger is accompanied by a woman, the proprietor of the establishment glances at her. If she is ugly, the terms are severe. If she is passable, discussion follows. If the woman is beautiful, the manager of the house places his café at the disposal of the husband. A handsome woman will draw customers for the house and more profit will be derived through sales to the players.

So M. Balbi had no difficulty finding a faro table in one of the most popular cafés in San Francisco. A new attraction had been added to the program, for the beautiful Carlotta was the one who dealt the cards. Their foresight was justified. Within three months enormous profits were made without a single shadow having been cast on Madame Balbi, either as a woman or a banker. On the contrary, her virtue was extolled, for the beautiful Carlotta spurned fabulous sums.

After this initial venture, the three Italians decided to try a hand in the mining country and to speculate for gold in the localities where it was found. After reaching one of the best known placers, they opened a faro game similar to the one they had operated in San Francisco. Here their luck doubled, a thousand, two thousand, dollars were made day after day; on all sides the talk was mainly of the beautiful Carlotta.

But such fortune proved fugitive; a rumor soon circulated among the miners, no doubt erroneously, that the fair card dealer assisted fortune with her own dexterity, that her fingers were far more agile than good luck was constant. The miners gave the signal, and as Carlotta was about to deal the cards eight or ten revolvers were levelled at her. She demanded the reason for this hostile demonstration.

"Because you are tricking us, beautiful lady," replied a miner, "and at the first card you touch, you die."

Carlotta turned deathly pale, but, despite the revolvers, continued to deal the cards. Her husband, unfortunately, did not have the same presence of mind; he leaned over toward her ear to whisper a few words, perhaps the one word "courage!" The miners inferred that he was instructing his wife how to rob them. Five or six pistol shots rang out; miraculously, none touched the beautiful Carlotta, but her husband was hit in the shoulder, three gamblers were killed, and two or three wounded. Carlotta dropped in a faint under the table. Then a violent combat broke out among the miners. Some believed Carlotta was dead; others, thinking she was still living, sided with her and fired in turn on those whom they believed to be her murderers.

Meanwhile, under cover of the confusion, M. Balbi and Chevalier Cellani removed the lady from under the table and carried her outside. The blood that flowed from the husband's wound and fell on his wife's garments made her appear to be dead, or at least seriously wounded. Once outside the room M. Balbi and Chevalier Cellani realized that Carlotta was not yet out of danger. They did not re-enter the hotel. This was a wise precaution, for the enemies of the fair Carlotta were in the majority. Having subdued their adversaries, they decided to exterminate this dangerous siren who simultaneously won both gold and hearts, and started for the hotel. But the Italians were no longer there. The miners then surrounded the town, threatening to burn it unless Carlotta were delivered into their hands. But they could not surrender Carlotta who, without losing an instant, had escaped.

Two days later she was back again in the city of Sacramento where, temporarily at least, she was out of danger. The city was reached just as the waters were creeping in. However, this was not unusual for the Sacramento; the river often overflows more or less violently, frequently carrying away in its wrath houses, sections of the city, and even the entire city. Two months later it will be rebuilt, only to be carried away again. But did not the inhabitants of Torre del Greco rebuilt their city seven or eight times after it was destroyed by lava pouring down from Vesuvius?

Those coming from the other side of the river told of the discovery of new and extremely rich placers. In Sacramento in the midst of disaster nothing could be done, so a decision was reached by the trio to attempt to establish themselves not in a café, but in a house of their own, and to open a faro bank among these new placers. This move, it was believed, would assure M. Balbi a fortune of at least one hundred and fifty thousand dollars. The new proposal was accepted by the beautiful Carlotta.

Nothing, however, could be done until the Sacramento resumed its normal channel, a matter of some three weeks. With the unquenchable thirst that seems to assail all who seek gold, a delay of three weeks appeared to mean a loss of perhaps fifty or sixty thousand dollars. Despite its swollen waters, despite the rapidity of its current, despite the debris with which it was loaded, they decided to cross it. Only a boat and two rowers were needed, which one hundred dollars would provide. The day was set for the departure. It was like a challenge to the river. Everyone whom the three speculators consulted advised them to wait. More than three hundred persons were at the landing place.

Madame Balbi wore a black velvet robe and had a rose and black opera wrap thrown over head. She was bedecked with diamonds. M. Balbi carried some ten or twelve thousand dollars in gold dust and nuggets. The boat put off from the bank and began to buff the current. The swollen river was a mile or more wide. The boat carried M. Balbi, Carlotta, Chevalier Cellani, a dog, and a parrot. It was propelled by two rowers.

After crossing two-thirds of the river, the boat appeared to struggle against an invincible force, and those who were riding in it were seen to give definite indications of distress. The craft was then drawn into a whirlpool; in place of moving ahead, it upset, overturned by some irresistible force. From both banks cries were heard; obviously the boat was sinking. Suddenly it disappeared; over the place where it had sunk waters now poured.

The dog swam toward the shore; he was the first to reach land. Next came the two rowers. Carried by the current which he lacked strength to combat, Chevalier Cellani tried to follow. Finally, supported by a reed, seaplant, or plant resembling the willow, appeared Carlotta, whose head sank lower and lower in the Sacramento. M. Balbi had disappeared, never to reappear. What effect the sight of this disaster produced on the spectators can be readily imagined. Amid the cries that arose, a man rushed up and asked: "What is it?"

"The beautiful Carlotta, she is drowning."

"Where is she?"

"Over there; she is still visible."

"There is still hope. Ropes! Ropes!"

Ropes were brought; having disrobed, the man adjusted them under his arms and hurled himself amid the floating debris into the icy waters of the Sacramento. The man was an Italian called Julian. He swam with considerable effort toward Carlotta and finally, after battling the current for three-quarters of an hour, succeeded in reaching her.

Rigid with cold, her two hands, one after the other, had lost their hold on the willow bough, but she had gripped it betweeen her teeth, where she still held it. Fortunately the colder she grew the more her

contracting jaws locked. Julian had brought another rope; this he
passed around her body. The men on the bank held the ends of this
second rope which they now pulled, bringing Carlotta and her res-
cuer to the shore. Carlotta had fainted; Julian's condition was
scarcely better. At this instant a cry for help resounded over the
waters, a cry of supreme distress that drew all eyes toward the river.
At the sound Carlotta shrieked: "It is my husband. Save him, save
him!"

Julian entrusted Carlotta to the men on shore and plunged back
into the water, swimming this time toward the man who was battling death with barely enough strength to keep himself afloat on
the water. At the end of sixteen minutes he reached the swimmer
and passed a second rope around his body. But before he regained
the bank he realized that it was Chevalier Cellani and not the husband of the beautiful Carlotta whom he had just saved.

While the two men were swimming toward the bank, Carlotta,
who had fainted again, had been carried over to the Hôtel de France
and placed in a well-warmed bed where she slept fitfully, calling in
a loud voice for her husband. Her delirious cries lasted throughout
the night. By the following morning the fever had subsided; tears
had succeeded nervous spasms, and Chevalier Cellani was allowed
to enter Carlotta's room. Carlotta held out her arms to him, but he
remained as if glued to the threshold. He regarded her with haggard
eyes, clasping his head between his hands searching in vain for
words, his vocal cords paralyzed by surprise and horror. Finally his
voice returned. "Carlotta," he cried, "Carlotta with white hair!"

For during the hour she passed in the Sacramento, hovering between life and death, more dead than alive, during the day and
night of delirium that followed, Carlotta's hair had grown white
as snow.

She believed Cellani was insane. However the latter, taking a
mirror, held it up before her eyes. The Italian woman uttered a
cry, and fainted. Notwithstanding her white hair, she lost none of
her beauty; she is still called the fair Carlotta, and only recently
word was received from California that she is about to marry one
of the wealthiest bankers of San Francisco.

CHAPTER III

APPLES AND ONIONS

WHILE WE were visiting San Francisco and becoming familiar with the country, our apples, onions, sweet potatoes, and syrups were held in the customhouse,[1] and we were powerless to secure their release. This delay at the customs lasted six weeks; meanwhile, eight or ten ships carrying cargoes of the same type reached port. Although this duplication was unintentional, yet the announcement of what each new ship arriving at the Bay carried resulted in a lowering of current prices. I was blissfully unaware of these complications and continued to anticipate the joy of making four hundred thousand dollars.

Finally, at the end of six weeks M. Giovanni was summoned to the customs to pay fifteen hundred dollars. He took that amount and rushed joyfully to the revenue office. Never were taxes more cheerfully paid. Although our imports had shrunk in value, yet they had arrived in port in prime condition and while the price had declined below what had been refused at anchorage, nevertheless a handsome profit could be made. Oh noble La Fontaine! What philosophy in the tale of Perrette and the pot of milk![2]

Receipt in hand, M. Giovanni asked where his merchandise was stored. An employee was instructed to take him to the place where it had been housed. This proved to be under an immense shed. M. Giovanni, upon arriving within sight of our future fortune, gave a cry of terror and despair. Every box had been broken; the apples, onions, and sweet potatoes were scattered on the ground, and as the rain had come down through the roof of the shed, the apples had rotted, the potatoes had sprouted, and the onions had tails like comets. Our profit of four hundred thousand had vanished so completely that M. Giovanni cried: "If you will only refund the customs' charges, that is all I ask."

But at San Francisco everyone becomes, if not easily, at least rapidly, philosophical. Catastrophes of the kind we experienced descend like hail, and what seems like certain fortune here is invariably ephemeral.

"I must sell my shipment in one lot," M. Giovanni said to the commissioner as he was leaving, "try to find a purchaser."

The next day a man arrived, who, after seeing the shipment, offered two thousand dollars for all of it. After bargaining for some time a price of twenty-five hundred dollars was made. The lot had cost us approximately sixteen thousand dollars.

We realized that, by adding our second speculation, our sweet potatoes, onions, and potatoes, to the first, the sugar we had been forced to throw into the water, we were having a run of bad luck. Since our departure from France we had lost approximately forty thousand dollars.

But to return to the purchaser of our apples and onions. He took the entire load away and had it placed under a shed. Two days later resounded the cry "Fire." Half of the city was, as usual, burning,[3] and our purchaser found only grilled onions, baked apples, and roasted sweet potatoes left out of our shipment, on which the wrath of heaven seemed to have descended.

Inasmuch as he had paid us in cash and had invested his last cent in this venture, eight days later he was selling us greens for salad. Naturally we gave him the benefit of our experience.

Having just burned our fingers in the fire, a few words about fire in San Francisco will not be amiss. San Francisco, as I have explained, was built of wood. This timber, which is imported, comes from another part of the United States, and arrives dry as a match, with the result that it burns furiously. At the time of our arrival in 1851, an hour was sufficient to destroy an entire street. The houses, furthermore, were built without chimneys, and every precaution possible taken against fire; but at San Francisco they did not catch; they were set. Such a conflagration served many purposes. First of all, it paid the debts of those who were burned out; it gave work to carpenters, locksmiths, etc.; it provided a pretext for bankruptcy; and, finally, it stimulated speculation of a kind revealed by the following incident.

An American lady and her family arrived in San Francisco by steamer; their furniture and goods consigned to an agency in San Francisco followed in a sailing vessel which, forced to round Cape Horn, naturally would not get in until six weeks or two months later. In due season their belongings reached port, and were placed in a warehouse. About this time two or three fires broke out in San Francisco. The agency and part of the warehouses burned.

Several days after the fire, the American lady sent to ask when she could remove her furniture. She was aware that the agent had had a fire; but as she knew he had several stores, she hoped that her furniture had been stored in one of those that had escaped the disaster. The agent replied that he was chagrined to report that all her furniture had been destroyed by fire, that she must adapt herself to the situation, as nothing could be done about it.

Six months later a friend of the American lady, who had known her in Boston and had often visited her house in that city, came to see her and asked to speak to her in private. She consented, although somewhat astonished that an old friend should be so formal upon such an occasion. The latter, with an air of considerable embarrassment, told her that he had just recognized in a house of questionable standing part of the furniture she had brought from the East and which she thought had been burned. Naturally her friend's hesitancy came from being obliged to reveal the place where he had found the furniture.

The American lady, an extremely serious-minded person, was amazed at the discovery, and, with as much discretion as possible, implored her friend to seize the earliest opportunity to return to the house and definitely ascertain with the aid of a mark she had made on her furniture when packing it, whether the pieces were actually hers. The gentleman, whether he found a pretext or not, was obliging enough to return to the house. The mark was on the place indicated. The furniture of the American lady had not been burned, but removed and sold. A lawsuit followed. The furniture was returned to the lady. *A mistake had been made.*

Furthermore, during this period no one in San Francisco had time to verify errors, as in the instance just cited, a case typical of thousands of others that were made in other forms of speculation.

It is only just to observe that, in addition to houses addicted to errors of this type, there existed a few in whom complete confidence could be placed. Today, furthermore, such things could not happen, but then they did occur, and occurred often.

This reminds me of what happened to French, English, and American merchants who, upon news of the discovery of gold in California, lured by the glamour of immense profits, shipped entire cargoes of every kind of merchandise to the coast and received in place of the money they expected, notices bearing the fatal words "burned or damaged," which meant, in either case, heavy losses.

On the other hand, merchants frequently sent shipments of inferior articles, justifying themselves by the current slogan, "Good enough for California!" Even if the cargo were "burned or damaged" in transit the shipper lost nothing, for his merchandise was of slight value even before it was sent to the coast. Usually these consignments, after costing the owner double their value in customs charges and storage, served to fill up the port or pave the streets.

Moreover, in all justice, it should be said that persons interested in unloading inferior articles on the California public showed undue zeal in handling the consignments with which they were entrusted, thus encumbering the ports and streets with nocturnal auctions, in the hope that under cover of night the defects of the merchandise would not be obvious and the open-handed California miner would purchase them.

Now the man who is duped in California is the miner; that is, the man with a belt full of gold; the extravagant man par excellence; the man with foolish desires who rebels at the idea of being considered a simple target for speculative purposes, merely because he pays all his bills without haggling.

M. Giovanni, while strolling one evening with his friends at the end of Kearny Street near the port, stopped at one of these auctions [4] that was unusually noisy.

The auctioneer was extremely clever. Just as these men stopped, he was about to put up a box containing three hundred cigars. Were these cigars good? Were they poor? Were they made of real tobacco? Were they mixed with the leaves of walnut trees? Did they come from Havana, or Belgium? That was beside the point; they had depreciated primarily because of the place and hour at which he was selling them.

The auctioneer held the box of three hundred cigars above his head, shouting: "A box of three hundred excellent cigars from Havana for one dollar."

Then, with the colorful vocabulary which is the exclusive possession of the California auctioneer he cried: "One dollar, gentlemen! One dollar, one dollar, one dollar, one dollar, one dollar!"

But no one was inclined, despite the recommendations that accompanied the object to be sold, to remove a dollar from his pocket. Thereupon the auctioneer was forced to reduce his offer, modest as it was, when the fact is recalled that in California a good cigar costs eight cents and an ordinary cigar only a few pennies. The auctioneer then repeated with the same volubility: "Three-quarters of a dollar! Three-quarters of a dollar!"

This was already a reduction of a quarter. The same indifference in the bystanders. Do not imagine that the auctioneer was easily fatigued; no, he continued with a courage worthy of a better cause: "Half dollar, half dollar, half dollar!"

That is, one-half dollar. The silence continued. Then, attempting to market his merchandise in any way possible, he called: "Then, gentlemen, for nothing, for nothing, for nothing, nothing, nothing, nothing!"

What he meant was, "Come, gentlemen, I will give it away!"

Everyone kept his hands in his pockets; no one wanted these excellent Havana cigars even for nothing. The auctioneer, apparently amused almost as much as he was amusing the crowd, wished to see how far the indifference of the bystanders would go. He drew a large round dollar from his pocket.

"Gentlemen," he cried, "a good and excellent dollar, warranted from the United States mint, for seventy-five cents, seventy-five cents, seventy-five cents!"

In other words, a good and excellent dollar, guaranteed coined by the United States, for seventy-five cents. This was twenty-five cents under the market price. But everyone was fully convinced that even if he had offered it at half price, the dollar was worth no more than the cigars; so the auctioneer, finding no purchasers, laughingly replaced it in his pocket.

Since sales were now over for the day, M. Giovanni and his friends, entirely satisfied with the spectacle which they had just witnessed, smiled and went on their way. The chicanery of auctioneers is obvious from this incident. All major failures in California are based, furthermore, on the following principle: Sell goods that should not be sold. On the other hand, first-class merchandise coming from France, England, and other parts of the United States, finds a ready market in San Francisco.

To return to the fires. Fires, as already explained, pay debts, create work, provide an excuse for bankruptcy, and permit fraudulent transactions. There is one more type of speculator that it serves to conceal; namely, the operations of criminals who take advantage of the confusion to rob. From the moment a fire is well under way, the police, as well as the investigations of the Vigilance Committee invariably find the following coincidences.

The point where the fire starts, except in some few rare instances, is always exposed to winds blowing from the land side, which spread the fire from east to west, in other words, to the outskirts of the city on the bay. The inference is that the fires do not break out accidentally, but are started by human beings.

What happened, on a small scale, in the fire of 1851 to Madame Plume,[5] wife of one of the foremost bankers of San Francisco, is typical of San Francisco when a fire starts, and the gong—that terrible sound that always made me jump trembling and terrified from my bed—rings. These gongs, by the way, often rang three or four times in the same night. Whenever I heard one, I thought only of saving my chest. Every Californian keeps his valuables packed in a strong-box near the door of his room, and when a fire starts, this is moved immediately to some point of safety near Telegraph Hill.

The alarm gong, then, was sounding; Madame Plume ran to the box that held her jewels, money, and laces. The fire was now within ten feet of her house, sending out tongues of flame preparatory to consuming it. Clad only in a simple dressing gown, she rushed into the street, the case under her arm. No sooner had she appeared in the street than she received a blow from the butt of a revolver and fell over backwards, dropping her box. By the time she regained her senses, the box had disappeared, carried off by the man who, aware that she would be forced to leave, waited for her at the door where he had struck her.

Among these first fires sounds like formidable sparks were heard that proved to be pistol shots. They were fired by the owners of burning houses and the Vigilance Committee, who were shooting robbers as if they were ferocious beasts. Such criminals were not taken to trial but were either killed on the spot, or hanged. As already indicated, this method of punishment was in accordance with the Lynch Law, or the law of Lynch.

These dreadful fires spread with such rapidity that it seemed as if no one could escape from them. As they invariably started at night, half-clad women could be seen running through the streets toward Telegraph Hill. The men, however, remained behind and attempted to save something from the flames. If they succeeded, they carried whatever they had rescued to the hill, then returned and attempted to move other objects.

A strange and abnormal world! Robbery in the houses, assassinations in the streets! Death awaited the man who left his own house with his own property. But there are no instances on record of goods carried to the mountain having disappeared. This led to the belief that a circle had been drawn around its base, over which robbers never passed.

By daybreak, in the section where the fire started, usually nothing remained but a mound of ashes and some dense smoke. Do you believe that all these ruined proprietors were tearing their hair in despair? Not at all! No sooner had they been chased from their houses by the flames, than they began to run to the wharfs where construction wood was piled.

While the house was still burning, wood to be used for another house was being purchased and this wood was taken to the vicinity of the fire, where it was left until the dying embers were extinguished.

Three days later the house would be rebuilt, business would resume its normal course; thus it would seem more like a dream than a reality that this sinister spectacle, passing with the rapidity of lightning, had actually been witnessed. This is an opportune moment to observe that San Francisco has been built or rebuilt almost fifty times.[6]

Turning from this strange tableau of typically American activity, where life and death pass in rapid pageant, to Telegraph Hill, the visitor looks upon an amazing scene of desolation. Here women and children of every nationality have congregated. Half-clad, wet by the chill dew of the night, and trembling with cold, they crouch over objects rescued from the flames. Children watch anxiously to know if they will see their fathers again. Women fear they will never find their husbands. With eyes fixed on the smoking ruins, they listen to the hideous sound of flames which, growing closer, indicate the progress of the fire, or, slowing down or dying out, bring hope that the fire has been conquered. Suddenly the flames, gaining fresh force, make every heart pound with terror and despair. Amid this confusion a man, wearing half-burned clothes, rapidly ascends the slope of the mountain; women and children flock hopefully around him. Soon his features are distinguishable. Those to whom he is a stranger stop, but his family rushes forward, accelerating their pace when they are certain he belongs to them. Then sobs of happiness, cries of joy resound; caresses and embraces mingle. Since the father, since the husband is safe, what was lost is forgotten.

But what of those who are lost? Enquiries are made about the missing, and all the poor exiled colony hangs on the lips of the narrator, greeting each word he utters with joy or grief. Then gradually the mountain is depopulated, everyone returns to the city and, following the head of the family, all enter their new abodes. At the funeral bivouac remain only those whom the fire made widows or orphans, or those who, having regained their father or husband, lost their entire fortune. But I am attempting to portray scenes that beggar description; so I shall stop.

In the early days of California, a group of American firemen was organized but, having no pumps, they were compelled to depend on buckets.[7] However, there was a shortage not only of pumps, but also of water. These two defects were soon remedied. Pumps were ordered from America and engineers were procured to dig wells at every street corner.

Inspectors watch these wells so that they are always in good condition and today the entire city of San Francisco at the first sound of the gong, is prepared to face fire. Often one, two, or three houses will burn, but the great fires that demolished entire sections no longer occur. In addition, a law has been passed so that a wooden house once burned must be replaced by one of stone.

CHAPTER IV

BRIC À BRAC

WITH notes amounting to approximately two hundred dollars, we for our part were as completely ruined as our dealer in Irish potatoes, sweet potatoes, and onions. Mature consideration is advisable before undertaking a speculation; these last bills did not leave us with funds to return to Europe. M. Giovanni did me the honor of consulting me about the situation. "What are we going to do, Jeanne?" he asked.

"That is quite simple," I replied. "We shall become dealers in old furniture and curiosities."

"How can we be dealers in furniture and curiosities?"

"Easily; we have splendid furniture and my New Zealand collection."

"Well, well, well," said M. Giovanni, "that is an idea."

"I hope so."

"But think it over, Jeanne."

"I have already done so. Begin to look for a house today; rent it tomorrow; and the following day we will open a shop."

That same day M. Giovanni began his search and found on Dupont Street a shack built of laths which he engaged at the modest price of three hundred dollars a month. However, there was a small room in the rear. After three days' heavy work on the part of my husband and myself organizing the bric-à-brac shop, we were ready to open Monday morning. I had some exquisite furniture, a piano, a library composed of choice books, and a cabinet of curiosities worthy of gracing a fine establishment. At the end of eight days, our store was known throughout San Francisco as the Antiquarian Shop. Its success exceeded all expectations. True enough, I had for crier at the door of the shop the eighth wonder of the world. This was a charming parrot with a yellow face and purple brow, who danced, sang, and talked. Her triumph, in song, was the dance *"Gustave."* But she always started off a half tone too high. The result was that when she reached a certain note, her voice cracked. Then she would shake her pretty head like a person saying to herself: "How foolish I am! I made a mistake, let's begin again."

Then she would start a tone lower and finish with ease. As a sign of satisfaction, she would utter a joyful shriek of laughter. She was a droll little beast, this little parrot, and seemed at times endowed with a certain intelligence. She would say in one breath and without stopping, "God bless Queen Victoria, her august husband, Prince Charles Albert, and all his royal family!"

The crowd stopped at the door of our house, first to listen to the parrot, then, seeing furniture in good taste, a fine library, an ethnological museum, a collection of minerals, some magnificent laces which I announced as English point, but which were in reality only Valenciennes and Chantilly, they entered and purchased. The Americans in particular bought without haggling. At the start M. Giovanni and I held long discussions, my husband not wishing to have me appear in the shop. I have already mentioned the dangers in San Francisco to which women were exposed. But I insisted and gave M. Giovanni so many excellent reasons that I succeeded in winning him over.

Among the many customers who flocked to our store, I observed one in particular who seemed consistently to purchase whatever seemed to have the greatest value; he would ask the price of an object, and upon being told would pay for it in cash, and carry it away. He showed such perseverance in coming to purchase throughout the week that he empied the shop of its most precious specimens. Every time we saw him enter, joy entered with him, so we welcomed him with many little attentions. One day I even went so far as to attempt to explain to him the origin of certain curiosities. But he merely shrugged his shoulders.

"What do you think all this means to me?" he said, "keep this information for the collector for whom I make these purchases when he comes to see you."

Two or three days after this conversation, the bric-à-brac house was almost empty, but our pockets, on the other hand, were full. In the evenings M. Giovanni went out for a time, while I remained alone in the shop. One evening, five minutes after his departure, Sir George entered. I gave a cry of surprise; I was wholly unaware that he was in San Francisco. He approached and greeted me.

"When will you be through with your store, Madame?" he enquired.

Surprised at his unexpected appearance and this strange question, I replied: "As you see, Monsieur, it will not be long now; within three or four days I hope to be sold out."

Sir George looked around, and observing all the shelves nearly bare replied: "For the love of God, bring this farce to an end and may I never see you again at the cashier's desk, even in California."

Having asked the price of several objects, he paid for them and carried them away. From then on I felt certain that the intermediary who showed so little interest in the scientific aspect of the objects he purchased was acting on behalf of Sir George.

When M. Giovanni returned, I told him of Sir George's visit and our conversation. But to my great surprise, in place of laughing he said: "He is correct, in the future you shall not participate in my businesses, especially in California. I am grateful for the assistance you have given me, but from this time on something else must be found."

As a matter of fact, M. Giovanni, upon seeing money coming in, had decided to undertake a large venture. We had thirty thousand dollars between us, and in California, although such a sum may not represent wealth, yet it is adequate to establish a business.

So I went to stay with an American family whom we knew, while M. Giovanni rented a large store and became associated with a merchant to engage in a wholesale business and purchase commodities of all kinds, not only supplying provisions to the mines, but also buying gold dust.

The business flourished. M. Giovanni realized immense profits, and as fast as they were made, they were used to make new purchases. These purchases, and their trade in general, consisted of wine, flour, sugar, tea, coffee, and preserves from Marseilles. This method of speculation has its advantages and disadvantages. The advantage is that funds are never idle, and are always making a profit. The disgreeable feature is that our entire fortune was tied up, and any losses would be on a heavy scale.

From time to time I came to see my husband at the store, where I was in the habit of remaining for an hour or two upon each visit in a small room at the rear. One day M. Giovanni happened to be alone, his associate having left to assist in the sale, at auction, of a shipment of tea, and the assistants were in the rear court, engaged in placing bales of merchandise in the cellar. Just at that moment, an Irish-American came into M. Giovanni's room to give him an order for a load of merchandise to be delivered to one of the mines. Unfortunately, at the very time he entered, I was leaving the small room to go into the court. The American saw me.

"Oh, oh!" he said, "who is that woman?"

"That is Madame Giovanni," replied my husband coldly.

"The devil," said the Irishman, laughingly, "Madame Giovanni, you say?"

"I said Madame Giovanni, my wife."

"Your wife?"

"My wife."

"Your own wife?"

"Mine."

"Come now, it is really somewhat presumptuous to assume that any man has a wife all his own in San Francisco."

"Then I must be presumptuous, for I believe just that."

"I should certainly like to see her, this wife of yours; have her come out a moment."

Fortunately one of M. Giovanni's qualities is composure. He believed that this was the best weapon with which to oppose this strange attack.

"Monsieur," he replied, "I have told you that it is my wife, Madame Giovanni, that should be adequate; since she is my wife, you should understand that she is not here to be summoned to appear at the call of the first comer."

The American shrugged his shoulders and left. Ten minutes later he returned, accompanied by a friend. M. Giovanni saw them enter with a certain anxiety, but although uneasy, he concealed the fact. The American came toward him with a brazen air. He indicated M. Giovanni to his companion: "There is the fellow," he said. "Behold the rascal who allows himself to have a wife entirely to himself in San Francisco! What do you say to that?"

The two Americans began to laugh in guttural tones. Then, having jeered to their satisfaction, and since M. Giovanni did not move from his seat, the American remarked, placing his hand on his revolver: "Monsieur Giovanni, do me the favor, I beg of you, to go and look for the lady; we want to see her, you understand, *we want to see her!*"

My husband immediately realized that something terrible was about to happen. However, he resolved not to weaken, but to make a firm stand. He extended his arm and, indicating with the end of his finger the door of the room where I was to be found, replied: "The lady you wish to see is there. I dare you to go and look for her; but I warn you, you go at the risk of your life."

The American leaped from the place where he was standing to my door. No sooner had he done this, than M. Giovanni, jumping over the counter, stopped him, seizing him by the hair, just as he was about to place his hand on the key.

In a second the intruder was knocked down on the ground and forced to lie there on his back. Although in this awkward position, the American, firing at close range, pulled the trigger of his revolver, aiming at M. Giovanni. Fortunately the bullet passed between his neck and shoulder, barely grazing the shoulder, and burying itself in the ceiling. With one hand M. Giovanni seized the barrel of the revolver that was still smoking, and with the other drew his own from his belt. In the meantime, with his free hand, the American grasped his knife, plunging it into M. Giovanni's thigh.

M. Giovanni realized that it was foolhardy to be lenient with this maniac; drawing his revolver from his belt, he placed the gun against the man's temple and blew out his brains. The fact that he had jumped back, after having dodged his shot, saved his life. The dead man's friend now came up and also tried to fire. M. Giovanni turned, but his adversary was obliged to cope with a newcomer. This newcomer was our associate who, unaware of what was happening, rushed to my husband's assistance. With a movement of his arm, he knocked the pistol from the hand of the American; the shot went off in the air.

Disarmed, and confronted by two adversaries, the American, aware that his friend was dead, turned and ran. Aided by his associate, M. Giovanni pulled the corpse of the American outside his shop, placing it near the threshold of his door. Then, utterly oblivious to his knife wound, which, incidentally, was not dangerous, he took his hat, lit his cigarette, and went to make his declaration at the office of the sheriff, requesting him, at the same time, kindly to have the body which was blocking traffic, removed. No charges were made against M. Giovanni; such scenes were not extraordinary at a time when the lack of definite authority forced everyone to be on the defensive, and, in the case of offense or attack, to defend his honor.

## CHAPTER V

## FIRE

A MONTH after this tragic scene, which was made known to me by the percussion of three successive pistol shots, just when our speculations were progressing smoothly and just when the surplus for our part of the venture amounted to one hundred and twenty thousand dollars, the ominous fire gong, so well known to all Californians, rang, announcing a fire.

The fire started on Jackson Street; [1] fanned by a strong wind, within a few seconds it reached our store. Before M. Giovanni could dress the roof was in flames. The brave firemen rushed from all sides, but the shortage of water so hampered their efforts that M. Giovanni did not hope for an instant to escape disaster. Notwithstanding, he went to work and, although our fortune was completely lost, he was courageous enough to occupy himself saving the possessions of others. In fact, he displayed such remarkable courage that for several days everyone in San Francisco was talking about him. It was not until the bells ceased to toll, thus announcing that the fire was under control, that he looked around.

Where our store once stood and, incidentally, our entire fortune, there was merely a smoking mound of ashes. This time the situation differed from that following our disastrous speculation in apples and onions. The only thing M. Giovanni now had in the world was his watch. He approached his associate—the one who had saved his life in the encounter with the American—and clasped his hand.

"My dear friend," he said, "I wish you courage and luck in your future enterprises; but California is "a devil of a land.""

"Where are you going?" asked M.V.B.[2]

"My God, I am going to see what has become of my wife during this terrible night. Good-bye!"

After searching in all his pockets, he finally found a cigar which he calmly lighted. This done, he bowed, and started up the street toward my boardinghouse. How anxiously I was awaiting him can be readily understood. At the first sound of the fire gong I, like everyone else, jumped out of bed. Then, learning that the fire was actually in M. Giovanni's store, I rushed out of the house.

Scarcely had I gone fifty steps in the direction of the fire, when I was joined by Mr. Wood,[3] the husband of the lady with whom I was boarding. He stopped me and, despite my desire to continue on my way, made me understand to what an extent my presence would distress my husband. Since there was, as usual, great confusion, it seemed extremely dangerous to venture forth into the crowd. Furthermore, Mr. Wood said he personally would go and bring me the news.

I waited for him with anxiety; it was not until two hours later that he returned. He had made the rounds, and informed me that M. Giovanni was still working furiously, although his wares were the first to burn. On toward four o'clock in the morning, he appeared, his face black from the fire, his beard and hair burned, and his clothes in shreds. He had been through the flames three times, and the front of his shirt was burned away. He entered, saw me weeping, threw his cigar away, dropped into an armchair, and with a reaction that to me seemed quite natural, since I knew his excellent character, began to sob. Then I went over, knelt down beside him, and attempted to console him. "My friend," I cried, "be brave."

"So," he replied, "you do not know?"

"I know everything; we are completely ruined, are we not?"

"Completely."

"But we are young, we can work. Whoever commences badly ends well, and we have our whole future before us."

He let his head fall on mine. "You are right," he replied. "Talk to me, console me, give me strength."

I continued to talk to him and he listened without replying, allowing himself, as it were, to be quieted by my words. As a matter of fact, I soothed him so well that at the end of a few moments, exhausted by the fatigue and strain of the night, he fell asleep. I was on my knees and bent over in a most uncomfortable position, but I had such profound pity for the man who, after seeing his own stores burn, had forgotten his own losses to assist others, that for an hour and a half I did not even stir. Daybreak found us in the same position. M. Giovanni slept profoundly. I, in turn, was now weeping, but softly, not to waken him. Finally he opened his eyes, tried for a few seconds to collect his senses, then suddenly remarked: "Poor Sir George. I must go and find out how he is."

"What! Find out about Sir George," I replied, "why is that?"

"First, because he made such valiant efforts during the brief quarter of an hour the fire lasted in our store; next, because, following my example, he worked as I did, and by my side, and I believe I heard some one say he had broken his leg, dislocated his knee, crushed his foot, or had some more serious accident." And M. Giovanni reached for his hat.

"What are you about to do now? I asked.

"I am going to find out about him," he replied. "I owe it to him, by God, indeed I do."

He picked up his cigar. To see M. Giovanni light a half-smoked cigar was, to say the least, surprising.

"Why do you do that?" I enquired.

"We are ruined, Jeanne," he said, "it is necessary to smoke cigar-butts."

Then he left with the courage and calmness of spirit that he invariably revealed in times of stress. An hour later he returned. Sir George, he said, had nothing more than a badly wrenched back; he was in the hands of the best doctor in San Francisco, Dr. Oleivéra.[5] He knew all about M. Giovanni's difficulties, desired to hear from him again during the day, and sent his compliments to me.

About eight o'clock large crowds began to enter and leave our house; everyone came to hear the news and acquire first-hand information about the losses we had just experienced. Americans, Frenchmen, and Indians [4] came to sympathize with us, complimenting M. Giovanni on his fine conduct and, it must be added, according to their fortunes and resources, offering assistance with a disinterestedness and generosity only to be found from 1849 to 1852 in California.

My husband thanked them, but accepted nothing. He had the air of a man expecting someone. On toward nine o'clock, Mr. Argenti, the banker, entered. M. Giovanni arose with alacrity and, with a beaming face, extended his hand.

"I knew you would come," he said.

Mr. Argenti, who was born in California, had amassed a vast fortune which he used in instances like the one I shall now narrate. Incidentally, he was a man of unusual distinction of spirit, heart, and manner, and had always shown a deep interest in M. Giovanni. My husband, on the other hand, never undertook any important business venture without first asking his advice.

"I wish to thank you," he said to M. Giovanni, "for having relied on me. I have come merely to tell you purely and simply, my dear compatriot, that I am placing thirty thousand dollars at your disposal.

Then he came over to me: "Come, be brave, Madame," he remarked, "do not take the situation too much to heart. You must need some rest; lie down, and try to sleep quietly. I shall request your permission to take your husband out for dinner."

"Madame," said M. Giovanni, "this is an embarrassing situation. You see the condition of my suit and my linen; moreover, what I have on are the only suit and linen I have; everything else was burned.

Mr. Wood offered to place his wardrobe at my husband's disposal; but M. Giovanni thought it would be wiser to go to a clothing store and replenish his wardrobe. Moreover—and I do not say this to deprecate the recognition we owe Mr. Argenti—experiences similar to the one just described were not uncommon in California.

In the same fire that ruined us, two American merchants also lost their fortunes. They had known one another only in a business way since their sojourn in California. As the last embers of the fire were dying out, they met on the street corner.

"Well," one asked the other, "how did you come out?"

"I lost everything."

"Everything?"

"Everything. I did not even have enough to buy breakfast this morning. And you?"

"I," replied the first man, "suffered a heavy loss, but luckily I had some funds in reserve. I still have twenty thousand dollars, and since you are poorer than I, allow me to begin the day by begging you to accept half of this sum. I can start just as well with ten thousand dollars as with twenty, and I believe that what I am doing will bring me luck."

The two men shook hands; that was all. Each began again with ten thousand dollars. Heaven blessed their new enterprises; they are now two of the wealthiest merchants in California.

CHAPTER VI

MORE SPECULATIONS

EXHAUSTED by the excitement caused by the fire, I followed Mr. Argenti's suggestion and went to bed. He was correct; the strain on my emotions had been so great that I could no longer remain standing. When M. Giovanni returned, Mr. Wood told him that I had retired; that I had a bad attack of fever, that I was asleep, and that I needed rest.

My husband was somewhat distressed to learn that I was ill, but he confidently believed that good news and the disclosure of his new plans—for he had already made new plans, thanks to his friend, Mr. Argenti—would soon effect a cure. He left me in charge of Mr. Wood, begging him to quiet me and assure me that everything was progressing favorably and that he, M. Giovanni, had been obliged to leave to avoid losing any time, time in California being the only thing that once lost can never be regained.

A hundred steps from the house he met Sir George, who was walking with a limp and leaning on a cane. Sir George approached him.

"It is you for whom I am looking, Monsieur," he said. "I have come to beg you to grant me a few moments' conversation."

"With the greatest of pleasure, Monsieur, but unfortunately I cannot take you to my wife; she is suffering considerably, and is so ill that she is obliged to remain in bed."

"Will you present her with my sincere regrets, Monsieur, for the misfortune that has occurred, and every wish for the best of health. But here we are within ten feet of a café. Will you not enter? I must beg this favor, because, since I still suffer with my foot, I find some difficulty in standing."

M. Giovanni and Sir George entered the café, sat down at a table, and asked for whatever was ready to serve. Considerably embarrassed and begging M. Giovanni to regard him as a compatriot—since all Europeans should feel like compatriots in other parts of the world—with all the delicacy possible, after commencing by telling him that he was extremely rich, Sir George offered my husband either his purse, or credit to the amount needed to reopen a store.

In order not to offend my husband by having the air of rendering him a gratuitous service, the Englishman offered to lend him the money at six per cent, which was extremely reasonable in a country where the legal rate was fifteen. M. Giovanni, smiling, stopped him and took his hand. The gesture was so expressive that Sir George was not deceived."

"You refuse me, Monsieur," he said, "I understand. In your eyes and those of Madame Giovanni I must seem ridiculous. You must forgive me, believe that I have recovered from my folly, and regard me from today on as a sane man."

M. Giovanni allowed him to finish, then replied: "It is not because you love my wife that I decline the kind offer you have made me. Aside from my complete confidence in Madame Giovanni, I assure you that at our first meeting, the first time I saw you, I judged you for what you have just proved to me, that you are a *perfect gentle-man,* incapable of a mean act; however, I must decline, my dear Monsieur, but only because a countryman, an intimate friend, has already come to my assistance; furthermore, I have accepted his proposal. I am leaving San Francisco, having decided on an excursion north into the mountains of the Sierra Nevada."

"And you plan to take Madame Giovanni on such a journey?" cried Sir George.

My husband smiled. "No, Monsieur, I shall go alone," he replied. "Madame Giovanni is wonderfully comfortable in the house and with the family of Mr. Wood. She has been living there for quite a while; after I have my foot in the stirrup and affairs are running smoothly once more, she will go to France to visit her family and my father. Then I shall rest easier, for as I was saying to my partner this very morning, California is an accursed land."

Whereupon, again thanking Sir George and making him understand how imperative it was for him to leave, M. Giovanni rose. Sir George requested the privilege of presenting me with his respects the following day. Needless to say, this favor was granted, and the two men parted on the most amicable terms.

Having, as he said, no time to lose, M. Giovanni went down to the wharf used by the steamers that were bound for Sacramento and Marysville. There he passed half an hour collecting information indispensable to the accomplishment of his new project. Everything seemed to favor his plans; one of our friends, meeting him walking rapidly back to his lodgings with the air of a man much preoccupied, asked him if he were already on the trail of some new venture. To this query M. Giovanni replied that he believed he had just found a speculation that would prove highly favorable.

"So much the better and good luck," replied the friend, and continued on his way without asking M. Giovanni what this new speculation was, so rushed is everyone in San Francisco.

M. Giovanni, upon his return, found me awake and waiting for him with considerable impatience. I was very ill, but I ignored my own condition. Mr. Wood did not consider it wise to keep him in the same ignorance about my health, but told him, on the contrary, his frank opinion. Immediately, M. Giovanni gave orders to have someone go out and look for an old friend of his, a physician, in whom he had full confidence; while waiting for the doctor to respond to the call, he entered my room.

I was as joyful to see him thus properly clad, as I had been depressed by his departure. He was dressed in new garments, not, however, from a clothing store, but from one of our extra trunks that had been stored in a stone cellar and that contained all our best garments, useless in California, and our fine Parisian linen. He had just recalled that, several days before the fire, he had had this trunk stored separately, and had discovered where it had been placed. He clasped my neck as if he were returning from a long voyage, as if he had not seen me for twenty years. At this embrace I could no longer restrain my tears.

"Come," he said joyfully, "do not weep, my dear Jeanne. Many things have happened since morning, and all is for the best. You heard what Mr. Argenti offered me; I have accepted, but he has given me more than money; he has given me an idea."

"What idea?" I asked.

Then M. Giovanni's expression suddenly changed, and he hesitated to disclose this thought, aware that what he was about to propose would chill me with horror. He became diplomatic, used charming phrases, and made inconsequential remarks to pave the way for the main discussion. He told me he intended to take a trip north to see what might develop. The result of these digressions was that instead of quieting me, as he had intended, he only succeeded in frightening me.

Confessing that I had not understood a word of what he had said, I implored him not to treat me like a child. I told him that if he had any new projects, and if these projects were reasonable, he should take me into his confidence, so that I might judge them sanely. Thereupon, he took my hand and, with his mildest air and most intimate language, which he used only on extraordinary occasions, said: "My dear Jeanne, as soon as you have recovered from your slight indisposition, I am leaving for the Sierra Nevada. Mr. Argenti assured me today that I could make a fortune if I had the courage to go and establish myself in the placers with a large assortment of merchandise such as clothes, miners' tools, merchandise, sugar, tea, flour, wines and brandy, in other words, whatever should be stocked for the use of miners in the various mining centers now being exploited on the banks of the Yuba."

"But," I asked, looking at him fixedly, "what am I to do?"

"You," he replied, "will remain here until I see how my affairs are progressing, then you will make your trip to France while I try my fortune in the mountains. Have no fear, dear one, everything leads me to believe that this fortune will not be difficult to make. We may fall quickly in this treacherous land; after all what is most consoling is that the ascent is equally rapid."

M. Giovanni had been fully aware of what would happen; that is why the dear man had taken this indirect way of telling me, as agreeably as possible, that he was about to place his life and fortune at the mercy of the first miserable wretch in whom he aroused a longing to send a bullet at him. Although the mountains were quite remote, yet each day fresh rumors drifted in of atrocious crimes recently committed in these centers where authority is unknown, and where strength makes law.

I began to sob, then told him that such a thing was out of the question. I implored him to abandon this idea; but, with a mildness that proved his determination, he begged me seriously to reflect on what he had said and, leaving aside all dangers which, moreover, were inevitable, he attempted to have me look at its brightest aspect. He told me he had already secured information from the captains of steamships and other well-informed persons, and that everyone whom he asked assured him that the mining season at Downieville was certain to be extremely rich, and that if he had the courage to go there and open a store, he could undoubtedly make a fortune in eighteen months.

Well as I knew M. Giovanni, yet I continued to raise objections. My appeals were futile. Under his mildness M. Giovanni concealed an unbending will, and his decision had been made. His physician having told him that, with good care, I would recover in a few days, he devoted himself to nursing me, in order to see me recuperate more rapidly.

During the next two or three weeks he purchased merchandise at auctions, having it baled, by day, under his own eyes. In the evening, while watching me—although I was gaining in strength and had no further need for a nurse—he and I discussed what would be suitable to take along. These items he jotted down as I dictated, and so there was nothing to do the following day but make purchases. By the end of three weeks he had assembled in the warehouse at the wharf fifteen or twenty thousand dollars' worth of assorted merchandise that had been carefully selected, awaiting shipment.

Meanwhile, Sir George came to visit me. As my husband had told me what had passed between them, I was somewhat reconciled to his call. Inasmuch as he had received from my husband permission to renew his visits, it so happened one evening that I found myself alone with him. I took advantage of this opportunity and, drawing my armchair near his, I begged him, now that we had become good friends, to explain his puzzling attitude toward me and the real reason for his sojourn in California.

With the utmost formality, and in the language of a perfect gentleman, which M. Giovanni believed him to be, he told me that he loved me deeply, that for a long time he had lost all hope of having it reciprocated, but that, lacking any other happiness, he found joy in seeing me from time to time. I put forth every effort to convince him that this was merely empty happiness, and at best slight consolation. Then I told him in all sincerity, which an intelligent man could not fail to understand, that he had nothing to hope from me but friendship and the promise of always being glad to see him. We separated the best of friends, he, fully cognizant of my friendship, I, happy that this frank explanation had placed me at ease with a gallant man. As he was about to leave, M. Giovanni entered. I told him everything.

"Can you understand," I asked, "how a man who has an annual income of three hundred thousand pounds, who might, thanks to this vast fortune, live like a great lord in England, France, or Italy, will waste his time in the muddy town of San Francisco, paying court to a woman who does not love him?"

M. Giovanni pursed his lips like a man who thinks that all tastes are natural. "He has his own way of finding amusement," he said, "why bother?"

CHAPTER VII

SACRAMENTO

WHEN THE month of April [1] arrived, which was the time set for the departure to the mines, I summoned all my courage and informed M. Giovanni that I had decided to accompany him. But M. Giovanni merely laughed in my face, considering such a thing impossible.

But my decision, as I have said, was made. I begged him, I implored him, I asked him if I had ever been a handicap or a burden on any journey; I reminded him that I was strong, courageous, valiant. In view of all this, I asked, what was there to fear? He replied that such a trip was even more than a strong man could endure, and implored me not to torment him further. However, nothing could induce me to abandon my project. I went to See Mr. Argenti, and told him what I expected of him as a friend; namely, that he urge M. Giovanni to permit me to accompany him, allowing me to return after he had become established.

Using all my persuasive powers, I convinced him that I would be extremely useful to my husband as a companion during the journey. He finally admitted that I might be right. Mr. Argenti having been won over, M. Giovanni soon yielded. At heart he did not care to be separated from me; but he was afraid some calamity might occur.

"Come then," he said, "since you are so determined. Only I warn you that in the middle of the journey you will be forced to return. Women must have their own way."

Accordingly, the departure was arranged for the following day. At three o'clock in the afternoon I embraced my hosts, Mr. and Mrs. Wood, promising to return within a month. Happy not to be separated from M. Giovanni, at four o'clock I found myself on the small steamer, *Camanche*.[2] Added to the joy, the supreme happiness of not being separated from my husband, was a secret desire to see new things. In fact I enjoyed every phase of travel.

Sir George came to wish us a safe journey. Our sudden and unexpected departure had hurled him into the depths of despair. He had believed that I would return to Europe, and undoubtedly had made preliminary preparations to make the trip at the same time. I, for my part, was so happy that I was ready to respond most cordially to all the wishes for a pleasant journey that were made, and so I replied to those of Sir George: "Come and see me in a month at Mr. and Mrs. Wood's house; you will be most welcome."

Finally the funnel smoked, the wheels churned the water, and we were off. The day was a Saturday early in April. On Sunday morning we reached Sacramento City. We breakfasted in port, at the Hôtel de France; then continued at once on our journey toward Marysville, reaching there some time in the middle of the night. We procured lodgings at the Oriental Hotel.[3] While I slept, M. Giovanni supervised the unloading of our merchandise, for our journey by water terminated at this point.

The river is called the Sacramento from San Francisco as far as the city of that name. There it changes and becomes the Feather River. I was enchanted by the route through which we had just passed; to me it was as beautiful as a journey along the road to paradise. In fact, from my point of view, much of the interest the trip held was in the splendor of the scenery. In my estimation, nothing can approach the majesty of these new regions, which appear to the traveler to be endowed with an almost celestial beauty.

But I must not forget to describe the journey itself. Upon leaving the Bay, that is, San Francisco, the steamer enters the Sacramento where salmon fishing is carried on on a large scale. Along both sides of the river extend magnificent carpets of flowers of infinite variety, interspersed here and there with patches of cultivated land that indicate the infancy of agriculture in California. Occasionally, attractive American cottages already surrounded by flowers, vegetables, and groups of trees planted by the hand of man are seen.

In certain areas the river appears to be completely covered, like a gigantic cradle, by branches of fine large trees that adorn its banks, uniting and interlacing above the water, but at so great a height that steamers with their smokestacks pass beneath them without lowering their masts and without touching a branch. From this vault of green, falls, with the poetic and divine grace of a still virgin nature, a wealth of parasitic climbing plants, among them pliant bindweeds that flutter in the wind, whose tips brush the surface of the water.

The stations that at convenient intervals supply the wood used by the steamers also attracted our interest. All these places are newly organized and of recent birth but, since they are operated by energetic Americans, they are run as if they had been established and in operation for several centuries. These stations are located on the banks of the river, and employ many men. The wood is stored in piles ready to be moved with the result that when the steamer stops all hands energetically throw aboard vast piles of logs. In less than ten minutes the load is complete, the steamer whistles, then moves ahead, leaving proudly in its wake seething masses of foam.

This was my first trip on a riverboat and, I must confess, since that time I have come to realize that this was a mediocre example of a United States vessel; however, it was managed to the satisfaction of all passengers.

Every cabin had two exits, one leading into the interior of the boat, the other to the exterior. The latter opened on a grilled gallery. The inside doors were kept open or closed, depending on whether cordial or unfriendly relations had been established between neighbors. The result was that after the second day many whom I saw enter alone left in couples. Since I knew what time was worth in California, I believed that when I left the steamer, I had not wasted mine, since I had spent it observing what was going on around me.

The three cities of San Francisco, Sacramento, and Marysville, I should add, each has its destroying plague. The first is fire; the second is fire and water, that is, fire and flood; the third is yellow fever, that destroys the population in a hideous manner.

The two latter cities just enumerated are the gateways to the gold mines, the placers being at their doors. Sacramento City and Marysville are the marts and shipping points for all supplies and equipment used by the miners. Because of this activity, the cities are almost as important, both as regards size and commercial activity, as San Francisco. Manners and customs have had a similar development, and when one of the plagues just indicated destroys them, they emerge from the ruins with as much alacrity as San Francisco itself.

It is impossible to conceive of anything more beautiful and more delightful than Marysville [4] surrounded by forests, gigantic oaks, and verdant prairies. Although fevers invariably prevail, no place in the world would appear to be more salubrious and favorable to health. The prairies mentioned were enormous carpets of flowers or odoriferous herbs that perfumed the air we inhaled. Among these flowers were hyacinths, tulips, irises, ranunculus, and a thousand other bulbous plants, for it is from this country, so the scientists say, that the Dutch have procured all the plants with whose cultivation they are popularly credited with having perfected. Possibly they may have improved the colors and multiplied the number of shades, but I question whether the hand of man has ever enhanced the perfume of these suave daughters of the prairie that appear just as they were when they left the hands of their Creator. I confess that I was almost convinced that mankind in this environment enjoys the most favorable conditions that have ever been provided.

While I made some excursions into the country that surrounded Marysville, M. Giovanni constantly watched the unloading of our merchandise and secured information as to the best way to prepare for what at that time was one of the most arduous of all trips, in other words, traveling north into the Sierra Nevada. This information disclosed the fact that the remainder of our trip must be made on muleback, in view of the difficulty of the roads, or rather the absence of roads, and that we would require at least three full days traveling as rapidly as possible.

We were also told—and it was not without astonishment that we learned this, for the heat was intolerable at Marysville—that we would encounter considerable snow and intense cold while crossing the mountains. But at the same time we were informed that if we had enough courage to face these perils, formidable as they were, we would be amply and richly compensated for our effort by the colossal success of our venture.

Despite our keen desire to continue our journey without further delay, we were obliged to remain eight days at Marysville, primarily to buy merchandise, find mule drivers or Mexican guides who knew the local trails, and finally to await the departure of the Express [5] from Downieville.

The Express, in California, is composed of government employees, whose duties consist in carrying once a week all mail, which, after reaching San Francisco from various parts of the world, is brought to Marysville by daily steamer, and finally transported to Downieville, Chafla City,[6] Valliga,[7] etc., and then distributed on foot to the neighboring placers. In addition to the mail, the Express also handles gold dust that has been collected at the various placers and consigned to some designated banking house, by whom it is forwarded to the Bay.

On their trips, the Express is armed to the teeth and invariably accompanied by at least two or three armed men. Further protection is afforded by miners, who often join the Express, going back and forth to the mines.

The Express, which appeared to have the full confidence of the public, was exclusively controlled by Americans. Thus its employees were usually men not only of energy and courage, but also delightful traveling companions. Their compensation was extremely high, but the fatigue, incidentally, was intense; each week the employees traveled two or three hundred miles and the manager of the Express from Downieville, Mr. Greathouse,[8] with whom we made the journey, said that his skin during the three years he had been engaged in this task had actually turned to leather. The danger was also great, as much because of the reports of the wealth the Express carried, as because of the difficulties invariably presented by the routes, which lead through mountains and over precipices and at times even among arrows that are occasionally discharged by Indians in ambush, who await travelers on the outskirts of the forest.

During the week we were forced to remain at Marysville, I witnessed one or two deeds that indicate the strange character of the population of California, which is made up of so many heterogeneous elements and which is commonly believed to have only vices, yet never fails, whenever the opportunity arises, to do a kindly and generous act. The impression should not be given that out in this land it is merely necessary to bend down to gather a handful of gold. What should be said is this: only a little work is required to collect armfuls of gold, which is the main harvest of the country, but once in the pocket of the reaper, the gold leaves as easily as it entered.

Throughout this narrative, whenever I offer an opinion I invariably cite instances to illustrate my point. A certain Frenchman called Father Giraud had resided for many years in New Orleans, where he lived modestly and quietly with his family, consisting of his wife and two sons. When news of the gold discovery reached them, the two sons, who were still very young, soon caught what the Americans call gold fever; in other words, a thirst for gold. They decided to leave for the mines as all their friends and acquaintances were doing. Despite his sixty odd years, the father did not wish these lads, young and inexperienced as they were, to travel alone to the mines and so accompanied them, taking his wife, in the belief that a mother was never useless to her children, and still less so in the upheaval which he fully expected to find in California.

Having reached San Francisco, they shared the universal fate; that is, in two or three years, luck favoring them, they acquired a fortune. Finally a series of disasters fell on the poor family. The two sons were drowned in the inundation that preceded our trip to Sacramento; the fact was definitely proved, for the body of one of the lads was recovered. This was a tragic blow to the poor parents. The mother, already in poor health, died from the shock. The father, meanwhile, had become blind, soon exhausted his last resources, lost the ability to work, and overcome by chagrin and exhausted by privations, was finally reduced to being led one morning when he had nothing for breakfast to the corner of one of the principal streets of Marysville where he knelt, cap placed on the ground before him, silently begging charity from those who passed.

The sad spectacle—almost unknown at this time in California— of a beggar kneeling in the street, was the signal for universal charity. Father Giraud was known at Marysville as well as at Sacramento City as one of their oldest and most respected residents.

In the humble posture just described, he was noticed by a Frenchman, who began to run at top speed to the Hôtel de France to relate to his compatriots what he had just witnessed. After holding a consultation, several Frenchmen who had gathered decided that this scene must not be repeated the following morning. Separating by common accord, they went out and knocked at every door in Marysville to make an appeal to all citizens, rich or poor, on behalf of Father Giraud.

Then some Americans joined the Frenchmen and went as they did, from house to house, until a personal request for funds had been made to every resident of Marysville. What they asked was for every citizen to go out that day and place small coins in the hat of Father Giraud. An hour after this appeal for relief was made, an immense procession was organized in which the entire city took part. A Frenchman and an American placed themselves on each side of the poor blind men to collect for him the rich harvest they knew would be gathered. Then came a veritable rain, not of small coins, although a certain amount of these were donated by men who were too poor to give more, but of dollars and five dollars, including many gifts of two and one-half dollars. Each donor attempted to add to his gift some kind word to console the poor blind man. The latter, however, failed to realize what was going on; and when anyone spoke to him, silent tears fell drop by drop on the harvest of dollars displayed nearby.

The collection was almost finished. Night was approaching, and Father Giraud's chair was about to be moved and the old man assisted to carry away his fortune, when two men approached; one was a Frenchman from New Orleans, the other an American. The American emptied his pockets, turning them inside out, then shaking them; they contained between six and seven hundred gold dollars which he had just, as he said in his Yankee dialect, won at one of those *damned gambling games.* The Frenchman from New Orleans, who had known Father Giraud for years, emptied his belt of gold dust and affectionately clasping the hands of the poor blind man, said to him: "I had every intention of spending eight days at the Bay, but now I am returning tomorrow to the mines."

His contribution was estimated at five hundred dollars. The money was counted. Father Giraud received a total of six thousand dollars. The steamship line also wished to make a contribution, so they transported him free of charge, with the tenderest care, as far as New Orleans, as he expressed a desire to return there to die. This happened, I believe I have said, during my sojourn at Marysville.

CHAPTER VIII

ACROSS THE PLAINS

SINCE MARYSVILLE was the last important settlement on the
road to the placers for which we were bound, M. Giovanni
renewed his efforts to persuade me not to force him to take me
further. What he had heard about the difficulty of the route, the
cold, and the snow, had obviously alarmed him. Several persons,
behind my back and even in my presence, strongly advised him to
overrule what they regarded as caprice or obstinacy on my part.
But I had not come this far to turn back and I won out in the face
of these difficulties; I declared that I intended to go on and succeeded, as usual, in having my way.

In view of the amount of merchandise we had to transport, the
situation that confronted us as we were about to leave for the
mountains, is difficult to conjecture. The actual price we had to pay
for moving freight was twelve dollars for every hundred pounds of
merchandise, approximately sixty francs in our currency. We had
eighty mules each carrying two hundred pounds, so it cost us two
thousand dollars merely for transportation of merchandise. Moreover, food had to be supplied for the eighty mules during the trip,
as well as for the drivers who had charge of them. In addition we
had two mules for our own use, at fifty dollars the mule. Obviously
the total cost would be at least twenty-five hundred dollars.

For greater security against Indian attacks, several mule trains
usually assembled at one time and remained in the depot with their
respective packers until a large number had congregated. Then the
entire caravan moved ahead, traveling in short stages, unloading
every night beneath trees, where the packs were removed, in order
to allow the animals an opportunity to graze and rest. These formed
what resembled gypsy camps oddly grouped on the summit of
mountains or at the tips of valleys. Travelers themselves do not need
to accompany their trains of merchandise, and usually go ahead with
the Express, which proceeds three times more rapidly than these
caravans move.

We ourselves left the day after our baggage and merchandise

had been sent. Because I was the only woman in the train, Mr. Greathouse held a reception before the main door of the Oriental Hotel for all the travelers, who numbered thirty, in my honor. Some were miners going out to seek gold; others were merchants, lured by the urge to speculate; the latter, who were traders, expected to sell their merchandise on the side. All congregated at the hour indicated; that is, exactly at six o'clock in the morning. By daybreak the air was balmy and full of a delightful freshness.

I was the first one seated on my mule, and it was from the saddle—for I still feared that some accident or some discussion might prevent my departure—that I received the farewells and good wishes, not only of our friends and acquaintances, but even of strangers, who are invariably eager to assist at the departure of a group of travelers en route to the mines. Similarly at a seaport when a ship is about to set sail for a foreign country, the wharves are thronged with spectators, who as long as possible call farewells, signal with their handkerchiefs, and follow with their eyes the ship ploughing through the ocean waves.

A leading official of the city, who was one of my warmest friends, appeared up to the last moment to be considerably alarmed at my audacity, and as I turned around for a final time to assure him that there was really no great danger, he looked at me and sadly replied: "I hope so, but may you never repent of having had so much confidence in yourself."

After proceeding quietly through the village on our mules, we then found ourselves on those magnificent plains already referred to, which revealed on every hand such thick carpets of fresh verdure and dazzling flowers that it seemed as if eternal spring must hover nearby, shaking humid wings of dew.

As we were about to cross the plains by a path that was barely perceptible to us, but well known to the Express, the cavalcade began to gallop; in all my life I do not recall ever having looked upon anything more beautiful than the scene which now unfolded on this magnificent theatre, or anything more unique than this troop of hardy adventurers and gold seekers.

Our train comprised exactly thirty individuals: Spaniards, Mexicans, Italians, Frenchmen, Englishmen, and Americans, most of whom had the manner of well-bred gentlemen. They were garbed in costumes characteristic of their nationalities, but which, at the same time, were judiciously chosen for crossing the mountains of northern California. My own costume was merely a kind of riding dress of black cloth with a small coat of the same material, loose enough to permit complete freedom of movement. On my head I wore one of those large men's hats called a Panama. I was well gloved and shod and wore, if I must confess, heavy gray stockings and sturdy boots, which were the despair of M. Giovanni, who was accustomed to seeing me in elegant shoes, which he moved heaven and earth to procure at any price, even in the uncivilized countries through which we traveled.

Of course this strange make-up, so contrary to my usual costume, and above all my footgear, was not a matter of taste, but one of expediency and necessity, in view of the rain, mud, cold, and snow that we were confident we would soon meet.

As we traveled, the flow of conversation was incessant and although everyone joined in in his native tongue, yet my husband and I, much to the surprise of our comrades, spoke indiscriminately as need arose, the various languages. To be frank, I was not at this time very familiar with Spanish, for I had not yet traveled through Mexico; but by way of compensation, I spoke such fluent Italian, French, and English, that indulgence was to be expected for my somewhat defective knowledge of the language of Calderon and Cervantes.

How splendid it would have been if a painter like Delacroix[1] or Decamps[2] could have seen us at this time, with a glorious sun just rising, galloping across the immense plain covered with verdure and flowers that stretched before us, defined only by a far-distant horizon, with its bluish tinge and faint outline of high mountains, whose slopes we were so laboriously to ascend many hours later! How deeply I regretted that I did not have the talent of one of these men whose names I have just mentioned to paint this magnificent spectacle and offer it, like a veritable gem, to the world at large! Above all my heart was moved by profound and religious feelings at the sight of the divine beauty that surrounded me. While these first impressions lasted, my joy was infinite; for the time being at ıeast I was blissfully unaware that the goal, the miserable purpose of this magnificent trip, was the lowly task of finding gold.

Although I am somewhat reluctant to mention the fact, naturally I had the honor and distinction of arousing the interest of my traveling companions more than any other person. Eyes fastened on the mountains whose conquest, so it seemed, I was about to make, I rode at the head of the caravan with my husband and the members of the Express on one side, and two Spanish brothers on the other. The rest of the party moved in a helter-skelter manner as they chose.

Along the road various kinds of game, such as flocks of partridges and groups of hares ran to cover as we passed by, but none of the men, although each one was armed with a gun or carbine, ever thought of firing on the creatures; all were preoccupied with another hunt—the hunt for gold.

Toward ten o'clock in the morning the heat began to grow intense. This had been foreseen. Every traveler was fortified with a flask of wine or a gourd of brandy carefully hung from his shoulder strap. From time to time, I too had to drink my share of the common supply, upon the advice of the Express, who took excellent care of me, and who exercised every precaution, even to that of regulating the time to walk and gallop our horses and the best way to husband our strength now and again when confronted with the inevitable fatigue of the journey.

At midday, having made approximately twenty-five miles, we reached our first stop, called Oregon House,[3] where dinner was waiting. This same thing held true all along the route traveled by the Express; the meals were always ready and the quarters prepared, well in advance of our arrival.

Dinner was served under a kind of shed, a primitive caravanseraglio, and consisted of rump steak, potatoes, stewed meat, and flapjacks—a kind of pancake made with flour, water, and leavening. As for the seasoning of the various dishes, the traveler ate only because he must eat. In fact, no one paid much attention to what he ate. Dinner and the period of rest that followed consumed about one hour; we then proceeded on our way.

From this time on the journey was fatiguing. Soon the first ranges of the blue mountains that had seemed so picturesque in the morning and which, once we had attained them, seemed so arid, were reached. Farewell beautiful prairies, ravishing carpets of flowers scattered by God's hand from the portals of Marysville to the base of the Sierra Nevada! The ascent now began; we crossed the hills into the mountains and, without stopping, passed from peak to peak in the region of snows.

About four o'clock in the afternoon, a snowstorm descended, a terrific gale that brought with it intense cold. Every possible effort to protect me from it was made, but the sudden change of temperature had already done much harm. I had thought I had completely recovered from my San Francisco illness. But I had deceived myself; at the first intense cold all my former symptoms returned and only with difficulty could I refrain from weeping. From a person in sound health, I was transformed into one suffering in every part of the body. Finally—for I did not wish to complain—my strength suddenly failed. I fell in a dead faint from my mule, face buried in the snow.

This mishap caused grave consternation in our train. M. Giovanni was in despair. At the first signs of snow he had wrapped me in his own garments, but unfortunately this precaution had been of no avail. No sooner was I on the ground than our companions, jumping off their mules, clustered around me. Mr. Greathouse, as kind as he was courageous, immediately ordered the caravan to halt. Each one, after tying his mule, began to dig without delay under the snow for dry wood, which, after considerable difficulty, was finally lit.

What now showed the most gallantry, the most generosity, was the fact that many men offered me their warm garments, taking off coats or overcoats. And in an instant half my companions were in their shirt sleeves, while I reposed on the bed that had been made out of their clothing. Finally a hot drink was prepared; of this I was forced to swallow, willing or unwilling, a full glass, which brought a little strength to my poor, numb limbs.

By the end of an hour I had reached a point where I felt so revived that, to avoid delaying Mr. Greathouse, I insisted that we should continue on our route. M. Giovanni, with tears in his eyes, which he attempted to conceal, took me in his arms, lifted me as if I had been a feather, placed me gently on my mule, and we moved on.

The snow continued to descend; growing icier and icier, it made the trail almost impassable. At length, covered with snow, chilled with cold, and clinging with difficulty to our mules that slipped and fell at each step, we arrived about seven o'clock in the evening at Nigger Tent,[4] a supper and overnight house.

The ground was covered with two feet of snow. Fifty miles had been made since the day of our departure. I was so ill that I had to be lifted off my mule and carried to a kind of bed of hay placed in a corner of the main entrance hall used by the general public; there, after dining, all retire merely by stretching out on the ground, wrapped in the miners' coverings of red and blue with which everyone invariably travels in California. In a luxurious alcove which was made by a blanket hung on a rope, I was placed, fully clad and wet through and through by the snow. As for food, it was utterly impossible to eat; all I could swallow was a glass of hot spiced wine.

After M. Giovanni had partaken of the common supper, which was a repetition of the dinner, he came and stretched out by my side, placing one of his arms over mine, but resting his other hand on the hilt of a Colt revolver hidden under his overcoat. He tried to close his eyes and sleep for a few moments, urging me to do the same. Soon the rest of the travelers began to make their nocturnal preparations, and each one to suit his convenience or caprice, wrapped himself in his blanket and lay down on the floor.

My fatigue was such that, despite the fever that consumed me and made me tremble, I fell asleep, but only for a brief period. Two hours later I awoke; opening my eyes, I saw M. Giovanni leaning over me weeping in place of sleeping.

Obviously, he was thinking of our recent misfortunes, the precarious position in which we had been left; of me, ill and sleeping on the ground among thirty or forty men who tomorrow might be our enemies. The scene was indeed depressing. Through a low window that stood directly opposite us, we caught glimpses in the forest of great trees, white with snow that was falling in huge flakes. We were conscious of men scattered here and there around us; some snoring, others wheezing, some talking in low voices and in a mysterious manner. I recalled the night I had passed among the aborigines in a village situated a few leagues from Auckland; I remembered the terror that gripped me during my hours of wakefulness.

That time I had been wrong; it was now here in this new environment that the real danger lay. True, I was a seasoned traveler, a tourist accustomed to a nomadic life; but until that time my life had been full of comfort and luxury. Courageously I had made myself the companion of my husband, but I was beginning to understand that I had been led to do so by moral courage and that perhaps my physical strength was about to fail me.

I closed my eyes, but M. Giovanni knew I was not asleep; he now tried to persuade me to turn back. There was still time, he argued, and by the evening of the second day I would be back in Marysville. I must add that I did not hesitate for a moment, but refused. I begged him patiently to bear with my weakness, trying to make him understand how proud I would be, once all these fatigues were over and the journey accomplished, to have been his companion on this trip to the Sierra. Convinced that my decision was irrevocable, he concluded that the wisest course to follow was to increase my will power still further. This time it was he who assured me I was equal to it; it was he who urged me to be patient; he who gave me new endurance. The fine things he now said and the manner in which he said them, cannot adequately be described. Under the stimulus of these consoling and touching words, I slept, if one can term sleep the kind of stupor into which I fell.

## Chapter IX

## OVER THE MOUNTAIN

I AM UNABLE to say whether it was amazement at the spectacle that unfolded before my eyes, or excessive fatigue, but it was impossible actually to sleep. Whenever I made the slightest movement, I felt sharp pains. My legs twitched; my arms were rigid and aching. In addition to all this, I was sore from riding and my leg was so chaffed from constantly rubbing against the pommel of my saddle that the skin had come off.

Everyone, having passed a wretched night, arose at five o'clock. The air was bitterly cold; its intensity since the previous evening seemed to have redoubled. Breakfast, that included the inevitable American flapjack, was served immediately. I ate one cake, dipping it in a glass of warm wine. M. Giovanni appeared relieved when he saw that my appetite was beginning to return. After procuring some extra handkerchiefs from our good and amiable traveling companions, he bandaged my sore leg. Before he did so, however, he bathed the sore spot with gin, which burned my leg so much that I shrieked when it was applied. Nevertheless, the remedy soon relieved the pain. I now had to be lifted on my mule, and our fellow travelers before mounting their animals, surrounded me, waving their hats with one hand, lifting their glasses with the other, and shouting: "Three times three to the good luck and prosperity of M. Giovanni and his dear lady."

This was a strictly American salutation which meant: "Three times three to the success and future prosperity of M. Giovanni and his good wife."

M. Giovanni and I profited by the opportunity to return the compliment to these fine men, which cost us several bottles of wine at five dollars the bottle. We then climbed into our saddles. I had suffered considerably toward the end of our trip the previous evening, and I expected to suffer still more, especially when I saw, out in the open space, four or five feet of snow.

However, the panorama that soon unfolded before my eyes made me forget my sufferings, acute as they were. For here was one of the most magnificent spectacles of nature in all her pristine glory that could be afforded a European traveler. True, our trail forced us constantly to ascend mountains almost to their summits, and while descending this panoramic view disappeared from sight; but at the summit of each mountain scaled there stretched a plateau from which the eye could see in every direction an endless chain of ranges that unfolded like the waves of a swelling sea, all covered with dense forests of oak and pine that measured, almost without exception, from one to two hundred feet in height.[1]

Since the creation of the world to which the giants of nature seemed to belong, the thickness of their foliage had, I believe, prevented a single ray of light from penetrating to the ground. I have never seen anything to compare with the quiet and calm of this dense forest. Everything on these immense plateaus revealed the supernal force of its sublime Creator. The vegetation was luxuriant; under this lush growth the hand of nature had spread a carpet of green moss, thick, soft, and so deep that neither sun nor snow could penetrate to its depths. Upon several of these superb plateaus the "prospects" of an occasional miner were found. The term "prospects" is applied to attempts made to locate mines. I was profoundly and deeply impressed at the sight of growth so rich, so fertile, so fresh, and at the same time so primitive.

The remaining members of our party, slight though the artistic appreciation might be of the majority of those who composed it, voiced admiration by cries, exclamations, halts, and even by jovial remarks. From Nigger Tent, where we had rested, to Good Year Bar,[2] our next stop, the distance was only fifteen miles. This was reached literally by encircling a great mountain formed like a loaf of sugar, on whose summit stood Nigger Tent. Whoever has had, like myself, the privilege of descending and reclimbing this twice, as I shall soon narrate, cannot recall this mountain without a beating heart. The trail, which coils around it in spirals, is, at the outside, only two feet wide. Looking down, the traveler perceives in an abyss whose depth causes dizziness the swift blue waters of the foaming Yuba.

After traveling half the distance to Good Year Bar, the closer the Yuba is approached, the more clearly the Yuba placers may be seen stretching along its banks and forming a charming picture, not only because of their picturesque setting, but also because of the activity of the mining population. At the particular season at which we arrived, these miners were still engaged in their preliminary tasks of making excavations and flumes. Fluming, in Californian phraseology, means to deflect a river from its normal channel and to prepare another, into which, at some later day, the stream is forced to pass. This procedure allows miners to "prospect" in the old channel.

The flume constructed for any stream whatsoever is invariably built at a height of twelve or fifteen feet above its channel, an achievement which if not simple is at least feasible, even though innumerable streams descend when the snows melt from the Sierra Nevada. This structure is made of planks, well tarred, cemented, and clamped together. The wood from which it is built is as dry as possible, and water must not be allowed to drip through, inasmuch as work is carried on underneath the flume. The timber used, furthermore, must be solid enough to withstand any accidents that might occur, and, finally, solid enough to be able to carry an enormous weight of water. Construction of these flumes is a herculean task, and no one is better suited to such work than an American.

Some idea of the difficulty of the labor is afforded if the reader will recall that this is undeveloped country and that the worker must rely solely on his own personal resources. First of all, to provide material he must cut down a large number of pines several months in advance. No one, however, understands better than an American how to handle, cut, and fell the gigantic trees of these virgin forests. After the timber has been cut, it must be sawed and made into planks required for the huge scaffolding. The worker must personally prepare all his own pitch and cement. Then, when the time arrives to pass from preliminary to actual construction, he must work for weeks in the water, building the pilework.

Then comes the difficult part, that is, the construction of this artificial channel, a work that requires infinite care. At the same time, in direct ratio to the size of the flume, three or four windmills are erected at each end to draw off the surplus water constantly seeping down into the old bed of the river—water that comes from hidden sources. Flumes are more or less elaborate. Some are fifty feet long; others, two or three hundred. These vast enterprises, as already said, are usually undertaken by Americans who form companies to exploit claims on the river.

Before commencing such exploitation, however, four or five months of preliminary preparation is essential, months which of course produce nothing but prospects. This work is accomplished, notwithstanding, provided the American has flour, sugar, and tea. But if one of these three staples is lacking, then there is grave danger that the flume will also fail. This preliminary requirement both of time and money is the basic reason why these extensive projects are rarely managed except in a few isolated instances by Frenchmen.

The day when the river is diverted into its new channel, white and polished like a mirror, is a day of joy and hope for the miner. He is now about to achieve the reward of his prolonged labors. But the first question he asks when pondering over this gigantic task is: "What if all this work has been done in vain? What if there is no gold?"

And how can the poor miners know in advance that, by diverting a certain number of feet of the river they desire to exploit, in that particular place the mine for which they are searching will be found. Who can fail to admire their unbounded confidence, their laborious efforts, the amount of time spent in the solitary hope: There must be gold there!

But chance is not the only guide used by miners. On each side of the river rise mountains in the form of perpendicular rocks. Between the river and the walls thus formed, there is merely a small trail. The miner follows that trail. He notes by the color of the different layers of soil whether the mountains are auriferous. If the strata indicate this structure, he knows that at the foot of the part of the mountain where the rock contains indications of gold, their labor will probably be richly rewarded.

From time immemorial avalanches, too, have been uncovering rich strata, sweeping gold from the mountains in the furious currents of their waters, which are precipitated from the summits of the Sierra Nevada when the snows melt. There, where the bed of the river hides its treasure, invariably the mountains appear to have been overturned; they are studded with terrifying rocks suspended in the air, that seem destined to drop at the first breeze.

The wise miner, notwithstanding, does not allow himself to be deceived by the appearance of the rocks. He attempts to study the river itself, which he accomplishes by prospecting right in it. He descends to its bed. He removes the soil, which he washes and which usually contains gold, or some indication of the presence of gold. If he has no diving suit to enable him to remain under the water, he prospects along the banks of the stream and washes the sand, where indications, that are invariably reliable and adequate when they appear, incite him to renewed effort with that hope of success that spurs man on to colossal tasks, whatever they may be.

When he finds gravel that gives promise of being productive, he must work his claim with the utmost industry. Inasmuch as a period of only four months elapses from the time the late snows melt and the first fall, within this interval the miner must reap his metallic harvest; for when the snows melt, the waters pour down the mountains in torrents, swelling the Yuba River, which then begins to tear its furious way across the Yuba Valley, carrying with it, like so much kindling, even the most sturdy flume.

Fortunately, these floods are foreseen; when they approach, intrepid miners can be observed armed with long sticks that terminate in enormous hooks, stationed at regular intervals along the banks of the river, attempting to salvage from its depths some of the debris of this magnificent construction; this debris, which would mean that much salvaged for next season.

The mines called excavations are merely tunnels dug in the slopes of mountains bordering the rivers. These, too, are elaborate affairs that often resemble catacombs. Gold is found in them in the same manner; the method of separation from the soil never varies.

The claim, or common mine, is worked by digging a well. The miner—the man who does this work is called a "drifter"—descends as far as bed rock, but no farther. He must find his gold there, or not at all. He then branches out, digging to the right and left, but never going beyond the area of the exterior circle that belongs to him, and erecting scaffolding in proportion to his diggings. In the center of the mouth of the excavation a pulley is placed; here men are constantly occupied in piling up the debris and the dirt the drifter collects.

Drifters are the most highly paid of all miners. As a matter of fact, their work is extremely dangerous and many have been buried by holes that have caved in. They are hired by companies for fifteen dollars a day. The buckets carried by the pulley are in turn emptied into a kind of box, six by ten feet long, simply constructed of three planks, one at the bottom and one at each side. To one end of this box, which is called the long tom, is fastened a kind of sieve with holes the size of a cork; below these perforations is a second box that ends in a second sieve with much finer holes; the third box has no sieve.

The miners, as already explained, empty their buckets into the long tom. On each side of this machine stands a man with a pail who removes and clears away the surplus dirt; for his purpose each group of miners prepares water conduits of leather or sail canvas, which the California miners themselves make in their tents during the long winter evenings. These various conduits carry an ample supply of water into the long tom, and the men, stationed at each side, remove with their pails the sediment that collects. Then, after the water has been thoroughly washed through the gravel and the soil is well diluted, all the stones are thrown out of the box with such rapidity that the bystander might be inclined to ask why the gold, too, is not thrown away.

There is, however, absolutely no danger of losing it. The gold sifts through and drops heavily; it then falls through the holes of the first sieve together with a considerable amount of gravel that comes with it; finally, having been shaken again, it passes into the last box, where it is mixed only with fine sand. This latter box remains closed throughout the day, being opened only to remove the contents, an operation that takes place at the meal hour. Everything is then turned out onto a tin plate. The less substantial this plate, the better. The mass is now allowed to dry over the fire or in a frying pan; then, after it is dry, the sand, which disappears like dust, is blown off, leaving nothing but gold dust. At the end of each week the group weighs the total amount and distributes dividends to all the members, who wear "carrying" belts in which to place their share.

This refers, incidentally, only to gold dust or extremely small nuggets. There are also many mines where gold in free particles is found. To stand in such a way as to command full view of the long tom at the moment when the two men, placed one on each side, remove the mineral with their pails, is highly amusing. Particles of gold are seen glistening in the stream of water that falls through the holes of the sieve. The man with the bucket never places his hand in the box; this is not a law, but a self-imposed rule made by the miners, which they never fail to observe.

The poor wretch of a miner who has neither a long tom nor a claim, and who works at a prospect, has for his sole equipment nothing but a tin dish. He stops here and there—on neutral ground, of course—digs, fills his plate with mud, earth, or sand, then washes it in the stream, or the nearest body of water, using his hands in place of a pail. The gold invariably remains at the bottom of the plate. The miner-prospector thus makes from three to five or ten dollars daily. But it is a dreary life, a life hard and full of privations for these poor men.

I wonder how many of these unfortunate creatures are now exiled in California where, lured by false hope, they have finally stooped to this hideous task, a task in which both body and spirit are broken! Some day a list of the martyrs of California may be published and the world will be astonished at the number of victims this land of gold can claim.

I have explained, to the best of my ability, how gold is mined in California. Obviously the process is comparatively simple, for all that is necessary is to separate the gold from the soil, which is accomplished by washing it with water. This operation completed, the metal glistens before the eyes, as brilliant and as splendid as in a goldsmith's window. Later on I will have an opportunity to explain the difference between panning gold in California, and finding silver. Let us now return to Good Year Bar.

CHAPTER X

MARY'S CREEK

THE TRAIL over which we traveled while descending the enormous mountain, permitted only one person or one mule to pass at a time. In certain places it was so terrifying as to produce vertigo, for being scarcely eighteen inches wide, if the mule's foot slipped the traveler would undoubtedly roll with it to the bottom of the Yuba, that is, into an abyss two or three thousand feet deep.

Such terrifying accidents happened every day to poor beasts loaded with supplies that were being taken to the mines; few caravans reached Downieville without having to deplore the loss of some mule that had fallen with its load into the bottom of this dangerous Yuba. To give an accurate idea of the condition of this treacherous path, scarcely passable even in good weather, I might add that when we began our trip snow, which was thick on the ground, froze as it melted. I must confess I was seized with dizziness and fright when I saw what passes had to be crossed. I should never have believed that a human being could have attempted such roads without having the foot of a chamois, or the wings of a bird. I measured the precipice with my eye and began to weep silently.

M. Giovanni was already so depressed at having yielded to my desires and permitted me to follow him, that I calmed myself in so far as it was possible, not wishing to aggravate his chagrin by exclamations of terror. I accordingly remained quiet, but perspiration and tears came simultaneously, the perspiration on my forehead, the tears on my cheeks.

Mr. Greathouse, leader of our Express, traveled at the head of the train; I followed, with my husband behind me, then came the others in single file. I was told, in order that I might be reassured, to allow my mule complete freedom, although I was scarcely guiding it with one weak, trembling hand. So I gave the animal a free rein with more anxiety than I can describe. Every time the animal stumbled, I felt the blood surge anew through my body. Thus I traveled for four hours, four hours of the most frightful agony I have ever known. Dizzy and terrified as I was, I glanced at the surrounding country, however, and saw areas of the ice-clad mountain entirely covered with the most exquisite blue flowers I have ever seen. These flowers bore a striking resemblance to our own myosotis and, having taller stems, had pushed up through the snow, spreading over the surface. They appeared in great masses, affording a striking picture.

As we were making our perilous descent, we encountered an endless number of broken trees that had rolled down the slope of the mountain. After leaving the upper level, many of them in the course of time had reached the river and taken root in its waters.

By three o'clock that afternoon, Good Year Bar was reached. At the sight of a woman, a curiosity that had not been seen since the new town was established, the miners congregated and stood in groups before the boardinghouse where the Express usually stopped. Upon dismounting from my mule, I found myself ill from the combined effects of emotion and fatigue. As the train arrived late, soon after dinner the order was given to remount the mules and start off again.

I attempted to get on my mule, but failed. M. Giovanni was in the depths of despair; he now decided that we would remain behind. I was troubled more by my sore leg than by all the other pains that surged through my body. Upon examination, the three handkerchiefs that served as bandages were discovered to be soaked with blood. M. Giovanni showed them to my traveling companions; this provided a good excuse.

"I should have been very proud, Madame," said Mr. Greathouse, "to have entered Downieville with you at my side, but it will be impossible, I see. The rest of the road will not prove arduous after what you have just passed over so keep up your courage, and tomorrow, or the day after, we shall meet again."

Several members of the caravan volunteered to remain behind with us, but M. Giovanni would not accept any of the offers that were made; on the contrary, he urged all these travelers who, in two or three days, had become our friends, to depart. Having said good-bye, we promised to meet again in Downieville. Soon after the cavalcade had started, I retired.

The following day, since only a few miles of the trip remained and I was determined to continue, I begged M. Giovanni to resume our journey. This section of the country differed from what we had just crossed.[1] It was flat, covered with grass, and in many places the snow had almost entirely melted. Having reached the camp of an old Indian, we found that a large number of the local natives with their wives had assembled. One of these Indians was a hideous spectacle, with a face that was almost entirely wasted away by an ulcer. We gave these brave men some supplies; in exchange they lit our fire and heated water for us. Those who were not occupied in this task ground some acorns between two stones, which were then made into a kind of paste; it was used much like chestnuts, in place of bread. Then, after resting forty minutes, we resumed our journey.

At two o'clock in the afternoon we entered Downieville.² Already this had become a thriving settlement with streets swarming with miners, shops of all kinds, hotels, stores, and cafés. The village lies on the Yuba and is destined to acquire considerable importance, for it is surrounded by rich placers and has become the leading center for immigrants who work in the mines within a radius of fifty miles. The village had just been burned, but had been rebuilt as if by magic.

The Express came to meet us on the main street and led us to Virginia House,³ a hotel kept by Mr. Wood and his family. The mistress of the house appeared to assist me to alight from my mule; then, with the aid of her children she arranged for my comfort and at the end of a quarter of an hour I was in bed. There I remained four days.

Now that I was well cared for by these good people, the day after our arrival M. Giovanni, with a guide as his sole companion, started off on the trail. His idea was to inspect the placers extending further north, which he was able to do, thanks to information previously secured from San Francisco.

What he especially desired to see was a newly-discovered plateau called Twist's Flats,⁴ which was immensely rich. After a trip of three days, he discovered it. The fourth day he returned to Downieville, his face joyous, and told me he believed he had found what he was looking for. It was not, he said, forcing himself to smile, a very gay spot; anything but that; however, he had an opportunity to establish a good business, and that was what we had come for.

Up on this plateau he had purchased an immense shed built of wood, not unlike a barn. This barn, shed, or structure, such as it was, had been built by an aged American and his assistant out of anything they could find, with the hope of reselling it at a good price when the working season opened.

M. Giovanni purchased it for one thousand dollars cash. It was the palace of the plateau. In the immediate vicinity of the palace were one or two cabarets that expected to make considerable money. On this plateau gold had been discovered only during the last season, but, unfortunately, too late to begin work. The prospects, however, were good for the ensuing one.

On the Yuba, nearby, some flumes had been erected, while commodious shacks, extensive excavations, and claims were scattered on all sides. In the midst of it were innumerable miners at work digging wells and erecting buildings; they formed a population of from fifteen to eighteen hundred men.

The plateau stretched between two chains of mountain peaks and the Yuba River, and was as active as the world in the last hours of chaos. This activity, however, was indicative of its wealth. The settlement lay fifteen miles north of Downieville and only twelve miles from the village of Butte, the farthest point to which miners had as yet penetrated.

The day after M. Giovanni's return with the good news—as usual we had little difficulty finding good news—we climbed on our mules to inspect our property. Several of our traveling companions wished to accompany us and visit these unknown regions; so we joyfully accepted their offer to join our little party.

The road was nothing more than a narrow trail, rough and tortuous, cut through the foothills of the mountains that border the river. Often the path completely disappeared. At such times we were forced to use in place of a road the river itself, which we followed until the water reached the bellies of our mules. Yet the trail was not difficult compared with the other route with its many precipices and sheer cliffs. And so my spirits returned, and with them, my courage. Laughing and singing, we soon completed these fifteen miles.

En route I was seized with a burning thirst. As I had difficulty in climbing off my mule, M. Giovanni, with the aid of his two hands, attempted to raise the water to my mouth; before reaching my lips, however, it would trickle away. One of our traveling companions then urged M. Giovanni to use his hat for a cup, adding that it was foolish to be too particular when traveling through regions like those we had just crossed.

I preferred, however, to descend from my mule—which I did with the aid of two men—then I approached the river, knelt down, and quenched my thirst without difficulty in the crystal-clear water.

My example was followed by the entire company; everyone knelt and drank; and as the brook had no name, we named it Mary's Creek, or Mary's Brook; my second baptismal name and the name of the Madonna being thus honored.

On a leaf torn from a notebook and attached to a stick placed near the bank of the river, an appeal was made to miners passing that way to remember the name, which was that of the first woman courageous enough to travel so far north. Throughout the trip of fifteen miles, we did not pass over as much as six feet of flat ground. After climbing a hill, we reached the plateau about two o'clock in the afternoon, and, to my profound amazement, I saw a large number of men as busily at work as if they had been a colony of ants.

Their activity included felling trees, sawing, cutting, and trimming them to make benches, tables, chests, and, finally, household furniture. The workmen were miners, but since the season for working the mines had not yet opened, the poor had gone to work for the rich until such a time as they could find other employment.

We entered our palace on the plateau. There we found at the end of our large shed a small room already prepared to receive us. It was furnished with a rustic table, some chairs, and a primitive bed made from virgin timber found on all sides in the adjoining forest. On the table, built during the night preceding our arrival, we had our first banquet, which was, by the way, one of the gaiest banquets, from the standpoint of its novel and odd environment, in which I have ever participated.

Our repast had been prepared at the plateau cabaret. It consisted of excellent roast beef seasoned with the best sauce in the world, that is, a tremendous appetite, followed by wild squirrel, then one of those excellent waterfowl which you, no matter how much you pay, my good Parisian friends, can never procure even for your most elaborate banquets. All the gold in California is not enough to transport delicate game beyond the latitude in which it is born. How ungrateful I am! I almost forgot the Yuba trout, a pretty little creature, pale rose in color, with flesh more delicate than any fish I ever ate in Switzerland or in the Pyrenees. One thing, however, was abominable—the wine; but the water was so pure, so good, so fresh, as to provide a welcome substitute. Obviously, M. Giovanni had made preparations for my arrival, and that of our companions. He spoke little, promised little, but forgot nothing.

<br>

CHAPTER XI

## FOURTEEN DAYS IN THE PALACE ON THE PLATEAU

AFTER the repast celebrating our arrival on the plateau was ended, M. Giovanni removed his coat, our friends followed his example, and five minutes later everyone was assisting the workmen. The situation this time was quite different from what it had been at Hobart Town, Auckland, or Tahiti; here I no longer relinquished the comforts of the soft sofas and excellent armchairs of our hotel to travel through the country; here I merely got up from a three-legged stool that was not even straight, and in five minutes, or rather in five seconds, I was out in the open country.

From the first I felt my fatigue disappearing; dinner was scarcely over when the desire to explore seized me. So I went out, eager to see everything, to inspect everything. The miners looked at me with naïve surprise; they were disinclined, it seems, to believe that I was really a woman. Everyone, however, was extremely courteous.

Soon, in some mysterious manner, they had found out about us, our misfortunes in San Francisco, and what we had just done on the banks of Mary's Creek. Our courage pleased them; they were happy to know that we had come there to isolate ourselves among them and bravely regain what we had lost. And so there was universal mourning on the plateau when it was known that I was to leave at the end of a week.

We were now showered with small attentions; all these men, crude and half-civilized as they were, extended many courtesies to me, a woman. Some went fishing, others went hunting, and the finest fish caught, the best game killed, was reserved for my use. From the day of our arrival the atmosphere seemed to change; the desolate plateau, enclosed on all sides by gigantic rocks and lofty snow-capped peaks, took on a festive aspect.

Several hours after our arrival, the pack mules finally appeared.

They carried a bed, some material to carpet the room, and some articles indispensable in so uncivilized a country. My joy was great, I must confess, to see a real bed; the substitute on which I had just reposed resembled one so slightly that I thought it was in the process of construction and as yet incomplete. Supper on the evening of our arrival was a hilarious affair, lasting far into the night.

The following day I stationed myself, line in hand, on the banks of a brook, for merely by taking two or three steps out of my room I could dip my feet in the clear, pure water that had so wonderfully refreshed me in the hour of my thirst. When I was not fishing I was accompanying my husband, whom I followed like a shadow everywhere, addressing, according to my habit, endless questions to the sturdy groups of workers.

Perhaps this may astonish those who are interested enough to read this narrative; but I felt safer among these men so remote from all authority that to them might made law; I felt, I repeat, safer among these groups than in San Francisco, where a woman cannot walk down the street without being made the target of some coarse joke.

My husband shared my feeling of security and I was somewhat astonished to see him abandon himself to a noisy gaiety that was far from normal; yet, to be frank, he found unexpected joy in this novel and new position in which we found ourselves. Our mule train pulled in exactly eight days behind us, having been delayed by a snowstorm that had obliterated even the most clearly defined trails and completely closed the mountain road.

The last day of my visit soon slipped away, and I cannot express with what anguish I saw the hour of my departure approach. I urged M. Giovanni to grant me another eight days, and he allowed me to beg and implore him before he finally consented. His was the joy of a child each evening at supper when he saw me there, sitting beside him, laughing and happy. He enjoyed listening to some tale about the Maoris I had known at Auckland or Tahiti, or the sailors on our ships. His joyful face revealed what my presence meant to him; finally, he granted me this extra week, telling me at the same time to make the most of it, since it would be the last.

During that final week I had the pleasure of seeing my husband's affairs begin to prosper. I was asked to participate at the opening of a magnificent flume, the Orleans flume, owned by a company in which my husband had purchased an interest. The ceremony took place on a Sunday when an attempt was made to divert the river and force it into its new channel. I walked over, leaning on my husband's arm; we were followed by all the miners from the plateau, each one garbed in his finest red and blue woolen shirt, with hair and beard combed; in other words, these good men donned in honor of this occasion the best costumes they owned.

Finally we reached the flume. Accompanied by the owners I entered, while the other miners remained on the banks of the stream. I knelt and read the prayer; everyone listened on bended knee and I can assure you it was a solemn spectacle to see a European woman there on the banks of the Yuba, a woman alone among all these men, praying and asking God's blessing on the superhuman work of these immigrants, who had come from all parts of the world as if to infuse into the wilds of America the miracle of European industry.

The prayer over, I left the flume amid the cheers of the miners, who threw their caps in the air. My husband had ordered a barrel of excellent wine to be sent down to the banks of the river, and each and every miner received a full glass. The following day, my second week having ended, I left the plateau.

Mr. Greathouse and my husband accompanied me as far as Downieville. I was disconsolate; but M. Giovanni tried to console me by reminding me that our separation would not last long. The morning of my departure every miner came to offer me a present— a sample specimen of gold dust collected on the plateau. All these specimens taken together had considerable value. Some time later M. Giovanni told me that one of the miners who had presented me with a pretty incrusted specimen, weighing perhaps an ounce, did not have enough money that evening to buy a pipeful of tobacco.

It is unnecessary to add how unhappy the separation at Downieville made me. Lifting me in his arms, M. Giovanni placed me on my mule, and would not take his hands off my knees; on the other hand, I could not decide to make my animal start. Finally, the mo ment came to leave; I was weeping aloud, and he was sobbing softly as we separated. Having departed, I was now under the immediate protection of Mr. Greathouse, our good Express, who took excellent care of me. The train, upon our return trip, consisted of five persons; my four companions were Downieville merchants who had business in Marysville.

This time the trip was accomplished with a minimum of difficulty. The weather proved perfect; everything was green under foot and for miles around. Partridges passed over our heads; hares rushed between the legs of our mules. In brief, the morning of the third day, without further mishap than a slight feeling of fatigue inevitable on such a journey, I was tranquilly seated at the dining table between Mr. and Mrs. Wood, to whom I described my trip and M. Giovanni's prospects.

The day following my return to San Francisco Sir George came to see me; he had delayed this long to prove his reticence. He was eager, he said, to enquire about our journey. But he had been too impatient to wait and had secured information from others who had seen me, and so knew it had been successful. He now hoped to hear all the details and thus complete the picture.

These I now gave, and I must confess, whether real or whether due to the constant play of emotions visible in his expression, his feelings seemed more intense as he listened than did mine in the telling. The recital having terminated, I asked him in turn if he had selected California as a place for recreation. He told me he had decided to stay here as long as I remained. Then, in accordance with my usual custom at such declarations, I brought into play my most flowery words of rhetoric to convince him that he was making a false move. I told him I was indeed disconsolate to have had so unfortunate an influence on his life. I begged him to think seriously of how odd his conduct must appear, I did not say in the eyes of my husband, who had no reason to doubt me, but in the eyes of strangers. I begged him, if he loved me, and especially if he esteemed me as much as he did me the honor of avowing, to prove his feelings by adopting another line of conduct, the reverse of what he had followed up to the present time. As usual, since the question was always frankly discussed between us, we parted the best friends in the world.

Six weeks after I returned to the house of Mr. Wood, one Friday night as I was about to retire with a fairly light heart, having received good news from M. Giovanni, I learned from my kind hostess, who did not know the pleasure she gave me by repeating these words, that Sir George had said that same day that he was about to leave for England, traveling by way of the United States. At eleven o'clock in the evening, Mrs. Wood went out, leaving me with a feeling of profound relief at the information she had just disclosed in regard to Sir George. I was soon asleep.

My sleep, however, did not last long. About two-thirty in the morning, I thought I heard the fire bell. At the sound of this gong that had proved so well known and so disastrous to me, I awoke with a start. I was not mistaken; it was actually the ominous signal. Mrs. Wood rushed headlong into my room, crying:

"Fire! Dress quickly, dear child."

"Fire! Where is it?"

"In a house not twenty feet from ours; as you know, there is no time to lose, fire travels quickly in San Francisco."

No sooner had she finished than a man rushed into the room, wrapped me in a cloak, lifted me up in his arms, and carried me out, before I could protest, with my head resting on his shoulders. I was in my night clothes; he took me to a neighboring stone house, occupied by an English lawyer, who departed at once that I might be alone.

I looked around for Sir George to thank him and reproach him at the same time, but he had disappeared. He had gone to look for Mrs. Wood, who could not be forced from her house and was attempting to save some of her most treasured belongings that were stored away. He did not, however, consult her any more than he had consulted me, but forced her to follow him, telling her first to save herself and then go over and stay with me. He also advised her not to worry, saying he would look after her financial affairs.

Respectfully he opened the door of the room where I was, announced Mrs. Wood, motioned her into the apartment, and, without entering, closed it behind her. Then he went out again to the burning area. Sir George was known by all the firemen, for at every fire he exposed himself to such danger that many believed that in these fires that were so disastrous from a financial viewpoint, he would lose his life some day. With Mr. Wood and several of their good friends, Sir George succeeded in saving a number of things, among them, two trunks of mine containing my wardrobe for California.

We passed the night at the home of his friend, remaining there until noon the following day. At that time Mr. Wood came in person to look for us; with the rapidity that characterizes everything in California, he had already rented another little house on Jackson Street. By two o'clock in the afternoon we were installed in our new abode. About five o'clock Sir George came in to enquire for me. This time, I must confess, I thanked him from the depths of my heart.

Meanwhile, I learned from his own lips that he was about to leave California. The time had come, he said, to go far away, for if he did not take advantage of a respite to gain command of himself, he feared that some day or other he might go mad, and then, unintentionally, do something for which he could never forgive himself. He wept as he told me, and I admit that I, too, wept as I listened. As he left, he asked me to think of him sometimes, as one thought of a friend, a brother, then he gave me the address of his bankers in San Francisco and New York, telling me he had notified them to give M. Giovanni and me whatever we needed at any time. He also said that if we were ever without resources, he sincerely hoped we would go to them and not some one else for assistance. I promised I would do as he wished. Then he kissed my hand and left. I never saw him again.

CHAPTER XII

FIRE ON THE PLATEAU

WHAT news I had from M. Giovanni about his affairs at this time continued to be cheerful; he wrote that a large amount of his merchandise left the Bay every day for the Sierras. He had now been in the mountains four and one-half months and had already repaid the advances made by Mr. Argenti and was paying for all his orders in cash. On each trip made by Mr. Greathouse my husband sent me a well-sealed small package containing some fine specimens of gold, which I never failed to store most carefully in a place where in case of fire I could reach out my hand, seize them, and escape. He sold to all the placers in the vicinity merchandise and tools which miners require for their personal use, as well as for their work.

His and my own presence among these courageous men, his affability, the memories of the baptism of the flume, all had given him a monopoly of business on the plateau. Although other speculators had come with the hope of entering into competition with him and had settled nearby, yet their efforts had been in vain; not one made expenses, whereas M. Giovanni constantly received so much money, so many specimens, and so much gold dust that by evening he was so direly in need of sleep that he could not even balance the books for the day. He had three clerks, or rather three friends, associated with him; even these three friends were not able to fill all the orders. He retired at night exhausted, but with heart and mind at rest, and from his bed, between work and sleep, he wrote me letters that brought me equal tranquillity.

But human endurance has its limitations. After six months of residence on the plateau and intense work, M. Giovanni was forced to stay in bed, being exhausted by pains in his back and head. One day I received a letter telling of his illness. I replied by return mail, asking if his malady was serious, whether I was to come to him, or whether he felt strong enough to return. He wrote me to remain in San Francisco, also telling me that he was suffering too much to make the journey to the Bay himself.

At this news, the fear of some serious mishap seized me. I did not hesitate an instant, but left San Francisco without asking the advice of anyone, and without even considering the four or five days of hardship which I would be forced to undergo. I reached Marysville the evening before Mr. Greathouse was to leave for the plateau. Having located him, I explained the situation as if he had been my closest friend. He not only approved, but even commended my action. The following day I left again for the mines with the Express train, which upon this occasion was fairly large. Needless to say, I found Mr. Greathouse invariably the same; certainly he could have done nothing more for his own wife or sister.

I shall refrain from mentioning the perils of this second journey; in fact, I was not conscious of them. Four days after my departure from Marysville I entered the poor little room on the plateau and, weeping bitterly, embraced M. Giovanni, who could only utter a cry of joy when he saw me suddenly appear. Nevertheless, after the first joy of being reunited had passed, he reproached me, although somewhat weakly, for having come.

He told me that among the men on the plateau a certain number were worthless, but that the majority were good. For this reason he had to be extremely diplomatic to avoid making enemies. He had speculated in claims, but in this respect had not been very fortunate; the outlay had been heavy and the returns light; in fact, they had not covered expenses. He hoped, however, to make up the deficit in a short time. Within a day or two work was to be begun on a claim located on a property of which he owned one-third. The claim was situated directly opposite our building and, like his associates, he had great hopes in its future. The three clerks had worked well; although they were overburdened with business. I asked them if I could in any way assist either by keeping the books or balancing the accounts. They welcomed this suggestion and I became a fourth secretary, taking of my own accord as much pride in my work as if I had been a bookkeeper all my life.

When I returned, I no longer received the same attentions that were showered on me on my first visit, but I attributed this slight neglect to the fact that everyone was absorbed in his own affairs.

However, every time the miners saw me my presence was certain to arouse a welcome smile, or a respectful greeting.

After my work was completed, I would leave my husband's store and stroll over the entire plateau. I would then return to the invalid's bedside and describe everything I had seen to enable him to endure his confinement with more patience.

On the third day work began on our claim. Toward evening, expectations began to be realized; the ore, apparently, was extremely rich. Each bucket of mud or dirt taken from the hole contained at least one-half ounce of gold; one bucket alone held ten ounces. At the news, which soon spread over the plateau, speculators began to congregate as on the stock exchange. The place was beginning to show very heavy returns and everyone strongly advised the owners to sell out their interests. A certain man called Douglas especially urged M. Giovanni to dispose of his share, even offering him two thousand dollars, and the same amount for the other two-thirds. M. Giovanni, who has the reputation of being a speculator, refused, however, to sell.

Then a plot was hatched between this rascal, one of his friends named Davis, and a band of Irish Americans, by whom secret rumors were circulated against M. Giovanni. Whispers went the rounds that this foreigner, this Frenchman, had made quite enough money since he had been on the plateau, and that it was time he resigned in favor of an American who, prior to M. Giovanni's arrival, had had this locality under consideration. M. Giovanni knew all about these intrigues, but he wisely ignored them, cherishing the hope, or rather the conviction, that a small number of dishonest men could not get the upper hand of an honest majority.

Meanwhile, M. Giovanni's health, which he direly needed, improved so much that he was well enough to be present at the opening of his claim, which was being worked before his own door. During the first week the mine produced three thousand dollars; in the second, thirty-five hundred. It was proving to be the richest holding on the plateau. The main vein, for which a futile search had been made in other claims and which was known to exist, passed through this mine that at one time we had been about to abandon, but which was tested again at the urgent request of M. Giovanni.

Incidentally, M. Giovanni had made every effort to retain his share in the latter claim, having had comparatively few opportunities to speculate in the mines since he had been on the plateau. He had taken part, as shown, in the construction of the great flume; but despite the hopes based on this tremendous work, it had not done more than pay its expenses, and M. Giovanni, in place of receiving on Sundays his share of the week's work, frequently had to pay the day laborers who worked there for him. He had an equal interest in a saloon, but there again the output was inadequate to meet expenses. Out of ten other claims he held on the plateau, only one had produced anything; yet, taken as a whole, all these speculations involved a cash expenditure for production expenses of four or five thousand dollars, and he had not yet recovered, as I have said, the sums expended.

This new diggings, then, was the Hen that laid the Golden Eggs, and quite naturally, he desired to keep it.

Two more speculators came to him, asking him, in a sense challenging him, to sell his part of the claim by telling him that he should be quite satisfied with his commercial ventures and his speculation in merchandise and should not attempt to monopolize the miners' share. He wanted too much, they said, and should beware, or his greed might bring him misfortune, and he might end by not having anything.

This was merely a threat that indirectly came to him from the wretch Davis, who, inspired by the example of the Americans, his compatriots, could not endure the thought that a stranger might own a mine that could not be taken away from him. M. Giovanni replied with his habitual calmness that they would never have adopted such a tone if the claim had been unproductive, and that they had no right to pick a quarrel with him, in view of the sums of money he had expended for flumes, dams, and the development of other claims, money that had served to support at least twenty-five or thirty miners.

Then he added, as usual, coolly and calmly: "None of you feels any gratitude! You reproach me for having done a good business here for the past six months; but have I, at any time, failed to conduct it in all good faith? Have you ever found me, whom you reproach for being a Frenchman, other than a friend? Have I not been a father to you? Have any of you who have been unsuccessful ever found the door closed on days when you knocked without money in your hands? And those who had no money, have they not found my purse open? Tell me, where is there a company to whom I ever refused a sack of flour or a box of tea when they had no funds. Were you accustomed before I came to have credit at your placers? No! I shall now bring out my books and accounts; let us verify them together, and if you do not find that I have four thousand dollars in accounts receivable, then I am the one who is wrong, and you are right. These no doubt will be paid; in fact, I have no doubt of it. But admit, too, that if from your point of view I have done a good business, it was while rendering you a good service. When any one of you was wounded or ill, who dressed his wounds, who cared for him, who prepared his medicines? I, who am something of a chemist and surgeon! For such care that I have rendered possibly to some fifty persons, ask and find out where I have ever received any remuneration whatsoever.

"And now, so that everything may be clearly understood between us, I repeat, I do not wish to sell all or any part of my share of the claim; your pleas are futile; your threats are infamous. Furthermore, I will not be beguiled any more than I will be intimidated. Now go." With his hand he made a gesture of dismissal. They obeyed.

During the evening of the following Sunday, as we were enjoying our supper, the question of my departure arose. This M. Giovanni set within the next few days, adding: "Mine will soon follow yours, my child; I must be at the Bay by next January, and after tomorrow I shall begin collecting the amounts due me by the companies. Three months more, and I shall come back to you with the fruits of nine months' work, arduous work, but which will be ample compensation, for now I am convinced that my profits will amount to fifty or sixty thousand dollars. With this I can resume my commercial activities at the Bay; then, given a little good luck, we shall end, let us hope, by making our stake in a year or two."

M. Giovanni spoke in good faith, for he had on hand at this time about fifteen or twenty thousand dollars' worth of merchandise in the store; brandy, wines, liquors of all kinds, flour, tea, sugar, coffee, preserved fruits, vegetables, meats, Wellington boots, woolen shirts, and miscellaneous tools. Added to this were accounts owed by the companies, accounts that probably amounted to an equal figure. As for cash on hand, as fast as it came in it was sent, as I have said, to the Bay, returning in the form of merchandise. In addition to what has just been enumerated were the five or six thousand dollars M. Giovanni sent me during the past five or six months he lived on the plateau, which from time to time I deposited with Mr. Davidson,[1] his banker in San Francisco.

This conversation with M. Giovanni, as I have explained, occurred on a Sunday evening. During the following night, on toward four o'clock in the morning, one of our three clerks rushed into our room, crying: "Fire! Quick! Quick! You have barely time to save your lives!" At this cry which seemed to pursue us everywhere, to haunt our steps from city to mountain, my husband leaped out of bed. I, too, was awake, but paralyzed with fright and incapable of rising. My husband saw my prostration; he came to me, seized me in his arms, and pistols in hand left by the door that opened toward the river.

No sooner had M. Giovanni taken three steps outside of the house, than a man in ambush fired a revolver shot at close range; the ball grazed his chest, passing within two inches of my head. Without dropping me, but still holding me firmly in his arms, M. Giovanni removed one hand from my body and replied with a better-aimed shot. The man fell, uttering a groan.

M. Giovanni, upon seeing the man writhing on the ground, wanted to know who was responsible for this affair. He placed me on my feet and, leaning over the wounded man, found that it was Douglas. I had fallen on my knees, but lacked strength to pray and I believe that instead of clasping my hands, I was twisting my arms. Then I saw another bandit appear, and cried: "Watch out!"

Just as M. Giovanni was turning, the newcomer fired on him. This time the ball opened the old wound in my husband's shoulder. Nevertheless, Mr. Giovanni, despite his injury, aimed his revolver with seven chambers, only one of which had been discharged, in the direction of the assassin just as the latter, observing that his rival had not fallen and believing that he had missed him, was in the act of attempting to escape, and fired the second ball between his shoulders. He, in turn, fell. M. Giovanni turned him over with his foot and recognized in this poor wretch a man whom he had always believed was one of the most honest men on the plateau, one to whom he had often rendered services. Simultaneously came the sharp cry: "Look out, look out."

The warning came from the clerks who expected an explosion. Among other commodities, our store carried powder; the kegs containing it were carefully buried, it is true, but the store did not have a plank floor but merely one of earth tamped down like a threshing floor. Furthermore, all the other merchandise was so combustible that when the heat or flames reached the kegs, an explosion was inevitable. At this cry, M. Giovanni did not believe it was necessary longer to pursue his investigations of the two would-be assassins. Moreover, he recognized them and there was nothing more to be done. Both, by the way, were mortally wounded; Douglas succumbed at the end of three hours, and his accomplice two days later.

He now returned to me, raised me in his arms as he would have lifted a child and, carrying me to the banks of the river, left me for a few moments in charge of two or three of his friends to whom he knew he could entrust me in perfect security; then, quick as a flash, he disappeared. He was searching for the incendiary, the basic cause of all our troubles. He soon found the man for whom he was searching; it was the miserable Davis. From where we sat we heard three fresh pistol shots; from the noise of their reports, two of these bullets seemed to come from M. Giovanni's revolver.

I was not mistaken. Davis, the incendiary, had fired once at him; M. Giovanni replied with two shots; Davis, in turn, fell mortally wounded. M. Giovanni left him in his death agonies and, bleeding from the wound in his shoulder, went in search of the clerks, calling them with every ounce of strength at his command. But they had disappeared. During the fire, however, they had been seen attempting to save the account books and various papers that several men tried and had even succeeded in snatching from their hands.

One of our friends reappeared. He had just brought one of these vandals to justice; soon after, another was found gravely wounded.

The house burned like a match. We could save nothing, not even one of my robes, not even an overcoat for M. Giovanni. By five o'clock the fire was extinguished; it died out of its own accord when there was nothing more to burn. The adjoining cabarets and tents had burned like our own palace on the plateau. My husband and I were sitting silently on a piece of rock. All the miners looked at us with acute misery, for we had been the mainstay of many of them. Then, after a silence lasting for a quarter of an hour, M. Giovanni said, without in any way altering his voice: "We're ruined again, but at least this time we had our revenge. No matter! I still believe what I have always said: 'California is a cussed land!'"

# VOLUME IV

## Chapter I

## RETURN TO SAN FRANCISCO AND DEPARTURE FOR THE SANDWICH ISLANDS

IN THE midst of the confusion caused by the fire, the miners at once offered their services, which we accepted as gratefully as if the offer had been made by beloved friends and relatives. While some of the miners were occupied in finding out what we needed, others brought blankets to protect me, for I was clad only in a night-gown and a shawl I had thrown over my shoulders.

Notwithstanding, in the turmoil of a chorus of condolences and offers of services, a voice was heard murmuring in English: "Damned Frenchman! Why wouldn't he sell his claim? It serves him right!"

In this mysterious manner our rich claim faded away, and the season was too far advanced to recommence operations. This little episode, furthermore, occurred two days after the night the fire broke out and while we were at Downieville, where M. Giovanni had gone to make a statement of everything that had taken place.

A day or two after the declaration had been made out, my husband returned to the mines alone, leaving me in charge of an excellent family who offered their hospitality in this emergency. He attempted to dispose of his share of the claim that had proved so disastrous there where he seemed to have made enemies. He also sent messages to the outlying placers in an attempt to collect what money was due to him, but in most instances his creditors said they were unable to pay what they owed. Finally, after endless hardships, trials, and tribulations, complicated by the fact that M. Giovanni was still suffering keenly from the wound in his shoulder, we returned to San Francisco, thankful that our lives had been spared in the hideous catastrophe, as well as fifteen thousand dollars—in other words some seventy-five thousand francs!

We also consoled ourselves upon entering San Francisco, by recalling that only seven months ago we came to the mines with more than thirty thousand dollars of borrowed money and not a cent of our own, and that, after all, we were now returning, after the entire amount had been paid back, not only with our lives, which were more valuable than silver, but with fifteen thousand dollars and without a debt in the world.

The evening of our arrival, I handed a small folded paper to M. Giovanni with a smile; it was a receipt from Mr. Davidson, the San Francisco banker.

"What is this?" asked M. Giovanni, not understanding at first what he had just read.

"My friend," I replied, "this is the pin-money you sent me the past seven months from our poor castle on the hill. I hope it will assist you to make some new speculations."

"Yes," he replied, "but first and foremost this amount will serve to defray the cost of a winter I should like to pass in the Sandwich Islands as a brief respite from this abominable California. A winter in that beautiful climate will fortify us for the future, for, to speak frankly, I personally feel that I have lost my grip and no longer know what business to undertake." Thereupon, taking his hat, M. Giovanni started to leave.

"Where are you going?" I asked.

"I am going to find out," he replied, "whether there is any ship in port leaving for the Sandwich Islands. Good-bye! Take care of yourself and don't be discouraged. I shall return for dinner."

One day, as we were about to dine, M. Giovanni came in and remarked that there was a small brig in the bay leaving within two days for the Sandwich Islands. We decided to sail on this ship, and began at once to prepare for the voyage.

Once the decision to leave California had been made, we were undoubtedly the happiest people in the world. No one watching us gaily pack our trunks would have said that we had recently experienced a long series of disasters. I, for my part, was as giddy as a young girl. I laughed, sang, and danced, then went out to make purchases for new friends I expected to make in the Sandwich Islands, with an abandon bordering on folly.

The following day we made a farewell call on the delightful French consul, M. Dillon, who appeared to enjoy our visits and always took a keen interest in our welfare. The French consulate stands at the far end of Jackson Street; directly above the consulate, which is the last house on the street, we found the road closed by one of those mountains of sand which I have mentioned before.

The French consul lived in one of the most delightful houses in San Francisco. In front of it stood a charming garden through which a walk led to the main door. The garden, which was entirely of flowers that had been arranged under the supervision of Madame Dillon, was a refreshing sight in a land where verdure is not classed among the known luxuries.

We did not take advantage of our cordial relations with M. Dillon to enter, as many of his friends did, through a private door, but followed the crowd, intending to register and see him when our turn came. After we entered, we found a crowd of at least thirty persons waiting in the anteroom. Upon closer inspection, these visitors seemed to consist of a motley assortment of human beings of French extraction, from courteous and elegantly-clad gentlemen to men with ragged garments and repulsive countenances, who looked capable of any crime.

I sat down on one of those comfortable Chinese armchairs that are found throughout California. My husband stood and chatted with the chancellor and a person whom I did not know. I amused myself by observing in detail the different changes of expression and listening with attentive ears to the various conversations that were going on around me. I continued to look at and listen, without appearing to do so, to two men who were chatting in a low voice, unaware that their words might be overheard.

From their appearance it would have been difficult to tell to what class of society they belonged; on the whole their clothes were good and from the standpoint of boots and gloves, even elegant. Their hair, however, was somewhat greasy, like that of men who use a small amount of poor oil in order to make it shine at all costs. The hat that one of them held in his hand, however, was of good quality, and the hat, as we all know, is one of the badges of a gentleman. Finally, left to my own investigations, had I not listened and overheard fragments of their conversation, I should still have been at a loss to know what type of men these two strangers were. As one of them carried a traveling cap of oilcloth I named him the Man with the Cap; the other, the Man with the Hat. While I was listening, I heard the Man with the Cap say to his friend: "By the way, did you know that our consul was held up again in the street today and robbed of twenty thousand dollars by a man named B.?"

"No, I hadn't heard about it," replied the other man, somewhat listlessly. "But I do know this, I am still hoping that the tale I invent will make him hand over a gold slug either willingly or by force. I have been reasonable, I have not asked any favors for more than two months. But I am not going to die of hunger, while there is a French consul in California."

"The devil! Don't be so grasping," said the Man with the Cap. "Ask only half that amount and give me a chance to get the other half. My turn comes after yours; you will discourage him, and I shall secure nothing for myself."

"That depends," replied the Man with the Hat, "in any event I get only what he decides to give me; he is too well guarded here for me to take advantage of him."

That was all I overheard. When they saw that I was listening, one of them touched the other on the shoulder and led him away. Then I began to pity the kindly M. Dillon, so ready with his gifts, from the depths of my heart. I thought to myself that if half the men who were waiting for an audience with him were there on the same errand as the Man with the Hat and the Man with the Cap, the post of consul at San Francisco was scarcely an enviable rôle.

Since I was the only woman who was waiting, the so-called chancellor, aware that we were friends of M. Dillon, was good enough to allow us to pass in ahead of the others, to the mumbled protests of those who had been waiting an hour or more. We told M. Dillon, who had not seen my husband or me for seven or eight months, that we planned to leave for the Sandwich Islands.

The Consul had lived there before coming to California, and it was our knowledge of this that induced us to pay him a special visit. He encouraged us to make the trip, congratulated us on our good fortune in being able to leave San Francisco, and gave us some valuable letters of introduction to use in the Islands. In return, I warned him to be on his guard when interviewing his two compatriots, telling him what I had overheard in the anteroom. This did not surprise him in the least, and he said with a melancholy smile: "You are the only visitors who have come to see me this week with a disinterested motive. Unfortunately, many of these men who come begging are genuinely in need of my assistance. For them and even for others who are less deserving, I do what I can, perhaps more than I should. I am a *pater familias.* The difficulty is to distinguish between those who are actually in need and those who make a business of extorting funds."

Then he shook my husband's hand, embraced me in a fraternal manner, wished us a pleasant voyage, and said good-bye. The following morning, that is, early in November, 1853, we went aboard the small brig *Lilly,* in command of Captain Woods. She carried eight passengers; as usual, I was the only woman.

Among the eight were two Jews, brothers called Luzar, who planned to establish a commercial house at Honolulu. The elder might have been thirty years old. In addition to these two Israelites, four of the other travelers were seriously ill with inflammation of the lungs. These invalids were going out to spend the winter on the islands, which, incidentally, are the Italy of the West! The poor men coughed enough on the way over to rupture their lungs, yet moved around the ship as if they were in good health and ate bountifully, each of them consuming at least as much food as either M. Giovanni or I, whose appetites are always normal.

The cabins on the *Lilly* were poor, and the saloon small and narrow. Under other circumstances we should have found it taxing to travel with a group of consumptives and with so few comforts. But, to our surprise the voyage was delightful; throughout the entire trip we were in the best of health and spirits. I had provided myself by way of diversion with needlework; M. Giovanni laid in a generous supply of books for his own amusement, and inasmuch as the voyage would not last more than fifteen days, we had tacitly agreed to make these fifteen days pass as pleasantly as possible.

The distance separating San Francisco from Honolulu is approximately eleven hundred miles.[1] Our brig slipped along the waters like an agile sea bird. We had the finest sea possible—what is called in nautical language a tractable sea. For the first three days most of the passengers wisely kept to their cabins, then gradually appeared on deck and finally came to the dining saloon at meal hours.

The captain, who was a fine man, did the honors of the table and managed the distribution of food in a skilful manner. However, we found the table somewhat long and the food somewhat short—this proved especially annoying to our two companions, the brothers Luzar, who having the advantage over our four consumptives of being in good health, cleared everything off their plates, leaving comparatively little work to be done by those who had charge of washing the dishes. In the evening, at the supper hour, they assuaged their incessant hunger by eating endless sardines and colossal potatoes cut in quarters. What these two gentlemen tucked away was astounding. On the other hand, our invalids were more difficult but less costly to nourish. Our captain had them served morning and evening with a kind of corn meal stew, which the Americans call mush.

On the first day out of San Francisco the passengers decided to make the voyage a friendly and harmonious one. With my needlework I often sat on some extra rigging, a camp stool, or a chair, while several of the passengers formed a circle around me. Often a French romance was read aloud, or we discussed California and the Sandwich Islands. The recent events of my life, however, made me at times a little depressed. There were moments when I felt sad in spite of all I could do; often I turned around just to glance at M. Giovanni, who had had such a miraculous escape not only from the fire at the mines, but also from the revolvers of those who intended to murder him. I felt I wanted him nearby, seated or standing, so that I could stretch out my hand to him, or feel his hand locked in mine, and know that he was actually safe. Then a strange sense of well-being would spread over me, and I would realize that since we were together, our tiny capital, scanty as it was, was still a tidy fortune compared to what might have been our fate had we not been protected by Providence.

Meanwhile, the small brig continued its rapid voyage over this exquisite sea, calm as a lake. Nothing worth recounting occurred during the short and delightful passage, and we came in sight of the port of Honolulu the eleventh day after our departure, at ten o'clock in the morning. The day before, while passing twenty-five or thirty miles off Oahu, we saw the silhouette of a great volcano clearly outlined against the sky.[2]

CHAPTER II

THE SANDWICH ISLANDS

THE PORT of Honolulu has one grave disadvantage; ships cannot enter without danger because of the bar, and must stop a certain distance out at sea. A mile or two off the island, our ship lowered sail to await a pilot, for the trip into port must be made under the guidance of one of the natives of the country. Within an hour or so the Kanaka pilot, who had sighted our vessel approaching, came out and brought us into port.

Most of the passengers did not remain aboard ship while it was being guided into the harbor, but went ashore in one of the many small boats that swarmed about the ship looking for passengers.

Viewed from the sea, Honolulu is enchanting; the lowlands extend gently to the edge of the water like a ribbon of verdure, leaving glimpses through and over the trees of the tops of buildings that give somewhat the aspect of an Asiatic city when seen from afar. The gallery of the Belvedere and its handsome castle, as well as the cupola of a church, gave an altogether delightful charm to this city, hidden in an immense garden which appeared to the traveler to resemble an oasis placed in the middle of the ocean.

Although several passengers had previously visited Honolulu, a spontaneous cry of joy and pleasure escaped not only from the lips of those who were viewing it for the first time, but also from those who were seeing it on their third or fourth visit. By way of concluding the description of this port, I might add that although the entrance is difficult to maneuver the departure is even more hazardous. To leave the island a certain wind is imperative, but this is often slow in arriving. Of this condition the poor whalers are fully aware, and the majority of commercial vessels are always more or less delayed by lack of it.

Notwithstanding, this harbor is chosen in preference to other ports on the island by the whalers, for it affords the best opportunities and has the most activity and commerce. This is the only island port, incidentally, where the American, who is the embodiment of activity and commercial acumen, has pitched his tent. The Americans came here to establish trading posts and discharge oil from their whalers, a time-saving procedure that makes it possible to have two fishing seasons instead of one. Commercial vessels, bringing out merchandise from Boston and New York to Honolulu, thus find cargoes awaiting them at this port; upon their return trip, they carry back oil to America. As a result, the prosperity of the Sandwich Islands is derived primarily from American commerce. During the season when the whalers put in at Honolulu to take on supplies and unload oil, they arrive in the following ratio: one hundred or perhaps one hundred and fifty American whalers; eight, ten, or twelve French whalers; eight or ten English whalers. These statistics indicate that there are many more American than French and English whaling ships.

In addition to these facts, it might be said, with the same truthfulness I attempt to inject in whatever remarks I make, that neither Kamehameha III,[1] the former ruler, nor Liho Liho I,[2] who recently succeeded his uncle and is now master of Honolulu is actually in control of the port, but rather the Americans.

For six months of the year commerce in Honolulu is at low ebb, but by way of compensation, during the remaining six months, that is, from September to March, the city leads a dual life, being active both night and day. At this time a steady stream of ships enters and leaves the harbor, coming to discharge oil and to take on a complete load of fresh supplies. During these six months amazing sums of money are placed in circulation throughout the city, not only by the sailors, but also by captains of commercial vessels. Small shops, large stores, open air merchants, all flourish.

The central market of Honolulu is one of the main points of interest in the city. Here, every morning, farmers from the interior display great piles of fruits, vegetables, and miscellaneous supplies that arouse the admiration of foreigners. These markets open at three o'clock in the morning and close at five or six o'clock in the evening. At opening time, everyone makes his purchases with lantern in hand, for daylight does not begin until six o'clock in the morning and only lasts until six o'clock in the evening. By a quarter past six the merchants leave and the market is deserted.

The meat stalls are unusually well-handled. Here all the meats of Europe, both domestic meat and fowl, are cut up, decorated, and arranged, as in the finest markets of London and Paris. All the Honolulu butchers lack to complete the resemblance to the butcher shops of Europe are the fine white marble tables on which our meats are kept cool. Notwithstanding, those used in Honolulu are kept clean and immaculate.

Of equal interest is the market where fish from European waters is on sale, as well as those of the Pacific Ocean, including a kind of whitefish peculiar to this island, which is caught by the millions in adjoining waters. Soaked in a concoction of seaweed and eaten raw, it provides the daily food of the natives.

The markets are usually managed by natives, although a few butchers are French. Near these markets, as in the neighborhood of the Parisian stalls, natives selling coffee or cakes in the open air or in tents congregate. Most of the regular patrons of these democratic restaurants, who eat either standing or seated at the tables, are the local merchants of the islands, who come in, bringing produce from the interior. These local cafés, which move from place to place wherever it seems likely that sales might be increased, are in general excellent.

Travelers visiting the Sandwich Islands find them, on the whole, quite unlike Tahiti. On the latter island only the men work, while the women appear to have no responsibilities beyond resting or making love. In the Sandwich Islands, on the other hand, men and women share the same tasks. The general attitude of women toward work differs so radically in Tahiti and the Sandwich Islands that anyone who has visited Papeete is surprised to see manual labor performed by the fair sex in Honolulu.

In the Sandwich Islands supplies vary in price according to the time of year. In the dull season, a chicken is usually worth twenty cents and a turkey forty. In the busy season, prices are doubled. Living at the hotel is not extremely costly; at the Hôtel Globe,[3] run by Franconi and Medaille, tourist rates are quite moderate. The same holds true at Victor's.[4] Victor, who runs the Hôtel de France at Tahiti, also owns a hotel of the same name at Honolulu. Fifteen dollars a week is charged for board, and five more for a room, that is, twenty dollars each week; however, the traveler probably lives as well there as at the leading hotels of Paris.

Of all the hotels I have seen the Globe, which I shall have occasion to mention again, is the most pleasantly situated. For the time being, the city as a whole will be described, and more specific information given in another chapter.

The streets of Honolulu are impressive both in length and breadth; like our boulevards they are lined with a double row of perpetually green trees. These afford shade at all seasons and, whenever the wind blows, a delicious freshness. King Street [5] traverses the city throughout its entire length; it is one of the most magnificent streets I have ever seen. Indicative of its size is the fact that it extends from sea to sea. On this street, as the name indicates, stands the King's palace. This is protected by an elaborate iron fence enclosing the royal park which is as fine as any garden of the Tuileries. The entrance to this park is guarded by a corps of sentinels, as in a European capital.

Nuuanu Street [6] bisects King Street, as well as the entire city, finally continuing out into the country where it ceases to be known as Nuuanu Street and takes the name of Nuuanu Valley. Thus it becomes the route that leads the traveler through a valley which perhaps has no equal in the world. For six English miles the traveler gallops over a delightful road, shaded by an arch of immense trees whose heavy foliage intercepts the intense rays of the sun. At the end of six miles the formidable Pali is reached. Here the route terminates abruptly, cut off by an immense precipice. This point is famous in the history of the Sandwich Islands.

The great chief Paki, father of the present chief Paki,[7] chamberlain to King Kamehameha III and, incidentally my good friend and landlord, inasmuch as I lived in one of his houses when I visited the Sandwich Islands; this great chief Paki declared war on Kamehameha II,[8] and their two armies met in the celebrated Nuuanu Valley. There Paki repulsed the enemy with such vigor that the entire army was forced over the precipice. Then the conquerors descended into the abyss, an immense and sterile crevice in the earth, and buried the vanquished chiefs of the conquered army where they had fallen.

Today this valley of Nuuanu is the promenade of Honolulu, a promenade bordered on each side of the road by charming villas and attractive houses occupied by leading merchants, ministers of the King, and governmental officials. The tourist never fails to go out and promenade in these Champs Élysées and in this Oceanic Bois de Boulogne, and, after reaching the abyss, to glance over the precipice and gaze with curious eyes at the place where the vanquished chiefs are buried. For the sole convenience of these curiosity-seekers, a tiny path has been made in the rocks; the stranger can satisfy his curiosity not only by inspecting the tombs at close range, but also by touching them with his fingers.

Now, if after having visited King Street and the fine beaches to which each extremity of this street leads; if, after having traveled by horse or carriage through the area separating Nuuanu Street from the precipice and the tombs, the traveler desires to visit the interior of the country, there he will find a luxuriant growth that bears a certain similarity to the verdure of Tahiti but excels the latter in the lavishness with which mother nature has planted what man can use.

Thus in the forests grows a large quantity of fine light moss, known to the natives as *pulu*,[9] that resembles reddish silk. This can be used in the same manner as our finest linen, even for making mattresses and pillows. An abundance of coffee is also found in its native state; sugar cane grows into a veritable forest; and there are more delicious fruits in one small group of the Sandwich Islands than in any other island of the Pacific.

Honolulu has many charming residences, invariably hidden behind gardens; the majority, of simple frame construction, have much the aspect of English dwellings. The curious stranger who glances through the iron fences surrounding these houses and penetrates with his eye the wealth of foliage shading them, will usually see an attractive two-story house built of stones cut from rocks and laboriously carried up from the shores of the Pacific by the Kanakas. The stranger asks the guide or the friend who is accompanying him and who is familiar with these places who owns the various houses. Three times out of four he will be told: An American missionary.

I refer any of my readers for whom the article, *American Missionaries,* may have definite interest, to accounts published in 1852 and 1853 in the newspapers of San Francisco, by an American lady of high standing who now runs a boardinghouse for young girls in San Francisco, Madame Parker.[10] With a frankness almost unbelievable among her compatriots, which does great honor to her courage, she publicly exposed the abuses of which these missionaries were guilty in the Sandwich Islands.

The government of the United States, according to Madame Parker, sent men to the islands to attempt to check the progress of bad customs, which both in Honolulu and in Papeete had attained amazing proportions; oblivious to the objective of their mission, however, the majority of these men were able to acquire fine homes for themselves with comparative ease. They came to reform, but stayed to grow rich. The licentiousness they were sent to combat was practiced near their own doors, under their very eyes. The wives of these same missionaries, who, too, had a mission to fulfill, arrived with loads of bright-colored cloth in the form of blouses and ridiculous hats, which they sold to Kanaka women at prices as high as those for which fashionable articles could have been purchased in London or Paris. Moreover, who gave silver to these poor creatures so that they might purchase hats? The wives of the missionaries realized that this money came mainly from debauchery, but they were unconcerned, so long as they received the money, where it came from.

Madame Parker exposes all this and much more. In San Francisco I had all the articles she wrote—which I regret not having brought to Paris—articles whose accuracy was verified during my sojourn in Honolulu. Notwithstanding the slight usefulness and even the dangerous influence of many of the early American missionaries in the Sandwich Islands today, these men enjoy the full confidence of the public; all are wealthy, and nearly all of them have derived their wealth from the source mentioned. And if an investigation into their past lives were made, they could also be censored for the tyrannical manner they displayed toward the Catholic clergy and every member of our mission in Oceania. Throughout the decades when Protestant missionaries first flocked to the Islands, our own worthy French missionaries were forced to submit to outrages and persecutions—a period of which the American missionaries, on the contrary, speak in the highest praise. Now, however, French priests and American ministers are on an equal basis, and if our countrymen seem humble, it is merely because we are more noble and more simple than American Protestants.

To return to Honolulu. The city, as I have said, was like an immense garden. Every house had its veranda, which was equipped with hammocks and chaise lounges. The houses I preferred above all others were those with thick clay walls and thatched roofs that invariably gave the interior, which was always dark, a fresh coolness. Usually the interior was not only comfortable, but even elegant.

On the other hand, the palace was decorated entirely in the European manner; most of its furniture was given by Queen Victoria and King Louis Philippe to his majesty, Kamehameha III. The reception room was so regal that it recalled Fontainebleau. There were also elegant carriages and magnificent horses, cared for, curried, and exercised by liveried grooms like the hostlers and jockeys of London.

The King, whom I often met, was kind and simple; his family was charming. The two princes, his sons, seemed almost like the type of elegant young men seen on Boulevard Tortoni. One of them will be King some day and I am of the belief that throughout his reign he will continue to be as gracious and amiable as he was before his advance in rank.

I had the honor of being presented to him, and I saw him often. I was a good friend of his father, as well as of Mr. John Young,[11] head adviser to the King, who was half English and half Kanaka. The two princes traveled in Europe with the celebrated Mr. Judd,[12] Minister of Finance under Kamehameha III, whose conduct caused the entire population to rise in rebellion until he was overthrown in an insurrection. He accompanied the two princes, as I have already said, to Europe; there, he carefully studied the politics and arts of our country on his own behalf. However, he contented himself with having his wards survey European civilization in much the same manner that cab drivers of Geneva tour Englishmen in small covered carts in which travelers ride sideways. Upon leaving Geneva with their backs turned toward the lake, the Englishmen returned three days later, unaware that they were entering the same place. They had completed their journey, but had seen only the reverse of what they expected to see.

The minister was afraid that any information these two young men might gain in Europe would only instill in them the desire to govern independently and that his ministry would be shorn of power. Hence, though these poor princes were ignorant of the names of M. Guizot,[13] of Lord Palmerston,[14] of M. de Metternich,[15] of Biron,[16] of Lamartine,[17] and of Victor Hugo,[18] they were thoroughly familiar with every shop in Paris or London that made superfine tailored garments, and knew where trousers were cut in the latest fashion.

I ask the reader's indulgence for this digression; it is now time to disembark, for I perceive that I am still aboard ship, from whose bridge I have been watching the turret of the Belvedere [19] and the cupola of the church [20] rise like the minarets of an Asiatic village above the tops of the trees.

CHAPTER III

SATURDAY AT HONOLULU

POSSIBLY SOME one might ask how, before disembarking at Honolulu, I have been able to describe the city as if I were already familiar with the palaces, hotels, promenades, missionaries and young fashionable princes, one of whom now reigns as the successor of Kamehameha. This can be explained in a few words: I am thoroughly familiar with the subject. On our voyage from Tahiti to San Francisco we put in at the Sandwich Islands, and remained there several days. Had I not returned to Honolulu, I should have described at that time what I had seen while passing through the capital of the archipelago; but having returned later, and having lived there several months, I decided that it would be wiser to defer to this second voyage the results of more serious study and profound observation. So I was in reality returning to a familiar land.

Without waiting for the ship to pass down the channel, M. Giovanni and I jumped into one of the boats that swarmed around the ship. Ten minutes later we were ashore. We went immediately toward the Hôtel Globe, where we stopped two years before. It was now one o'clock in the afternoon and, under the ardent sun whose warmth was mitigated by the trade winds, a new vigor seemed to infuse our beings, all was so green, so harmonious, so tranquil.

At one o'clock, however, the entire city takes a siesta and not until four o'clock does it arouse and resume the activity of the morning. Along our road leading from the port to the hotel only a few natives accustomed to the climate or some Chinese coolies for whom differences in climate did not exist were in evidence. Having reached the miniature park that surrounds the Hôtel Globe, M. Franconi, garbed in the vest and white trousers of the colonist, his face protected by a broad hat of Panama straw, came out to welcome us. His unexpected appearance under the green trees caused us keen joy, for here was a familiar figure, the figure, furthermore, of a friend. Having recognized us, he hastened toward us. The hotel was filled to capacity, for we had arrived at the peak of the season—in other words, toward the end of October. M. Franconi, however, in some way arranged to have us occupy one of the delightful guest houses in his park.

Imagine, in order to have some idea of our environment, the Hôtel Globe as a large and somewhat elegant building with a veranda extending all around the ground floor, which opens on the park. Above the first veranda was a second porch, lighter than the first, that entirely covered the first floor and was furnished with sofas, chaise longues, and hammocks, shaded first by large trees that towered above the house, then by window blinds that enveloped the first floor, just as the ground floor was protected by the floor above.

The ground floor contained the offices. On the first floor, which was reached by an imposing outside stairway, were the dining rooms, which were spacious and lofty, as is customary in warm countries. There excellent dinners were served, which I recommend to tourists of all lands and gourmands of all nations. From the windows of this dining room and the balustrades of the balconies, glimpses could be had here and there in the park of charming small houses, cottages, and huts, all mysteriously hidden in clumps of trees that protected them from the withering sun. The guest houses were delightful retreats, consisting merely of a sleeping room, bathroom, and sometimes a salon. The furnishings were simple but quite suitable and their general air of comfort impressed the traveler the moment he entered.

Chinese matting, fine and white, covered the floor and often the walls as well. An immense bed with *pulu* mattresses and pillows was the principal object in the room; it was enveloped in a graceful valance of muslin called mosquito netting. Most of the furniture, the red chairs, lacquer tables, and the bamboo desk were Chinese, articles from that country being not only abundant, but also extremely cheap in the Sandwich Islands. Near the door were banana, guava, and other tropical trees whose names I did not know. Even now I can still recall their beauty and fragrance. Beneath these trees, hammocks hung and in the center of the garden a gathering place was provided with chairs and rustic seats, where hotel guests could congregate for afternoon tea or to rest in the evening. Imagine this paradise for two dollars a day!

Here the men smoked their cigars, while we joined them in our light robes of silk or mousseline, to chat and relax with the pleasant informality that is inspired by a certain hour of the evening in these warm latitudes, that seem, far more than in our European climate, to radiate the warmth of God.

M. Franconi prepared a special dinner in our honor, and the first dinner ashore, after a voyage, no matter how short, always seems excellent. That evening, which was pleasant and mild, we happened to meet several persons whose acquaintance we made two years before. I asked them if the usual Saturday fiestas were still being held, and was told that they were more popular then ever. Since we arrived on Friday, I promised myself to attend the following day in a leisurely manner, for I had had only a glimpse of them on my first visit. Every Saturday, Honolulu has a festival; thus every Saturday corresponds in a sense to our Mardi Gras.

Where did this weekly folly originate? I asked the wisest Sandwich Islanders in vain about this custom. Not one was able to enlighten me about the origin; it exists, because it exists—it is a custom, that is all.

And so, every Saturday between nine and ten o'clock in the morning, the Kanaka women appear in their doorways, decked with flowers, flowers made into garlands, wreaths, and bracelets, exactly like the voluptuously perfumed Tahitians whose customs I have attempted to portray. From ten to eleven men and women leave their homes on horseback—they will deprive themselves of food all week to save the dollar necessary to hire a horse on Saturday.

The men wear shirts and trousers of every color, sashes around their waists, whose ends float in the breezes, and flowers woven by their mistresses around their heads and necks. The women, who ride astride, are clad in a large piece of cloth, usually of orange calico, which they tie around their waists and hips, then roll into a sash, which falls on either side of their legs like a kind of sheath. This, hanging loose from the hips, leaves the legs and feet bare, and is allowed to drop over the two flanks of the horse. Fabrics are manufactured expressly for this purpose and supplied by the Americans, who are always alert for new business.

Wealthy women of the island wear, first of all, a large hat with black plumes as a mark of superiority; then a robe of black satin; then over the robe caught up between their two legs like Turkish trousers is a piece of cloth, a national ornament that is inseparable from the Saturday fiesta. The poorer women are clad in nothing but wrappers under this piece of cloth. Of course, every sailor off the whaling ships who has a dollar to hire a horse dons his finest vest and his best trousers to take part in the cavalcade, and in the end nearly everyone, including all the strangers, joins in this general movement that resembles a moment of universal folly, and is, furthermore, an extremely curious spectacle.

The rendezvous is in King Street. An hour or two after the crowd arrives, the foolish and senseless races, in which every rider joins in a mad frenzy, begin. Some participants do not leave the city, but merely go from King Street to Nuuanu Street; others, on the contrary, rush toward Nuunau Valley, as if they intended to hurl themselves over the abyss that terminates this charming promenade. Everyone seems to have lost all self-control and to be the victim either of drunkenness or madness. At five o'clock King Kamehameha III departs. The King, who appears to be about sixty years of age, has a benign and kindly countenance. At the races he wears a blue coat with gold buttons, and black trousers, and has the appearance of a good bourgeois citizen who rides his horse well. His close friend, John Young, is usually to be found nearby.

John Young, the companion, counsellor and minister of His Majesty of the Sandwich Islands, is a descendant of the first Englishman who set foot with Captain Cook on the island. John Young's father, the son of this English adventurer, was the close friend of Kamehameha II, as John Young is of Kamehameha III. Upon their deathbeds the two fathers expressed the wish that the same friendship that bound them should also unite their children. The children have respected the last request of their fathers.

The King, who now rules under the name of Liho Liho I, or Kamehameha IV is, as I have already said, a handsome and elegant young man, who has traveled extensively in England, France, and Italy. His trip was the result of a strange situation. To study European progress, King Kamehameha II and his wife made a trip years ago to London, and while returning from England contracted smallpox and died within sight of home. At that time Kamehameha III, with whom I subsequently became acquainted, took an oath never to leave the Sandwich Islands. Despite it, one day the news spread that the King was about to leave for Europe. This rumor caused a riot. The King renewed his pledge in public, never to leave the Islands; in his place the two young men made the journey. And so young Liho Liho and his brother Alexander were sent with the Minister of Finance, Mr. Judd, their tutor, to tour Europe. They traveled, as indicated, in the same manner that the Englishmen from the Hôtel des Bergues toured Lake Geneva.

Obviously so good a prince, so popular a King, would never interrupt or restrain the amusements of these good Kanakas, who continued their follies and their excursions until nightfall; in other words, until six o'clock in the evening, the hour when each one dismounts, returns his rented horse, disrobes, and eats poi.

Poi, a kind of mush made with taro, is the daily food of the Sandwich Islanders. Taro, a root that is extensively cultivated in the Sandwich Islands, sprouts in water, in basins expressly prepared for this purpose. When fully mature, it resembles a turnip. Before being used it is crushed in a stone mortar; the Kanaka, as he pounds, works the mixture with one hand and with the other adds water. The preparation of taro requires at least five hours. but at the end of this time it is reduced to a pulp.

Taro is the universal food of the Sandwich Islanders, from the King down to his most humble subject; but the richer the man who eats poi, the thicker the poi; the poorer he is, the thinner the poi. The result is that since the Sandwich Islanders do not use spoons, but their fingers, the King proudly eats poi with one finger, the bourgeois with two fingers, and the poor, between whose fingers it slips, with the whole hand. Poi closely resembles starch after it has been boiled and is even used to wash linen, for the Kanaka women, who are excellent laundresses, have no other substitute for starch. Due to the low price of this commodity, a Kanaka can live on a few cents a day and still have bananas for dessert.

At the instigation of the missionaries, King Kamehameha III forbade wine and intoxicating liquor in his kingdom and, ostensibly at least, adheres to this prohibition. In public His Majesty drinks only water; hence he rarely drinks in public. The King prefers champagne, which is the wine he always drinks in private. The two proprietors of the Hôtel Globe and the Hôtel de France keep him supplied with champagne, sending him full hampers which are returned to them empty.

The palace is not the only place where King Kamehameha III disregards his religious and hygienic creeds. Often he goes out with his friend John Young about seven o'clock in the evening, and arm in arm both stroll down to the Hôtel du Commerce,[1] run by Macfarlane on Nuuanu Street, to play billiards. When the King is seen approaching, the owner of the hotel has the billiard room, if occupied, vacated—this is the only tyrannical act the King exercises over his subjects—then receives the King, hat in hand, has him enter if he wishes to play only with his friend John Young, brings out some champagne, and closes the door behind them.

If His Majesty wishes to extend the favor of his company to others, the élite are called in, introduced, and invited to play and drink with the King for that evening. But usually, on toward eleven or twelve o'clock, the party breaks up, when the King, anticipating trouble when he feels his legs tremble in a distressing manner, indicates his intention of leaving. At such times John Young reveals the influence he has over His Majesty; courteously urging the latter to take his arm, he leads him back safely to the palace, thus proving that he is not only the supporter of royalty, but also the sustainer of the King.

Owing to the fact that M. Giovanni had a certain knack at billiards, he had the honor of making the acquaintance of His Majesty. Mr. Macfarlane had spoken to the King about him as a stranger who had an easy cannon and an expert double, and so the King expressed a desire to meet this stranger. Thus it came about that M. Giovanni had the distinction of beating His Majesty at the Russian match, the Italian match, and even at doubles, and soon found himself in such favor that he was nearly made minister to King Kamehameha III, as Chamillart, under similar circumstances, was appointed by Louis XIV.

After the King, the two princes, and John Young, the most important person on the island is the son of the great Paki, the conqueror. He is chamberlain to His Majesty, and his house is as fine as the palace. Paki is a powerful Kanaka lord; he has two wives, one in the country and one in the city, who exchange visits in an amicable manner. I was fortunate enough to meet the two wives at the same time, for Paki brought them to call on me when I was recuperating from what is known as Panama fever.

Panama fever is the only scourge in the Sandwich Islands, a land where the air is perhaps the purest in the world. It was introduced about twelve years before our visit by an infected ship, and is nothing more than yellow fever, whose force is lessened by the salubrious climate. Notwithstanding, the victim suffers intensely for three days. The treatment used comes from an old Kanaka remedy that consists in following the pain wherever it strikes and applying soothing herbs to the afflicted areas. At the end of three days the patient is as weak as he would be after a long illness. However, it is rare, in fact almost unknown, for the disease to prove fatal. During convalescence the sufferer, despite the religious and hygienic protests of the missionaries, is forced to drink the most tonic wine that can be found. Yet even with the use of these wines, strength is slow in returning.

Honolulu has a theatre [2] with a troupe of English or American actors. When the Queen attends, there is a grand celebration, and, as in Italy, considerable commotion. I attended one of their performances when the King, the Queen, and the princes participated in the festivities. Upon this occasion John Young, who was also present, was thirsty and asked for something to drink. Because of the local law prohibiting wines and liquors, he was offered water in a gourd that had been cut in half and that resembled a chalice. He moistened his lips with this water—a beverage for which he did not conceal his dislike—then decided to punish the man for the indignity that had been offered, and so, amid the applause of the bystanders who were watching him, he poured what water remained in the gourd over his head.

The most important church in the Sandwich Islands is Bethel Church,[3] which is the Saint Roch of Honolulu. This was the favorite church of Princess Victoria, a good and charitable person, but withal a zealous and proselytizing Protestant. She sang in the Bethel choir and occasionally was even heard in solos, her august voice mounting clear and pure toward the heavens.

Princess Victoria's two brothers had a harem in the interior of the island where they kept twelve mistresses, an equal number of women to wait on them, and at least a dozen servants. There each favorite had her own personal maid, who spent most of her time making wreaths of orange blossoms, necklaces and amulets of jasmine, and girdles of various kinds of flowers. The Kanakas of the Sandwich Islands, like those of Tahiti, as I have already said, adore flowers.

The beds of these women consisted of piles of mats covered with tapa cloth. Near each bed was a bathtub, so that the favorite merely had to pass from bath to bed and from bed to bath. The princes, accompanied by their friends, usually came out on horseback to visit their harem; and there, I believe, as at Macfarlane's, amused themselves playing billiards and getting drunk.

Sandwich Islanders celebrate the first day of their year, which does not coincide with our New Year, by holding a great festival in the city. What we call New Year's gifts are called in the Sandwich Islands *lualua,* and consist of plates of food that are carried on litters by servants and left at the houses of the donor's friends.

At the end of fifteen days passed at Hôtel du Globe, having found a house for rent that was completely furnished, we decided to take it. Our new habitation consisted of a magnificent suite on the ground floor, situated between two gardens with a salon, a sleeping room, a bathroom, a dining room, and a veranda that surrounded the entire house. The sight of my bed made me utter a cry of joy. Even in Italy I had never seen one so imposing. At least six persons could have slept on it in comfort.

Having only recently recovered from yellow fever, I had an overwhelming desire to sleep, a desire to which I yielded with a pleasure I never experienced in any other place or under any other circumstances. As soon as my strength returned, I began paying calls throughout the island, for my introductions provided entrée into the homes of the leading families. I was soon on friendly terms with several women in Honolulu and especially with Miss Benedict, sister of Mr. Vincent, known locally as the carpenter-proprietor. Why he was called by this title was a secret that the wealthy Mr. Vincent kept to himself.

Who was this Mr. Vincent? [4] He is an American from New York who left home when quite young without the knowledge of his parents who were members of a well-to-do and highly respected family. Lured by an overwhelming desire to see the world, he shipped as cabin boy on a trading vessel, but, having been punished, perhaps somewhat cruelly, for some slight misdemeanor, he deserted his ship at Honolulu and reached the interior of the island.

After his ship departed, he returned to the city and, having apprenticed himself to a carpenter, remained on the island, working diligently. Later, when he succumbed to a serious illness, he was nursed back to health by the young daughter of a powerful chief, called Maria, who was so devoted that he fell in love with her. Since their affection was mutual, after considerable difficulty he obtained her hand in marriage, and with it a great fortune in cultivated lands and plantations which she possessed. He continued the profession he had recently adopted, but on a larger scale, until he became the leading building contractor in Honolulu.

I spent New Year's Day at the house of Madame Vincent, who invited me to participate in a *lualua* in honor of her husband. The feast arrived, carried by sixty servants of the carpenter-proprietor, all newly clad for the occasion. Madame Vincent rode at the head of the procession on horseback, for the celebration was to take place in the country.

Her husband, having preceded her, dismounted and embraced her, then both entered the house together where the *lualua* was served on a huge table around which we sat during the repast. Maria, as Mr. Vincent's wife was called, did not join us, however, but waited on us like a servant. After we had finished dinner, she shared the repast of her parents and her Kanaka friends in a side room, where everyone sat on mats.

Madame Vincent preferred the country to the city and usually lived in her country house which, by the way, was a delightful spot. This retreat was near the Pali; I often went out on horseback with her sister-in-law to visit her. Maria always welcomed us both like sisters and asked us to remove our riding habits and don those loose silk garments that are the delight of Kanaka women. Then, clad in dishabille, we would saunter through her beautiful gardens, eating strawberries, peaches, prunes, and other country fruit. One evening while strolling through these gardens, I fell into a patch of taro— taro, as I have said, is raised in what resembles huge bathtubs sunk in the earth—from which my friends had considerable difficulty extricating me.

A word now about the various consuls who reside in Honolulu. Mr. Allen,[5] the American consul, was by reputation and accomplishment the most estimable and the bravest man on the island. His daughter, Mrs. Patterson,[6] was as charming and handsome as any American woman on the main continent, but as eccentric as she was beautiful. However, her eccentricities should be allowed to pass unnoticed. The only person who had any right to reproach her was her husband, and he refrained from making any comments about her conduct.

General Miller,[7] the English consul, was so reserved and quiet that I seldom heard anyone mention him. Never having heard any comments about him, I am unable to say anything definite about him.

At the time of my visit there was no French consul in Honolulu. M. Perrin,[8] the regular consul, being in Europe, his place was temporarily filled by Baron Thierry,[9] the same individual who once called himself King of New Zealand. I called to see the French consul only to find myself facing a dethroned King. Having known his life at Auckland, I was fully aware of his romantic past. Unfortunately, M. Thierry had the same difficulty filling the post of vice consul that he had when acting as king. At the time M. Perrin reached the Sandwich Islands to become consul, he engaged Baron Thierry for the position of vice consul pending the arrival from Europe of the regular appointee.

The baron served in this capacity for several months. Then one morning M. Frick,[10] who had been sent by the Minister of Foreign Affairs to occupy the place that Baron Thierry was holding in the interim, arrived. Apparently some kind of an agreement had been made between M. Perrin and M. Thierry that was adversely affected by this arrival, but there was no way to alter the appointments made by the Minister of Foreign Affairs and Baron Thierry had no alternative but to resign in favor of M. Frick. Several days later M. Perrin, who was preparing to make a trip to France, suspended M. Frick from office, reinstating Baron Thierry, whom he instructed to take charge of the consulate in his absence. It was after his departure that I called at the consulate.

One fine day in December not long after my visit, guns were heard in the bay. These proved to be cannon on the sloop-of-war, *Brillante,* which coming into port fired a salute of twenty-one shots in honor of King Kamehameha III. Soon the news circulated that the warship was carrying M. Perrin, now consul plenipotentiary of the French government to His Majesty, Kamehameha III. Two hours later he appeared in Honolulu and entered the Hôtel de France. But to the intense astonishment of Baron Thierry, who believed he was to remain permanently as vice consul, M. Perrin

had with him a new official, M. Letellier,[11] appointed, as was
M. Frick, by the Minister of Foreign Affairs.

M. Letellier was accompanied by his wife, and although they had
taken passage on the same boat as M. Perrin, throughout the entire
trip the relations of the two French officials had been so strained
that the new vice consul could scarcely anticipate a happy future
in his new post in Honolulu. Then, the very morning of the day
that M. Letellier assumed his new duties, merely because the muster roll of the crew of Captain Cronier's whaling vessel had been
improperly prepared, he was suspended from office, Baron Thierry
being given his place. M. Letellier returned to his hotel sick at heart.
His wife was ill. Neither one was rich, neither one spoke English,
the principal language of the country, and eight or nine months
would elapse before his protest could reach France and a reply be
received.

Several days later the consul was received amid great ceremony by
King Kamehameha III who desired him to deliver the official cre-
dentials he carried. At the same time, Baron Thierry appeared as
chancellor of the French consulate. But only fifteen days later, to
the amazement of the entire city, Baron Thierry and M. Perrin had
difficulties, and the baron for the third and last time found that he
had lost his title of chancellor.

I have no prejudices against anyone. I knew M. Thierry slightly;
I knew M. Letellier somewhat better; I knew M. Frick fairly well,
and do not know whether he was right or wrong. Yet from a purely
Christian point of view, I must add a few remarks, with the hope
that they will not be misunderstood. The day M. Frick lost his place
he was without funds. If he had only had something to live on,
he would not have seen so distressed. A man, especially a distinguished man, can always extricate himself from a dilemma. In his
case, the family which consisted of himself, his wife, four boys,
four girls, and his sister—eleven in all—was a heavy burden to a
man in his financial condition. Of this number, however, the two
eldest sons were leaving for Australia where they hoped to find
work in the gold mines at Port Phillips, and the eldest of the four
girls was married to M. Franconi, who had charge of the Hôtel du

Globe. That made three mouths less to feed; but still there were eight to support.

Fortunately, M. Frick spoke excellent French and English. He began to give lessons in order to earn his daily bread; then, having some idea of natural history, he turned his attention to conchological research, and, devoting his energy to making collections, increased by a large amount the total number of specimens that form the family of achatinella which are found exclusively in Hawaii. Thus he succeeded in amassing what at the present time ranks as one of the finest shell collections in the world, a collection including two million land shells and one hundred and ninety thousand marine shells. All this he has classified, labeled, numbered, and placed in a vast room, used as a museum, which would create a sensation even in London or Paris.

Every whaler, every stranger, reaching Honolulu comes and asks the privilege of inspecting his treasures, which the misery of his wife and the hunger of his children inspired him to assemble with such zeal and at the cost of so many sacrifices. From time to time he has been induced, at the urgent request of amateurs, to sell a small collection of less rare objects to keep the family pot boiling. But when he knows that the pot will boil tranquilly for eight or ten days, he takes his pack and walking stick and, accompanied by natives who assist him in his task, leaves again to explore mountain peak and seashore that supply him with specimens, nourishing himself like a bird from heaven—that is, by drops of dew and grains of millet that the good Lord chooses to send him. At such times he subsists on sugar cane and wild bananas, supplementing this frugal nourishment by a little poi found in the huts of Kanakas that live in the interior, sleeping here and there, wherever the impulse for research lures him, traveling at times six, eight, and even ten days to discover a new species. Then, when he has found some rarity previously unknown, he returns and presents it to his family.

As he displays his treasure, shrieks of joy resound throughout the house. To his family the day brings a dual happiness, for it is a day both of return and of enrichment. Singing and dancing, they encircle the good man who now calls in a dozen natives who have often assisted him. Showing them the latest addition to the conchological family, which has just been discovered, he tells them to keep its color and form carefully in mind and sends them out to search for similar objects.

The Kanakas leave eagerly and return at the end of a certain time, each one carrying any shells he has been able to collect that resemble the specimen, for which M. Frick pays them. And how do you think he pays them? With marble billiard balls, rosaries, images of the Virgin, and a few glass trinkets purchased from whalers or received as gifts from men who have seen his collection. To understand his method, it is essential to watch the parsimonious and solemn way he rewards them by passing out to the man who has brought him a small box of shells—the fruit of three or four days passed in the mountains—a dozen assorted billiard balls, and to hear the infantile quarrels of the Kanakas, who want vari-colored marbles in place of red or white balls! And it is both inspiring and pathetic to watch this man struggle against poverty in order to keep intact his collection, for which he has already been offered a good price, but which he is holding for the future, intending to sell it in Europe.

Would you like to know, furthermore, with what Christian resignation this family martyr endures the poverty brought on him by the enmity of the consul? Then read the following letter written to me at Honolulu on January 2, 1854.

Honolulu, Jan. 2, '54

"A happy New Year to Monsieur and Madame Giovanni and Co. from papa, mama, and big and little chicks of the Frickian tribe.

"My very dear lady,

"M. Friart has brought me your pleasant messages so full of kindly feeling toward us. They were very precious New Year's gifts and the only ones that so far have passed the lowly threshold of our door. Here, as elsewhere, everyone is weary even of pretending a little sympathy for those who remain so long in distress. If Athenian citizens were thoroughly weary of having invariably to call Aristides virtuous, is it surprising that everyone is tired of calling me a ragamuffin? This, in the end, is an incurable condition; we grow accustomed to considering it normal; no one is interested in us any longer, and our door is shunned as if smallpox reigned within. But rest assured, fine spirit, with your message of courage; we are not so easily conquered. At the moment I write, one of my small daughters comes pathetically to me. 'Everyone is rejoicing,' the poor child remarks, 'everyone has presents, but no one gives me anything.' I swear that my philosophical spirit sinks at the words. But I shall survive. Misfortune, like vice, becomes a habit, and misfortune is one of the curses of our advanced civilization. Perhaps you have heard, as a piece of bad news, that my two sons have recently returned from Australia without gold. But don't be deceived; the return of these children so long absent was a joyful day in our desolated home. God is good. For now they are both working and each one brings back at the end of the week's labors what he has earned. What should we have done without them at present, when the echo of our voices is no longer interrupted by the moving of furniture which has gone, piece by piece, to enrich other homes, in plainer language, now when we no longer have anything we can convert into bread?

"Sometime ago I wrote a play for the theatre which brought me twenty-five dollars. A poor price, you will say. But the theatre is also poor, and poor without doubt is the work of a poor man! In a box I have a comedy of high society in two acts, *An Old Girl*. I refused twenty-five dollars for it, hoping by some means to realize considerably more from the land where gold is near the melting-pot.

"My son-in-law makes, I am told, considerable money at his hotel; but I see his profits only from a distance. His wife dines with us daily, and our departure would leave her as isolated as a ship-wrecked mariner on deserted strands, for she has no inclination to ally herself with American dolls who only know how to bedeck themselves in their finery and sit idly on their doorsteps.

"Since the sale of our piano, our interior has become as solemn as a Quaker assembly, except for the noise of my small girls and boys who are happy because they understand nothing of our serious preoccupations. Our health continues to be good; of the caprices of wealth, I cannot say as much!

"Inclosed you will find a letter from Mylira. Better late than never. I presume she will give you any news that has escaped me."

CHAPTER IV

CAPTAIN COOK

AFTER a sojourn of three months at Honolulu, M. Giovanni began to think about business, and soon had an opportunity to undertake another speculative venture in California, which consisted in procuring a cargo of chickens, turkeys, pigs, coffee, sweet potatoes, and miscellaneous supplies that Americans consider luxuries, on equal shares with the captain of a brig that was about to set sail from port. In the handling of these various commodities, there was a chance to make enormous profits; chickens, for example, worth four or five cents in the Sandwich Islands brought four or five dollars at San Francisco; turkeys selling for thirty or forty cents at Honolulu had a value in California of twelve or fourteen dollars. To reach port safely with this cargo, however, certain precautions had to be taken, but even under the most unfavorable conditions, since the trip from San Francisco to the Sandwich Islands had been made in eleven days, not more than fifteen days would be required for the return voyage to this port in California.

After the agreement had been completed, we set to work in earnest and began making purchases, but since everything was decidedly expensive owing to the whaling season, it was agreed that the load should be completed at Hawaii, an island situated three days' journey from Honolulu, where the port of Karakakoua,[1] often visited by ships, is situated. We left Honolulu and on the third day reached Haina,[2] as the natives of the country call Hawaii or Owyhee.

We came into the port of Karakakoua on Sunday just in time to attend mass, but found the harbor and shore as sad, deserted, and abandoned as Honolulu is gay, well-populated, and teeming with activity. The streets, that were lined on both sides by trees, were like carpets of verdure; and we walked over what seemed like veritable lawns of green sod. As we left and retraced our steps to the port, one of the supply merchants observed: "This is where Captain Cook[3] was assassinated."[4]

I am unable to pass by this historic spot without giving a few details regarding this murder, well known as it may be. Discovered about 1512,[5] these islands we were now visiting were rediscovered in 1778 by Captain Cook, who gave them the name of Sandwich, in honor of the Count of Sandwich. After Captain Cook had remained a month at the port of Karakakoua, the *Discovery* finally arrived, and the two ships left the islands to reconnoiter the west coast of America. There Captain Cook continued his explorations until, checked by the ice, he was forced to return to the Sandwich Islands. On January 17, 1779, he anchored less than a quarter of a mile off the northwest coast in the bay of Karakakoua.

"Scarcely had the boat anchored," [6] said Captain Cook, "when we were surrounded by a flock of canoes. I had never before, on any of my voyages, seen so large a crowd assembled at any one spot, for, in addition to those who arrived by canoe, the shore of the bay was thick with spectators, and still more swam around us, in groups of several hundred, that might have been mistaken for schools of fishes. The singularity of this scene struck us forcibly."

These were the last lines written by Captain Cook; at this point the narrative of his voyage was violently interrupted by the catastrophe we shall now recount. The bay of Karakakoua lies on the west side of the island of Hawaii, in a region called Akona and is about a mile in depth. Captain Cook, in the belief that he could careen his ships and take on food and water at this point, anchored on the north side, about a quarter of a mile offshore. After the inhabitants perceived that the Europeans were preparing to remain in the bay, they approached. The crowd, as on the previous evening, was immense and all signified their joy by chants and cries. Soon the sides, decks, and rigging of the two ships were covered with native Hawaiians, while a throng of women and small boys, who had been unable to secure places in the canoes, swam out to the vessels. The majority of them passed the day in the water, apparently no more fatigued by keeping themselves afloat on the waves than they would have been lounging on the sandy shore. All went well from the eighteenth to the twenty-fourth.

On the twenty-fourth the Englishmen were somewhat surprised to see that the chiefs did not permit any boats to leave the shore, and that the natives remained near their huts. Several hours passed before any explanation was offered as to the cause of this embargo.

Finally the discovery was made that Chief Terreoboo had tabooed the bay and had prohibited communication of any kind with the Europeans. That evening it was impossible to procure any supplies whatsoever, and despite threats and promises not a native dared approach the vessels.

In the afternoon, however, a visit was received aboard ship from the great Chief who had come devoid of escort or clothing to inspect the vessels. He had with him only one canoe, in which sat his wives and children. After remaining on board until six o'clock in the evening, he returned to his village.

After Captain Cook saw Terreoboo start for land, he followed him, reaching shore at approximately the same moment. Upon the invitation of the local chieftain,[7] he and Captain King accompanied him to his dwelling, and as soon as they were seated, the latter threw the cloak he was wearing over his shoulders, placed a feather headdress on Captain Cook's head, and slipped a fan between his hands. Then he laid at his feet five or six coats of great value. Simultaneously, his retainers brought four large pigs, some sugar cane, cocoanuts, and breadfruit. The native chieftain terminated this ceremony by uttering Captain Cook's name; in the Oceanic Islands, this is the most favorable sign of friendship that can be extended by a Kanaka chieftain. Soon a procession of priests appeared, led by an aged individual with a venerable countenance. Behind them followed a file of men, some of whom led live pigs, while others carried sweet potatoes and bananas.

The day of departure had been set for February fourth, and on the third, Terreoboo asked Captain Cook and Captain King to accompany him to the residence of Kaoo. Upon their arrival at this place, they found the ground covered with bundles of material, a considerable quantity of yellow and red feathers, a large number of hatchets, and a quantity of iron instruments, which the natives of the country had obtained by barter from the Europeans. A slight distance away lay an enormous pile of vegetables of various kinds; near the vegetables were several pigs. The two officers believed at first that these various things were gifts, but they soon learned that they represented tribute paid to the chieftain by the local inhabitants.

Terreoboo now chose for himself approximately one-third of these presents brought by the natives of the country, and gave the other two-thirds to Captain Cook and Captain King, who were astounded at the magnificence of this present; it surpassed those they had received up to that time in any of the other islands of the Pacific. The English leader immediately summoned his boats to have them carried aboard; he set aside the large pigs that were to be stored and salted, then distributed to the crews thirty smaller pigs, as well as many vegetables.

Early in the morning of the fourth the anchors were hoisted and the two ships left the bay. As they moved off a flock of canoes followed. Captain Cook proposed at this time to complete the exploration of the island of Hawaii before landing on the other islands of this group, for he hoped to find another anchorage that would afford better shelter than that of Karakakoua. On the sixth day of the month, as he passed the most westerly side of the island, he discovered that he was opposite a large bay. The pinnace was sent out to examine it, while the other vessels tacked, preparatory to entering.

The eleventh day and part of the twelfth were spent taking down the foremast and sending it ashore with the carpenters. But after the vessels had anchored, the English perceived to their amazement that the islanders' attitude had changed. No more cries of joy were heard; no more friendly faces appeared. Finally, as the crowds vanished, there was an ominous silence. The bay appeared deserted; only occasionally was a boat sighted, disappearing down the coast.

Meanwhile, Captain Cook was informed that several thefts had been committed on the ships and pinnaces. He was somewhat gloomy because of the situation and said to Captain King: "I fear the islanders will force us to take violent measures; it is not wise to allow them to think they can steal from us with impunity." [8]

The following morning at daybreak, Captain King, who was returning to the *Resolution,* was hailed by the *Discovery*. He learned that during the night the islanders had swum out and stolen the ship's longboat by cutting the buoy to which she had been anchored. When Captain King came aboard, he found that the marines were arming and that Captain Cook was already loading his gun with a double load, one side with small lead and the other with balls. As Captain King was making his night's report, Captain Cook interrupted him: "The longboat of the *Discovery* has been stolen," he said with an air of animation. "You see the preparations I am making to recover it.[9] By force or ruse Terreoboo or several chieftains of the island must be lured on board and held as hostages until they have returned the stolen articles. I have just given orders to stop every canoe leaving the bay, and I shall destroy them all, if necessary, one after the other, if I have no other way of regaining the longboat."

In fact, under Captain King's very eyes, Captain Cook dispatched across the bay the small boats belonging to the *Resolution* and *Discovery*, well-armed and equipped, and ordered two cannon shots to be fired on two large canoes that were attempting to escape.

Between seven and eight o'clock in the morning, Captain Cook and his associate left the ship. Captain Cook climbed into the pinnace, taking with him nine marines and an officer, while Captain King started out in the small canoe. The last orders he received from his chief were to calm the excited natives and assure them that no harm would be done, not to scatter his troops, and to keep constantly on his guard. Then the two captains separated, Captain Cook marching toward the village of Kowrowa, the residence of Terreoboo, and Captain King toward an observatory the English had erected.

Captain King's first act, upon reaching shore, was to order the marines under no condition to leave their tents, but to load their guns with balls, and keep them ready at hand. Meanwhile, Captain Cook signalled the small boat of the *Resolution* to rally the pinnace; escorted by it, he then continued his route toward Kowrowa. There he disembarked with the nine marines and the lieutenant, and marched toward the village, where he received the same marks of respect that were usually extended to him. The natives prostrated themselves before him in the dust and, according to their custom of hospitality, offered him some small pigs. Aware that no one suspected his mission, he asked where he could find Terreoboo and his two sons. As he was talking several islanders appeared, accompanied by the two princes; they conducted Captain Cook to the place where

Terreoboo was asleep. Having aroused him and told him in a few words about the theft of his longboat, Captain Cook invited him to come as was his custom to spend the day aboard the *Resolution*.

Terreoboo accepted the offer without hesitation and at once rose to accompany Captain Cook. So far everything seemed to be progressing in a satisfactory manner. The native chief's two sons were already in the pinnace, and the rest of the little group was down on the shore and about to embark, when an old woman called out in a loud voice to Kanee Kabareea, the mother of the two princes, and one of the favorite wives of Terreoboo. The latter, after exchanging a few words with the old woman, approached her husband and with prayers and tears begged him not to go out to the ship. At the same time two chiefs who were with her held Terreoboo by his cloak, warning him not to move and, laying their hands on his shoulders, forced him to sit down.

The islanders who, while this was taking place had assembled along the bank, apprehensive for the safety of Terreoboo in view of the hostile preparations that were being made in the bay, now began to crowd around Captain Cook and their leader. Then the lieutenant of the marines, aware that his men were being crowded by the natives and would be unable to use their arms should the need arise, advised Captain Cook to prepare to fight along the rocks near the shore. As the crowd cleared a path for him without protest, the lieutenant went over and stationed himself some thirty paces from the place where Terreoboo had remained seated.

As he did so, the chieftain's face revealed fright and despondency. Captain Cook persisted in remaining near him and continued to urge him to embark. Terreoboo now got up and prepared to follow him. But the priests, conscious that their prayers and entreaties were useless, pulled their chieftain away, declaring that even if they were forced to use violence, he was not to follow the stranger to his ships.

At that moment, the excitement on every hand seemed to increase. Then an event occurred that made the situation even more tense. As the boats stationed across the bay fired on the canoes that were attempting to escape, their guns unfortunately killed one of the leading chieftains. News of this calamity reached Kowrowa at the very moment that Captain Cook, cognizant of the resistance being offered, ceased attempting to persuade the chieftain to embark and walked toward the shore to enter his own boat. Observing him depart the natives ordered the women and children to leave, donned their war coats, and armed themselves with stones and lances.

One of the men, holding a flint in one hand and a long dagger in the other, approached the English leader; he brandished his sword and threatened to hurl a stone at him. The Captain coolly ordered him to cease his threats, but his calmness was mistaken by the natives for fear and so their insolence merely increased. Then Captain Cook took aim and emptied one of the two chambers of his gun that was loaded with small lead in his direction.

The islander, however, was covered with a war cloak that was impervious to buckshot. This led him to believe that European guns were powerless, so he hurled himself on Captain Cook. The latter then emptied the second chamber of his gun, loaded with two bullets, and killed the native. His fall was the signal for a general attack. Stones rained on Captain Cook and the soldiers, who replied, as did the sailors from the boats, by a discharge of musketry. But to the intense astonishment of the Europeans, the Hawaiians withstood the fire courageously, falling on them with hideous cries and yells, before the marines were able to find time to reload their guns.

While their comrades were being slaughtered three paces away, four marines were snatched from their oars, three of them being dangerously wounded. The lieutenant received the blade of a sword between his two shoulders but fortunately, having conserved his bullets, he was able to kill the man who struck him. As for Captain Cook, the last time anyone actually saw him, he was waving his hat and calling to the boat to stop firing and approach as close as possible to shore so that he could embark. Suddenly he disappeared; for having failed to keep his eyes on the islanders, whom up to this time he had held in check by his glance, he was struck in the back and dropped forward into the sea. As he fell, a crowd of natives rushed toward him, pulled him up on the shore by his feet, and since he had only one sword, one native after another lifted this weapon and vented his fury on his corpse, striking it long after the Captain had expired. The exact spot where the illustrious traveler died was pointed out to me by the merchant.

Captain King, meanwhile, was on the other side of the bay. Through his spyglass, although he could distinguish nothing clearly, he noticed a considerable amount of commotion, accompanied by several shots that gave him an inkling of what had happened. Then he saw the savages withdraw into the interior and rush toward their villages, followed by firing from the canoes. Finally, the officer in command, convinced that there was no hope of saving the English leader, decided to go aboard and ask his superior officers what he should do in this emergency. He was ordered to burn the village and kill every native he could find.

Almost immediately after this command was given, a chief called Eappo, who had come bearing gifts at the instigation of Chief Terreoboo and to seek peace, was announced. Eappo was told that terms of peace would not be considered until the remains of Captain Cook and his sailors were returned. The envoy replied that the flesh of the seamen, as well as their breast bones and stomachs had been burned, and that their arms, hands, legs, and thighs had been divided among the island chieftains. The body of Captain Cook, he added, had been disposed of in another manner: the head had been cut off and given to a powerful chief called Kahoo Opeon; the flesh from his breast had been given to another chief named Maiha Maiha, and the thighs and lower limbs to Terreoboo.

Demands were made for the immediate return of these remains of Captain Cook, such as they were, and the village was threatened with complete destruction if this request was not granted within twenty-four hours. On the nineteenth, between eleven and twelve o'clock, a group of islanders came solemnly down the hill that overlooked the beach, in single file. As they approached, Eappo, who was clothed in a feather garment and appeared to be carrying something carefully in his hand, signalled from a high rock for a canoe to be sent out. Captain Clerke,[10] confident that Eappo was bringing the remains of Captain Cook, took the pinnace, ordered Captain King to follow with the longboat, and approached shore. When he landed, Eappo entered the pinnace, handed Captain Clerke some objects, whose shape could not be recognized, objects that were wrapped first in a piece of new cloth and then covered with a mantle decked with black and white plumes, and attempted to make him understand that this was what he had requested.

After Clerke and his men returned aboard the *Resolution,* they opened the package. Within were found intact the hands of Captain Cook, which were readily recognized by a large scar that separated the thumb from the forefinger. The metacarpal bone was next discovered, then the head, stripped of its flesh, and with the hair cut off and facial bones missing. The bones of the two arms from which hung the skin of the forearm were inclosed, however, as well as the leg bones and thighs in one piece, but without the feet. All these seemed to have been in the fire, except the hands that retained their flesh, but had been cut in several pieces and filled with salt, probably to preserve them longer. On the morning of the twenty-first, Eappo and the chief's sons came aboard, carrying the remaining bones of Captain Cook, two bullets from his gun, and his shoes. Eappo was sent back and ordered to place a taboo on the bay. The bones of Captain Cook, having been deposited on a bier and weighed by a chain holding two cannonballs, were cast with the usual ceremonies into the ocean, and the Captain given a sailor's grave, that is, the abyss of the sea.

CHAPTER V

## RETURN TO SAN FRANCISCO. WHAT OUR SPECULATIONS PRODUCED. WE RENEW OUR ASSOCIATION WITH M. B. I LEAVE FOR FRANCE, TRAVELING BY WAY OF MEXICO

AT FIVE o'clock one evening, two hours after the last sack of coffee and the last chickens and turkeys which we had spent six days loading on our ship the *Hamilton,* to be transported to the markets of San Francisco, had been stowed away, we raised anchor and set sail from the Islands with our perishable cargo aboard. Our turkeys and chickens had been bought at an extremely low figure, as had the coffee, which grew wild in the woods and had cost only five cents a pound.

Our intention, or rather M. Giovanni's intention, was to put in at Honolulu, where I was to arrange for another cargo and then proceed to San Francisco in a better boat, ours being scarcely more than a tub, and, although adequate to transport two-footed feathered creatures, was not suitable for animals with, as Diogenes says, two feet and no feathers.

Under the guidance of our Kanaka pilot, the *Hamilton,* as our ship was called, passed safely down the channel. No sooner were we well out at sea then a black line, approaching from the horizon with the rapidity of a racehorse, appeared. The pilot and the captain looked anxiously at one another. A terrific squall was sweeping down on our vessel! The captain immediately called all hands to reef in sail, come about, and head up the channel. Every member of the crew now began to work with an energy that revealed full knowledge of our danger. The maneuver was rapidly executed and the *Hamilton,* retracing its course, entered the port, safely negotiating the channel just before the storm broke. Soon the tempest was queen of the sea. Beyond the channel towered great waves black as mountains of ink. Three whalers foundered, losing men and cargoes. Ten or twelve more entered the port of Honolulu with heavy damage, and of the many fishermen who were out at sea, only a few escaped. Had we been three miles farther out, we too should have been completely lost. Death had never come so close before.

The following day the sea was too rough for us to be able to retrace our route, and so I spent the time having masses said for the poor unfortunates who were out in the open sea the previous evening. Most of these masses were the *"De Profundis."* A day later, on toward three o'clock in the afternoon, we set sail again, starting once more across the ocean that had almost proved our tomb. The storm had blown over; the sea was calm as a mirror; during the day across its limpid surface that reflected the broiling rays of the sun, beautiful fish of all colors were visible. After the storm, barely enough wind remained to fill our sails. By morning, however, the breeze became so unfavorable for a return to Honolulu that the captain warned M. Giovanni that it might take five or six days to reach port, which would seriously weaken our cargo, while on the contrary, if we chose to profit by this wind to set a course for San Francisco, we could arrive there within twelve days.

Inasmuch as it was primarily on my account that M. Giovanni wished to return to Honolulu, I insisted that we continue as we were going, promising to adjust myself to conditions on board. Accordingly we decided to allow our agents to arrange for a second cargo, and to skirt Honolulu. I regret that I have nothing of importance to narrate about the twelve days our voyage lasted, except that I have never eaten so many cocoanuts as I consumed during that time, for I passed my days idly grating the kernels of these fruits for myself and the poultry. Our cargo, moreover, was highly satisfactory and did not suffer from seasickness. We inspected it daily, M. Giovanni and I, and at the end of each survey my husband remarked: "This time I definitely promise you, Madame Giovanni, that if I am offered as advantageous a price for my chickens, turkeys, pigs, coffee, sweet potatoes, and gourds as I was offered for my potatoes and onions, I definitely promise you that I will seize the opportunity I have missed only too often."

On the twelfth day we arrived in port and on the thirteenth, M. Giovanni was approached by at least twenty commission merchants who offered to handle our entire cargo. In these days there were so few farms raising produce of this kind near San Francisco, that supplies brought in from the Sandwich Islands were considered a great luxury. The cargo cost us between twenty-five and twenty-six thousand dollars and netted one hundred and twenty thousand dollars, which M. Giovanni divided with the captain.

So we found ourselves the following morning at the hotel with sixty thousand dollars in our possession, enough to reestablish new business connections as a merchant, a profession with which my husband was far more familiar than speculations of a hazardous nature. I do not know whether he was satisfied with the voyage, but I myself was immensely proud to have accompanied him and shared the dangers. Two days after our arrival as M. Giovanni, his face beaming, and as full of antics as a sailor, was strolling down Washington Place smoking a cigar, he met M. B., his first business associate. The fire, it will be recalled, had forced them to sever their business connections.

M. B. was also walking with his hands in his pockets, but he was somewhat less buoyant and gay than M. Giovanni, who, having recently returned from a trip to the Sandwich Islands, was full of energy and enthusiasm. After exchanging a few gracious words of friendship—M. B., without amassing a fortune, had nevertheless acquired a sum nearly equal to what we possessed—the two former cronies renewed their former partnership and entered the house to announce the glad news that they had joined forces again.

As I was quite satisfied with the arrangement, my husband and M. B. rented a fine house on Kearny Street—this time of stone, for after three fires had ruined us from garret to cellar, we had scant respect for wooden buildings. From that time on, we began to deal again in wholesale commodities. Our agent, as will be recalled, had been left at Honolulu to procure a second cargo, and one morning we were informed that it had reached port. M. Giovanni went aboard with M. B. Everything proved, after turkeys, chickens, and pigs had been inspected, to be in good condition; fifty chickens and turkeys and a hundred pigs had been thrown overboard, but that was unimportant as the remainder still brought M. Giovanni thirty thousand dollars as his share of the venture.

But upon learning of our success, many of the ships lying in San Francisco Harbor set a course for the Sandwich Islands, hoping to realize the same remarkable profits we had just made. But in most cases the eye of the master and the hand of the mistress grating cocoanut for the chickens and turkeys and secretly giving tips to the sailors to see that the pigs were well cared for, were absent; cargoes arrived in port in so deplorable a condition that those who got back the cost of the venture considered themselves fortunate.

Our business transactions were progressing serenely when M. Giovanni entered my room one morning and remarked: "My dear Jeanne, our affairs are in good shape. Thanks to Almighty God we seem to have won out over bad luck. The time has now come to gratify your desires and those of our families and to return home for a visit. Make all your preparations for a trip to France, and, if you wish, to Italy. At Carrara, or San Giorgio, you can visit my poor father and tell him that in a year or two I will be back to embrace him in person." I was both happy and sad at the prospect of this journey; sad to leave my husand alone in a land where he had been so miserable; happy at the thought of seeing my own parents again and of becoming acquainted with his relatives.

From that time on, my main concern was this interesting trip; and to my great joy, it was arranged that I should pass through Mexico, where I hoped to be able to establish new business contacts with the Mexicans.

Before I left I had no idea I should arrive in the midst of the unrest caused by the affair of Raousset de Boulbon and Pronuncia-mentos of Álvares, and would have to travel through country torn by civil war. On March 1, 1854, I embarked on the luxurious American steamer, *L. Stevens,* of the Panama Line, amid a group of all our San Francisco friends, including M. Dillon, our dear and kindly French consul, who had always been so helpful in times of misfortune.

CHAPTER VI

## THE MAIL STEAMER, THE *L. STEVENS*

THE DAY of my departure for France finally arrived, and on March 3,[1] 1854, I went aboard the *L. Stevens* accompanied by M. Giovanni and our dear consul, M. Dillon, who had invariably under all circumstances been so good to us, and by Mr. Garrison,[2] the mayor of San Francisco. The *L. Stevens,* a ship of 3700 tons, on which I had booked passage, was the finest vessel on the Pacific Ocean and made the run from San Francisco to Panama, touching en route at Acapulco. Furthermore, whether the passenger disembarked at Acapulco or went on as far as Panama, the price was invariably the same.

To those who have not seen the ship, it is impossible to give any conception of the grandeur, or better yet, the majesty of this magnificent mail steamer. Her length was immense. I did not measure her, but I know that, during evening promenades, when we strolled around the deck, after we had walked from one end to the other six times, we were tired out. At one end of the deck were awnings, couches, and armchairs for the promenaders.

The deck was polished like the floor of the finest drawing room and, to give an idea of the influence this Dutch cleanliness exerted over the passengers I will disclose something that is one of the most improbable things in the world; namely, that the Americans, who usually expectorated everywhere, restrained themselves on the *L. Stevens.* For if they misbehaved, there was a repetition of what happened during the days of the Bourbons when a citizen inadvertently kept his hat on his head in the anterooms or foyers of the Théâtre Français: A Swiss came to remind him where he was and request him to remove his hat.

On the *L. Stevens* the quartermaster came up, politely tapped the culprit on the shoulder and, hat in hand, said to him: "Sir, cuspidors are provided for that purpose." Then to the consternation of the American, two sailors arrived, one with sand, pail, and broom, the other with a brush; all traces of the accident were removed and both scrubbed until all signs of the crime had been eradicated. Anyone who has never seen Americans expectorate, has no idea of the skill which they achieve in an exercise that seems extremely simple at first glance, but which, perfected by them, rivals the most eccentric caprices of the fountains at Versailles. At ten feet an American can expectorate into a cuspidor; at twenty feet, he can clear the ship's railing. If bets were laid, I know I would wager on the Americans.

I was familiar with the magnificent steamer *L. Stevens* by reputation, but this was the first time I had been aboard her. I confess that I was amazed, upon examining this floating city, to find that the ship was carrying approximately twelve hundred passengers, of whom three hundred and fifty, or four hundred were traveling first class. The captain, Mr. Pierson, who knew me, came up to me and, aware that I was French, treated me with all the courtesy of a Frenchman. With his white gloves, polished boots and black suit, he had the bearing of a courtier and the quiescence of a gentleman.

We had come aboard half an hour in advance, and were told that three strokes of the gong would give the signal when the time to depart approached. There is nothing that passes more quickly than the time that precedes the moment when the traveler is about to leave those whom he loves. No sooner had we come aboard and been welcomed by the captain, than—at least so it seemed—the gong rang three times. At the third stroke of the gong, I was forced to part from my husband and the kind friends who had come to see me off. At the last moment M. Giovanni was strongly tempted to withdraw the permission he had given me and take me back with him to San Francisco. Then, as the wheels of the ship began to turn in the water, we left the docks.

The visitors lingering on the wharf began to cheer. I shall not be exaggerating if I say that without counting the curious bystanders, three or four thousand friends came down to see the twelve hundred passengers off. Handkerchiefs and hats were waved both aboard ship and on the wharf, sounds of weeping were heard, and if those who had nothing to leave were affected, how much more deeply moved were the ones who left relatives or friends behind.

The *L. Stevens* moved majestically away. I remained for a time near the gangway, replying to the group of hats and friendly handkerchiefs that were waved in my direction. Soon we were half a mile from the wharf and at this distance could scarcely distinguish the various faces; even by straining our eyes we could not be certain that we were responding to the gestures of friends. Then suddenly the *L. Stevens* was saluted with such a hurrah that Captain Pierson decided that one courtesy deserved another. He gave orders to come about and headed back toward the wharf at full speed so we could see the crowds and all the friendly faces that had become so blurred in the distance once more. As we grazed the wharf, we were able to send a last farewell, another tender message to our friends. Then, after passing so near the docks that we could almost touch them, our ship moved off like a bird that, having touched the shore with the tip of its tail, flies swiftly away. This time the captain did not turn back, but steered directly for the Golden Gate.

A quarter of an hour later, the seven or eight thousand spectators on the wharf were only a confused blur of faces. As the handkerchiefs and hats faded from sight, I began to weep bitterly. Just then the captain came up to me. "My advice to you, Madame," he said, "is to go to your cabin and lie down. No matter how fine the weather, the sea will exact its toll, and the sea is less harsh toward his subjects whom he finds in their berths than those who are caught standing. Although he desires to have everyone acknowledge his power, yet he is generous toward those who admit defeat."

Experience had taught me that the captain's advice was sound; after the wharf receded in the distance I followed it to the letter. By the third day I was acclimated to the ocean, and able to go down to dinner. Dinner aboard the *L. Stevens* was an impressive function. Strict etiquette was observed, full dress being required. A placard framed and hung on the wall announced that ladies would not be admitted except in low necks and short sleeves, and men only in black coats and trousers. Thus everyone knew that formal evening attire would be required and so dressed for dinner.

In the dining saloon there were four large tables in four corners of the room, the central space being left open for greater freedom of service. These four tables were: the captain's, which was not open to the public, but was filled only by invitation; the purser's, which ranked next the captain's; the second mate's, which was below that of the purser; and, finally, the fourth table, which was the least popular. After places had been assigned in the dining saloon, they were retained throughout the voyage. A seat had been reserved for me at the captain's table.

Champagne was the only wine served at dinner. It is unnecessary to add that, following the English and American custom, toasts were exchanged from table to table. Usually the Americans, the busiest men in the world, eat as fast as the great Napoleon. An American dinner often lasts ten minutes and yet the diner does not feel rushed. Our dinner on the *L. Stevens* was a real dinner in the French manner, lasting an hour and a half. The table was set with English porcelain and magnificent silver plate; the food and service were lavish.

The appointments on this ship were magnificent; the ladies' saloon, the dining saloon, the smoking room, all were entirely constructed of glass and gilt. Everywhere there were carpets, which were renewed after each voyage. Here is the meal schedule: breakfast at nine o'clock, drinks at eleven, dinner at two, tea at five, and supper at eleven. This seemed reasonable to the French passengers; the Americans, however, found a way to eat and drink between meals.

Our ship also had a barber whose shop was located directly opposite my cabin. A line of customers waited in front of his door from seven o'clock in the morning until ten at night. Not only did our barber shave the men; he also dressed the ladies' hair. Whenever a woman was having her hair arranged, the outside curtain was drawn. At the dinner hour, much to the dismay of the barber, there was a sudden exit from his place of business.

The journey from San Francisco to Acapulco lasted eight days and at the hour scheduled we reached port. The trip had been perfect; the winds had been equable; not a drop of rain had fallen. Although the sun had been terrifically hot, an awning had been stretched over the ship's deck and as a breeze was usually blowing off the ocean, the heat was bearable.

Acapulco proved to be a typical Mexican port, poor and unimportant, either because of the indolence of the natives, or the unhealthfulness of its climate. Yellow fever is prevalent three months of the year at Acapulco and is often fatal. Earthquakes that constantly rock the city and *pronunciamentos*,[3] together with yellow fever, give some idea of the charm of Acapulco. For the benefit of the reader who may be unfamiliar with the term *pronunciamento,* an explanation of the word will soon be given.

I disembarked from the *L. Stevens* on the arm of the captain. As the only hotels that existed in Acapulo were nothing more than wretched lodgings, the captain assumed charge of finding quarters for me, and took me to the agency of the Panama Line where he believed rooms would be found. By the time we reached the office, we realized that something unusual was occurring. Had yellow fever broken out? Had there been a recent earthquake? Or was it a *pronunciamento?* For a time we did not know into which of these three Mexican plagues we had fallen. Soon the noise of the drums and the activity of the population dispelled any doubt in our minds and we realized that we had fallen directly into a *pronunciamento*. Of the three plagues, this was both the least deadly and the most interesting.

merchants from whom they had purchased large quantities of fruit and liquor.

I should observe at this point that the four persons who were to remain, like myself, at Acapulco, boarded with a Chinese called John. Let me repeat what I have just said; namely, that to the Americans, all Chinese are known as John. Furthermore, he was the only Chinese living in Acapulco and, true to tradition, ran a low-class rooming and boardinghouse. The time will come when the Chinese will spread out like a rising tide, whose source is in the celestial empire, over the entire surface of the earth, wherever the land lures them. Chinese make the best servants I know.

I was still down at the port with my companions, returning the greetings that were being sent this time to me from aboard ship, when the French consul came to place his services at my disposal. When I told him that I was remaining at Acapulco—a situation incomprehensible to him—and was going overland to Mexico City, he uttered a cry of surprise and dismay, remarking that I was attempting the impossible; and that the state of Guerrero, which would have to be crossed from end to end, was in open revolt against the government of Santa Anna. The English consul supported him, as I may add, did, the common rabble, who were called in by these dignitaries to give advice and who declared that only a French woman could have conceived such an idea, and that it was utterly foolhardy to make the attempt.

As I have already remarked, I had firmly determined to surmount these obstacles, not to prove unwomanly in the face of danger, nor to regret having made the decision. The result of this perseverance was that my companions, who at first hesitated, were finally ashamed to abandon the trip when a woman was not afraid to go ahead. Finally a decision having been reached to proceed despite any dangers to which we might be exposed, we planned to depart within two or three days.

In this time we intended to apply ourselves assiduously to making preparations for this trip and to leave nothing undone that would insure a safe and successful journey.

Aware that we had definitely determined to proceed, the consular agent and Mr. Tyler did everything in their power to assist us to procure whatever might aid us in completing this perilous journey safely. The first obstacle that arose was to find means of transportation, an omnipresent difficulty that invariably complicates a situation. Transportation was absolutely unprocurable. Thus failure threatened the expedition at its base. The revolutionists had laid violent hands on every available animal—donkeys, mules, and horses—within a radius of fifteen miles. Mules, donkeys, and horses, furthermore, afforded the only mode of transportation in the country. I might also add that no other method of transportation was possible, for the state of Guerrero, which we were about to cross, was the Switzerland, or Pyrenees of Mexico. Moreover, the traveler passes endlessly from summit to precipice and is forced, by fording or swimming, to cross three or four rivers which do not have, and never will have, either bridges or boats, unless, as seems fairly probable, the Americans some day absorb Mexico as they have absorbed Texas and California. Until that time, however, travel in Mexico is bound to be hazardous and unpleasant; moreover we were unable to wait for the Americans to conquer and improve the country.

Mr. Tyler and the French consular agent, after giving orders that mules should be provided at any cost, assumed that mules would be found, and so turned their attention to procuring safe conduct passes for us from General Álvarez, who was known to be two or three days' journey on horseback from Acapulco on the route to Mexico City.

This request for safe-conduct caused considerable astonishment on the part of the local commander, Señor Comonfort,[5] who persisted in saying that all the safe-conducts in the universe, even if signed by Almighty God himself, would not pass us through Álvarez' camp; and that even if they did it was absolutely foolhardy for us to attempt such a venture. I told him first of all to issue the safe-conducts and that I would assume the responsibility of obtaining from the rebelling general a pass for myself and my companions.

"Oh, these women!" cried Señor Comonfort. "They will attempt anything."

"It is our sole strength," I replied, "allow us to exercise it."

"This is your wish?"

"Certainly."

"I will give you your safe-conduct; but I wash my hands of all responsibility."

"I will hold the basin if necessary."

"Good! But first will you do me the honor to dine with me, Madame, and then, since you wish it ..."

"Since I wish it?"

"I will sign your pass."

"I accept."

So I had the honor of dining with the commander of Acapulco; afterwards, faithful to his promise, he signed the following passport, which I carefully preserved as evidence of my journey.

But on whom or on what should I blame the orthographical errors? Are they due to the Mexican idiom or corruption of Spanish? Or are they inevitable in such a decision as Señor Comonfort had just made, a decision that, to my way of thinking, was far more serious than my determination to proceed with the journey.

| sello quinto | Here the Mexican arms: an eagle fighting a serpent | medio real |

El ciudadano Miguel García, teniente colonel de exercisio y prefete ode con destrico.

"Concedo libre y seguno paso porse à la Señora dona María Luisa Giovanni (Francesca) para que pasa à Méjico y Vera Cruz por embarcarso. Por tanto, supplico à las autoricatos si civiles como militaras, no le pungao inguno ion barazo, ase tes tien le facilitar con aucios que necessite, payando hos por un precio dado en Acapulce.

A doce de Marzo de mil ochocientos cinquente y quatre—
Alexandre Ganina." [6]

This pass was accompanied by letters of recommendation for General Álvarez from our consular agent.

With my pass and letters, I now felt confident of the future. In fact, that same day word arrived that mules had been procured, and that final arrangements would soon be made with the muleteer. In

Spain and Italy, as we all know, such agreements are drawn up in writing. In Mexico, this same wise custom is observed.

Terms were accordingly arranged in the presence of our consul, who agreed to prosecute if these were not kept. The muleteer assured us that if we were unable to pass beyond Peregrino,[7] the place where Álvarez' camp was located, he would bring us back to Acapulco.

Arrangements having been completed, these gentlemen, in the belief that they had done everything in their power, first, to discourage us from attempting the journey, then, after the trip was decided upon, to point out the dangers, did what Señor Comonfort had done the evening before and what the proconsul Pilate did eighteen hundred years earlier, in brief, they washed their hands of the consequences.

Our departure had been set for March 13, 1854, at four o'clock in the morning. As March 13, 1854, was the next day, I decided I had no time to lose. Furthermore, through the acquisition of letters and passes issued to me personally, I had become the head of the party, and either through courtesy, or inefficiency, I had been tacitly recognized as competent to direct all operations, and no one thought of contesting this power.

With safe conducts obtained and mules procured, all that remained were the preparations indispensable for a trip of fourteen or fifteen days through the mountains. This necessitated the purchase of a thousand small articles. I bought first of all a hat of Panama straw with a broad brim for protection against the intense rays of the sun. Under this in Mexico is worn a silken fold of an enormous handkerchief which is first placed on the head beneath the hat, thus affording protection at the same time to the neck and shoulders, while the four ends, hanging loose, fan the traveler. The silk handkerchief presented to me by Mr. Tyler was charming, and added a coquettish touch of local color.

I realized too late that an unusually fine woolen riding habit that I had had made in San Francisco must be discarded because of the heat. I was thus forced to buy a light-weight cotton habit and hastily to have made a wrap supplemented by an immense pelerine. This costume together with the broad-brimmed hat had much the appearance of a Quaker's traveling costume. Next came a search for gloves. Fastidious as I was, I had provided myself merely with kid gloves, and these I was soon compelled to abandon because of the heat. Fortunately the gentlemen here were in the habit of wearing cotton gloves; and since all of them have small hands, there was keen rivalry among them to see who would have the honor to present me with a pair of gloves. Next I purchased some alkali to use against poisonous insects.

Then finally—less on my own account than that of my traveling companions—I allowed myself to be persuaded that it was necessary to lay in some liquid supplies, such as brandy, liqueurs, etc. This was done. We had been told by reliable persons that we could buy what food we needed along the road. The purchase of a hammock, an indispensable article, so I had been told, that would not be provided at any of the inns en route, completed my shopping expedition. Inasmuch as all these preparations had been completed by two o'clock in the afternoon, I decided to spend the rest of the day visiting Acapulco and its superb harbor.

## Chapter VIII

### VISIT TO ACAPULCO. THE BAY. THE FORT. DEPARTURE. ENUMERATION OF MEMBERS OF THE CARAVAN. OUR FIRST DAY'S JOURNEY

WE DECIDED to start off by visiting the bay. Mr. Tyler and Mr. Van Bran, head clerk of the agency, who were placed at my disposal, procured a boat in which we glided over the bay, propelled by four stalwart rowers. What had attracted me from the decks of the steamer was the amazing transparency of the water, which seemed like liquid azure. I had seen this water at various depths aglow with gold and silver lights; I had known that fish caused these lights, but I had not known to what species these fish belonged. From the boat I could now watch them at closer range, and by the dorsal fin I saw that they were merely sharks. In the bay of Acapulco sharks usually travel in schools. With me in the boat were two Spanish ladies; I confess that I shivered slightly as I watched these terrifying dogfish pass a fathom below; but the Spanish ladies, accustomed to such spectacles, appeared wholly unconcerned.

I was carrying a charming Chinese fan that in San Francisco, where these objects are unusually cheap, had cost some forty-five dollars and so would have brought at least one hundred in Paris. In the center of the bay I had the misfortune, while toying with this fan, to drop it. The fan was still on the surface of the water, with the cord hanging from my fingers, when it was immediately snatched away. I regretted it far more than I should have otherwise, had it not been so invaluable to me in this land of intense heat.

Here, anyone who made the mistake, as so often happens on our own lakes and rivers, of allowing a hand to touch the water, would be extremely fortunate to escape being pulled in by the arm. My comrades told me that when a man falls overboard in the bay of Acapulco, he disappears as quickly as the crumbs of bread that are thrown to carp in the pools of Versailles or the Canal at Fontainebleau.

I refused to believe that my unfortunate fan could disappear so rapidly; I insisted that the rowers stop rowing and tarry a moment, but at the same instant a cannon was fired from the fort, which drew, and I might also add, completely absorbed, our immediate attention. This was the final signal for the proclamation whose preparations I had witnessed the previous evening. The moment had arrived when the official proclamation was to be made, a fact indicated by riddling with bullets the old hull of a ship that seemed to have survived the political events and geological upheavals that had stranded it on the other side of the bay, only to serve as target for the revolutionists. At each new proclamation, the old wreck, which has two or three dozen bullets in its stomach, fulfills its function.

A signal indicated that it was time to leave the bay, which we should have done, moreover, without this signal, expecting at any moment to see bullets fly over our heads. Steering for Acapulco, we pulled rapidly back to shore. Excited by the bombardment from the fort, which I had not known was on the program, I begged my escorts to take me into the city, so that I might see more of the revolution. We followed the old Spanish road leading to the fort and found ourselves face to face with wartime preparations that were advancing with unbelievable activity. Through the doors—one of the fine features of the fort, which is a magnificent specimen of a sixteenth century fortification—men were carrying all kinds of supplies for a siege, especially food, consisting primarily of an endless quantity of strips of meat prepared for drying. These were being fastened to cords suspended from trees that lined the walks around the fort, despite the enormous numbers of dogs that roam the streets of Acapulco and make such a hubbub during the night, that it is as necessary in order to sleep, to become accustomed to their barks, as it is in Paris to become accustomed to the sound of carriages. Not one of these quadrupeds, whose manners we greatly admired on this occasion, ventured to approach within fifty feet of this display of meats, which they regarded sadly from afar, sitting on their haunches with a piteous air and melancholy howls. The miserable creatures seemed to understand that they too would be caught and salted down if the need arose.

Incidentally, all foreigners, Englishmen, Americans, and Frenchmen, took part in the movement and, being carried away by the confusion, shouted: "Viva Álvarez!" A motley army was assembling; everyone, children included, who could produce a sword, saber, or bayonet, was having his own little proclamation. The situation promised to be as interesting by night as by day, but as our departure was scheduled for four o'clock in the morning, sleep was imperative. I retired and began seriously to consider what I had undertaken, when suddenly I imagined I was dreaming that I was on a ship at anchor, and that the boat was beginning to move and take her departure. But it was not the boat that was making the motion; it was the whole house. Providence, who wished to satisfy my curiosity on all points, had arranged an earthquake in my honor!

I was awakened by the movement of the floor and the creaking of whatever was jointed in the house. There was a light in my room. I leaped out of bed and rapidly donned a dressing robe. At the same instant Mr. Tyler entered my room. He was running, for he knew I would be awake and badly frightened. He was correct.

"My God," I said, rushing toward him, "what is happening?"

"Nothing," he replied, "only a slight earthquake, that is all; we are accustomed to them here in Acapulco."

As it was two o'clock in the morning and we were starting at four, I did not consider it wise to retire again; so, sat up, waiting for the arrival of my comrades. Notwithstanding, we were told as we were about to leave on our journey to Mexico City, that what was merely a slight earthquake during the night had destroyed four stone houses used as residences.

On Monday, March 13, 1854, as agreed the previous evening, we left Acapulco at four o'clock in the morning. We were already seated on our mules when Mr. Tyler, the French consul, and other officials in the city arrived to speed us on our journey, imploring us, with the most touching solicitude, to abandon the trip, and further attempting to persuade me at least that the perils to which I was exposing myself were insurmountable.

Already mounted on my mule and clothed in my Quaker costume, I laughingly bade them farewell. We then departed at full gallop over a fine old road constructed entirely by the Spaniards, and well shaded for several miles. After retiring at midnight, I had been awakened at two o'clock in the morning. From two o'clock in the morning to four o'clock, I had not slept an instant. Consequently I was overcome by fatigue, and dozed on my mule. Amid the confusion this slight incident caused, Doctor D—— suddenly cried: "Well, I must have lost my pistols, I ..."

Then without further explanation, he departed at a gallop along the route over which we had just come. The heat was already excessive; however, we did not intend to desert him and waited for him by the road under a sun hot enough to cook eggs. At the end of an hour and a half he returned with his pistols that he had lost just as he was leaving the city, and which he had found exactly where they had fallen. This will give an idea of the amount of travel on Mexican highways. We now resumed our journey. I had been so drowsy when we started out that it was only after this second halt that I glanced over our caravan.

Here are the heterogeneous elements of which it was composed: First—let us give honor where honor is due—two brave Hungarian officers who left, as I have already said, good prospects in San Francisco to start for the Orient to fight the Russians. They were armed to the teeth, and carried enormous swords that were suspended from their belts, and pistols on the pommels of their saddles; one of them also possessed a gun with two chambers. I am careful not to speak disrespectfully of the latter in view of the invaluable services this gun rendered during our journey.

Then there was Doctor D——, a Frenchman who was carrying dispatches from the Mexican consul at San Francisco to President Santa Anna, that dealt with the overthrow of the expedition of Raousset de Boulbon in Sonora.[1]

At San Francisco I had known M. Raousset de Boulbon quite well and what I shall subsequently narrate about this brave and adventurous young man will not be among the least interesting episodes of the final stages of my journey. Taken together, Monsieur D—— and I were like La Fontaine's fable of the *Chauve-Souris*.[2] He had dispatches for Santa Anna; I had recommendations for Álvarez. If we were captured by Álvarez, we were to say, "See our paws." If we were disturbed by Santa Anna, we were to say, "Touch our wings."

Our fourth companion was another Frenchman, a brave and excellent man who in my eyes, at least, had only one fault—he had a name impossible to pronounce. I rectified this difficulty by calling him the Man with the Rifle. And in fact he carried in a formidable manner over the pommel of his saddle, a large rifle that had never, at least to my knowledge, been loaded. He was returning to Mexico and from there proceeding to Vera Cruz, where he expected to join his brother, who was a merchant. Finally, there was I, myself, accompanied by my servant. Then came Rubio, our guide, a jolly fellow well known along the route from Acapulco to Mexico City, and vice versa, and whom I suspected of being less in touch with honest men, who are rare in this neighborhood, than with robbers who are numerous. Three *arrieros*,[3] owners of our mounts, whose task was to care for the baggage mules, and a man who led an extra mule for me in case any accident should happen to mine, completed the caravan that consisted in all of eleven persons.

On toward noon we reached the inn, a kind of Indian tent. There we stopped. My hammock was soon hung; I lay down and slept while the servants disappeared into the country in the hope of finding something we might put between our teeth.

By offering money we found a hen and some eggs; but they were more costly than at San Francisco. We had bread as well, so we dined as best we could on a chicken and eight or ten eggs. But if we had only had the ingredients to make tortillas! The person who told us we could buy food along the road apparently had reference to the route in time of peace, not in time of war. Fearing pillage, the Indians had taken refuge in the mountains, taking along everything they possessed. We had neither spoons nor forks; some of us fortunately had knives, and the Hungarians had their sabers; but at that moment I would willingly have exchanged two sabers for one casserole without consulting them. Lacking casseroles or spits, the chicken was cut in small pieces and roasted over the coals. As for the eggs, they were allowed to harden in the ashes. This was characteristic of the entire trip, except that later I succeeded in finding a spit composed of two props held together by a rod; from it the chicken, securely tied with a string, was hung. To all appearances, God, through the medium of our two Hungarians, had miraculously provided us with food. Breakfast over, we rested, not to digest our meal—that would have been too luxurious—but to allow the intense heat to pass.

At four o'clock we remounted our mules and went on to the inn of Legido, where we arrived about eight o'clock and where we slept, after a supper even more frugal than our dinner, consisting merely of eggs and fresh water. My sleeping room was two large trees, from whose lower branches hung my hammock. In this I slept fully clad.

Its installation in the open air disarranged the nests of the parrots that had established their domiciles in the upper branches; they chattered furiously throughout the night, complaining no doubt of the way I interfered with their habits. My other companions, who did not have the same luxury of a hammock, slept nearby on Indian mats, and acted as outpost sentries in the event of nocturnal surprises. I recall these first nights of the journey as among the best. Rarely have I slept so well!

CHAPTER IX

## CONTINUATION OF THE JOURNEY—FAMINE—THE GREEN PARROTS

AT TWO o'clock in the morning our guides wakened us. So magnificent was the moon that it stimulated us to cover as much distance as possible on foot to avoid traveling during the intense heat. But if the moon was magnificent, the road was frightful, being little more than a maze of mountains—much as if the ancient Gods of Olympus, in Mexico as in Thessaly, bore a grudge against the Titans. No sooner had we ascended Pelion than we were forced to ascend Ossa.[1] The roads were maintained by the Spaniards, which is merely a courteous way of saying that they had been abandoned. The route skirted terrific precipices and frequently, on the surface, had a pitch of forty-five degrees.

Having escaped rolling down these precipices at least twenty times, at seven o'clock we reached the Venta de los Arroyos, where we stopped. I was overcome by fatigue and scarcely capable of retaining my seat on my mule; but, as can be readily understood, I did not confide my condition to anyone. For it was I who had organized the party by every means at my command. I recalled the famous adage: "You desired this, Georges Daudin."

After this halt, during which it was necessary to deprive ourselves of our breakfast, since we had no supplies, we weakly resumed the route, traveling on until one o'clock. At that hour we reached the hut of a poor Indian; by rare good fortune he had not yet fled. In his house we found some eggs and excellent water. After sleeping until four o'clock, we resumed our journey. By seven we reached another Indian *venta,* or inn, but the latter was deserted and desolate. Here, as on the previous evening, my hammock was hung beneath two trees. The question then arose as to what we should eat for supper. There was not even one lone shrimp anywhere. Upon counting the party, we discovered that the two Hungarians were missing. Were they lost? Had they deliberately abandoned us? The world looked black; and I was inclined to support the latter theory, when we saw them arrive, through the dusk, at a full gallop on their mules. These two brave hussars whom I had slandered—all Hungarians are hussars—instead of abandoning us, had been engaged in replenishing the larder and had returned to us with twelve green parrots which they had brought down during their excursion. I had never liked live parrots; I confess that I did not have much sympathy for dead ones, and I imagined that if I tasted the flesh of these birds with their idiotic chatter, my stomach might waken me the following morning with the words, "Have you had breakfast, Jacquot?"

The covetous looks the *arrieros* cast on our macaws made me overcome my repugnance. I told myself that it was not necessary to judge birds, possibly delectable within, by plumage more or less green, or beaks more or less large. Then I followed the example of my comrades, took my parrot, removed its feathers, trussed it, and placed it on the famous spit I had longed for when I was half-famished and sleepless at night from hunger. Overcome by fatigue, we each devoured our parrot sadly, without exchanging a word. I, personally, felt somewhat feverish; stretched out in my hammock, I began to cry softly. In some such manner as this usually terminated, it will be recalled, all my valorous efforts.

Upon starting out I was a man, full of imagination, fired with hope; with fatigue and weariness I was merely a woman who could only weep. Then, as pride struggled to overcome fatigue, I sobbed more quietly. But in the end I did not weep less; possibly I could not have cried more. I fell asleep, with tears still falling. By three o'clock in the morning, everyone was up and on muleback. A few moments before daybreak we reached General Álvarez' advance guard and his son, Commander Diego. The outposts allowed us to pass, but the former stopped us; an officer whom I had summoned and to whom I showed my pass, told me it would be necessary to appear before General Álvarez in person. I inquired where General Álvarez could be found. The man indicated a mountain peak that towered three thousand feet above our heads. "On top of that mountain," he replied.

I could scarcely refrain from congratulating him on the foresight he displayed in adopting so inaccessible a spot for his camp, but from my point of view, since I had to search for him high up in the mountain, I might have preferred a place somewhat inferior in strategy, and more readily accessible. Since there was nothing more to discuss, I departed. I asked the other members of our party to wait for me, taking only Doctor D—— as my escort.

Provided with passport and letters, we began laboriously to ascend the sheer slope of the mountain called El Peregrino. On this dreary pilgrimage at times we used hands as well as feet.

After two hours of climbing barefoot—my shoes I had dropped on the way—with hands and feet bleeding, we finally reached the summit of the mountain that terminated in an immense plateau, one that commanded an extensive view, dominating the most stupendous panorama imaginable. Following constantly in the wake of our guide, whom I suspected of not having led us over the best trails, we encountered for the first time, a company of soldiers training, each corps being separated from the others to permit greater freedom of movement. Next we saw the bivouacs of the soldiers, the butchers, who were already at work, and the tents of women making *tortillas*,[2] all of which made the mouths of poor Doctor D—— and myself water.

Finally we found ourselves directly opposite the abode of General Álvarez. The tent of General Álvarez was formed quite simply of interwoven branches placed against immense rocks. The sole furniture of this camp consisted of a bed, on which the father and son were sitting and, when we appeared, dictating orders to a secretary seated somewhat less comfortably on the ground. The first ray of sunlight was just creeping over the opposite mountain and casting its light on the two men, when I reached the threshold of their dwelling.

Near the entrance to this tent hung a hammock reserved for visitors; this served as a substitute for sofas, cushions, and armchairs. The interior was resplendent with various kinds of weapons and before the door were two soldiers standing guard, who walked constantly back and forth in opposite directions, passed one another, marched with backs turned to one another to a given point, then pivoted on their heels, approached face to face, then began the same interminable maneuver again.

A short distance away in the shade of great trees, sat a group of staff officers writing at a table; they were constantly receiving orders from their chief and reports from the outposts. All this had the aspect not of a minor riot, but a major revolution, and even seemed to reflect the grandiose aspect of the environment, borrowed by these individuals from the surrounding countryside. When they saw us the father and son rose, offered me the hammock, and presented the doctor with a small wooden stool. After we were seated, they sat down.

The doctor opened the conversation, explaining that we were strangers forced to cross Mexico by business that called us to France, and that I, personally, was carrying a passport from Señor Comonfort, in command at Acapulco, a passport that was addressed directly to Álvarez, and to Don Diego, his son, so that they would consent not only to permit us to continue our journey, but also to protect us against parties of Indian bandits. I waited until the doctor had finished his discourse before handing my letters to the commander.

General Álvarez read them with great interest, then addressed his remarks to me: "My God, Madame," he said, "I am truly sorry to say so, but it is impossible for me to allow you either to proceed or to turn back."

Without listening to my protests, he ordered his aide-de-camp to have a tent placed at my disposal, and dinner served. Then the rest of our party was notified that we were being held pending new orders. The situation was a disagreeable one, but when we saw our dinner arrive, we could not refrain from admitting that even the worst calamities have their bright side. Had we not been made prisoners, we should have been obliged to eat those pretty green parrots, so charming to the eye, but so hard on the teeth. Personally, the sight of knives and forks gave me extreme pleasure; I had been accustomed to this luxury of our civilization too long to abandon it so suddenly. Later we learned that while Doctor D—— and I were enjoying Álvarez' dinner, the latter sent a messenger to Acapulco to find out as much about us as possible. That evening General Álvarez invited us to take tea with him.

At this point I shall digress and take advantage of the sojourn under the general's tent to say a few words about this illustrious chief of partisans and his son, Diego. At that time he was an old man sixty or sixty-five years of age, extremely handsome, with a noble countenance and hair white as snow. He was large, well proportioned, had the physique of a soldier, and was the idol of the Indian *pintos,* who were numerous and formidable in this southern area and on whom he counted in case of defeat, to save and protect his life.

An explanation should be made at this time as to why these Indians are given this name. They are called *pintos,* in other words, painted, not because they are tattooed like the natives of the Marquesas Islands or New Zealand, but because the tones of blue, red, and brick color that tint their cheeks are natural, and caused, according to anthropologists, by a blood disease. These Indians who make up the bulk of Álvarez' army, have certain advantages in their favor: they are not fed or paid. They serve enthusiastically and eat whatever they can find, living like good patriots on the insects or reptiles, familiar to them, that inhabit the air, land, or sea, on which white men could not subsist.

In those days Don Diego, the son of Don Juan Álvarez, was a man forty years of age. He was extremely well built, being graceful and quite tall, and had a fine military carriage. He has been accused of being not only wicked, but even cruel, but nothing about his outward demeanor justifies this accusation, and I have never seen or heard any concrete instances cited of his barbarity. At the time of the *pronunciamento,* that is, when he had just raised the standard of revolt against Santa Anna, he had two sons still at college in Mexico City. These two youths, who were afraid of being taken as hostages, fled with their tutor, a Frenchman from the college and, according to rumor, reached Don Diego safe and sound.

Álvarez, I have been told, owns immense herds of livestock, a type of wealth that permits him more easily than any other to wage a partisan war. The day following our arrival at camp, on toward noon the general had our luggage inspected—an excellent idea, but one he should have had thirty hours earlier.

In my trunk I had several Chinese objects that he greatly admired. These I at once offered to him, and, if appearances are to be believed, the offer flattered him; after a consultation with his son he remarked, while offering me a cigarette, that he could not see any further reason why the caravan, of which I was the leader, should not continue on its way. He merely exacted from Doctor D—— his word of honor that he would not give Santa Anna any information about the location of this camp. He then informed us that our Acapulco passport would no longer be of any service and might even prove a handicap, after we had entered the "tyrant's" territory.

Thereupon Don Juan Álvarez and his son, Don Diego, graciously shook hands with us, and wished us a pleasant journey as we departed. An hour later the formidable mountain that we had ascended with such difficulty, was descended, and we rode our mules with joyful hearts in the belief that all difficulties would henceforth vanish.

## CHAPTER X

## CONTINUATION OF THE JOURNEY. ABANDONED MINES. THE HUNGARIAN HUNTER AND THE HUNGARIAN SWIMMER. A SYBARITICAL SUPPER. A CONJUGAL QUARREL IN MEXICO

SCARCELY HAD we passed the last outposts of the camp at Acapulco, than we began to enter rough and horrible roads, where our poor beasts could only travel at a walk and even then with great difficulty. Several rich gold mines on which the government had suspended work were also passed. Apropos of the gold mines, the comment might be made at this time that the policy of the Mexican government is to drive all foreigners out of Mexico, and to prevent the continuation or completion of any important developments that have been undertaken. After the suspension of work undertaken by the individuals, if the government allows them to organize companies or create societies, there will be a wave of emigration and foreign speculation which is exactly the reverse of what, under any circumstances, it desires. In Mexico, however, it is a well-known fact that a man cannot walk one hundred steps without treading on auriferous soil.

We reached a river so broad that we had to pass on muleback. The current of this stream, called the Mescala River, was at times so rapid that it bent the hamstrings of our mules, the water coming up level with the tops of their necks. While crossing the river, that is, when the situation was perilous, we counted our party. As usual, our two Hungarians were missing. They had vanished from sight and we thought they were out hunting. A shot from a gun heard approximately one hundred feet away, confirmed us in this belief. We looked around; the shot came from the middle of the river. Our fellow travelers, in water up to their necks, were hunting wild duck and woodcock, as well as having chased doves and parrots. The one who had the gun and not the sword, that is, the officer, fired and killed the game; the other, who did not have a gun, but did have a sword, filled the rôle of "dog," swam over to the game, and brought it in. We applauded both the shooter and the swimmer, for they were working only for our dinner.

The river, which we crossed and recrossed time and again on our trip, not only delayed us with its dead branches and tree trunks, but also at the main channel, which proved a serious obstacle. During the rainy season, this river is so swollen that it ceases to be fordable; fortunately, when we reached Mexico, that is, in March, the river was almost normal, so that by putting forth considerable effort we believed these difficulties would prove surmountable and our animals would be able to swim over. Thus we reached the other side without accident, and although our Hungarians were drenched up to their ears, they required no assistance to reach the bank, and at the end of ten minutes were dry.

The night of that same day was passed at the Venta de los Caminos where, to my profound joy, I found a good old Mexican woman and her husband, who received us most hospitably in a typical Indian inn, and served us—what do you imagine? The national dish, the dish of hunters, onion soup. This onion soup, incidentally, was a masterpiece of the culinary art. These good people begged our pardon for having nothing better to offer and remarked that they had brought out a spoon and fork, which were usually kept hidden away, in my honor.

Forks and spoons were what I missed most of all; at meals, these were the things it was most difficult to do without. So when, after I was given a fork and spoon, they asked my forgiveness for not having treated me better, I was tempted not only to pardon them, but to fall on my knees and kiss their hands.

And while we used these precious implements, it was with the idea of resigning ourselves to their loss, in the event of a surprise attack by the enemy. Inasmuch as I was a woman, all kinds of delicate little attentions were showered on me. For example, my traveling companions arranged that temporarily I should have the exclusive ownership, or rather use, of the spoon and eat my soup alone from the pot. Napkins were not provided. After I had finished, my right-hand neighbor was handed the spoon which was then passed to the next diner. Each one used this spoon to dip into the common soup pot. When this was done, the conventions having been faithfully complied with on the part of each individual, we next passed to jugged woodcock and duck; then came roast doves and green parrots. I received my portion of the stew in the cover of the pot; mine removed, these gentlemen fished into the same casserole as delicately as possible with their fingers. In an instant the stew disappeared. The roast which was now passed proved easier to eat. Each one received his portion in his hand; everyone insisted that I take the two wings of a dove. The Hungarians, who were extremely solicitous for my comfort, pretended they preferred parrot.

Never was a dinner served in the most formal manner and with splendid silver plate more enjoyable. Our hosts were astonished to see us so gay; they looked at us with amazement, and expressed keen admiration for France, whose women made merry at a time when life and death were at stake, when our fate hung so much in the balance that any one of us might, without running the risk of heavy losses, gamble his existence on the short straw.

Under ordinary circumstances this place of sojourn, this laughter, this improvised dinner, would not even merit being described, but in an Indian hut, among Indian rebels, on a deserted road, at the base of wild mountains between Juan Álvarez and Santa Anna, threatened almost equally by friends and enemies, this scene indeed was a memorable one in my life and a memorable one, I am convinced, in that of my comrades. Laughter was followed by fatigue;

the moment supper was over, we all retired. The men slept outside the hut on typical Indian beds, that is, on mats or a latticework of sticks interwoven and tied together in such a way that they could be folded and unfolded like a roller blind fastened to two trestles.

Since the night was chilly and since the physiognomy of these good men, my hosts, inspired confidence, I allowed them to hang my hammock inside their hut. While they were engaged in this task, I went over to a hanging that cut off approximately one-third of the length of the cabin, from behind which I had intermittently heard the wails of an infant, and thought I also heard a woman groaning. Having asked and received permission to lift this curtain, I found myself in the presence of a young woman and her new-born child. Every time the child cried, the mother fed it, to quiet it. The child knew nothing but its needs; these were satisfied, that is all. The mother, too, was weeping, but apparently the tears came not from hunger, but from grief. I exchanged what few Mexican words I knew with the poor woman and this much I was able to understand.

She was the daughter of the house, married to a kind of bandit who, it seems, made her extremely unhappy, since she loved him dearly. I asked her where her husband was, but apparently she knew nothing about him. She seemed jealous. I recommended, as best I could, patience; I assured her that a mother had to endure many things from the father of her child. She shook her head; obviously she had no desire to be consoled.

Then the good men called me back, as my hammock was hung. I took the dry and feverish hand of the young woman, and we exchanged wishes for a good night, a wish that failed to bear fruit either for her or for me. I entered my apartment, not by opening and closing the door, but by allowing the blanket to fall. I did not disrobe that night any more than any preceding nights, but slept in my hammock wrapped, by way of covering, solely in my shawl.

My hammock had been hung in the center of the room. On my right, behind the hanging, was the bed of the young mother and child; on my left, in the same compartment with me, was the bed of the two kind Indians. After I retired, the aged mother visited me; she had heard me speak to her daughter and child, and this had touched her; anticipating that I might be cold, she came to cover me and ask me if I needed anything. I experienced a certain feeling of quietude and well-being such as I had not felt since leaving Acapulco. I thanked her, and feeling drowsy, wished her a good night, as I had her daughter. In that dim borderland that precedes sleep, that borderland which is, in a certain sense, the twilight of the soul, I could still distinctly see her on her knees, and hear her muttered prayers.

I tried to follow her example, but my will power failed; fatigue overcame me, and I fell asleep while listening to the sound of the dying conversation of my comrades, the rumble of flying and humming made by insects that in Mexico appear after dark, not awakening until evening and living only in darkness, and the murmur of birds that rustle their feathers voluptuously at the invigorating contact of fresh breezes during the night.

At the end of an hour everyone was sleeping soundly, I, as well as my two companions. Only the young woman might have been awake. Suddenly, I was aroused by the approach of a galloping horse. My first idea was that we were about to be victims of a surprise attack by the Indians. I confess that the idea struck terror into my heart and the thought came to me to cry out and spread the alarm.

But just as I was about to do so, the horse suddenly came to a halt by the door at the rear of the hut, and the appearance of a Mexican half-breed, who entered bounding like a panther rather than walking like a man, froze the words in my throat. I dropped low down in my hammock, ready to swoon from fright. For some unknown reason I had a premonition that something dreadful was about to occur. However, a feeling impossible to analyze restrained me; it was a mixture of terror and curiosity that robbed me of the strength to cry out or flee, but one that served to intensify the acuteness of all my senses. My eyes were riveted on this man to see what he was about to do; my ears were strained to hear what he was about to say. The newcomer went behind the curtain that formed a separate compartment in the hut and hung down before the mother and child. This curtain, which he now pulled back, left an opening through which my gaze traveled.

The end of a candle burning near the wall cast a light, a kind of faint dusk, over the bed of the young woman, scarcely visible in the night. I saw the figure of a man silhouetted against the light. His features were terrifying; he appeared to be not dead drunk, but madly drunk.

"Is it you?" asked the woman with a sigh.

"Yes," the latter replied. "It seems to me you should be able to see perfectly well who it is."

"Where did you come from?" she continued.

"From the house of the devil."

"That means you have lost, as usual."

"I tell you, I was robbed."

Then the woman, sighing again, uttered a few remonstrances. These reproaches seemed to exasperate the gambler. Next passion began to enter into the conversation. Since they now spoke rapidly and in dialect, I could not clearly understand the words they were exchanging, from what I could infer, however, not only was she reproaching him for losing his money, but she was complaining especially because he had completely forgotten her, abandoned her, and was spending his time with other women.

The husband replied in abusive language; the poor mother, whose heart was torn by jealousy, could no longer contain herself; she burst into sobs, and, weeping softly, uttered in an insulting manner the name of a woman. Scarcely had this name escaped her lips when a sound resembling a kind of groan was heard and a weak cry, followed by these words: "Help, mother, he has killed me!"

Upon hearing this cry, this appeal, the mother leaped out of bed and rushed to the aid of her daughter; I, personally distressed by the grief that I fancied I recognized in the cry of the young woman, hurried to her side. The man passed near us in the shadow, like a ghost silhouetted against the flaring candle. I suspected some grave calamity. I was not deceived; the poor woman was stretched out, faint and bleeding, on her bed.

She had been stabbed by a knife below her right breast. Scarcely had I seen the wound when I rushed toward the door, waking my companions, and enlisting the doctor's services. A general alarm was sounded. Everyone woke up and a few minutes passed before we fully realized what had happened. The doctor clung obstinately to his belief that I was the one in trouble. I made him understand, by pushing him in the house, that he was quite mistaken, and just as he was disappearing through the door to go to the aid of the wounded woman, I swooned. I had reached the end of my strength.

Chapter XI

FROM THE VENTA DE LOS CAMINOS TO<br>CHILPANCINGO

WHEN I revived I was sitting in my hammock on the veranda. While I was unconscious, my two Hungarians had moved me; some drops of fresh water that had been thrown on my face brought me to life. I asked for news of the young woman. I was told that the doctor was with her, but had not as yet made a definite report. A moment later the old woman left the house and came toward me. The poor creature was sobbing; she did not know how to atone for the scene I had just witnessed. I told her not to think of me, but to tell me about her daughter. She shook her head and said: "He did not get her this time, but one of these days he will kill her."

By this time the doctor had come out. The wound was serious, he said, but he believed the knife had slipped to one side striking the heart muscles, and had not penetrated the cavity of the chest. Although it was not mortal, yet the invalid was in some danger from the many complications that under such circumstances might, as the result of sudden shock, weaken a woman who had recently been confined and who was nursing her infant.

As we talked, I heard the wounded woman call weakly for her mother; I forced the old woman, who was determined to remain near me and to look after me, to return to her daughter. Finally she acquiesced and the door closed on this pathetic little drama, that had moved me so deeply. After the woman left, the gentlemen insisted that I sleep, or at least attempt to sleep.

The trip the following day would be fatiguing; we were to leave, as usual, at three o'clock in the morning. After the scene I had just witnessed, obviously sleep was impossible. However, in order that my friends might be able to rest, I rolled up in my shawl, and made a pretext of acceding to their request. There I remained wide awake until three o'clock. Whenever my eyes closed, I could see the entire tragedy again, hear the grief-stricken cry of the young mother.

At three o'clock the guides clapped their hands to call us. My toilette was soon made, for I was entirely clad, and the stream that had been diverted to make water accessible was not ten steps away. I did not wish to leave without saying good-bye to the young woman. She was in her blood-drenched bed sleeping with a feverish sleep. By the gleam of the dim candle we had lighted, the muscles of her face, twitching as if she were having a nightmare, were visible. Her mother was on her knees near the bed, praying. I knelt nearby and also prayed. It was all I could do.

On behalf of my companions and myself I left some money for our hosts; I must confess we had considerable difficulty making them accept it. As a matter of fact, this same thing occurred all along the route whenever we had business dealings with any of the Mexican Indians.

At three o'clock that morning, as I said, we left. What became of the young woman? Did she die from the knife wound? I never knew. Perhaps if I were to return and pass again over the road I traveled at that time, I might secure some information, for if any incident has remained keenly alive in my memory, among a thousand memories collected during a life that, as is clearly apparent, has not been wholly free from danger, I may say that it is this episode.

The morning was icy. Aware that I was shivering, one of our Hungarians wanted to cover me completely with his cloak. At first I refused; thereupon he threw it down on the road, declaring that he was going to leave it there if I did not place it instantly on my' shoulders. I had to yield.

And now a few words about my two delightful traveling companions. My ignorance of the art of narration, as I believe it is called, compels me to write as my memory dictates and without striving for certain effects. I have said little about my two Hungarians, because in the beginning I paid no more attention to them than to other members of the party; however, as their individualities became more pronounced in view of the services they rendered to the expedition in general, and me in particular, which were innumerable, both my attention and interest were drawn in their direction. A more complete contrast between two men would have been difficult to find. One was small, quick, alert, gay, full of life and movement, as boastful as a Gascon, a brave Hungarian. The other was large, serious, usually sober, reserved, never boastful, and always active.

The small one had a riding school at San Francisco and gave lessons in fencing. He rode his horse like Baucher,[1] and was adept at handling the large saber with which he struck the flanks of his horse. When he learned that the Turks and Russians were going, as he said in his comical French, "to get a sound drubbing," he closed the door of his riding school at the peak of its prosperity, put gold in his pockets, gold in his valise, gold everywhere, and departed, invariably accompanied by his large saber, whose point and edge he confidently expected to try on all the Russians.

His traveling companion was a Hungarian officer of large stature who won a reputation for bravery during the last Hungarian wars that followed him as far as San Francisco. I do not know what his record was, but I do know that he was in control of an independent and honorable fortune. Our two companions, as I have said, kept the caravan supplied along the road with doves, ducks, woodcock, and green parrots. I was thankful for the services rendered to our party; I should have been ungrateful indeed had this gratitude not been inspired as well by the undue attentions paid to me in particular.

At first, about five minutes after setting out from the place where we last stopped and after ascertaining, in the language that was spoken only when talking to me, whether I needed anything, the two Hungarians would disappear, not to reappear except at places designated for breakfast and dinner. From time to time, however, we heard the sound of the officer's gun, or when we were least expecting it, suddenly saw them on top of a mountain or at the bottom of a ravine, where the riding master's saber, reflecting the sun's rays when it struck the sheath, gleamed.

At the rendezvous, as I have said, we invariably found them with the game that was the result of all this varied activity. Upon starting off I usually had a bone to pick with the riding master; he wanted me to mount my mule as an accomplished rider does, handle my bridle according to the rules of good horsemanship, and force my poor, weary, sick body to hold a pose like that prescribed in the *Manual of the Perfect Riding-master*. All this was utterly impossible.

Thereupon, a struggle followed, one in which the Hungarian was always vanquished. He then retired, consternation painted on his countenance, and, urging his mule to a trot in a manner befitting an expert horseman, rejoined his companion, who shrugged his shoulders and said to him gravely: "You will make yourself detested." Then both disappeared.

I have mentioned the agreeable manner in which they reappeared. The incident of the coat thrown on the road touched me deeply. I now paid more attention to these two men than I had before, and I remember that during the night, at the moment I believed I was in danger, it was to them I turned; and that when a new peril appeared, it was of them I thought first of all. I placed the cloak over my shoulders and we continued on our way toward Venta Daccahuisla, where we were to stop for breakfast.

We found the place almost deserted. Even when inhabited, Indian villages present the most miserable aspect. I do not know why people who have to live in the houses they build so often select for a site some open spot devoid of trees or verdure in a sea of dust. There they group their houses that consist simply of huts placed three or four inches apart and that look like immense chicken coops, through the openings of which, at a mere glance one may see the entire life of the household. As I have said, the village was absolutely deserted; all the food we could find were eggs and water, some were eaten hard, others from the shell. Our providers had keen ears, not the smallest little green parrot escaped their guns.

After taking a siesta until the intense heat had passed, we started off along the road in the usual order: first Rubio, then I, the doctor following, and the Man with the Rifle bringing up the rear. As for the Hungarians, like M. Arlincourt's solitaire, they were everywhere and nowhere.

On the outskirts of Chilpancingo [2] we stopped at a sugar plantation, where the owners hastened to extend hospitality. Scarcely had

I descended from the mule when—just as in France, a chair is offered, in Holland, a cigar, or in Africa, a cup of coffee—I was offered a stalk of sugar cane three feet long together with a knife. I used it to cut the stalk which was then sucked. The sugar cane and knife as handled by the Mexican made me think of the American whittling a stick of wood with a penknife.

I cut my stalk in small pieces and began eating it while waiting for dinner. The evening repast was a veritable banquet; each one had his own glass, knife, and fork—a rare luxury. After it was over our Hungarian, the riding master, of course, having enumerated the number of Russians he intended to put to death, demonstrated with his sword for our benefit how he planned to accomplish his object. The small hero, I might add, was a miracle of speed and skill. This was an extremely odd spectacle for all the inmates of the hacienda, who watched these demonstrations, leaning over the wall and sunning themselves while the sun set. Thus was the evening passed.

When night came we retired, I, as usual, to my hammock; the gentlemen to their mats, wrapped in their covers and coats. I do not know whether they slept, but I do know that I, personally, passed a wretched night, literally besieged by swarms of mosquitoes and armies of cockroaches. Here in Mexico again I encountered my ancient and hideous enemies of the Indian Ocean. I arose without having closed my eyes for a single moment. It was unnecessary even to think of offering our hosts payment for their hospitality; however, I presented my hostess with a gift of some perfume, and also a bottle of Bully vinegar that proved highly acceptable

By two o'clock in the morning we were on our mules once more and hoped to reach Chilpancingo in time for breakfast, although we had twelve leagues—some thirty English miles—to make. But this time, except for a few pranks that seemed rather the vindication than the assertion of a right, our Hungarians remained faithfully near us. At eleven o'clock we recognized Santa Anna's outpost sentries. Our passes having been viséd, we went on into the city.

## CHAPTER XII

## CHILPANCINGO

CHILPANCINGO was the first important village we found on the route after leaving Acapulco; here, as I have said, we encountered Santa Anna's first sentries. Behind the walls, for Chilpancingo was a walled city, there was a garrison of four thousand men. The road leading into the city was one of those old Spanish streets that are so important in the life of the community. Of course, before venturing to appear in this quasi-European environment, I stopped outside the gates and made myself presentable.

This consisted of placing my riding skirt over my Quaker costume, turning up my Panama hat, and discarding my veil. Had a brook been nearby, upon this solemn occasion, my small Hungarian, the man with the fine saber, the swimmer, would have gone in, so that I should not have had to descend from my mule, and dipped my handkerchief in it for me.

The large Hungarian seemed satisfied with merely looking at me; furthermore, he appeared far too dignified for me to expect similar attentions from him. Then there was a definite barrier between us, for although each of us spoke three or four different languages, he German, Hungarian, Swedish, and Russian; I, English, French, and Spanish, the result was that when he tried to understand me, he had considerable difficulty. So he spoke to me only with his eyes, but I must confess that he used this mute language with the utmost eloquence.

In the distance, we heard the beating of drums; the garrison, it seemed, wished to indicate for a distance of a mile or so on every side that it was prepared for action and on its guard. When they saw us appear by the southern route naturally they were considerably surprised; we were the first travelers whom Álvarez had allowed to pass through. Crowds followed us, interviewed us, questioned us, gathering in groups near the inn where we stopped. This inn, the leading hotel in the village, had been converted into officers' barracks, and so no rooms were available. Finally, the couple who owned the hotel had a bed prepared for me in their own room, and the other members of the party were forced to camp on the veranda outside the house. Arrangements were made to meet in my room for meals.

Incidentally, a few words should be said about the curious persons who were our hosts; the master was ninety years of age and the mistress eighty. The little attentions these old people showered on one another were so remarkable that they outdid even Philemon and Baucis.[1] Their honeymoon had lasted for a period of sixty years. Apparently this was not the only happy couple in Chilpancingo, for I can truthfully say that thoughtful attentions seemed to be characteristic of all these happen Chilpancingaños, from whom I received nothing but kindly treatment from the time I reached their village.

Every morning the old woman, with a step as light as if she were not more than twenty years old, went down to her garden while I was still asleep and cut an enormous bonquet, which she placed near my bed. When I awoke, with my first waking breath I inhaled perfume, and my eyes opened on a mass of flowers.

Fifteen minutes after our arrival, the rumor circulated that a party had arrived who had passed through Álvarez' camp, and (a detail indicating that everyone doubted the fact) that quite a young and pretty woman was also in the party. Their curiosity, as you can imagine, was intense. Chilpancingo is a land where life offers few diversions; so few foreigners ever came there that I was a rare event. Everyone wanted to see what I looked like.

Now the French describe a stranger who is the center of attraction as being as "restless as a French hat," for the French are so polite that upon the slightest occasion they will lift their hats. Of a woman constantly under surveillance it might aptly be said: "As uneasy as Madame Giovanni's door"; for the first day I arrived, under one pretext or another, my door was probably opened a hundred times. My hostess had placed a large screen before my bed, and only when retiring behind this screen, was I in my own home.

That evening I ventured to put my nose to the window; this was foolhardy, and soon I had cause to regret my indiscreet conduct. Every soldier attached to the garrison was on the veranda; each soldier had a woman, either one he brought with him, or one he acquired in the neighborhood. These women have no other homes except where their husbands or lovers are; they live with them out in the open air, on the veranda. It was a revelation to watch this group of warriors and women, for these modern amazons had even less innate modesty than the amazons of antiquity.

No sooner was I installed than I received a visit from the aide-de-camp of the commander, who came on behalf of the general to advise me that if we continued on our route we would run the risk of losing our lives. For this reason, he added, he believed he should assume the responsibility of prohibiting us from leaving Chilpancingo until he devised a plan that would insure our safety. As a matter of fact, the road was infested with robbers; the evening before we arrived some troops carrying dispatches from Mexico City had been stopped by three hundred bandits, twelve thousand dollars seized, four officers made prisoner, and two soldiers killed. The other members of the squad had been led behind the rocks where, it was feared, they might have been killed.

An officer who swam across the river and was rescued after he was almost exhausted, brought us the news. The bandits, however, had removed all his clothing. For the past eight days, Chilpancingo had been trembling at the name of Bealva, leader of the robber band. He and his son, who served under him in the capacity of lieutenant, were unbelievably bold; they had even reconnoitered as far as the gates of the city.

Upon learning that our traveling companion, Dr. D——, was carrying dispatches, the commander of Chilpancingo was even more insistent that we should not run even the slightest risk of falling into the hands of these robbers. He asked us to delay our departure two or three days, promising that he would provide us with an escort at the end of that time. This guard was to accompany us until we met a detachment coming from Mexico City that had some mission to execute along the route and could assist us.

To encourage us to remain, the aide-de-camp was instructed to invite us to dine the following day with the local commander. The invitation was accepted. The following morning, the eighteenth, we learned when we awoke that two captures had been made during the night. One of the two prisoners was Bealva's son—the man just mentioned as being his father's lieutenant—who had been taken upon information supplied by General Bravo from his bed. That excellent man was ill when I was traveling in Mexico—he has since died. An adage among military men is: "Brave as his sword." Of General Bravo it might be said: "Brave as his name."

The second prisoner was Colonel Thores,[2] one of Ávarez' superior officers. While reconnoitering he had ventured too near the city and had been surprised by a party of men so superior to his own forces that resistance was futile. At first it was believed he would be shot within twenty-four hours; the general, on the contrary, had given orders to keep him alive to exchange for officers who had fallen into the hands of bandits who declared that they were allies of Álvarez'.

Our dinner proved wholly delightful. The Hungarians had visited the wine cellar and larder in person and had taken out the best they afforded. Moreover, the Hungarians had been fraternizing since the previous evening with the Mexican officers, and in ten or twelve hours they had all become excellent friends. From six o'clock in the morning, that is, from daybreak, they had been indulging freely in various drinks both large and small; then, having mounted their horses, had made a tour of inspection throughout the city. During this little excursion, our riding master gave an exhibition of his prowess, with the result that after dinner a deputation of Mexican officers—all Mexican officers are excellent riders—came over to persuade our acrobatic Hungarian to be so kind as to give them a demonstration in the courtyard.

This invitation afforded our Hungarian riding master an opportunity to display his skill, an opportunity that could not be overlooked. He applied the spur, grasped his imposing saber, and descended into the court. The other Hungarian followed. He, too, was an excellent equestrian and skilled in handling arms. From my room I could hear the applause that greeted the dexterity of our two Magyars. But I was so accustomed to the prowess of my two traveling companions that I deprived myself of the pleasure of watching them, and began to jot down notes about my journey that are now being used to write this narrative. Then, after my notes were complete, I began to brush up my Spanish; my hosts, with whom I chatted, displayed inexhaustible patience in helping me.

When the dinner hour arrived, my two Hungarians entered, the large one smiling, the small one full of irrepressible spirits. The latter repeated in somewhat garbled language a series of more or less amusing anecdotes he had just heard. His main concern seemed to be to ascertain whether I was being treated here in the local barracks in the way an honest woman has the right to expect. He told me that if anyone was rude to me, to report the matter to him; he had his saber, and would guarantee to cut off the ears of the person failing to be courteous.

Soon after dinner, a call was announced from the officers on the commander's staff who had come to pay me a visit in a body. We discussed music. In Mexico, as in Spain, almost everyone has a guitar. One of the officers reached for his instrument, played some chords, and began to sing. As this one guitar alone was insufficient to provide a concert, his friends knocked at the door of three or four neighbors and located several others. Bored with this music, the Hungarians disappeared, returning with an enormous bowl of blazing punch.

From this time on this musical soirée proceeded according to the usual custom. At eleven o'clock the musicians retired; however, in place of going directly home they stopped and began to entertain me with a serenade under my window. At two o'clock in the morning the singing still continued. When I awoke the table was too small to hold all the bouquets that had been sent.

# VOLUME V

## CHAPTER I

## THE MESCALA RIVER

THAT same night the commander sent off three or four hundred men to guard the road leading to Chilpancingo until the detachment of troops believed to have been sent down from Mexico City arrived.

At eight o'clock the following morning, we were entertained by feats of horsemanship staged in the courtyard. The equestrian skill of our famous Hungarian riders had aroused the jealousy of the Mexican caballeros, who were as much at home on horseback as our friends, the Hungarians; the Mexicans in self-defense challenged our traveling companions to an exhibition of their respective merits.

Having been asked to attend as queen of this tournament, as usual I was honored by many little courtesies; I was offered a place at an open window, a cushion was arranged under my arm, I was presented with a bouquet and a fan, and was given permission to return to my room when I grew tired of watching the sport.

The tournament proper began at half-past nine. At ten-thirty, however, a rustling sound was heard in the air; the sun seemed to disappear behind a dark veil; clouds of dust darkened the atmosphere. A moment later the house in which I sat began to shake like a drunken man; two or three horses staggered and fell, throwing their riders. The bystanders—men, women, and children—dropped on their knees and began to pray. I grasped a corner of the window to avoid falling, and joined in the general cry: "Earthquake, earthquake!"

The earthquake lasted just thirteen seconds. In this short time the Hungarians had managed to speed up their horses and so did not fall, but when the swaying of the earth suddenly ceased, the little Hungarian placed his hand on his heart, saying: "I feel almost seasick. My heart is still pounding, but so far as I know it is in the same old place."

The horses and hearts of both Hungarians were perhaps the only things that had not changed places during the earthquake. When the earth finally regained its normal tranquillity, we collected our senses, and although our heads still felt dizzy, merely remarked that the earth had just had a bad attack of ague. The Mexicans, however, are so accustomed to earthquakes which occur five or six times a year, that they were not in the least disturbed by it.

As the local commander ordered a detachment of three hundred men to clear away the debris left by the earthquake immediately, our departure was set for the following day, March 20th. We planned to start at three o'clock in the morning, as usual, expecting to meet our escort at Zumpango, our first stop. Upon reaching the opposite bank of the Mescala River, we hoped to find the first detachment of troops from Mexico City; we had also been told that we would meet more troops at various points along the road.

At noon on Sunday, March 19th, we received counter orders to the effect that we were not to remain at Chilpancingo until the following morning, but were to leave at once for Zumpango.[1] Having packed and ordered our mule drivers to saddle our animals, we left the city about three o'clock that afternoon amid the farewells and best wishes of the commanders. At least a dozen officers expressed a desire to accompany us and escort us for a few miles beyond the city. After a round of farewells our good friends sped us on our way with as much solemnity as if they were responsible for the state's treasury.

The journey proved to be full of amusing experiences. One of the officers was a regular clown and made me laugh so heartily that I was almost prostrated; my sides ached by the time I reached Zumpango. As a result each step my mule took felt like a knife blade, and hurt so that I even considered urging the party to go on ahead and let me turn back.

As we started off we noticed several men winking at one another ominously. During the trip the little Hungarian with the large sword exhausted all his eloquence trying to persuade our escort to accompany him to Constantinople. All his persuasive ways proved futile; the brave Mexicans had too many of their own problems to face with General Taylor [2] and also, at times, with Don Juan Álvarez, to join the Hungarians and fight in foreign lands.

At ten o'clock that night we reached Zumpango. The city occupied a charming site in a delightful wood, and is notable for the beauty of its sixteenth century Gothic cathedral. The tranquillity of the moonlight evening added to the beauty of the scene. Since March 20th was the nameday of the patron saint of Zampango, bonfires were burning in the streets and every five minutes a rusty cannon was fired from the fort.

As there were no inns in the town, we went to stay with the alcalde, [3] for the ancient Spanish custom of hospitality still prevailed at that time throughout Mexico. From the alcalde's house could be heard the church organ and the chants of priests and nuns in the church nearby.

As my side still ached from the trip, I went into the neighboring cathedral to pray for strength, then went back to the house of the alcalde. The pain having disappeared within an hour, I returned to the cathedral to express my profound gratitude to the Lord.

This time the two Hungarians asked permission to accompany me to the church; I was extremely happy to have their companionship, for I had been somewhat frightened the first time I entered the door and found myself in semi-darkness before an altar of holy Joseph, clothed in a long black robe, standing with one arm stretched out toward me. Only after I had somewhat recovered from my fright did I kneel down in a corner of the church and thank God from the depths of my heart for His blessed protection during the many dangers to which I had been exposed.

By the time we had returned, after my second visit to the church, to the house where we were stopping, we found that the alcalde had prepared a large sleeping room, the only quarters available, for our common use. After my comfortable hammock was hung and my comrades' traveling blankets and mattresses were arranged in this room, we joined our host, who had invited us to tea.

The tea proved to be a light supper, and was served by the alcalde's charming and capable daughters. While these stately Mexican maidens served us, the patriotic alcalde questioned us about our trip through enemy territory, for he was keenly interested to know how we had crossed through the country and past the military forces of General Álvarez. Having promised not to reveal this secret, we were forced to leave the curiosity of the alcalde unsatisfied, for whoever travels in foreign countries must decide above all else to remain aloof from political entanglements and not to take sides.

Although we were as friendly as possible toward the alcalde and expressed our warmest thanks for his hospitality, we did not mention Don Juan Álvarez and Don Diego. Of course the local residents regarded us with the utmost amazement. In fact, the members of our party were so odd and conspicuous that everyone wondered why we were traveling together, since we were so unlike in appearance, manners, and character. The man with the mysterious bag was unusually silent and went quietly about his own affairs. The doctor, on the other hand, was arrogant and gossipy. The two Hungarians, as the reader already knows, were utterly unlike one another. I was invariably serene and pleasant, and, after the pain in my side had ceased, I laughed as much as usual.

The alcalde finally realized he could extract nothing from us. Aware that we needed rest, he suggested that we might like to retire to our room.

Tired as we were, we were unable to sleep in our own quarters, for two reasons: there were at least a million fleas and several million bugs in our room; and our good host, the alcalde, kept a number of his pet fighting cocks nearby. In fact, much to our surprise, our room was a kind of annex adjoining the cages that held the vivacious creatures, which our host fondly called his "menagerie." Our nearest neighbors proved to be three hundred of these birds, in the corners of whose cages tablets had been placed on which the pedigree and the victories of the inmates were tabulated.

All night long I could hear a constant commotion nearby, but did not know just what the noise indicated. Finally, the little Hungarian strapped on his cavalry sword, which was invariably near at hand, took a light, and we all went out to investigate. The fighting cocks, whose night's rest was not interrupted by this disturbance, watched what went on with their bright, yellow eyes. One of them, mistaking the burning candle for the dawn, began to sing and crow.

The little Hungarian, among whose talents was the ability to crow, answered him in his own language. The martial fever that burned in his breast appeared to have expressed itself in the vigor and force of his outburst, for the three hundred plumed combatants apparently believed that he was challenging them to a contest. Those already awake replied, while those who were nodding opened their eyes to find out where the noises came from, and then joined the general chorus. Within a short time a full-fledged concert resounded through the night air, with bass singers, baritones, and tenors, striking every note in the scale.

We went hastily indoors, for the noise was deafening, and awaited as courageously as possible to see what the outcome of this warlike demonstration would be. The mere thought of the bugs and fleas indoors kept us wide awake; even the Hungarians who, like Achilles, had been dipped in the Styx and emerged unharmed, could not close their eyes.

Although we were ready to set out on our journey at two o'clock, the promised escort failed to appear. A verbal order, so the commander reassured us, had been given them to guard us, but in Mexico, as in Spain, good intentions often fail to materialize. This seemed to be the situation with our guard. However, we preferred to be exposed to any danger rather than live another hour with those dreadful insects. As we had expected, with the approach of dawn the crowing grew louder and louder, hence we retired from the field of battle and beat a hasty retreat.

At half-past three we left Zumpango with Rubio, our guide, in the lead, the man with the mysterious box following, and the two Hungarians bringing up the rear. We were fully aware that a long, hard day lay ahead of us, and that we were entering dangerous territory near Mescala. What form this danger might take was largely a matter of conjecture, but I could feel my heart beat with something akin to fear. In order to be prepared for any emergency— for I knew the country was infested with bandits—during the preceding night when I could not sleep I had put on two dresses, one on top of the other, hoping the robbers would be satisfied with the first layer, and would leave me the second.

Although we looked back at frequent intervals, we failed to see any signs of our promised escort. My companions urged me to remain at the rear of the procession during the trip, but I refused and, despite my secret fear, kept my place in the lead. This added responsibility of protecting me at the end of the train made my Hungarian friends extremely angry, for they knew that in case of an attack resistance would prove futile.

The distance to Mescala was approximately thirty miles. The heat was oppressive, not a breath of air was stirring, and, to add to our misery, we were plagued by myriads of insects, especially mosquitoes, that caused us indescribable torture. Although I had covered my face with two veils and put on leather gloves, yet I could still feel the bites of these tiny creatures. The Hungarians even swore the mosquitoes were stinging them through their boots.

Finally we reached the Mescala River; there, so we had been told, we would have to wait either for a ferry, a boat, or some other means of transportation. Our Hungarians rode back a short distance, for we knew that half an hour from the Mescala there was a Mexican post, where we hoped the escort whom we expected to meet at the river would be found. But this hope was soon dissipated, and we were obliged to remain on the bank of the river, exposed to the tender mercies of gadflies and mosquitoes.

When the Hungarians returned with the news that the Mexican post knew nothing about our promised guard, we decided to pass over the river without it. Some Indians were called in to assist us, and after the usual amount of proscrastination they pointed out a shallow place where we could cross. The water level, however, was extremely high.

The two Hungarians plunged into the water at the point indicated, in an attempt to ford the stream, but after they had gone about ten paces they found we would be forced to swim through deep water. Instructing the Indians to guard me on either side of my mule and, if necessary, keep the animal's head above water, they waited on the opposite bank ready to come to my assistance if the need arose. I leaned over on my animal with a throbbing heart and without hesitation gave the signal to start. The other members of our party remained behind, ready to follow as soon as I reached the far shore.

CHAPTER II

PINTO INDIANS

I PLUNGED into the river. For a time my mule moved steadily forward, but I was soon aware by his nervous twitching that the poor animal had lost his footing and had begun to swim. The two Indians remained on either side of the mule and held onto the bridle to guide him and keep his head above water while I clung firmly to his mane. In the deepest part of the current my head suddenly felt dizzy; as I heard the water splash against the flanks of my mule, I thought I was about to faint. Then I heard the voice of the large Hungarian call: "Don't look down at the water; look up at the mountains."

Realizing that this advice was meant for me, I lifted my head, and riveted my eyes on the mountain. The dizziness passed. After climbing up on the opposite bank I reached into my pockets and gave each Indian a piaster, or Spanish dollar. The men could scarcely believe their eyes when they saw this munificent gift; they knelt down and thanked me in the most profuse manner. The other members of our party followed us into the water. Everyone made the trip across the river safely; the doctor silently, the man carrying the mysterious box, with his usual profanity.

The natives, however, cross the stream at low tide on a float of hollow gourds covered with planks. On this makeshift ferry they are able to pass in comfort and safety.

After looking around in every direction, we discovered about half a mile from the banks a small village that was entirely deserted. Here we decided to seek shelter for ourselves and animals from the broiling rays of the sun. For once the two Hungarians could find no way to exercise their talents, for the shabby village was quite empty; even the wild game had disappeared. There was absolutely no sign of man or beast. The only live creatures that remained behind were swarms of mosquitoes that tortured our hands and faces no matter what we did. To be frank, I probably suffered much more from the annoyance of these insects than from the pain in my side.

We were now entering the danger zone. This land was known to be overrun by bandits, and the more we inspected the place, the more we were forced to admit that this barren and deserted village, hemmed in by wooded plateaus, was just the spot where robbery and even murder could be committed without danger of detection.

I glanced at my hammock that was fastened between two large trees. Above my head perched a flock of green parrots that at the slightest hint of danger would sound the alarm. One of the Hungarian officers intended to shoot at the chatterers to silence them, but I persuaded him to have mercy on them, assuring him I did not intend to eat any more roast parrot.

Notwithstanding the loud cries of these birds and the fear of robbers, I finally fell under the spell of the great magician, sleep. Rubio and our mule driver had already set me a good example, for they were stretched out on the ground and snoring long before I closed my eyes.

I slept profoundly for at least three hours, the deep sleep of the righteous. When I opened my eyes the entire company was already up and, I might almost say, already in the saddle. Although the hour was late, no one had cared to rouse me, for all felt that I, a member of the weak sex, had withstood the terrific hardship of the journey well, and deserved a rest.

With thoughts of bandits uppermost in my mind, my first words as I awoke were: "What, aren't they here yet?"

Surmising what I meant, they replied: "No, not yet. Aren't you surprised?"

This was the first surprise; the Hungarian with the cavalry sword afforded the second when he handed me a large piece of watermelon and two sweet lemons. These made up my noonday meal—a a veritable feast, since I had expected to fast the entire day. After searching for some time in a garden, the Hungarians had found two watermelons and a lemon tree loaded with fruit. How often, during my travels, have I realized the profound wisdom of the words of the apostle: "Let each day be sufficient unto itself"

My frugal but welcome meal that had been supplied by the two Hungarians was soon over. The attitude of these two Magyars, who grew more cheerful the nearer we came to danger, seemed inexplicable. The smaller of the two who, as my riding master, felt entitled to a few special privileges, grasped me unceremoniously by the arms and placed me on my mule while Rubio was taking down my hammock and loading it on my pack mule.

"Now let's move on," said my instructor after I was seated in the saddle, "we've waited long enough for the bandits and might as well go out and look for them."

The big Hungarian said something to him that I could not understand. "I am inclined to believe," replied the brother with the sword, "that your suggestion is a good one." Then, turning to us he said: "Has anyone a pencil and paper?"

"I have," I replied, tearing a leaf from my notebook.

The Hungarian Nimrod had decided that the robbers should be informed of our three-hour sojourn in the deserted village. So with the aid of Doctor D——, the only member of our party who spoke fairly good Spanish, the following message was written in large letters on a sheet of paper: "Two well-armed and well-mounted Hungarian officers, two ditto Frenchmen, and a beautiful Frenchwoman, with a large amount of baggage, stayed here three hours and then left for Chilpancingo, after making a quiet search for the bandits whom they had expected from Mescala. The party had a good rest, but not much to eat."

After the message had been nailed to a tree, we departed. The two Hungarians led the way, laughing at the top of their voices. I failed to share their confidence and courage, but was extremely careful not to let anyone suspect my nervousness.

The jokes of the Hungarians, however, kept up our high spirits for some time, until the intense heat began to dampen our ardor. After traveling a mile or more in total silence, we finally reached Zalitu, a poor settlement inhabited by Pinto Indians.

Pintos are one of the ethnological curiosities of Mexico. The following information about their origin has been supplied by my erudite friend, Dr. J——, who has often discussed affairs pertaining to Mexico with me. Pinto Indians, according to scientists, present an extremely interesting study, and the various kinds of tattoos which I had observed while traveling through the country are the result of this peculiar form of metabolism.

"What," you may ask, "is a pinto?" [1] He is, first of all, a normal person who is either white, yellow, red, or black, Indian or mestizo. Suddenly his body undergoes some kind of chemical change and a round, milk-white spot tinged with yellow, copper, or black appears. As this spot grows larger and larger, other spots appear on various parts of the body, giving it a mottled or speckled appearance.

Sometimes the spots grow together in such a way that the victim looks almost like an albino. Although I have not seen this remarkable phenomenon myself, yet I have heard about it from reliable sources, and know several persons who have described striking examples of such transformations. Pinto markings are not always white; slate-colored or bluish-red shades are frequently seen, but are less noticeable on the bronze-colored skin of the natives, and are not so apt to attract the attention of travelers. The mottled effect is usually the most conspicuous on white skin before it has turned to bronze under a tropical sun.

I recall one amusing tale told at a college in Mexico about this strange metamorphosis. A certain young merchant was traveling through various parts of Mexico but had not been in the country long enough to know that young men were often victims of its pernicious climate. Finally business took him to the southwestern province of Tabasco. There, in the city of San Juan Bautista,[2] he met a well-dressed man who came up and took his arm in a friendly manner.

"What do you mean," said the traveler, "by this familiarity? Kindly apologize."

"We are old friends," replied a well-known voice; but the face was that of a stranger.

The traveler looked at the man who said he was "an old friend," but could not remember ever having seen him before.

"I repeat," replied the traveler, "that I don't know who you are."

"Do you really mean it?"

"Yes, I don't remember you."

"Well, I am your old friend, Francisco de N."

Then the traveler recognized, underneath the slate-gray countenance, the face of a merchant whom he had not seen for some time. Within a month the man had changed from a white man to a pinto, so that even his best friends did not know who he was.

Another friend told me some more tales about pintos. I could not, or rather would not, believe all he said. Yet I marveled at the sublimity and the capriciousness of nature, which in some mysterious manner caused this fascinating, surprising, yet repulsive phenomenon.

My friend, in his speculations about them, believed, from his own observations and from what he could find out from other sources, that this change was conclusive proof of the divine brotherhood of man. At the risk of seeming tiresome, I should like to make a few more remarks on the same subject.

Pintos, it is generally believed, transmit their characteristics to a pronounced degree to their descendants, and it is not unlikely that an entire colony of them will ultimately develop as our negro settlements do. Let us hope this will not occur; that the human race will be spared this unfortunate type. Not only is the pinto affected externally, but his entire system seems to suffer internally. Like the albino, he lacks vitality, and there is every reason to believe that this hybrid population in the course of time will develop into a race of cretins. Such are the deductions of Doctor J——, who has seen every kind of pinto, as to the future of this mottled race.

After a long, tedious, and anxious journey, during which I had eaten only a piece of watermelon and two lemons, we found at our Indian village nothing but eggs of questionable freshness. These we had to boil for some time to avoid the danger of eating embryonic chicks.

After finishing the evening meal, the doctor thought it would be wise to pack some of my most valuable garments in among the hay or straw used to stuff the saddles of our pack mules. His idea met with universal approval; everyone set to work under the doctor's direction to dismantle the saddles. The work was, of course, retarded to some extent by the darkness, and we were afraid to use lights for fear of attracting spies.

First, I hid some beautiful Chinese material that had cost two hundred dollars in San Francisco, where such things are extremely cheap, and some other objects of considerable value. A part of the gold we carried was also concealed in the same manner. I might also add that a purse of gold coins, which I was taking home as gifts to my friends, was tucked away with the gold.

The longer we considered our situation, the more we were convinced that, since we were well protected by the Hungarians, if we offered no resistance in case we met bandits, the danger would not be very great. So we agreed not to antagonize any robbers who might appear, settling the point, as was our custom, by a majority of votes. Thus our Hungarians were obliged to promise that they would not resort to arms if stopped by bandits.

Thursday morning, at the early hour of three o'clock, we started off once more. Nothing menacing having occurred that day, we considered ourselves out of danger. Our route led over a marshy plain, but although the air was bitterly cold, we were protected by a range of mountains on both sides.

Through this land we traveled for several hours; notwithstanding the admonitions of the Hungarians, I crouched down on my mule and slept from time to time, for I was very tired. At each sudden noise, however, and whenever my animal made a sharp movement, I woke up. Every time this happened I thought we were being attacked by robbers.

Now I had secured from both Hungarians a solemn promise that under no circumstances were they to offer any resistance; as I expected, they gave me this promise willingly. But I was skeptical whether they would keep their promise.

Suddenly we came to a narrow ravine and our guide, Rubio, made the ominous observation that this spot was the haunt of cutthroats. It was now five o'clock in the morning. We were about to descend into what Rubio called the "den of cut-throats" and had taken only a few hundred steps when we heard a noise in the adjoining woods. Three Indians with heavy beards and long black locks rode up, ordering us to halt.

CHAPTER III

ROBBERS

THROUGHOUT the trip we had been afraid of meeting bandits; now the moment we so dreaded had at length arrived. My one thought was the danger to which we would be exposed if we offered even the slightest resistance to these fiends. The conduct of the doctor and the other Frenchman in this dilemma did not alarm me, but I was distinctly nervous about our two Hungarians. I glanced swiftly back at them. To my dismay, I saw that one had drawn his sword and was preparing to attack; that the other was about to shoot and exhibit his skill in marksmanship.

I could feel the blood pound back and forth through my veins. "My God," I cried, "remember what you promised!"

The grimaces with which the one replaced his saber in its case and the other laid down his double-barreled gun were so ludicrous that I burst into a fit of laughter which I feared would make my side ache as it had near Chilpancingo. The Indians stood nearby watching me in such amazement that they merely caused my hysterical laughter to increase. I suppose they thought I was only a silly young woman. This uncontrollable mirth, however, actually caused me the keenest kind of anguish.

Finally the two Hungarians began to laugh, too; although I do not know whether their pain was as great as my own, yet they laughed almost as loudly as I did. The doctor and the man with the mysterious box had already complied with the bandits' request to dismount, and now called to the Hungarians: "These men are only part of the band; the main group is hiding about twenty feet back in the woods."

Realizing how serious the situation might prove to be, the Hungarians sprang from their horses. The doctor, who usually acted as an interpreter, called out to the bandits in his best Spanish: "Don't harm us; take what you want."

Eager to set a good example, I emptied my purse. Cursing and swearing, the two Hungarians now threw their watches and purses, full of gold, on the ground. The smaller of the two, who was wearing a ring, added this to the spoils with so wry a face that I laughed even more than before. The doctor and the man with the mysterious box followed with more contributions.

Dissatisfied with this loot, the bandits now asked for the large Hungarian's double-barreled gun and the tiny Hungarian's sword. Their greed nearly precipitated trouble. "Doctor," said the little Hungarian, "tell them for me in Spanish that the first man who lays hands on me will be killed like a chicken."

"Doctor," said his big companion, "you might add that I intend to shoot them down like dogs if they refuse to be satisfied with what we have already given them."

Apparently the doctor translated this warning to the bandits in an effective manner, for they seemed to understand what he meant and ceased to annoy us for the time being. Yet they continued to watch us even more closely than before.

During the trip I had been carrying my riding habit and shawl strapped on the saddle behind me with my other luggage. The bandits now broke the strap and appropriated these garments. I did not make even the slightest protest. Encouraged by this success, the thieves prepared to steal our mules. Suddenly the sharp report of a gun was heard from the depths of the woods; the brigands disappeared in the direction of the shot, as quickly as they had descended upon us.

The whole affair had not lasted more than ten minutes. After the outlaws vanished, we looked at one another in amazement, wondering if it was all a dream, or whether we had actually been robbed. But the curses of the two Hungarians and the consternation on the faces of the doctor and the man with the mysterious box clearly indicated that we had actually been held up. I was ready to faint from excitement.

"This time we got off rather easily," remarked Rubio. "Well, let's move on."

We decided to follow his advice, and started ahead under his guidance. The little Hungarian, who by this time felt somewhat ashamed of having given away his ring and watch and was trying to find what comfort he could in the possession of his sword, took my arm and assisted me to my mount.

The other members of the party jumped on their animals and we trotted off. The mules seemed instinctively to sense what Rubio called this *mal sitio,* or bad place; they seemed eager to get away as fast as possible. But within a short time the ardor of the animals diminished; exhausted from the long journey, they dropped back into a slow walk. We speculated as to what unexpected circumstance accounted for the disappearance of our tormentors, and what the shot we had heard in the woods might mean. As our packs were following about an hour behind, we fully expected that another attack would be made and that our three bandits had gone back to take part in a second assault.

Since we were still in the dangerous gulch, we urged our animals to move faster, and soon reached safer ground. By that time I felt that the worst was over; my fears that had been expressed in uncontrollable hysterics now gave way to an indescribable feeling of relief. My nerves, stretched almost to the breaking point, relaxed; I was able to draw a free breath and feel normal once more.

I rode on silently for a mile, then began to weep. This reaction was probably better than the hysterical fits of laughter that had seized me twice before and threatened to become chronic. I thought with constant feelings of gratitude of how God had watched over me in times of danger, and of my beloved husband so far away. Dear old Giovanni! Fortunately he knew nothing about the Mexican revolution that had exposed us to so many dangers. Perhaps at this very moment he was sitting quietly with his friends at breakfast, thinking: I wonder where Jeanne is now? How surprised he would have been to know that at that very moment I was being held up by bandits and had been forced to dismount and watch my riding clothes and shawl disappear into the woods.

Riding ahead at a rapid rate, we finally came to a tiny settlement. Rubio, from whom we derived most of our information, told us that this was Venta Pallula. Our adventures had given us a good appetite; we were ravenous by the time we reached the inn.

Fortunately, the Indians of the village proved to be somewhat civilized. The owner of the inn brought out eggs, and also offered to kill some chickens for us. Of course we told him all about the robbers. He did not seem especially surprised, and merely said he doubted whether the bandits we met belonged to Bealva's band, which, everyone believed, had left the country. The robbers who stopped us, he added, were probably local Indians who occasionally harassed and robbed travelers.

Not understanding the conversation, the two Hungarians asked the doctor to translate what the inn keeper said. They appeared so dejected at these remarks that I was afraid my foolish laughter would break out again. They looked back at me, shook their heads, and talked together in Hungarian.

Although I could not understand their language, yet I felt I knew exactly what they were thinking. It was something like this: Poor Jeanne, your two traveling companions, notwithstanding their gallantry, wish you were in Hades. For your sake, we were robbed by three bushrangers, when a little courage, not to mention the use of our guns and swords, would have prevented this misfortune.

Conscious of how annoyed these two courageous men must be, I began to regret that I had compelled them to make the solemn promise, for we felt certain that the bandits would return with their accomplices and take our animals after robbing us.

As he had plainly indicated, the little Hungarian said he would like to kill the bandits like so many chickens; the big Hungarian, who regarded them as so many dogs, had also expressed his feelings in no uncertain language. From these men at least, the three bandits could expect no mercy.

Incidentally, our Hungarians were determined to find some excuse to pick a fight, and to them one time was as good as another. Both men had every intention of settling the score in full! They knew exactly what to expect from me, for when confronted by bandits I had meekly given them all my cash.

The little Hungarian, who was not entirely happy over his imposed self-restraint, broke his promise by declaring he would settle matters any time during the journey that our mules were touched. He then showed me four ounces of gold he had salvaged in his pocket. He and his brother had not been searched and had managed to cheat the bandits. The man with the mysterious box had also saved something: he still had his gun—a pure luxury so far as he was concerned—and about twenty louis in gold.

I looked at the doctor and the doctor looked at me. We both knew we had acted foolishly. The bandits, as a matter of fact, had been frightened when they saw three armed men in the caravan, which accounted for their leniency toward the Hungarians and the man with the unused gun.

After breakfast we decided to take a siesta. There was nothing further that could be done for my comfort, and the tranquil sense of relief, added to fatigue, made me feel drowsy. I experienced the sense of well-being of those who have had yellow fever and so entertain no fear of contracting the disease again; in other words, to use a purely medical expression, *non bis in idem.*

Lying in my hammock, I blessed the bandits who had indirectly been the cause of this pleasant peace of mind, and soon sank into a profound sleep. I believe I have just quoted from Virgil, but I devoutly hope no one will ask for the exact words of the Latin poet.

CHAPTER IV

MAN PROPOSES, BUT GÒD DISPOSES

ARRANGEMENTS had been made to leave this Indian inn, Venta Pellula, at five o'clock, and as we had but little baggage with us, Rubio had only a few trifles to place on our one and only pack mule. Most of our luggage had been left behind us, and God alone knew what had become of it. We were soon in our saddles, for there was no time to lose since we hoped to pass the night at Altomator, about twenty miles away.

Less than a quarter of an hour had passed after we resumed our journey, when we heard a loud report; instinctively we felt that it was a bandit signal. I turned back at a gallop, the doctor and the man with the mysterious box following me, while the two Hungarians remained behind to protect the party. This time I felt certain that the enemy would not get off so lightly if they tried to molest us.

In another five minutes we were back at the inn, where, much to our joy, a surprise was in store for us, for there drawn up in front of the door were our pack mules and long-lost baggage. The drivers, upon being questioned, told us they had not seen or heard anything of the bandits. In fact, not only the treasures that were hidden in the packs, but also all our luggage had been saved; our mule drivers had traveled over the same route we had taken without meeting a living thing, with the exception of a wild cat which they shot and brought in with them.

I almost wept with joy to find intact in the chest all my laces and linens that I had given up as lost. Although I had been traveling in a costume that made me look like a Quakeress, my feminine vanity was still as strong as ever, and I had no desire to appear in Mexico City, which has at least three hundred thousand inhabitants, looking like a scarecrow.

We now stopped long enough to allow the mules and drivers time to rest, and decided that in the future our entire party would remain together. By this time the two Hungarians had discovered that the country was full of game, and hence made a number of short detours, both to reconnoiter and to hunt. Now and then we heard a shot and knew to our great delight that a good dinner was probably in store for us. Upon their return our hunters brought us several doves and partridges; I was delighted when I found I would not have to eat any more parrot.

About nine o'clock that same morning we entered Altomator where we pulled up before an Indian hut. Our principal interest was breakfast. Hunger made us unusually nimble; the preparations for the feast were undertaken not only with joy but with the utmost cheerfulness. We had three main things to be thankful for: our lives had been spared; with the exception of a trifling sum, our gold and luggage had been saved; and, finally, we had half a dozen doves and partridges to prepare and cook.

The question that now arose was how they should be cooked; as we removed the feathers from the birds we discussed this point at considerable length. Our cooking and dining equipment consisted of two pots and a casserole, two or three plates, and about as many forks. This limited supply of pans accounted for the serious manner in which we debated whether we should roast or fry the partridges, and make soup or stew out of the doves. Finally, after consulting the various tastes, we decided by a majority vote to stew the doves and roast the partridges.

This decision was reached as we sat on the ground like tailors, removing feathers from the birds, and while two old women squatted in a corner preparing tortillas. After watching them make this latter delicacy, I came to dislike it as much as roast kangaroo or parrot stew.

Traveling, I have been told, is the most satisfactory way to learn the manners, customs, and traits of other peoples, as well as one's own personal characteristics—although psychologists say that no one ever sees himself as he actually is—and on this trip I came to know my comrades as they actually were. For instance, Doctor D—— was invariably insufferable and usually disappeared whenever we needed his assistance; as he was carrying dispatches, he considered himself an extremely important person, however. I invariably thought whenever I saw him of La Fontaine's delightful fable that describes just such a selfish, conceited character. Incidentally, his exalted opinion of his own importance was not shared by his fellow travelers.

During the journey the doctor seemed quite perturbed upon discovering, while we were packing our gold and miscellaneous papers in our saddles, that I, as well as he, carried a letter addressed to the President of Mexico; he asked many questions in an effort to find out what my letter contained. To his dismay he discovered that, like a veritable daughter of Eve, I would not disclose anything I did not want him to know.

The man with the mysterious box was singularly silent as we traveled, although now and again, he allowed a few mild oaths to escape, like the doctor. Yet on the whole, he was one of the best and most harmless men I have ever known.

I believe I have already said that Rubio had made plans to steal some of my baggage. I should like to warn all travelers bound from Acapulco to Mexico City against cunning rascals like Rubio. During the entire trip my countryman with his box, which was, of course, as harmless as he was himself, rode near my pack mule. Thus our train was constantly protected by this loyal man carrying his precious box, from which he was never separated, for he never let the pack animals out of his sight until we reached our hotel in Mexico City.

As loyal fellow travelers our two Hungarians were also worth their weight in gold. They were courageous, determined, cheerful, obliging, and indefatigable. Not once during the entire journey did they fail to provide refreshing lemons, or neglect to find a suitable place to hang my hammock. They also foraged constantly for game, and probably no travelers who had made the trip before lived as well as we did. We were indebted to them and them alone for the bountiful and delicious evening meal we were served at Altomator, a meal such as no one from time immemorial had probably ever enjoyed there before.

And after this delectable repast how I rested in my hammock! My comrades stretched out as usual on their blankets, and thus we chatted until late that night. In fact, we talked until about one o'clock in the morning, when an Indian came up and told us that Santa Anna had just left Mexico City for Iguala, a small town where Don Agustín de Iturbide [1] declared the Independence of Mexico in 1823. At this time we were not more than an hour away from Iguala, but unfortunately, in spite of the report, we refused to believe anything based on Indian rumor, and so traveled thirty miles out of our way.

On Wednesday, the twenty-second, we left Altomator at two-thirty in the morning. For some two miles the route led through a pleasant forest where great branches filled with brilliantly-colored, warbling birds formed a veritable roof over our heads. At the end of this paradise, we were stopped by a steep mountain, or rather a mass of rocks. I started toward a side road, but as the wily Rubio rode directly toward the mountain, which is known as Paya, we were forced to follow him up, and climbed three hours without stopping, hoping to reach the summit before the intense heat set in.

In many respects the mountain resembled Peregrino, except that it was four or five times higher and so steep that I was forced to cling to the pommel of my saddle with both hands to avoid falling off the mule, and from the ground, in all probability, down a sheer precipice. Finally we reached a plateau at the summit of the mountain. We had just dropped the reins and were about to rest ourselves and our mules, when we saw three riders coming up the mountain; they reined in their horses as they approached us.

One of the leaders, who was wearing a uniform somewhat French in style and a light overcoat with gold embroidery on the collar and cuffs, acted as spokesman. This was General Cespides,[2] who was accompanied by two officers. Behind them came a long train of mules carrying baggage and supplies and two servants leading extra riding horses.

General Cespides spoke to us with the utmost courtesy, asking us where we came from; he seemed astonished to learn that we were from Acapulco and had traveled through the territory of the insurgent general, Álvarez. He told us in turn that he had come from Mexico City and was en route to Iguala to join President Santa Anna.

The Indian, as events subsequently proved, had told us the truth; we were not more than an hour away from President Santa Anna, whom we had expected to find at the capital. We had made a fifteen-mile-detour, not to mention climbing a steep mountain, to reach him, whereas we could have found him in less than an hour.

General Cespides seemed inclined to doubt the real object of our journey, and although he did not mention it, his amazement over our fortunate escape from the hands of the bandits was obvious. To convince the doubting Thomas we finally showed him our passes from Álvarez. The general now urged us to turn back and accompany him to Iguala, and seemed to feel that if he took us with him, he would be certain to receive a good reception from the President.

We, too, recognized the advantages of such an arrangement; since what the Indian had told us about the arrival of the President in Iguala had been confirmed by General Cespides, we rebelled at the thought of the tedious detour we had made. During the final stage of the journey, I rode on the right and the doctor on the left of the General. Behind us came the two Hungarians, the man with the mysterious box remaining with the two officers.

CHAPTER V

## SANTA ANNA

WHEN I learned that this laborious trip up Paya Mountain had been useless and that I would now have to descend the steep slope, I had an overwhelming desire to weep. General Cespides seemed to know how I felt and attempted to divert me by conversing with me in French that was even worse than the gibberish of the two Hungarians. Before we started down, he procured a horse, which he ordered saddled for me; then he handed me a basket of fresh oranges and bananas. This fruit proved a veritable bonanza, and in addition to what the chest supplied, provided an enjoyable repast

After a brief rest, we mounted our horses and began the descent. Taken as a whole, our party now made an impressive display of strength and appeared able to ward off any attack. The reinforcements seemed to annoy our Hungarians, however, whose sympathies were not with President Santa Anna [1] but with Sultan Abdul-Mejid,[2] so they galloped on ahead in disgust. No other human beings but these daring officers could have made the return journey at this swift pace down the mountains. By traveling slowly, I found the trip endurable, however, and after three-quarters of an hour, we reached the foot of the mountains. The entire party now broke into a gallop.

After traveling for some time, toward noon we reached a delightful valley in which lay the beautiful city of Iguala. To weary, dust-covered travelers the gardens and shrubbery surrounding the houses seemed like a green oasis in a sandy desert. Yet even here the sun's rays were almost unbearable, so intense was the heat. We rested for a short time under a shady tree while the general's aide-de-camp went to look for a house.

In Iguala the houses consisted of the three types of dwellings that are invariably found throughout Mexico—Indian huts, peasant dwellings with straw roofs, and adobe structures. The latter, which are usually built near the main plaza, are fairly substantial in appearance. Many of them are found either near the barracks or the palace where the President and his staff reside. Notwithstanding the outward charm of Mexican houses, they are not pleasant to live in because of the numerous insects, including poisonous scorpions, that infest them.

Less than half an hour after our arrival at Iguala, the General's aide-de-camp, who had been sent out to find accommodations for us, came back. He reported that the city was filled with troops and that the only place he could secure for me was a crude shelter. After hearing the messenger's report, General Cespides glanced at me as if to say: "Well, are you satisfied?" I assured him that anyone who undertook the trip from Acapulco to Iguala must expect to be contented with whatever accommodations could be found.

The General now left to inform President Santa Anna of our arrival, so I had the aide-de-camp take me to my bivouac. He apologized time and again for not being able to find better quarters than the shabby native dwelling. Upon reaching it, I was so tired that my eyes closed involuntarily.

An hour after my arrival, I was aroused and told that General Van der Linden wished to speak to me. General Van der Linden proved to be a Belgian who passes in Mexico for a Frenchman. At the time of my visit he was a superior officer in General Santa Anna's army and held the rank of general. Whether he was entitled to this honor or whether it was merely a courtesy title, I was unable to discover, not being well versed in military etiquette.

I received General Van der Linden while I rested in my hammock. He was a man forty or forty-five years of age, with a stately carriage and pleasant countenance. I expected that he, like the other officers, would discuss our journey and attempt to find out military secrets. But I was mistaken; he did not seem interested in our adventures and spent the entire time talking about himself.

Such loquacity seemed to indicate only one thing: that the General seldom had an opportunity to talk with anyone in his own language. I was forced to explain to him, however, that some mistake had been made, and that I was not a Belgian. So far as I was concerned, his garrulousness was a blessing in disguise, for I was so tired that I infinitely preferred to listen rather than talk.

Within an hour I had learned all about the heroic deeds of my pseudo-countryman and, much to my surprise, discovered that he considered himself the luckiest man in the world. He was delighted with his dual rôle of surgeon-in-chief of the army and personal physician to the President, positions that brought him in twenty thousand piasters a year. He also told me he had a wife living in Mexico City.

While we were talking, the aide-de-camp to Santiago Blanco,[3] Minister of War, came in. The Minister, having learned from Doctor D—— that I had a letter for the President, courteously extended an invitation to me to accompany General Van der Linden to call on him. I felt obliged to accept this invitation, and so rose, dressed, and, accompanied by my Belgian caller, went to see the Minister of War.

General Santiago Blanco was extremely friendly when I arrived, and urged me to call on his mother and sister when I reached Mexico City. He expressed regret that we had been forced to turn back, and requested me to give him my letter of introduction to the President, promising to deliver it in person. The doctor, it seems, had already given him his dispatches, which told of the defeat of Raousset de Boulbon[4] and the destruction of his guns.

I wish I could tell everything I know about my bold and unlucky countryman, Boulbon, and about his vast enterprise that met so tragic an end and created a sensation on the other side of the Atlantic, particularly in France. I could relate, if I chose, many intimate and little-known facts about his defeat, and I believe that no one except myself knew the real circumstances connected with the case. Raousset de Boulbon, by the way, was an intimate friend of my husband in San Francisco, and was shot while I was in Mexico.

After visiting Santiago Blanco's headquarters at Iguala, I returned to my house, or rather my Indian hut, where dinner was waiting. The food, although poor, was somewhat better than what we had had earlier on the journey. A special treat upon this occasion was the bottle of Bordeaux sent by General Van der Linden from his own, or rather, from the President's table. At the request of my traveling companions, to show my appreciation I drank half a glass. This was the first time since my illness in the Sandwich

Islands that I had tasted a drop of wine. Among my most pleasant memories of my travels are the days I spent in the Sandwich Islands, and time and again my thoughts dwell on them, especially when I am traveling in more civilized lands.

At four o'clock that afternoon, General Van der Linden came back and told me that at five o'clock President Santa Anna would receive me. Punctually at five o'clock I sent in my card. Upon entering, I found the President in a large reception room, beautifully illuminated. Nearby on the veranda a military band was playing. I could not decide whether this display was merely a stage setting for the President, or whether it was planned for my own edification. Unwilling to admit anything derogatory to my self-esteem, I assured myself that everything had been arranged in my honor.

As I entered the large reception hall, I looked around the room for the glittering, gold-trimmed uniform of President Santa Anna, whom I expected to recognize by his wooden leg. Among the elaborately-dressed members of the general staff I noticed a man wearing a simple white coat and colored trousers, who was sitting at the end of an oval table covered with a green cloth.

He rose and greeted me. This modestly-dressed man, who resembled a Mexican ranchero, proved to be President Santa Anna. General Van der Linden now informed me that the President, according to the English custom, would like to shake hands—a form of etiquette he reserved only for very special occasions. After saying a few cordial words the President rose, offered me his hand, led me to a comfortable chair, and resumed his seat at the table.

Throughout our entire conversation, Generals Santiago Blanco and Van der Linden acted as interpreters, while I used my fan to emphasize any doubtful points. The conversation soon turned to the insurgent Álvarez, and with my fan I indicated on the table the various positions of the revolutionists. Then the President took the fan from my hand and asked several questions. Finally he told me how many men he had and asked me whether I believed that the enemy had equally large forces.

"I do not know what condition their troops are in," he added, "but I believe that twenty-five Vincennes sharp-shooters could turn the tide in my favor." Having ascertained the route we had taken, the President's final questions were about certain strategic locations, points that a scouting party could settle far more readily than I.

"How does it happen," I replied, "that you don't know these facts? If this were France, scouts would be sent out for at least twenty miles in every direction before the enemy realized spies were nearby."

The President laughed, and began to talk about Raousset de Boulbon. According to Santa Anna, Boulbon was far more important and infinitely more dangerous an enemy than Álvarez, for Boulbon had come to Sonora with the intention of conquering the country. The President was still indignant that his own army had but narrowly escaped annihilation at the hands of Boulbon's forces, who had come dangerously close to conquering Sonora.

I confirmed all the information he had already received from the dispatches Doctor D—— carried. The President then asked me what had become of Raousset de Boulbon himself. I replied that before leaving San Francisco I had heard that he had gone to hunt bear in northern California, and this information seemed to reassure him to some extent. As events subsequently proved, the importance the President of the Mexican Republic attached to this daring adventurer was not without reason.

At six o'clock President Santa Anna, after inviting me to attend the ball the ladies of Iguala were giving in his honor that evening, excused himself.

## CHAPTER VI

## THE BALL AT IGUALA

PRESIDENT SANTA ANNA, one of the best-known men of our day, whom I met for the first time at Iguala, is about five feet six inches tall. His face, although alert and animated, is gray and pallid from the incessant pain in his leg, caused by the wound received at Vera Cruz, which makes walking difficult. Notwithstanding his suffering, his dark, fiery eyes glow with a light that seems to come from the inmost depths of his soul.

Before giving an account of the ball to which President Santa Anna so kindly invited me, I should like to recall the historic events

at Vera Cruz in which the President led the Mexican forces in
opposition to the French squadron under Admiral Baudin. The
famous French expedition to Vera Cruz with which Santa Anna's
name was so closely linked is known to the world at large.[1] Both
before and after this event Santa Anna had been dictator and president of Mexico, but when it occurred he was a general in charge
of the Mexican forces, and Bustamante [2] was president of Mexico.

At the time of the accident, Santa Anna was leading the Mexican
forces against the French who were blockading the Mexican port of
Vera Cruz and demanding through Admiral Baudin, for all French
citizens living in Mexico, the right to participate in the privileges
accorded other powers. A short time before, in a conference held at
Jalapa,[3] the Mexican Minister of Foreign Affairs had refused to
yield to this demand backed by the French navy, and in the time
gained by the delay caused by these negotiations, the Mexicans
rushed five hundred extra men to the fortress, an act that incited
the French fleet to begin hostilities.

For four hours the French, having trained their guns on the
fort, shelled the Mexican garrison, strengthened by these reinforcements. A truce was subsequently arranged between the Mexican
and French forces, and, at a later date, articles of capitulation were
signed by the opposing leaders. By the terms of this tentative agreement the Mexican general, Santa Anna, guaranteed to deliver all
guns, ammunition, and supplies in the fortress to the French, to reduce the garrison at Vera Cruz from four thousand to one thousand
soldiers, and to indemnify the French, who had left the city during
hostilities, for all their losses. On the other hand, the French admiral agreed that the fort and all remaining equipment would be
returned to the Mexicans as soon as the contending nations had
reached an agreement. In accordance with the terms of the agreement finally arrived at, the French took possession of San Juan de
Ulúa and opened the harbor of Vera Cruz to commerce.[4]

At Mexico City, however, a distinct attitude of hostility toward the
French still prevailed, even after the affair seemed to be settled, for
the haughty Spanish-Mexicans at the capital were so incensed at the
capitulation of such an important post after only a four-hour attack
that from their doorsteps they shouted: "Death to the French!"

Groups assembling in various parts of the city aided in fomenting fresh discontent. The outcome of this dissatisfaction was a spirited declaration of war against the French residents of Mexico.

Bustamante, who was then president of Mexico, protested that the Mexicans were acting contrary to the terms of their agreement with the French, and openly addressed to the Mexican people a proclamation in which he called attention to the terms of the treaty of San Juan de Ulúa.

On the same day that President Bustamante's protest was made, that is, on December 1, 1838, a meeting was held to discuss an edict recently issued, that ordered all Frenchmen to leave their dwellings, and, within four days, to leave the Republic of Mexico.[5] Frenchmen living in or near the capital were expressly ordered to assemble at the desolate little port of Acapulco, where there was no opportunity to find passage on a ship.

In view of the fact that the journey to Acapulco was long, difficult, and beset with robbers, and that at certain times of the year a deadly fever was prevalent on the west coast, this edict was equivalent to a death sentence. I myself have traveled over this tedious road infested with bandits, and I cannot emphasize too strongly the fact that I have in no way exaggerated the dangers, but have rather minimized them.

Let me now turn for a moment to the political situation. Politics, as I have already remarked, is apt to be dull and uninteresting, yet it adds variety to my narrative, and variety, as a professor once told me in an informal lecture, is the spice of life. So I have followed his suggestion in describing my travels in foreign lands.

The French leader, Admiral Baudin,[6] faced with the hostility expressed by French residents of the capital, by President Bustamante's inability to handle the situation, and by the publication of the aforesaid edict, landed a company of troops on December fifth, only four days after his protest was made, at Vera Cruz, conquered the city proper, hoisted the French flag in the plaza, and then returned to his vessel.

But before the soldiers reached their ship, they took possession on the shore of the harbor of a fine cannon, which was used primarily for display, rather than for defense. The cannon was loaded, but the retreat of the Mexicans had been so rapid that not a single shot had been fired from it. The French marines, deciding to salute the Mexicans with their own gun, pointed the cannon toward a door in which a Mexican general was standing, and fired. The General was Santa Anna. He had seen the match flicker near the fuse of the gun and had attempted to escape, but he was too late. A cannon ball shattered his knee. The French marines seemed to enjoy the little joke they had just played and embarked, laughing and frolicking like little children, or rather like Frenchmen.

In the meantime, Santa Anna was being carried into the house, where he dictated a report in which he claimed a complete victory for the Mexican forces. He said that he had turned back the French with a bayonet charge and forced them to board their ships; that a hundred French marines had been killed; that many wounded were left lying in the streets of Vera Cruz; and that he had captured an eight-pound cannon.

General Santa Anna, in the belief that he was on his deathbed, then dictated what he believed was his final message: "As my life blood ebbs, it gives me keen joy to see the beginning of amity among Mexican leaders. General Arista,[7] with whom, unfortunately, I was not in accord, I embrace for the last time and send to convey on my behalf to the President of our republic my profound gratitude for the confidence and trust he has reposed in me in times of danger.

"I beseech my countrymen, in the name of their afflicted fatherland, to banish all strife and to unite in erecting an impenetrable barrier against French attacks. I request the government to allow me to be buried here on the spot where I was wounded, so that all my fellow soldiers may know what line of battle I had planned for them. Finally, I request my countrymen not to fail to protect and defend our land, and to avenge our losses by victory.

"To all Mexicans who have opposed my political aspirations and have forced me to remain a simple Mexican citizen, I leave this one final message: God and Freedom."[8]

While Santa Anna was dictating this message, Admiral Baudin, having heard that the wounded man was the great general himself and that he did not have proper medical assistance, offered the services of his own personal surgeon.

General Santa Anna, however, declined this offer of assistance, apparently fearing "Greeks bearing gifts." Instead he acted as his own surgeon, amputating the leg himself. The unscientific method used by the General caused him excruciating pain and the wound is still troublesome. This accounts for the pallor of his countenance, so obvious when I first saw him. Santa Anna's subsequent recovery is known to the world at large.

But I have already dwelt far too long on incidents in Mexican history. To go back to my invitation to the ball given in honor of President Santa Anna. When General Van der Linden was accompanying me to my house, or rather to my veranda, he said many flattering things to me, among others that when Santa Anna, who was now President of Mexico, was talking to me he had laughed for the first time since leaving the capital.

As soon as I reached my abode I opened my favorite traveling case which, together with my laces, dresses, and jewels, fortunately had escaped the bandits.

In preparing to leave San Francisco I had, of course, considered the possibility of attending a ball, and so, having suitable evening clothes with me, was fairly well prepared for such an emergency. In fact, I found I had everything I needed, and yet, like a seasoned traveler, had not brought too large a wardrobe. Thus I was able to devise a little evening costume in Iguala, as I had in Sydney. I had had two days to prepare for the governor's ball in Sydney; in Iguala, however, I had just two hours. In Sydney I had been able to pick my favorite violets on the banks of the river for my costume; in Iguala, on the contrary, not a single flower could be found.

I took out my pearl-gray moiré gown and added a lace collar to it. This completed my costume. Since Mexican women are invariably overloaded with cheap jewelry, I did not need my pearls, which I had not brought with me and which would have been far too ostentatious for a place like Iguala, where the President came to the ball in civilian clothes, wearing a blue dress coat and a white cravat.

During the ball General Blanco, the Minister of War, came over and told me he had placed two hundred pesos [9] to my credit, adding that since we had been robbed we might need some extra gold for traveling expenses. He requested me to share this sum with the doctor, saying we could repay him in Mexico City.

I could not refuse this friendly contribution and I saw nothing wrong in taking advantage of this unexpected opportunity to acquire some additional funds that could ultimately be repaid.

At midnight I said good night to President Santa Anna and left the ballroom, the doctor accompanying me to my door. The dear, vain little man was quite excited, because he had been entrusted some time ago with the delivery of an important dispatch to the President. Napoleon, he seemed to feel, was quite insignificant compared to Santa Anna; he imagined himself a Croesus in comparison with whom the Rothschild Brothers were only poor money lenders.

At the houses we found the two hundred pesos which General Blanco had sent in advance, and a letter from him to a rich landowner called Miguel Mosso, whose magnificent hacienda lay directly on our route. The General had already urged us to visit his friend, Don Miguel, who, he assured me, would be delighted to entertain us overnight.

## Chapter VII

## ARRIVAL AT MEXICO CITY

WE STARTED off for Mexico City at four o'clock on the morning of the twenty-third from Iguala, where I had received such a courteous reception from President Santa Anna and General Blanco, both of whom I admired deeply. As we traveled my Hungarian comrades treated me, as usual, with the utmost consideration and courtesy, chatting about everything they thought would divert me as we climbed the steep mountain on whose summit we were to meet General Cespides for the second time. Not a single parrot or dove had been shot along the route by either of the two Hungarians, and so we anticipated with keen enthusiasm arriving at some place where we might have breakfast.

Having traveled at least fifteen miles, we reached Venta Negra about eleven o'clock that same morning. By this time it was obvious that our guide, Rubio, was one of the worst scoundrels I have ever had the misfortune to meet in all my travels. A typical instance of his deviltry occurred again at Venta Negra. Now Rubio, who often served as a guide for travelers and who was constantly contracting debts along the road, and indulging in much petty thievery, would stop at all his familiar haunts, yet skirt any large settlement where, because of his past deeds, he knew he would not be welcome. For this reason he would often take us out of our way to reach unimportant villages where his fellow rascals congregated. To suit his own dark purposes, he led us over a devious route known only to himself. Unfortunately for him, Venta Negra was located in a narrow valley which it was impossible to avoid, and the nearer we approached the more restless our friend Rubio seemed to grow. Before long we were to learn the true cause of his distress.

As we approached the village, a Mexican came to meet us with such speed that the little Hungarian galloped up to him to find out what the trouble was. The man informed us with the utmost courtesy that he had come to see not us, but our guide.

Meanwhile Rubio slipped quietly into the inn, and as he did not come out again the Mexican went inside to look for him. A moment later the stranger reappeared, dragging Rubio by the collar. The two men, who were quarreling violently, were kicking and hitting one another with their hands and feet. When Rubio seemed about to lose in the struggle, I told the two Hungarians to pull him away from the husky Mexican. They complied with my request.

However, the Mexican turned to them and said in a courtly manner: "Señor, three of my mules have been stolen by this rascal; you can readily understand that I want my property back again."

The Mexican continued to argue in a forceful manner, and from what I could deduce he appeared to be entirely right. Thereupon Rubio, having escaped from the fists of this Mexican, indicated a certain mule, the very animal, in fact, that the doctor was riding. During the trip I had remarked that this was the best mount in the entire caravan.

The Mexican went over to the mule, inspected it from head to foot, nodded, and led it away. The doctor considered protesting, but as he understand Spanish and hence knew what had been said, he realized that the owner had more right to the mule than he did.

But there were still two mules to account for. Having accomplished this much, the irate Mexican released his grip on the miserable Rubio.

Since the other two mules he had stolen were not in our caravan, Rubio decided to settle for them in gold. After considerable argument as to price, both parties were finally satisfied. Rubio paid what he owed; the Mexican apologized to us for the trouble he had caused, stuck his gold in his pocket, got on his mule, and rode off.

After that we had an extremely simple breakfast of eggs and coffee. As we rode off we remarked that we were not far from Mexico City. The doctor, meanwhile, had taken possession of Rubio's mule and was following us. Upon leaving the inn Rubio cursed and shook his fist at the Venta Negra. Fortunately, the Mexican was too far away to see this, or undoubtedly he would have done what he had threatened to do—give Rubio a good beating.

We planned to stop that night at San Gabriel, as the well-known hacienda of Don Miguel Mosso was called, but when we reached there at five o'clock, we discovered that the owner was absent and that we would be obliged to continue on our way.

The two Hungarians now traveled ahead of us on the road, while the man with the mysterious box remained near our baggage. But our Rubio had mysteriously disappeared. We were thus forced to find our way without a guide, so I led the train, riding with the doctor. By the time we left Don Miguel's hacienda it was already growing dark; within half an hour we could not distinguish the road. The doctor and I both called, "Rubio," but he failed to appear. Only an echo, as the romanticists and poets say, came back.

Although in grave danger of losing our way, we continued to ride ahead. From time to time, however, we reined in our mules, calling "Rubio" at the top of our lungs. Finally we thought we heard an answer behind us. We stopped and waited. We were not mistaken. Soon, not Rubio, but the rear guard, the man with the rifle, the mule drivers, and the pack appeared. As the mule drivers were thoroughly familiar with the road, we traveled confidently on ahead under their guidance. Finally lights appeared. We were now about a quarter of an hour away from the bridge at Isola.

Not far from the village we saw a man approaching in the darkness; it proved to be the rascal Rubio himself. Without taking the slightest notice of us, he hurried on. Aware that I was powerless to stop him, yet I rode up, made a few unpleasant remarks to him, and struck him in the face with my riding whip. He slunk shamefacedly away.

Everything seemed to go wrong that day. No suitable place could be found for my hammock, our evening meal was poor, and we did not sleep well. Added to this, there was an insane woman in the inn. Had we known about her, we could easily have gone to another inn and not been forced to come into contact with this absent-minded and queer individual.

So long as we were up, nothing happened; the poor woman merely sat in a corner and ate her supper out of a bowl made from a gourd. However, as soon as I retired to my hammock she got up, came over near me, and began to make the sign of the cross all over her body. Not knowing what she wanted, I called for help only to be told: "She's crazy, but she won't do anything dangerous. Leave her alone, she won't touch you."

As a matter of fact, the woman proved to be quite harmless, yet she kept me awake all night, a serious matter to any traveler. Our night's rest was further interrupted by the arrival of couriers who travel back and forth between Iguala and Mexico City, changing horses at the inn.

On Friday, the twenty-fourth, we started out at three o'clock. After traveling twelve miles, we stopped for breakfast, which was somewhat better than usual. All signs now indicated that we were approaching the outskirts of a large city. The two-hour siesta that followed was more than welcome after the sleepless night we had just passed.

At Cuernavaca we had no difficulty finding a resthouse and a bed, a real one that could truthfully be called a bed. I was almost overcome with joy. This was only the second time within twelve days that I had been so fortunate; the last good bed I had was at Chilpancingo. I slept soundly.

The following morning, to my keen delight, I discovered that I was in a veritable paradise, a classical paradise somewhat like the gardens of Versailles, with cascades and fountains and high clipped hedges. Yet all this magnificence was in what was only a roadhouse garden.

Versailles, however, does not have such splendid rose arbors as those I then saw, which were as long as the famous arbors laid out by Napoleon at Compiègne for Maria Louisa. Those I now inspected at Cuernavaca [1] had not been the gift of a king to a queen, but revealed the lavish hand of mother nature, who creates a miniature paradise wherever water is available. Each day at Cuernavaca is stamped indelibly on my memory. I regretted that I was not free, for I felt that here I could end my troubles and sorrows.

From Cuernavaca the traveler can reach Mexico City by stagecoach. Our two Hungarians who were as independent as a pair of centaurs decided to remain behind and follow later. The banality of the stagecoach did not appeal to them. Furthermore, by riding horseback they saved the coach fare. The man with the rifle also fell behind, not as a matter of courtesy, but to wait for the pack train to pull in. Throughout the entire trip this conscientious friend assumed full responsibility for our baggage and seemed to feel obligated to deliver me unharmed in Mexico City.

On this final stage of the journey I was accompanied by the doctor. At three o'clock we departed in a gray coach, erroneously known as the fast mail. The Hungarians and the man with the mysterious box called after us, wishing us a happy journey, as the antiquated conveyance started up the road.

Forty miles in a Mexican stagecoach is an ordeal I would not inflict on my worst enemy. The road was unbelievably rough and uncomfortable, but fortunately I was so tired that on toward evening between villages I fell asleep.

A sudden stop that almost broke my ribs awakened me. I looked out. The coach was standing between two rows of ragged, armed men, some of whom were on horseback and some on foot. Through my mind flashed memories of the robbers of Mescale. "Bandits," I shrieked, "bandits, bandits!"

"Calm yourself, Madame," said a spectator. "These men whom you see are not robbers. They have not come to make trouble, but are the escort sent to protect us from robbers."

When I was able to breathe freely once more I looked around, but did not feel a great amount of confidence in our guards.

The manner in which the springs and axles of the coach jarred, shaking and disturbing the unfortunate passengers, belies description. Conversation was utterly impossible, yet I longed to converse with my neighbor who had reassured me about the escort and who, I now felt certain, was the same Don Miguel Mosso at whose hacienda we had expected to pass the night. When I was thoroughly convinced that it was he, I decided to introduce myself, and so handed him my note of introduction from the Minister of War.

Don Miguel was a keen admirer of Santa Anna, and took a deep interest in us when he learned that we carried letters from him. He invited me to stay at his house as long as I remained in Mexico City, and to consider myself a member of his family.

At eleven o'clock the stage stopped at a Mexican roadhouse that served breakfast. The appearance of Don Miguel acted like an electric shock on the servants. The waiters moved with incredible alacrity; the proprietor made every effort to provide his distinguished guest with something more than the customary stagecoach breakfast.

Finally an excellent meal was served. When the doctor asked for our bill, he was told that it had already been paid. In France I would have regarded this act with disfavor, but since my visit to San Francisco I had learned enough about Mexican manners to take this in the courteous spirit in which it was offered. So I thanked Don Migual Mosso for his kindness.

An hour later we reached Mexico City. Notwithstanding Don Miguel's urgent invitation to be his guest, I decided to stay at a hotel called the Grande Société.[2]

We had left Acapulco on March thirteenth; on the twenty-fifth, some twelve days later, we reached Mexico City. En route we had stopped one day at Mt. Peregrino and two days at Chilpancingo. By eliminating the detours that Rubio had made us take to avoid meeting his creditors, the journey could have been made in eight days.

Upon arriving at the capital, we learned that Bealva's son, John, and the adjutant of the rebel general, Álvarez, had been shot on the twenty-third at Chilpancingo.

CHAPTER VIII

## LIFE IN MEXICO CITY

WHEN our coach reached Mexico City, all the travelers
scattered to find suitable accommodations. I engaged quarters
at the Grande Société, the best hotel in the City before the large
Iturbide, which was opened after I reached the capital, was built.
The doctor was the only other member of our party who took a
room there.

The time had now come to part from our two Hungarians. During the journey they had talked occasionally of attempting to join
the army of Álvarez, or the President, as superior officers, but they
did not like the idea of participating in a civil war. They felt, too,
that it was their patriotic duty to join the war at Constantinople.

For this reason they remained only three days in Mexico City,
scarcely long enough to have more than a glimpse of the city and
its fine palace. Then they went to Vera Cruz, where they secured
passage on a ship bound for Europe. From that day to this, I have
not seen them or heard from them. I can only say that throughout
the long, tiresome trip they were not only invariably agreeable and
considerate, but even took an almost brotherly interest in me.

As I have already remarked, I reached Mexico City at two o'clock
Sunday afternoon. I engaged quarters immediately in the best room
of the hotel, a luxury I had been anticipating for some time. There
I went directly to bed, into which I sank with an indescribable
feeling of peace. Later, after a bath, I rested again and had dinner
in bed. After dessert I went to sleep and did not wake up until
eleven o'clock the following morning, when I was aroused, not by
the noise of chattering parrots that I had heard so often throughout
the trip, but by the lively tunes of a spirited military march that was
being played under my window as a regiment passed on the way to
church.

By this time my good spirits had returned. I forgot my recent
hardships and recalled only the interesting country through which
I had passed and the conversations I had had during the journey. I

jumped out of bed, donned my dressing gown, and opened the window.

Here, as in every part of the world where fine martial music is heard, the military band was followed by a large crowd. I was fascinated by the gay and festive appearance of the people. After my eyes had grown accustomed to the sunlight and my ears to the music, I still felt so exhausted from the journey that I went back to bed.

As I had dined the previous evening, I now breakfasted on my downy couch, then fell asleep again. This time, however, my sleep lasted not twelve, but fourteen hours. I know my eyes were barely open—although it was well toward evening—when I heard the good doctor knocking loudly at my door. I rose, dressed quickly, and, somewhat annoyed, opened the door.

The doctor told me he had already called at the French legation and had been received by the attaché, M. Dano.[1]

"What color is the attaché?" I asked, rather abruptly.

"What do you mean by color?" he replied in amazement.

"Well, out here we meet people of every color, brown, white, yellow, red, and copper color."

"He happens to be blond. Do you like blonds?"

"I will let you know when I am wide awake."

"After I tell you about my visit to the attaché, you will be wide awake. I was as cordially received by the attaché as if I had been an ambassador."

"So he was glad to see you?"

"He appeared to be. He is polite, amiable, and very much of a gentleman. I told him all about our trip up from Acapulco."

"What comments did he make?"

"He jumped up from his chair, and so did everyone else. 'What,' he said, 'you have come all the way from Acapulco?'"

"'Yes,' I replied, 'and among my fellow travelers was a woman.'"

"'A woman made the trip?'"

"'Yes, indeed, a typical Frenchwoman. If you saw her you would think she was the kind of woman that is never visible before two o'clock in the afternoon. But appearances are deceptive. She was always the first one in the saddle, and never delayed us so much as an hour during the entire trip.'"

" 'I should like to meet the lady', said the attaché."

" 'I know she expects to see you, for she has a letter of introduction to the French consulate. But until now she has been taking the rest she so greatly needs after her long trip and for this reason has been unable to call at your office.' "

"So you have reported my arrival at the consulate, doctor?" I remarked.

"Of course; surely you don't intend to travel incognito?"

"No, but I didn't expect to do more than send in my name. Later on I will see them, but at my own convenience. I dislike the idea of anyone knocking at my door and waking me, as you have done."

My bath having been prepared, I now left the doctor. Then, after something to eat, I had the thrill of reading of our arrival in the paper. By this time I felt completely rested and fully conscious of the fact that the luxuries I had been enjoying for the past sixteen hours were not a dream, but a reality.

The following morning I woke up at ten o'clock of my own accord. My desire to dress properly convinced me that my feeling of fatigue had passed, and that there was nothing to prevent me from visiting the central plaza of the city. I opened my traveling bag that had, fortunately, escaped the bandits, and took out the pearl-gray dress that had already graced the President's ball.

After completing my toilette, I went out, accompanied by a servant I had hired, to call on Madame Blanco, the sister-in-law of the Minister of War to whom I had a letter of introduction. When my name was announced, the door was thrown open and I was greeted by Madame Blanco and her family physician, Dr. Jourdanet, whom I now met for the first time.

Madame Blanco, the sister-in-law of the Minister of War, is the wife of the General Blanco who joined forces with Raousset de Boulbon at Hermosillo.

She was extremely cordial and inquired anxiously about her brother-in-law and recent events of the campaign. I tried to appease her fears by putting the situation in the best light possible. Having been born in New Orleans, where she had lived for twenty years, she spoke English fluently.

In the Mexican manner, she placed her house, or *casa,* entirely at my disposal. I accepted this courteous gesture in the spirit in which it was offered, aware that it was nothing more than a delicate way of expressing hospitality.

After leaving Madame Blanco, I went to the French consulate. The attaché, through the doctor's call, already knew that I was in the city; yet I was allowed to remain for an hour in his anteroom. However, I knew this was purely accidental and not maliciousness on his part.

Finally I was ushered in to see him. I handed him the letter of introduction that had been given to me by the French consul in San Francisco. At first glance M. Dano, like all diplomats, appeared cold and reticent, although elegant and courteous in manner. After remaining there a quarter of an hour, I left for the banking house of Jecker and Torres. I carried exchange on this house, as well as a paper package that Mr. Tyler, the banker at Acapulco, had asked me to give them. This important package that had been entrusted to my care had caused me considerable anxiety throughout the trip, and I had thought that the favor I had thus extended would give me the right to receive exchange from their bank in gold.

But in Mexico City, or at least in this particular banking house, exchange is handled in another manner, so when I made my request the attendant handed me a large sack of silver. This made me suspicious, not only of their chivalry but of their gratitude.

Satisfied that I had accomplished enough for one day, I merely located the place I intended to visit the first thing the following morning, then returned to my hotel. At that time I was not familiar with the famous Hotel Iturbide, but I should like to advise all travelers that the Grand Société, in which I was extremely comfortable for nine months, is first class in every respect.

Not long after I returned to my hotel, I heard a knock on my door. When I opened it, much to my delight a Californian entered. I had a letter for him from San Francisco and so had sent him word of my arrival.

The visitor was the rich merchant, Limantour, who now claims from the American government ten square miles of land on the exact place occupied by the finest section of San Francisco. Naturally Limantour's claim has created a tremendous sensation, for the government will owe him, when the case is settled, not less than twelve million dollars—some sixty million francs. He has already been offered a cash settlement of two million, which he rejected and began suit. The affair has been important and interesting enough to enlist the support of the newspapers, one of which has sponsored the claim of the rich landowner. Limantour is a native of Brittany.

CHAPTER IX

LIMANTOUR

THE following details regarding this singular lawsuit have been substantiated from a brochure published in English in Francisco by an American lawyer and general, James Wilson.

M. Limantour was born in France, but spent most of his life at sea as a merchant. In 1831 he came to Mexico, landing at Vera Cruz. The following year he made many trips between this important Mexican port and his homeland. By 1836 he had extended his commercial activities into the Pacific, trading in many countries along the entire coast north of Lima.

In September, 1841, he set out on a voyage that included all the Mexican ports of Upper and Lower California. On October 28, 1841, as he was attempting to enter San Francisco harbor, he had the misfortune to wreck his vessel. Although the ship was a total loss, part of the cargo was recovered through the assistance of residents of Sausalito, Sonoma, and other neighboring settlements.

Having saved his gold and a large portion of his cargo, he decided to stay at what is now San Francisco, known in those days as Yerba Buena. Unable to procure passage on a ship after months of futile effort, Limantour appears to have remained approximately a year in Yerba Buena.

Mr. Wilson in his brochure attaches special significance to the fact that M. Limantour reached Yerba Buena, or San Francisco, toward the end of October or the first of November, 1841, and that his enforced sojourn lasted until the fall of 1842. During this period he had an opportunity to inspect the fine bay and coastal lands, especially near the hamlet of Yerba Buena. In the eyes of M. Limantour, an alert merchant and capable sailor, the harbor had a great future.

In the year 1841, at the time that M. Limantour was living on the desolate coast near Yerba Buena, a ship came into the bay from Oregon. Among her passengers, in addition to some agents of the Hudson's Bay Company, was an envoy of the French government, Duflot de Mofras, who had been sent out to ascertain the importance and resources of California and Oregon Territory.

When M. Duflot de Mofras,[1] who subsequently published a book on California, learned that a Frenchman was staying in Yerba Buena he went to see him and discussed with him and an English agent at some length, the political and commercial importance of the bay of San Francisco. He spoke of the importance of the fact that this land might soon become English territory, since the Mexican government had borrowed a considerable amount of money from England which their government would probably use as an excuse and pretext for taking over this territory. Each conversation with the Hudson's Bay Company's agent strengthened M. de Mofras' faith in the future of the harbor, and so he advised M. Limantour, if he wished to become extremely wealthy, to secure land near the bay of San Francisco.

M. Limantour's reply was: "If you have so much confidence in its future value, why don't you attempt to acquire a grant yourself?"

"In my capacity as agent of the French government," replied M. de Mofras, "I cannot take advantage of such an opportunity."

This conversation made a deep impression on M. Limantour, who finally bought the lands, the possession of which is now in litigation. I shall discuss this purchase later on in my narrative.

While M. Limantour was living near the bay of Yerba Buena, that is from October, 1841, until the fall of 1842, he learned the history of these coastal lands from early settlers. In this way he came into contact with the most important persons living near the bay, many of whom became his close friends, for he spoke Spanish fluently enough to be able to carry on long and involved conversations with them in their own tongue.

After a sojourn of eleven months—in other words, in October, 1842—he procured a small ship from General Vallejo[2] which he named *Fanny* in honor of the general's eldest daughter. On this boat he started out with what goods he had salvaged from his wrecked vessel, visiting the harbors of Monterey, Santa Barbara, and San Pedro. By this time M. Limantour, through his commercial activities and enterprising spirit, had grown rich and acquired a large amount of property. On January 2, 1843, he entered the harbor of San Pedro and dropped anchor.

At this point certain important events that occurred in California and Mexico prior to 1842 should be mentioned. In 1835 and 1836 certain definite signs of unrest appeared in Mexican territory. Under the leadership of Don Juan Alvarado,[3] Upper California revolted and declared its independence. Mexico, which by this time had separated from Spain, believed that armed intervention was unnecessary and decided to appoint Alvarado to the governorship. By so doing Mexico hoped to open the way for the men who favored independence to unite with it.

For a time this diplomacy had the desired result. Alvarado assumed the title of governor, acknowledged the supremacy of the Mexican government, and thus ended the revolt in California. Alvarado retained this post until 1842.

Señor Don Antonio Lopez de Santa Anna had now reached the zenith of his power and was the undisputed master of Mexico. Profiting by a situation that arose through the jealousy of an official in California, Santa Anna felt that by appointing a governor of California with full powers, he would bind the territory more firmly to Mexico. He therefore appointed General Micheltorena[4] to the post of governor.

On February 11, 1842, he sent his instructions to General Micheltorena, whom shortly before he had appointed Governor of California. The Mexican treasury was, as usual, depleted, and the government was in no condition to supply the new governor with the funds needed for his office.

Micheltorena left Mexico in the summer of 1842, reaching Upper California in September. With him came four or five hundred men who scarcely deserved the name of soldiers. He lacked supplies, gold, ammunition, means of transportation, and every kind of equipment for his vessels. Forced to assume the responsibility of providing these himself, he remained for a month in southern California at the pueblo of Los Angeles. At this time M. Limantour dropped anchor in San Pedro Harbor and General Micheltorena sent him the following letter:

Los Angeles, January 8, 1843.

Dear Sir:

For nearly three months I have been prevented, owing to a shortage of supplies and equipment, from proceeding with my troops to the capital, and now find myself in an extremely precarious situation.

M. Louis Vignes,[5] one of your countrymen, has informed me of your arrival and of the fact that you have gold and supplies on board your vessel. I should be extremely grateful if you would place some of your gold and supplies at my disposal. Should you do so, in return I will give you a draft on the house of Jecker[6] and Company at Mazatlan.

I can assure you, furthermore, of a certain amount of governmental business that would be of material assistance to you in your commercial enterprises. In fact I would guarantee to exert all my influence to make your trading ventures as profitable as possible. Or if you preferred to acquire some land in this country, I could give you a grant in any place you might select, on condition that the land was not already held by some one else. I have been given extensive powers to govern the Californias, but the most pressing thing that now confronts me is to provide for my troops and to extricate myself from this embarrassing situation.

If you will be kind enough, M. Limantour, to grant my request without further delay, we can then proceed to draw up the details of an agreement that will prove mutually acceptable to both parties.

Awaiting with the keenest anticipation an early reply, I am,

Your devoted servant and sincere friend,

Micheltorena.

Limontour accepted the proposal made by the Mexican governor. The result of the conference was the following agreement, or rather series of agreements, signed by Micheltorena in his capacity as governor.

I, Joseph Près Limantour, captain of the French navy, make the following agreement with your excellency: [7]

1) I am prepared to accept the government's receipt for $4000 as payment on account of a larger amount owed me by the Mexican treasury.

2) For this receipt your excellency agrees to make over to me two unoccupied pieces of land as indicated.

3) The first of these grants lies near the pueblo of Yerba Buena, 400 Spanish yards southwest of Mr. Richardson's old home.[8] The boundaries of this grant are indicated on one of Mr. Richardson's special maps and certified by the owner and the alcalde (a complete legal description of the boundary now follows) "for a distance of about two leagues between the bank of the *estero* down to the harbor, exclusive of an area of 200 Spanish yards encircling the confines of the city proper."

I request your excellency in return for the $4000 to make over to me the two grants as indicated, with the clear understanding that I can take possession of the properties when I acquire them without being forced to submit to the existing colonial laws. It is not my idea to accept this land as a gift, but to acquire possession by purchase, so that I will have the legal right to dispose of it.

J. Limantour,
Pueblo of Los Angeles,
January 10, 1843.[9]

Governor Micheltorena replied as follows:

Los Angeles,
February 25, 1843

The claim,[10] approved by the proper authorities, entitles the French citizen, François Joseph Limantour, full rights to the following two land grants:

The first lies about a league [11] from the pueblo of Yerba Buena and some 400 yards from the house of Mr. William Richardson on the bay, extending in a straight line approximately two leagues from northeast to southwest. The second grant also of one-half league stretches from northeast to southwest to a point 200 yards beyond the circumference of the city proper.

This land, as indicated, has been selected by the aforesaid Limantour, captain in the French marine, to whom I now grant this property in consideration of services rendered, with full title.

Micheltorena.

If Limantour wins his case, he will own the finest section of San Francisco, for the city now stands on land granted him by Governor Micheltorena. However, at the present time the Mexican government is contesting his title.

The Americans believe that Limantour waited far too long before pressing his claim, and tried to avoid a lawsuit. The case has aroused considerable comment and discontent in San Francisco, where the Americans unanimously contend that his claim is without foundation, notwithstanding the important evidence disclosed in Wilson's publication.

In an issue of such magnitude, I would not venture to express my own opinion, but as a friend of Limantour I hope from the depths of my heart that he will win his suit. If he does win it, his birthplace, Lorient, will be materially enriched, since he has promised to give a large sum—a million dollars, I believe—to found a marine hospital. All French sailors should offer a prayer to Our Lady of Guérande [12] for Limantour to win his suit.

I gave Limantour the bundle of papers his lawyer asked me to deliver. He seemed quite depressed, and had little to say about his case. During the nine months I spent in Mexico I saw M. Limantour frequently and we often discussed his lawsuit. I found him invariably as reticent and quiet as he was the first day. He did not seem to question the attitude of the American government, but dismissed the matter from his mind and went about his affairs as if this unimportant case did not concern him. I recommend his splendid philosophy to anyone who finds himself in legal difficulties in Europe.

CHAPTER X

## MEXICO AND THE MEXICANS

AFTER M. LIMANTOUR, whose case interested me so deeply, departed, I still felt weary, notwithstanding my fourteen hours sleep. So I closed my door, went to bed, and slept until nine the next morning.

By the following day I felt that I had fully recuperated from the hardships of the journey. Having dressed, I now went out to make some purchases. The finest mercantile shops in Mexico are situated on what is called Calle de Plateros [1]—Silversmiths' Street. At first I imagined that after an absence of ten years I was finally back in Paris, for the dress shops along Calle de Plateros vie in splendor and luxury with those of Rue de la Paix and Rue Richelieu. This, of course, is not surprising, since all the merchants are French. I found everything carried by the finest shops of Paris; the styles are only a month late—in other words, the amount of time required to send them from Paris to Mexico City.

Although the quality and style are similar to those of Parisian articles, the prices are higher. What sells in Paris for a franc costs a dollar in Mexico City. A hat trimmed with feathers, that can be purchased for twenty-five francs in Paris, is priced in Mexico City at four times as much; that is, one hundred francs. A black taffeta dress, worth one hundred francs in France, will cost one hundred piasters, or four hundred francs in Mexico City. This same variation in price applies to all merchandise.

"What a large profit," fashionable Parisians would say. "Mexican merchants must make fortunes almost overnight."

But Mexican merchants are not so ruthless as they seem. First of all, there is an extremely high import tax on all garments; then at least a third of the merchandise is more or less damaged in transit; and, finally, prices are comparatively cheap in view of the difficulties encountered in bringing the latest Parisian creations from the Boulevard des Capucines, the Rue Royale, and the suburbs of Saint Honoré all the way to Mexico City.

I was delighted to know that I had at last found a friendly land with an abundance of good shops that supplied whatever I wanted. Mexico would lose half her charm if she became an industrial country like France.

I shopped until two o'clock in the afternoon, then decided to call at the house of Don Miguel Mosso, the wealthy owner of the vast hacienda of San Gabriel, whom we had met while traveling on the stage. This second meeting with Don Miguel confirmed my belief that he was one of the finest men I had ever met. He seemed anxious to have me know his wife and courteously arranged to have us meet in the near future.

I recall with keen joy the friends I made in Mexico, for everywhere I went I was received in the most cordial manner. I even became greatly attached to my Mexican maid, Demetrie, who was as devoted to me as if we had grown up together. Our parting was almost tragic.

Although I have been back just six months in my luxurious and beloved Paris, yet I have found no one to compare with Demetrie. The French maid I have at the present time criticizes my English accent and acts, much to the detriment of my purse, as if I were an extremely rich woman.

After shopping feverishly for two or three days, I finally found time to catch my breath and look around the city. The following day I decided to visit El Paseo.

El Paseo, as the name indicates, is the favorite promenade of the Mexicans; it is what the Champs Élysées, the Boulevard des Bois, or the Tuileries are to fashionable Parisians. I enjoyed El Paseo extremely, for everything I saw was new and strange. Of course I was in a carriage; in Mexico it is not customary to visit El Paseo on foot.

Later on, when I went there, I was usually accompanied by one of the prominent ladies of the city. I found the feminine custom of greeting one another with the hands extremely amusing, for the ladies used their fingers as rapidly as if they were giving telegraphic signals. A stranger seeing them might think all Mexican women were dumb, because while riding along the boulevard they seemed to talk only with their hands.

As I have already mentioned, I have a knack for languages, and always enjoy learning a new tongue. However, I must confess that I was unable to understand the meaning of their finger dialect, for when I attempted to decipher all the various nuances of the Mexican language as expressed in these signals, from the casual greeting to the most tender welcome, I was finally forced to renounce my studies as too complicated for a European. There were so many other beautiful things to see and enjoy in Mexico that I was soon consoled for my inability to master their mysterious signals.

The days I spent touring the city passed rapidly. Finally I made an excursion out into the country. There I visited the home of Don Manuel Eleandon, one of the richest land owners and most important financiers of Mexico City. He lived in a beautiful villa on Tambaya Hill.

Ten years ago the spot where this villa now stands was a deserted, sandy region, covered only with a little scraggly cactus. Within the short space of a month, this wilderness was transformed into a fine park; an elaborate hothouse, purchased in London, was erected on one corner of the property; it holds a profusion of exotic tropical plants, grown by skilful French gardeners.

The villa itself is of pure Italian architecture. The traveler, viewing the valuable art collection, the exquisite, rare old porcelains, and the graceful bronzes it contains, forgets America and feels that he is back in some fine old palace in Europe surrounded by old world culture.

Don Manuel, the creator of this almost miraculous beauty, has so many activities and interests that he has comparatively few opportunities to enjoy its charm. He is a plain, unassuming man who believes in making the most of what he has acquired. Although his tremendous energy and application have made him a man of vast influence, yet at the same time he does an extraordinary amount of good, which is kept secret at his personal request.

His position has not been entirely a pleasant one, however, and he has been made to suffer at the hands of his countrymen. Mexicans possess, to a pronounced degree, a feeling of envy. The possessions of others distress them, for wealth is their main source of enjoyment and the thing that above all else they strive for. According to Mexican ideas, what their fellow men amass rarely comes from lawful sources. This fact explains the strange disfavor with which Don Manuel is regarded, in spite of his many charities.

Don Manuel owns a large factory at Orizaba and has many prosperous haciendas in the vicinity of Córdoba, Guadalajara, Milpas, and San Andrés. He is also the largest shareholder, as well as one of the discoverers, of the silver mines at Real del Monte.

The employees, craftsmen, and workers of all kinds who depend on him for their existence and livelihood are so numerous that he must have at least fifteen thousand persons on his payroll. Indirectly dependent on him are some five hundred families of these workers.

Notwithstanding the number of men whom he supports, Don Manuel is, as I have said, unpopular. He is openly accused of being a usurer who speculates on the instability of the ever-changing Mexican government. I do not know on what these charges are based; I do know that they cannot be proved by facts. The Mexican republic, owing to the frequent change of government, is constantly in a state of political turmoil; as a result, the central government is somewhat corrupt.

National economy lies too far beyond the range of purely feminine interests for me to enter into discussions of a political nature, but the fact remains that every new government in Mexico is seriously handicapped by a shortage of gold. Drastic reforms in national economy, which no one has the courage to undertake, are desperately needed. Until these are made, the government, if it is to exist, must receive funds from outside sources. Government officials, however, are to blame for the fact that the public loans lack adequate backing and that the treasury is in a chaotic condition that would wreck any normal business venture.

Although capitalistic speculation in government securities may be legal, yet it is extremely hazardous. And if speculators who may at times have profited, lose heavily, the blame falls on them rather than on the shoulders of those who are responsible for the depleted condition of the national treasury. Obviously, any loans made to the Mexican government, backed by a lean treasury, are financially unsound. So how can capitalists be expected to have any confidence in a government that cannot put its own finances on a secure basis?

According to the latest reports, bonds of the Mexican government are not worth more than one-tenth of their par value. Thus those who have invested in these securities cannot hope to get back more than one hundred thousand piasters out of every million loaned the government.

From any angle the financial outlook in Mexico is serious; there is no assurance that back payments on bonds will be met, and interest on them is now being paid out of capital. Thus capitalists cannot be guaranteed proper security for their loans to the government and so are forced to protect themselves by asking extraordinary concessions. These demands are so great that although Mexico is now on the gold standard, the government cannot balance the budget. Yet Mexican officials make no effort to retrench, hoping through frequent fluctuations in the exchange to make back some of the deficit.

This has thrown a heavy burden on the treasury, and so long continued and repeated has been this abuse that each new government that comes into office is forced to liquidate the affairs of its predecessor. When this occurs, any former contracts or agreements that have not been consummated in a sound manner are valueless. This fact is well known to the capitalistic class, whose efforts to protect themselves against such contingencies are called usury.

Agreements thus made by capitalists with the Mexican government are not based on sound financial procedure; it would be unfair, however, to judge them according to our own laws or customs. Nor must the fact be overlooked that Mexican finances need, above all else, organization and sound management, for the entire economic machinery of the state is defective and corrupt. Thus Mexico is faced with a gold shortage and the lack of a sound method of replenishing the exchequer.

The same situation has occurred, and financial crises have arisen many times before, in other lands. Even Napoleon, the great organizer and financial genius of the early nineteenth century, was forced during the First Consulship to procure large advances from leading capitalists in a manner very similar to that used in Mexico, and yet French speculators who came to the aid of Napoleon were considered to have rendered invaluable services to their country.

CHAPTER XI

## CHAPULTEPEC PARK. POPOCATEPETL. DEL MUERTO. THE FESTIVAL OF FLOWERS

AFTER visiting Señor Eleandon's charming villa, I went to see Chapultepec Park, a sight that invariably inspires in the visitor, even in travelers who have already seen the glories of Tahiti and the Sandwich Islands, an extraordinary sense of wonder and amazement. Apparently, the trees have not been disturbed since time immemorial; from their limbs hang long, festive streams of white moss, as grotesque as the beards of venerable griffins. In fact, the magnificence and splendor of the luxuriant vegetation that rises on the heights surrounding the castle, belie description. The old castle in the park is now being used as a military college.

During my visit to the Mexican capital, this park was my favorite retreat; almost every evening I went there to revel in its beauty. My customary walk was to what was called El Molino del Rey— the King's Mill—a place famous for a battle between the Mexican and North American forces.

I often wondered why this park had not been converted into the governor's official residence. The property has been neglected for the past hundred years and some parts are entirely overgrown. This is especially deplorable, since it is only about a mile from the capital with which it is connected by a fairly good road.

The park,[1] as its name implies, is extremely old. The first to enjoy the shade of its gigantic trees were the wives of the Aztec kings. Prior to the Spanish régime this was also the retreat of the great Montezuma. The ruins of the women's baths that were destroyed by the soldiers of Cortés and Pizarro are still plainly visible. And at the foot of the lofty mountains on which the king's castle originally stood can be seen the crude bas reliefs, considered so remarkable at that day.

On the site of the old Aztec palace rises the castle, long used by the viceroys as a summer residence. Because of its location, this building is comparatively easy to defend. During the recent war with the United States in 1846, the Americans besieged this stronghold, which was defended only by the pupils at the military schools and some soldiers from the local barracks.

The besieged, however, put up a stubborn resistance, and in one of the rooms are shown the portraits of the courageous lads who lost their lives in its defense.[2] The Americans, too, suffered a large number of casualties in this battle, and Mexico would never have been conquered so easily if half as much resistance had been shown in other battles as at Chapultepec.

This skirmish at Chapultepec Park was purely incidental to the main Mexican-American War; but if Mexicans had fought as stubbornly in other parts of Mexico when the war first broke out as they did here, the outcome might have been quite different. The Americans early in the campaign concentrated their activities in the South, where the Mexicans offered comparatively little resistance, bending every effort, as did the French in the so-called Pastry War,[3] on capturing the enemy's guns at San Juan de Ulúa, besieging Vera Cruz, landing a regiment of soldiers at the latter port, and launching their main Mexican campaign from this point.

The castle stands on a high hill, surrounded by a park. The steep, winding road leading up to it is so thickly overgrown with grass that it was quite obvious that Mexico had very little interest in attracting tourists to this historic spot. From the hill one of the finest panoramas in the world is visible. To the right lies the city of Zumpango with its vast gardens and cozy houses, and beyond, glimpses of a picturesque little village. Scarcely visible in the distance are San Angelo and San Augustín; more readily perceptible are the capital, Mexico City, with its magnificent buildings, broad, straight avenues, and innumerable domes and spires, the shimmering waters of Jeroco,[4] dotted with thousands of water fowl, and finally, on the horizon, the two majestic volcanoes of Popocateptl[5] and Del Muerto,[6] with their snow-capped peaks towering toward the skies.

The former, which is cone-shaped like the majority of volcanoes, is the loftier and more imposing of the two mountains. The second has quite a different contour, resembling more closely a volcanic overflow of glacial activity than a typical volcano, standing out in the distance like a great ghost decked in a snow-white shroud. This

volcano is usually known as Del Muerto, although its real name is
the Indian term, Iztaccihuatl. These two mountain peaks, which are
visible throughout the entire valley, were an unfailing source of
interest on my daily excursions and I was never tired of gazing at
their grandeur.

A friend urged me to make the trip to the villages of Amecameca
and San Nicholás de los Ranchos that lie at the foot of the mountain
and from there climb Popocatepetl. Although I felt a keen desire to
do so, I finally decided the trip was beyond my strength.

Popocatepetl, which is nearly as high as Dawalghiri and Chimborazo,[7] is one of the loftiest mountains in the world, its peak being
nearly 18,000 feet above sea level and 4000 feet higher than Mont
Blanc. The crater contains a large number of sulphur baths that
were originally built by the same Mexican concern that now man-
ages them. While they were being constructed a number of workmen were obliged to live inside the crater.

All ice used by Mexico City, Puebla, and other neighboring cities,
comes from Popocatepetl. Although higher than Del Muerto, its
slope is easier to climb, and the peak of the latter has not yet been
reached. In 1852, however, an attempt was made by several Frenchmen who had lived at least ten years in Mexico City. Herr von R.
gives the following account of their experiences.

"Upon our first attempt we reached the pyramids of Cholula.[8]
This hill was one of the favorite retreats of the natives, who built
a temple that has since been destroyed and replaced by a church,
on its summit. The ascent of this hill is extremely difficult, for the
soil has been removed and replaced by great walls of masonry. This
remarkable and extensive construction reveals the innate power of
the early Mexicans.

"Our visit to this pyramid occupied one entire day. In the evening we returned to Puebla; there we took horses and traveled to
the delightful city of Atlixco. It was at the foot of Popocatepetl that
we had first conceived the idea of attempting to climb its slope, but
our plan was not so easy to execute, as permission had to be secured
from Puebla. This delayed us for another two nights and days.
During this time we were forced to sleep on the ground and eat

with wooden forks devised by the inventive powers of the ablest member of our party.

"Permission finally having been secured, we left on March fifth at four o'clock in the morning. For a time the way led through a deep but beautiful gorge thickly covered with pine forests. We then reached enormous blocks of lava. The higher we climbed, the thinner grew the trees, until we caught a glimpse of the enormous peak we hoped to reach, capped with its great glacier, glistening in the sun.

"After climbing six hours, we reached the small village of Tlamacas at ten o'clock, where we rested for nearly an hour. Some fifteen hundred feet beyond Tlamacas every vestige of vegetation had entirely disappeared. At last we found ourselves at the foot of a great, gray mountain whose sides were covered with sand, and whose cone-shaped peak was covered with snow. Up its steep slope we climbed in a diagonal direction. The trip was quite dangerous because the horses, unable to get a firm foothold on the sand, were constantly slipping. On this steep and dangerous trail covered with lava and gravel, our horses grew dizzy. Finally the poor animals refused to go any farther. Only by considerable effort were we able to make them move again, and even then they stopped every twelve or fifteen feet, trembling violently.

"Finally, after half an hour we reached a large block of rock covered with a wooden cross. This indicated the point beyond which travelers could proceed only on foot. After sending our animals back to Tlamacas, we began to ascend the steep peak.

"For the first hour we climbed laboriously up the slope, which was covered with sand mixed with ice and pitched off abruptly at an angle of forty or forty-five degrees, making us lose our foothold and fall down. After a time we reached some thick, white snowbanks. The atmosphere had become so thin that we were obliged to stop every six or eight steps and catch our breath. The higher we climbed, the weaker we became. About four o'clock in the afternoon, almost exhausted by a quarter of an hour of this fatiguing climb, we reached the edge of an immense funnel-shaped crater, whose outside diameter measured some six thousand feet. The inside diameter of the crater was nine hundred feet at its base and the depth two thousand feet.

"The first view of this crater was tremendously impressive. At various points smoke emerged, accompanied by a noise resembling steam escaping from the vents of thousands of kettles. The largest and most numerous bursts of steam came not from the edge but from the center of the crater. The smoke had a definite odor of sulphur [9] which, as it was wafted through the air, caused the climbers to experience a feeling of chilliness and fatigue not unlike that felt in an attack of seasickness. Our heads seemed heavy, breathing became difficult, and our stomachs were upset. The skin of one of my companions even broke out in tiny eruptions, while others were so overcome by inertia that only by exercising every ounce of strength and will power were they able to move. This state of affairs lasted until we were well down below snow level again.

"After climbing a steep footpath for almost five hundred feet, we discovered a workmen's hut built of boards and stones, which stood on a firm foundation of rock. In this hut, which was about twelve feet long, five feet wide, and four feet high, we spent what proved to be a most unpleasant night, eight of us being packed so closely together that we were unable to stretch our legs. We shivered with cold, for the fire that burned in the hut smoked so badly that we were nearly suffocated. Here we waited impatiently for day to dawn.

"Now and again a noise resembling thunder was heard, indicating that the hidden fire which filled the monstrous stomach of sand and rock inside the crater had erupted, but had not reached the surface. At any moment we expected the volcano to awake from its profound sleep.

"The floor of our hut was one of the horizontal slabs that formed the inside of the crater's mouth. This opening, which has a depth at this point of some fifteen hundred feet, slants off at an angle of thirty degrees. In the hut we were able to secure some rest, however, despite the penetrating cold.

"Finally day dawned. As we left our shelter the peak with the sun just rising behind it was visible. The horizon was not entirely clear, yet we could see for miles in every direction. In good weather probably Calaya,[10] some two hundred miles away, could be seen.

"Forty miles beyond on the plain lay Mexico City, where even the houses were faintly distinguishable. Toward the east we looked out over broad plains, toward the north on Mineleas Mountain,[11] and toward the west at the Orizaba range. On the south and south-west we gazed toward the warmer hill country of Matamoros and Cuernavaca that lie in the direction of Acapulco.

"After enjoying the stupendous panorama for a long time, we went back to our hut for coffee, the refreshment our stomachs craved. We then began to descend into the crater. One hundred and fifty feet below the top we were forced to use ropes carried for this purpose by one of the mountaineers, for the crater was so steep that we were unable to climb down without some support. At this dangerous point the guide fastened the ropes under our arms and one by one we were lowered slowly to the next level. In less treacherous places we climbed down by holding on to the rope with one hand and a stick with the other, a method of travel which proved satisfactory so long as we remained near the rope and kept looking into the crater. But, with a cavity over twelve hundred feet in depth far below, the sensation, to say the least, was unpleasant.

"In this manner we climbed down for a distance of approximately three hundred feet. Here we found a secure foothold once more and were able to step from rock to rock until we reached solid ground. At this lower level we discovered several large openings [12] in the rocks from which steam gushed forth with such force that stones as large as hens' eggs were thrown a distance of about thirty feet. When we placed some of these stones near one of the openings, they were soon coated with sulphur that crumbled to dust at the slightest touch. Near these steam-holes the earth was hot and covered with sulphur water, yet only a few steps away we saw ice an inch thick.

"After inspecting these phenomena and securing samples of the sulphur, lava, and stones, we started to climb out of the crater. The return was as difficult as the descent had been. I remained behind the party in order to feast my eyes on the magnificent spectacle, and

was so stiff when I reached the next level that I was speechless for
more than a mile.

"At eleven o'clock we began the journey down the mountain. This
was made partly on foot and partly on another unmentionable part
of our bodies. Half an hour after starting down, we were back in
Tlamacas. Having eaten nothing that day, I was so hungry and
exhausted by the time I reached the town that I did not have enough
energy to enjoy the beauty and sublimity of the landscape. An hour
after leaving Tlamacas, we were resting comfortably in the house
of a friend. Despite our recent experience, we felt that the trip had
been well worth the hardships we had suffered."

From this account of an adventure it is obvious that I am not
exaggerating when I say that the trip to the volcano requires the
strength of a superwoman.

The season when I climbed the mountain was the time of the
great flower festival. I had already heard a great deal about this
festival, which is half Spanish and half Indian in origin, and the
theme of many interesting legends. At the time of the flower festival
everyone is requested by the government to exhibit on the streets
and in the houses pictures of the Virgin adorned with flowers. This
request is obeyed with enthusiasm and when the great day arrives,
even the most aristocratic Mexicans leave their homes and mingle
with the crowds in Puente de la Lena to participate in the festival
of flowers. This occasion also affords pious Mexican women another opportunity to attend church services.

The flower festival has become a tradition with the women of
this beautiful land, who enjoy the fiesta to such an extent that only
with difficulty can they be persuaded to return to their homes. At
no other place in the world can so many flowers be seen at one
time as at this Mexican floral display. Masses of tulips, hyacinths,
roses, carnations, and lilies, are on display, filling the air with their
fragrance. The women pelt one another with blossoms, and wear
flowers in place of jewels as necklaces and bracelets. They come in
gay crowds to see the flowers, carrying away as many bouquets as
their arms can hold. They leave the gaiety of the streets only long
enough to adorn an altar or place a rose or carnation in their hair.

This passion for flowers is characteristic, as well, of the lowest type of Mexican. Like Ophelia, the entire Aztec race would pick violets in their last hours. Every humble dwelling reveals in some simple way the innate love of its Mexican owner for them. Every shabby Indian hut has its roses, every public square its dahlias and jasmine, and every grave in a year's time is a veritable bower of bloom. On feast days every house and church is lavishly decorated with them. The altars are then in the truest meaning of the word laden with riches; the stone pavements are strewn with blossoms; on both sides of the street the doors and windows of the houses display festoons and garlands of flowers.

CHAPTER XII

FIRE AND FEVER. HENRIETTE SONTAG

AFTER I had been in Mexico City about fourteen days and while the air was still filled with the fragrance of flowers, suddenly late one night the familiar fire gong rang.

I thought I must be dreaming. Could it be true that this dire menace of California, which at least had the excuse of wooden houses to burn, was about to pursue me among all these handsome stone edifices?

About an hour after the alarm sounded I heard the voice of the doctor, who was knocking at my door, call: "Fire, fire!"

I had not been mistaken; what I had heard while I was sleeping was actually the fire gong. Trembling from head to foot, I put on my dressing gown and went to the door. The fire alarm, which brought back many tragic memories, made me so weak that I had scarcely the strength to open the door.

The doctor burst into the room. He had not had time to pack all his things and so had tied them in a blanket, which he was carrying over his shoulder.

"Hurry, hurry," he urged. "Throw your things out of the window. There is no time to lose. Fire has broken out in the hotel!"

"Where?"

"I don't know exactly where. But you know how fire spreads. Flee, or in another half hour we will be roasted alive!"

Apparently the doctor was thinking of the houses in San Francisco, but my thoughts were wholly on the fire of the moment. Then both of us lost our heads. We pulled the trunk out in the middle of the room and rushed to pack whatever we could find. When the trunk was full, I began to open the various wardrobes. In one of them I discovered all my dresses, the most important part of a traveler's wardrobe. I now realized that I had packed only utterly useless things. So the trunk had to be opened and in place of odds and ends, silk dresses and shawls were placed inside. Everything was handled so hastily that our hands did almost as much damage as fire would have done. Fortunately the manager of the hotel, Señor Labardie, came to my room to reassure me.

"But the house is on fire," I cried like a crazy woman.

"Madame," replied Labardie, "you are frightened because you think this is like some of the fires you have seen in California. But Mexican houses are built in a more substantial manner. The fire is in another part of the building; if properly handled it will have considerable difficulty reaching this wing. Just keep calm and don't worry. I will let you know when it is time to leave the hotel."

Since we were not the only guests he had to quiet, he left us and went on to see our neighbors, who were equally frightened.

I was now alone with the doctor and one of his friends from the city, who had just joined us. Anxious to see how grave the danger was, I walked around the entire house on the outside balcony, where I was seized by another attack of hysterics brought on by the situation. This could be attributed partly to fright and partly to amusement. The balcony was crowded with half-clothed guests who presented a most ludicrous appearance. Some lacked trousers or had forgotten their shoes; others were struggling to save their baggage and threatening to knock down anyone who got in their way; many of the ladies were in their nightgowns; some were sobbing and wringing their hands.

I touched my head instinctively to find out whether I was dreaming. Although I was hatless and my hair was in disorder, yet at least I was not a scarecrow like so many of the women.

"When you write about your travels," said the doctor, "don't forget this."

"No pen can do justice to the scene," I replied, "it requires the brush of a painter."

In the meantime, the fire had completed its destructive work. Since fires seldom occur in Mexico City, no provision is made for handling them, and in emergencies soldiers and citizens are forced to act as firemen. There are no fire brigades and no fire engines; the latter, however, is a more serious lack than the former.

In front of our hotel was a well from which the water was drawn in buckets, the buckets were then passed from hand to hand and, as everyone dropped part of the water, by the time the pails reached the fire they were empty. Notwithstanding, the participants in this extraordinary scene displayed a vast amount of feverish activity.

The measures taken in Mexico City to prevent theft were highly commendable; the streets being guarded on both sides by troops. In all fairness to President Santa Anna, it should be said that after his election robbery was almost unknown. Anyone caught in the act or convicted of robbery under his régime, was hanged, a penalty that brought about a marked decrease in crime.

A high wall having brought them to a stop, the flames finally died out of their own accord. By that time it was already five o'clock in the morning. The guards then left and the volunteer fire brigade that had spilled so much water departed. Order having been restored, the guests went back to bed. I sent the doctor to his room, then attempted to get some rest myself. I slept fitfully, however, and dreamed of fire.

What damage the conflagration had done was comparatively slight; only the kitchen where it started was destroyed. After the disaster, the guests were obliged to dine outside the hotel at the Café Coquelet, which was run by the brother of our manager.

The evening after the fire occurred, a gâla performance of the opera was scheduled to take place at what was originally known as the Sonnambula, but was now called the Santa Anna Theatre. That evening the popular Sontag, who invariably attracted a large and fashionable audience whenever she appeared, was to sing. Sontag never failed to create a sensation in her rôles, and the élite of Mexico City invariably thronged to hear all of her performances. In fact, so great was her popularity that before each of her appearances there was a great crush near the main door, where her admirers waited hours for her arrival. For two weeks, opera fans had been anxiously looking forward to this evening, for only that morning had she reached Mexico City.

Five or six performances of the opera had already been given without Sontag, but so far I had not seen any of them. After my unpleasant experiences the night before, I felt the need of some form of diversion. As Don Miguel Mosso had offered me a seat in his loge any night I cared to attend the opera, I decided to accept for that evening. As he was unable to accompany me in person, he sent his carriage with his nephew as escort.

The opera house in Mexico City is as large, possibly larger than the leading one in Paris, and can accomodate more than three thousand persons. Each loge is elaborately decorated and furnished to suit the taste of its owner. Upholsterers are employed to hang curtains and change upholstery, place mirrors, provide comfortable chairs, sofas, and cushions, and convert each loge into a miniature drawing room.

When the curtain falls between acts, everyone leaves his seat and goes out to the lobby to smoke cigarettes. No one seems to mind the smoke, for in Mexico, as in Spain, everyone smokes.

A Mexican theatre presents a novel sight. The women, covered with jewels, recline on sofas and large armchairs in their loges. There are flowers everywhere. Even without the aid of mirrors the ladies invariably arrange these flowers with exquisite taste in their hair. Roses and carnations are worn by the women behind the ears, and often removed and waved like handkerchiefs, or gracefully used as a headdress.

When I entered the loge Don Miguel Mosso had so graciously offered me, the overture had not yet begun. But the rustling sound in the loges was music to which I was quite unaccustomed—music one could never forget—that of waving fans.

At least a hundred ladies were fanning themselves with a grace and delicacy even more pleasing than the coquettish charm of Spanish ladies. The fans rustled, purred, and crackled like silk embroidery. The rapidity with which the ladies closed them was amazing, as were also the coquettish flirtations they carried on with beautiful fiery eyes behind the fans. I can never see loges in a theatre without recalling the coy airs of these Mexican coquettes.

The orchestra began the overture. The curtain rose. The artist sang magnificently. How remarkable it is that Henriette Sontag, although close to fifty, still retains her appearance of youth and her superb voice. This was not only the first, but also the last time I saw her. She sang so enchantingly, so divinely, that little did I dream when I left the delightful performance and went back to my hotel where the fire had recently occurred, that this popular prima donna would soon meet a tragic fate.

CHAPTER XIII

SAN AGUSTÍN

WHILE the kitchen of the Grande Société Hotel was being rebuilt, while I was reveling in Sontag's songs, and while I was visiting the outskirts of Mexico City, the feast of San Agustín, one of the most important festivals in all Mexico, took place. For two weeks before this celebration no one talked of anything else.

San Agustín, where the fête was held, is an extremely beautiful spot four hours beyond Mexico City. It was here, during the Spanish régime, that many wealthy citizens maintained summer residences. After the Declaration of Independence took place in Mexico, the city lost a large part of its population, and when I was there it came to life only during Pentecost, when a general exodus took place from the Mexican capital to San Agustín, headquarters of the fête. There, on the holy days consecrated to the great saint, every gambling house was filled to capacity.

The Mexicans are the most indefatigable gamblers in the world, and during the four feast days of Saint Augustine, that is, from Sunday to Wednesday, they feel free to indulge this major passion. As a matter of fact, there are actually eight days of this freedom, since they engage in games of chance night and day. During my trip from Acapulco to Mexico City, I saw gambling in every Indian village.

At Chilpancingo I saw the entire garrison, officers as well as soldiers, playing cards. In fact, this pastime is universally popular on most of the islands of the Pacific. The New Zealanders are notorious gamblers, and the Kanakas of Tahiti and the Sandwich Islands stake everything they possess on cards. Whenever they have a moment's leisure they gamble, no matter where they may be. The games played are extremely simple; the players merely draw cards and say: "Pair, or not a pair." However, they are quick to learn any European gambling games when the opportunity offers, and find excellent teachers in the sailors, who often remain weeks or even months in the harbors of Auckland, Papeete, and Honolulu. But the heaviest gambling and the highest stakes I have ever seen were in San Francisco, the city that prides itself on the number of foreigners it attracts.

We went down from Mexico City to witness the Feast of San Agustín. The Saturday evening before Pentecost, crowds of people, traveling by wagon, horse, or on foot, poured out of the capital toward this gambling center. Every street was crowded with gay Mexicans. Card games were going on everywhere; every house, in fact, appeared to have been converted into a gambling den.

Playing went on not only in the houses, but even in the streets, main plazas, courtyards, and gardens, wherever space could be found. Gamblers sat on the ground, on planks, on stools, on tables. Everyone had with him his savings for an entire year. The banker brought his millions, the peon his few piasters. In some places the stakes were for gold alone; at other places, for only one or two piasters or centavos. The bankers, large or small, formed what were called discount companies. They knew the financial status of every player, and lent money with nice discrimination, from twenty to a thousand piasters.

Gambling is like a fever that recurs annually, one from which there is no escape. The leading gambling houses of Mexico City were connected with the most popular bars in the center of town, but these were never visited, at least openly, by respectable people. At San Agustín, however, all the people gambled, both for the sake of the sport and in order to watch the crowds. Everyone felt he must win or lose something.

Not even the attachés, or members of the diplomatic corps, refrained from playing at this time, and although they seldom gambled during the year, they indulged in this sport during the four feast days of San Agustín. At the various tables there could be seen young men wearing the latest French fashions, officers in elaborate uniforms, rancheros in picturesque costumes, and women who first watched and finally joined the noisy crowds at the tables, playing almost furtively and in silence for a time, then boldly placing their gold on the green-topped table.

The urge to gamble at San Agustín [1] and take at least some part in the festivities is so deeply ingrained in the Mexican character that those who are unable to spend four days away from the capital authorize others to act in their behalf. Thus visitors play, not only with their own funds, but with gold given them by friends to use for their gain.

Often gamblers who start for San Agustín have their pockets full of gold pieces, supplied by various members of the family. The ten-year-old boy rifles the contents of his toy bank; the grandfather sets aside part of his annuity; everyone contributes something. The calmness and deliberateness with which Mexicans, and, in general, players of Spanish extraction, wager even large sums of money is striking. As they play, their faces do not give the slightest indication whether they are winning or losing. The unfortunate friend who may be wagering his last coin will never see anything that suggests joy on the face of his opponent.

The Mexican who loses leaves his table, strolls off to one side, and with the utmost nonchalance smokes a cigarette, just as if he had won. The sight of a sinister or unfriendly face at a table is unusual, unless it is that of a foreigner. If an exclamation of joy or dismay is heard, it invariably comes from a Frenchman, German, Englishman, American, or other foreigner.

Notwithstanding the extremely high stakes involved, the bankers do not cheat their customers, but work fairly, conscientiously, and honestly. Stakes of eighteen or twenty thousand piasters are not unusual; gambling at Baden Baden, Hamburg, and other important German cities falls far behind that of San Agustín.

In 1854, the year I was in Mexico City, gold flowed literally in streams. On Saturday, Sunday, and Monday the banks often face losses amounting to several millions. Then on Monday evening the luck suddenly changes; bankers were often fortunate enough to win back by Tuesday what they had lost during the first three days, and even make heavy profits.

There are many interesting places in and near San Agustín. In the morning during fiesta week, short trips were often made by carriage, horse, or foot to the outskirts of the city. At dusk, dances were also occasionally held in the fields, in which not only the local belles and buxom country girls, but also the fashionable, richly-jeweled ladies participated. Later on a formal ball was held in a large, beautiful room.

There were other diversions, too. Probably the most popular, after gambling, was the cockfight. Among a pleasure-loving race like the Mexicans, they provide an easy way to lose money. In Mexico a fighting cock is as valuable as a thoroughbred horse, and these feathered aristocrats have no idea of the large amounts staked on their pugilistic talents. President Santa Anna, who is an ardent supporter of cockfights, has lost large sums in this pastime.

While we were still in San Agustín, suddenly, on Wednesday morning of fiesta week, a hideous rumor that shook the city like a thunderbolt circulated: cholera! As this ominous word passed swiftly from lip to lip, the visitors began to run as far as possible from the place where the cholera was known to have broken out. The rumor was accompanied by as much confusion as if a bomb were dropped among a flock of birds. The gamblers forgot they had placed their gold on the green table. Men and women who were traveling in their private carriages forgot they had started for San Agustín. Riders forgot they had horses. No one knew where he was going, but merely knew that he must escape from the cholera.

And yet the cholera spread its web over the fleeing Mexicans much as a spider spins one to catch its prey. Personally, I felt as if I were about to pay the penalty for my visit to foreign lands and that I, too, as well as the earlier victims of the cholera, would meet the avenging angel that hovered over the earth.

So I joined the crowd that was rushing back to Mexico City. The terror could not have been greater if a band of Indians had attacked the gamblers at San Agustín and scalped several of them.

Yet many would infinitely prefer to have lost their scalps rather than to face cholera. The crisis, however, clearly revealed the grip of the gambling fever, for many professional and amateur players, scoffing at the thought of cholera, refused for a time to leave their tables.

"Why worry?" one of them remarked. "The cholera will never come this far; anyway it's no worse than yellow fever." And so at San Agustín many continued to gamble feverishly until late that Wednesday night.

Meanwhile, fresh rumors of an alarming new number of cholera cases continued to reach the players but they merely shrugged their shoulders and did not even deign to reply when warned of the danger. Finally, their courage began to wane. Then, as the night progressed, fear of the terrible disease gradually gripped even the gamblers.

By the time day dawned, the face of every player revealed unmistakable signs of consternation and fear. At least one of these began to scream; his face became distorted and white, and, gripped by convulsions, he fell to the ground.

"He was always a poor loser," remarked one of the wags.

The "poor loser" was taken away and died within an hour. Soon a second, then a third cholera victim was carried from the room. By this time the situation had become alarming. At a large dinner party that lasted until three o'clock in the morning, the guests heard the tragic news that the great gambler, Monsieur Coquelet, was dying.

This information had a depressing effect on the others. By eleven o'clock in the morning the city was as desolate as if it had been raided by enemy soldiers.

## Chapter XIV

## CHOLERA. NUESTRO AMO

THROUGHOUT the entire day following the evacuation of San Agustín, frightened crowds streamed into Mexico City, spreading fear and terror as they went. Many returned from the plague-stricken metropolis only in time to lie down on their beds and die. In the great capital death snatched its victims with incredible rapidity on all sides. Those returning to it to escape cholera brought the disease with them, contaminating it everywhere. It seemed almost as if the curse of God, as in Biblical times, had fallen on a city steeped in sin. For six long weeks the dread disease raged throughout Mexico City. Yet outwardly the place gave slight indication of the real horror and extent of the epidemic.

Religious observances in Mexico are so salient a part of the national character that no Christian will face death without the solace of the final rites of the church, if it is possible to secure them. And so, when the church bells toll at any hour of the day or night, everyone knows that the final sacraments of the Catholic church are being said for the dying. As they ring it is customary for those hearing them to kneel and bow their heads in prayer. The observance of this religious ceremony is so universal in Mexico that prayers are offered for the departing soul not only by the casual pedestrian but even by merchants and entire families who emerge from shops or homes and in the streets join those who kneel in prayer. Everyone, from elderly men down to children scarcely able to walk, devoutly observes this custom. Everyone, whether bent on business or pleasure, stops at this solemn time to add his "Nuestro Amo"—Our Lord— on bended knees.

Priests bringing the final sacraments of the church to those about to depart this mortal life usually travel in humble conveyances when going to the poor, but in handsome carriages escorted by torch bearers when visiting the rich. During the tragic days of the cholera epidemic, the heavily-gilded carriages drawn by two white mules, that so often carried the holy sacraments to the sick, were never seen. In place of these few official conveyances, dozens of plain carriages were hastily secured for emergency use by the clergy.

In every quarter of the city as the plague spread, bells tolling for the dead were heard simultaneously. This situation made a deep impression, even on agnostics, for it was impossible to watch processions of priests, funeral coaches, and torch bearers, and to listen to church bells and litanies, without deep emotion.

During the epidemic many foreigners as well as Mexicans contracted the disease. The French colony in particular lost so many of its members, and those who escaped grew so despondent, that every French resident in the capital left his own affairs to come to the aid of these French sufferers, aiding all, whether rich or poor. Conditions in Mexico City were much like those that existed in Barcelona, Warsaw, and Paris during the cholera epidemic of 1833, when human effort was powerless to stem the tide of the disease, which broke out on all sides with such rapidity that nothing could check its force.

Many members of the French colony, as I have already said, died of cholera. Even the diplomatic corps was seriously affected, and of the ten or fifteen members of the foreign staff who were in Mexico City during the epidemic, eight contracted the disease and two died.

Most cases of illness and death, however, occurred among those who had attended the feast of San Agustín. The two great opera companies that were appearing at the capital lost many members in the epidemic; the bass, Rossi,[1] the tenor, Pozzolini, and Sontag,[2] poor Sontag who had gone with such enthusiasm to San Agustín, all died at the peak of their fame.

During the illness of these particular artists, the cholera was accompanied by peculiar complications. After the crisis passed and the sick artists began to recover, there was widespread rejoicing in the gloom-stricken city over their supposed recovery. But this joy was premature. After a convalescence lasting about fourteen days, these noted members of the opera developed an insidious fever that in the end proved fatal.

The profound grief felt over the death of these great artists, who were mourned throughout the city, was indicative of their universal popularity; the funeral services held in their honor were almost like those accorded persons of royal birth. Every carriage in the city turned out for their funerals—although its occupants by so doing flirted with death itself—to pay homage to the beloved operatic stars.

Among the mourners were the President of the Republic, the Minister of State, the various ambassadors, and the leading citizens of the capital. Others, who could not attend in person, sent representatives. The fellow artists of both opera companies laid aside their personal animosities at this time to render homage to their great rivals whom the angel of death called. The remains of the famous artists were placed in the pantheon at Santa Paula. Later, however, the body of Count Rossi was removed to Europe by a member of his family.

Many guests of the Grand Société Hotel, in which I was then living, contracted cholera at this time. Oddly enough, the plague seemed to concentrate on the upper floor, where the airiest rooms, overlooking the terrace which was planted with flowers and shrubs like the hanging gardens of Semiramis, were located. The first floor, where I had my room, did not have this same delightful outlook.

Although I tried to remain as cool and collected as possible when the plague reached our hotel, yet I had a strong premonition that I would contract the disease and so I remained quietly indoors. Then one day, after I had spent the previous night at the bedside of a sick neighbor, I too fell ill. I felt the first symptoms of the disease about four o'clock in the morning. I rang the bell frantically, and a servant opened the door. "Cholera!" she cried when she saw me, and fled without offering to help me.

Fortunately, Dr. Jourdanet arrived a few moments later. He brought help so quickly and looked after me so efficiently that I was soon out of danger. In fact, the expressions of kindliness and sympathy on the part of all my friends were touching.

M. Limantour, who was so ill with cholera that he could not leave his own bed, sent me a large feather mattress, a luxury that was almost unknown in the mild climate of Mexico City and that was invaluable during a siege of sickness.

Many foreigners who were living on the first floor left the hotel hastily when they learned that the plague, which had broken out in the rooms above, had finally knocked at my door on the first floor. As a matter of fact, a general exodus of every guest in the place who had not been ill soon took place, though the manager remained at his post. No one else, however, contracted the disease. Within a few days I was well again and cholera, having left his calling card only at my door on the first floor, disappeared from the hotel.

Chapter XV

## PHYSICAL CHARACTERISTICS OF MEXICO CITY. THE CHURCHES. THE GOVERNOR'S PALACE. THE MOUNTAIN ACADEMY. THE MINT. THE PICTURE GALLERY. THE TREASURE ROOM. MEXICAN ANTIQUITIES

UPON recovering from my illness, I spent the remaining weeks of my visit learning something about Mexico City and the surrounding country. A certain amount of activity and excitement is imperative, I must confess, to keep me in high spirits; nothing bores me more than too much peace and quiet.

The finest architecture in any Mexican or Spanish city is found in its churches. This holds true of Mexico City where the leading edifice is the cathedral.[1] This magnificent structure dates from the time of the Conquest of Mexico by Cortés, that is, from the second half of the sixteenth century. The façade of the cathedral is quite imposing, on the whole, although some of the details are both weak and architecturally incorrect. The interior of the cathedral resembles those of the cathedrals of Spain, with their lavish display of wealth. The ornamentation on the altar was originally solid silver, but later plated silver was substituted.

In Mexico City all the major important feast days are celebrated in the cathedral. After Mexico became a republic, some thirty of these celebrations were eliminated; but two or three still take place every week. In Mexico City, as in Rome, when celebrations are held all work stops. Incidentally, Rome is the only city in the world that has more churches than Mexico City, which has 180,000 inhabitants—20,000 more than Rome. The Order of St. Francis, one of the largest and richest religious orders in the world, had at one time not less than seven extremely rich churches in Mexico City.

One of the most fashionable I visited was La Profesa,[2] which draws the élite of the city, especially the women, who remain within for long periods, rendering homage to Our Lord.

Another point of interest is the magnificent convent of Merced, an edifice built in the Moorish manner, with elaborate entrance halls. The other churches in Mexico City are much alike and without points of special interest. All of them, like most churches throughout Mexico, have wooden, not stone floors; they have no benches, or pews, even for wealthy parishioners. Thus rich and poor, fashionable and unfashionable, come to worship God as they will mingle together on judgment day; elegant ladies and ragged *leperos*[3] kneel side by side.

On feast days Mexican churches present an interesting spectacle. Women attending services at this time dress in black satin and cover their heads with black mantillas. The mantilla, however, is gradually being discarded. The hideous French hat that affords protection neither against heat nor cold has become extremely popular in Mexico, where it has been introduced by Parisian shops, for English and Spanish milliners would not dare sell such atrocities.

Formerly, Mexican women did not wear hats to church, and when I was in Mexico they were never used in the provinces. The French introduced the custom of wearing hats to places of worship; the English, who respect the time-honored ways of the church, believe in covering the head with the mantilla, or *tápalo*.

The *tápalo* is a shawl that is thrown over the head; it derives its name from this usage. Any color or any kind of material may be used for this headdress. The *tápalo* and mantilla, however, are used primarily by the aristocratic upper classes. Poor women and Indians cover their heads with a sash, which they wear with coquettish grace.

Those whose interest is not so much in spiritual as in temporal matters consider the government palace the most interesting building in Mexico City. The street on which this stands usually changes its name with each change of government. Formerly it was known as the Plaza Real, or Plaza Mayor,[4] but these names are no longer in vogue, and when I was in Mexico it was usually called either the Plaza Nacional, or the Plaza de la Independencia.

The plaza is quite extensive and is reputed to be the largest and finest square of any capital city in the world. The government palace, which occupies one side of it, dates from the end of the sixteenth century and is of interest because of its size rather than its architectural merit, for it resembles vast barracks.

Sometime the Mexican officials hope to have all the central branches of the administration housed in the palace, which is so vast that it has five or six great central courts; at the present it houses the most important divisions of the government and contains suites for the president, the six ministers, the court of justice, the chamber of deputies, the treasurer, the postmaster general and the war department.

This central grouping of administrative offices expedites the handling of governmental affairs, which are hindered by the natural slowness and laziness of Mexican officials as a class.

A short time before my arrival in Mexico City a Spanish nobleman, Count de la Cortina, gave an elaborate dinner in honor of President Santa Anna, which was held in the great reception room now known as ambassador's hall. Upon this occasion the main court, which is as large as the central court of the Louvre, was covered with an awning and transformed into an exquisite garden filled with orange, lemon, and pomegranate trees in full blossom. No one knew where the mirrors, carpets, and statues with which the court and second floor were adorned, had been procured.

The banquet cost more than thirty-five hundred piasters. The next morning everyone in the city was asking: "How did you enjoy the party last night?" In this land of wealth, rich Mexicans base their enjoyment on the cost of the entertainment. This limits entertaining, and makes the city rather dull, for not everyone, like Count de la Cortina, has several thousand piasters to spend on one night's pleasure.

Simple evening parties, or *tertulias*,[5] are almost unknown among Mexicans, who prefer balls. If anyone entertains, his neighbor feels he must give a similar, or an even more elaborate function. This accounts for the lack of intimate little gatherings in Mexico City. Intimacy is further discouraged by the fact that wealthy Mexicans seldom pay calls, a local custom that has unfortunately extended to diplomatic circles.

Before the Mexican-American war, Mexico City was a gay capital, but since that time there has been a noticeable decline in the number of balls and entertainments given. So few parties are now held that today the quarterly ball of the Merchants' Association is the most fashionable event in the city. These balls are elaborate affairs, and are attended by all prominent residents of Mexico City.

In addition to the government palace, an important point of interest is the Minería, or Mining College,[6] up in the mountains, attended by young men who wish to study mining. The Minería, which was built at the end of the eighteenth century, is not so large as the governmental palace, although it deserves to be called a palace.

The scholastic standing of the Minería is high, and its graduates are as well equipped from a practical standpoint as men who graduate from the leading mining institutes of Europe. The director of the Institute, Señor Velasquez de León, is also Minister of Commerce and Public Works.

The mint is a single building in which immense sums of unused gold are stored. The officials at this mint were unusually polite and courteous; one of them showed me various kinds of gold and silver coins, including a tiny *cuartillo*,[7] worth three cents, and described many details about the manufacture of coins. The mint was so full of the odor of sulphur, however, that I could scarcely breathe. When the workmen enter the mint, they are required to undress and deposit any gold they may have, which is returned when they leave in the evening.

Mexico City also has an art museum,[8] a fine building which contains, unfortunately, a collection of Spanish copies of Italian and French masterpieces and comparatively few original paintings and works of genuine merit.

The art school has trained some renowned artists. A young Mexican painter called Cordero [9] created a sensation one year in Paris with his painting, the "Ehebrecherin," or adulteress, which met with universal favor. Original paintings of the great Spanish masters, Murillo, Velasquez, Morales,[10] and Zubaran,[11] that once hung in great Spanish homes and cathedrals, have almost without exception disappeared from the country.

In addition to the Museum of Fine Arts, there is an interesting museum of Aztec relics in Mexico City in charge of the well-known archaeologist, Fernando Ramiro.[12] Here I was shown treasures that date back to the time of the Conquest. However, these bas reliefs and inscriptions, which bear a marked resemblance to those of early Egypt and Assyria, failed to interest me. In fineness of detail they are far behind those of the Orient; many of them, in fact, I considered extremely crude.

My curiosity having been especially aroused by an immense stone, strangely like some of the old druid altars of Britain, on which Aztec priests placed animals to be used for sacrificial purposes, and in which even the old hole through which the blood poured had been pointed out to me, upon my return to Paris I made a point of comparing some of these ancient relics with those in the French capital, but found nothing there to equal them.

Throughout Mexico the tourist and antiquarian will find any number of Aztec monuments, and although I had an opportunity to see many of them, yet I was satisfied with what I found at the museum, for I was only mildly interested in urgly old stones and hideous crumbling idols.

Travelers, notwithstanding, usually enjoy the remarkable and well-preserved ruins near Texcoco, including the pyramids of San Juan Teotihuacan,[13] known to the Indians as the sun and moon pyramids, and above all the great pyramids of Cholula.

On the Mexican plateau some remarkable Aztec ruins not unlike those in Tabasco, Yucatan, and Central America are found. In fact, many travelers who have visited the ancient ruins in Egypt, Persia, and Mesopotamia, say that Palenque is fully as interesting.[14]

CHAPTER XVI

FIESTAS

EVEN more delightful than the churches, palaces, monuments and museums of Mexico City are its fascinating promenades. Like all cities of Spanish origin, Mexico City has its Alameda,[1] or pedestrian walk. Among Mexicans the Alameda is perhaps the least popular of all the local boulevards. This is odd, for the avenue is unusually commodious, consisting of an extensive promenade lined with poplars and adorned with a series of small shade gardens and masses of flowers. Half a dozen brooks materially enhance the charm of this retreat.

When I was in Mexico City, the Alameda was my favorite walk and although I went there every morning I met only foreigners taking a stroll. Morning in Mexico City is the best part of the day; since the elevation is 7800 feet, the air is crisp and pure. This high altitude, however, does not always agree with foreigners; often strangers have difficulty adjusting themselves to it.

Invigorating as the morning undoubtedly is in the high plateau country of Mexico, the evening often proves distinctly disagreeable. From July until October the mornings are invariably fine, perhaps finer than at any other season, yet as these months are usually the rainy season, by two o'clock in the afternoon clouds appear in the sky and storms of an intensity known only to those who have lived in the tropics appear.

When heavy rains fall the water, pouring down from the plateaus above the city and having no channel through which to escape, floods the city in a short time; as gondolas are not available, few people venture out. For inexperienced pedestrians to find themselves in Mexico City during these floods is indeed a calamity.

On some of the streets, however, porters are stationed; during the daily storms they are on the lookout for customers, and for a *medio*, about six cents—the equivalent of bus fare in Paris—anyone can be carried to his destination. But the porter does not guarantee not to drop his customer. Of course if he stumbles and trips, the passenger falls into the water and must reach the pavement as best he can. Such scenes, which I often watched from the sidewalk, sometimes gave rise to amusing and grotesque situations. The local showers, 'it should in all justice be said, usually stop about five o'clock, when the sky clears. At this time the distant mountains are as plainly visible as in the early morning.

Pleasant evenings are the rule after the rainy season, and occur in October, November, December, and even into January, but after these months have passed, the sky during the day is often overcast. In March, April, May, and June comparatively little rain falls, but almost every afternoon a north wind blows through the city, making an evening walk distinctly unpleasant. The evening promenade has its own peculiar code of etiquette. At five o'clock house doors begin to open and vehicles of all kinds begin to move toward El Paseo Nuevo, the favorite rendezvous in the evening.

This plaza, El Paseo Nuevo,[2] is situated at the west end of the city, between the street leading to Tacubaya[3] and the church of La Piedad. El Paseo itself is not especially beautiful; the trees look starved, although the view through them is superb. From El Paseo in clear weather may be seen in the full majesty of their beauty the peaks of the well-known volcanoes whose unpronounceable names I will not attempt to repeat. In fact, at times the air is so clear that villages and cities many miles away appear to be nearby.

Few capitals of Europe present as festive an appearance as Mexico City during the evening promenade along El Paseo, where more carriages turn out than in any other city of the same size on the continent of Europe. On important feast days El Paseo is as lively as Longchamps and at that time riders usually appear in handsome Mexican costumes with saddles richly ornamented with silver. The *jalano*,[4] a hat trimmed with gold and silver galoon, and *calzones,* trousers slit and adorned with silver buttons, white blouses, and long spurs are usually in evidence.

The carriages that pass up and down El Paseo Nuevo in the evening are drawn either by horses or mules. Prior to the Mexican-American war, only mules were used, but since that time these animals have almost disappeared, and in their places fine American horses are considered fashionable. Although Mexican horses have extraordinary endurance, the American breed is much faster. Most of the carriages are brought over from France or England, but shortly before our visit to Mexico, a carriage factory was started in this country which has even sent models to be exhibited at the Paris Exposition. This, however, employs mostly French and English workmen; a large part of the materials used are procured abroad. Foreign-made carriages are usually heavily over-decorated, many of them having gilded axles and wheels.

One section of this same promenade, the area known as La Piedad, planted with a fine avenue of trees, is at least two miles long. At first I could not understand why the trees along La Piedad were so beautiful and those of El Paseo so stunted, but I finally decided that the latter had been the victim of a *pronunciamento*. The trees along La Piedad are comparable to those of the Tuileries.

Walking seems about to become fashionable in Mexico City. At the entrance to the promenade of La Piedad, many women now leave their carriages and proceed on foot, some walking for ten minutes, others for fifteen, but none more than half an hour. This, however, is an entirely new fad. The charming setting of La Piedad is what has fostered this fashion, for at other places the ladies remain in their closed carriages.

Another interesting place to walk is El Paseo de las Vigas, which is visited only during fiestas, being at other seasons entirely deserted. I often wondered why this was so, for this Paseo is extraordinarily beautiful. No one could enlighten me on this point, but probably it is just another whim of fashion. One reason why the Paseo is neglected may be because the road leading to it passes through a poor section of the city. But during festivals all streets seem alike; no one seems better than the others. I did not allow this fact to prevent my visits, and when I did not go to Chapultepec, I frequently went to El Paseo de las Vigas for a stroll.

El Paseo de las Vigas[5] has as long a promenade as El Paseo Nuevo de la Piedad, but the avenue itself is broader. Its trees are also larger, more picturesque, and give more shade. There is a fascination about this walk because it leads to Chinampas,[6] or the floating gardens, by way of the canal of Santa Anita.[7]

On festive occasions this canal is crowded with boats, each holding boisterous, flower-bedecked Indians. Even the water between the boats is covered with lotos flowers and water lilies. The native women wear wreaths of flowers on their heads and necks; the men, on their hats. Everyone laughs, sings, and plays the guitar in a delightful manner. These Mexicans, in fact, reminded me of the Maoris, whom I so deeply admired.

In addition to their morning and afternoon promenades, the Mexicans have equally simple evening pastimes. They enjoy loitering on the main plaza, especially near the entrance, or what is called Trottoir de las Cadenas,[8] a name that refers to the heavy chain that surrounds the cathedral where crowds of men and women bring their own stools, sit, gossip, and listen to the music played by the President's band.

Any description of the leading aspects of Mexican life would be incomplete if the processions were overlooked. The first of these I saw took place during Holy Week; upon this occasion all the local religious dignitaries, who are unusually numerous in Mexican cities, participated in the parade, carrying the banners of their church. Bystanders, especially Indians and peons, frequently follow it or kneel down and worship the symbols of the church as they pass, thus lending life and color to the parades. After witnessing the devout ways of these low-class Mexicans, I understood the spirit of the sermons preached in Mexican churches, although my knowledge of Spanish was so slight that I did not always understand the words.

Maundy Thursday and the following days of Holy Week are consecrated to quiet, heavy traffic being prohibited. On Saturday noon, however, this quiet season ends in a riot of noise. By eleven, preparations for this outburst of hilarity are well under way; there are unmistakable sounds of activity as horses are saddled and carriages are brought out from the coachhouses. At noon the church bells begin to chime. House doors are thrown open, carriages begin to appear on the streets, riders gallop up and down. The city is now filled with noisy crowds of people, who congregate on each boulevard and plaza, bent on revelry. On every street, and before every house, the men give expression to their religious fervor by starting bonfires.

These conflagrations, of course, are nothing but Auto da Fés, where Judas is burned in effigy. The Judases themselves are represented by dummies stuffed with gunpowder; they have hooked noses and long beards, and wear long black coats. When the fire reaches these mock Jews, they explode with a loud report. Often, in their over-zealousness, the participants are slightly burned, which turns their thoughts toward the future world and the last day of judgment.

The entire city is abroad at this time; the rich travel in carriages or on horseback; the poor on foot. Much of the noise and confusion is made by these shabby pedestrians, who carry rattles which they shake continuously. Even a single rattle in the hands of a zealous reveler can torture sensitive nerves, and the ear-splitting noises made by thousands of *matracas* [9] is indescribable.

A prominent feature of this revelry is the long-established custom which requires every master to give a donation to his servants. On the last morning of Holy Week, each servant invariably asks his master for a gift, approaching him with this morning greeting: "Something for my rattle, Señor!" The master complies with the request, and the servant pockets the gold, brings out his rattle that has been hidden away for a year, and in appreciation of the gift tortures the donor and his friends with a hideous din.

In the midst of the general confusion, another group, the hounds, are the victims of equally mad pranks. On every corner of the street porters—I have never been able to find out why porters and not water carriers are used—are stationed. One porter stands on one side of the street, with another directly across from him, and each holds in his hand the end of a rope. When the dogs, alarmed by the noise of rattles, begin to run, the porters trip them with the ropes and throw them about twenty feet in the air. The dogs fall anywhere, often on the heads of the pedestrians. This, however, fails to disturb the porters, whose main interest lies in seeing how high they can toss the dogs. While the onlooker may enjoy this sport, the dog, to say the least, finds it quite annoying, not to mention the pedestrian on whose head the animal happens to fall.

During the evening, the entire city is a blaze of light. The Indians now sit in long rows around the main plaza, selling flowers, lemonade, tortillas, cakes, and other delicacies. At eight o'clock the fireworks begin and the streets are thronged with gay crowds shooting off rockets. At intervals guns, too, are fired. Bands play in the central plazas until the early morning hours. By two o'clock, the lights are finally extinguished and the gaiety stops.

The most important procession is that of Corpus Christi. On this holy day every house in Mexico City is decorated with carpets, bunting, and garlands of flowers. In fact, a fiesta in Mexico City is inconceivable without flowers. The procession travels through the city, headed by the archbishop, followed by the leading dignitaries of the city in official uniform, the troops from the local garrison, and at least twenty thousand persons from various cities throughout Mexico. Directly behind the holy image comes a gilded carriage, drawn by white mules. Those who are not out in the streets watch the parade from windows, the women wearing their best black dresses and mantillas.

The festivities in honor of Holy Week culminate in the Feast of All Saints' Day. In Mexico City this celebration assumes a weird, almost uncanny character; it seems to be a time consecrated to revenge for bloody deeds rather than to religious observances, for upon this sacred occasion more revengeful acts are committed than on any other day of the year.

And why has this feast of the dead become a day for exacting revenge? Does this deep-rooted custom actually serve a dual purpose? In Mexico, as in Italy, France, and all other Catholic lands, the day is reserved for visiting the graves of near relatives. Many a *lepero* who has lost some relative or friend from some act of violence, by visiting the grave vividly recalls how the victim met his death,—perhaps by a blow, or a knife—and as he knows who committed the deed, he decides to have revenge.

According to Mexican tradition, no man can rest peacefully in his grave so long as his murderer remains unpunished. To insure rest to the deceased, the friend will often take revenge with his knife, selecting for this purpose All Saints' Day as the appropriate time. Anyone who has an old score to be settled, and survives this sacred day, feels confident that his life will be safe for at least another year.

This abuse of a holy fiesta is so deeply ingrained in the national character, and is so generally known to the public at large, that everyone in Mexico City makes special preparations for emergencies at this time. Special guards are called out, and in the town hall, city jail, and hospital, extra beds are prepared, which everyone knows will be needed during the Feast of All Saints' Day.

# NOTES

## VOLUME I

### CHAPTER I

1. Mauritius, or Ile de France, off the coast of Madagascar. This was the locale of the famous novel *Paul et Virginie,* written in 1789 by Jacques Henri Bernadin de St. Pierre (1737-1814), one of the great novelists of his day. (Page 1.)

2. Aramis, one of the leading characters in *The Three Musketeers,* portrayed as a schemer, or politician, with leanings toward the church. (Page 1.)

3. Twenty-and-one, played by two or more players. The object is for each player to obtain from the dealer such cards that the sum of the spots is as near as possible to that number. (Page 2.)

4. Aimata, or Pomaré IV (1827-1877), was then reigning over Tahiti. (Page 2.)

5. Between 1841 and 1851 Dumas had published his first volumes of travel under this title, which included records of trips to southern France, southern Italy, Spain, and Algeria. His later volumes of travels postdate the *Giovanni.* (Page 3.)

### CHAPTER II

1. Meaning The Fish of Maui. Now North Island. (Page 5.)

2. South Island. The native name means, The Waters of Greenstone. (Page 5.)

3. The name Kanaka, in varying forms, is generally used throughout the Pacific where it usually means man or person. (Page 6.)

4. A food known as *aruhe* or *poi,* made by the natives from fernroot. This was first baked, then beaten to weaken the fibers. (Page 6.)

5. The *Kiore maori,* or native rat, which was supposed to have been brought into Polynesia from Europe. It was a small rat of cleanly habits and considered good to eat. This pouched rat or mouse is still found in outlying sections of the island and throughout New Guinea. Possibly a member of the Marsupial family known as *Notarycles typhlops.* (Page 6.)

6. The tui, *Prosthemadera novaesselandiae,* the most popular song bird of New Zealand, is distinguishable by its bluish, or greenish-black color, white spots, and tufts of curly white feathers. The range and quality of its notes are exceptional. (Page 6.)

7. The suckling of pigs, while known in New Zealand, is not so common as the *Journal* indicates. (Page 7.)

8. Yes, yes! (Page 7.)

9. *Maki,* in its freer usage, implies that an action has been done spon-

taneously, on impulse, for personal benefit. This use of the word is obviously incorrect. (Page 8.)

10. The *bibi* was a small hat in vogue in 1830. (Page 8.)

11. *Robes à la vierge:* a loose flowing robe of a style seen in paintings of the Virgin Mary. (Page 8.)

12. Queen Street, with its banks and commercial houses, is still the leading street in Auckland, where it follows the waterfront. (Page 9.)

### CHAPTER III

1. Sir George Grey (1812-1898) was appointed governor of South Australia in 1840 and sent in November 1845 to assist the English settlements in New Zealand which were threatened by destruction at the hands of the Maori warriors. After subduing the natives, he won their friendship, bringing peace to New Zealand. Much of his time was subsequently passed collecting their myths and legends. He was known as a real statesman, and a man of strength and character. (Page 11.)

2. May God protect you! (Page 14.)

3. The old Victoria Hotel was situated on the water front of Auckland. (Page 15.)

4. Tasmania. Discovered on November 24, 1642, by Abel Janszoon Tasman (1603-1659), one of the greatest of Dutch navigators, and named *Anthoonij van Diemen's landt*. Van Diemen, who had been connected with the Dutch East India Company, and was subsequently made governor, hoped to extend the control of his group into this new and unexplored region. (Page 15.)

5. Apparently Reunion Island, in the Indian Ocean. (Page 15.)

### CHAPTER IV

1. The *Journal* does not disclose how the intervening months were passed since Madame Giovanni left New Zealand in March. (Page 16.)

2. In 1831 the natives left for South Bruni and Flinders Island. By 1845, however, less than fifty remained. (Page 16.)

3. There is no record of a Hotel Gaylor at this period. (Page 16.)

4. "El Solitario", the sobriquet of Serafín Estébanez Calderón (1799-1867) a brilliant poet and lawyer of Madrid, who was known for his terse and clever epigrams. (Page 16.)

5. In 1805 several convicts from Norfolk Island were removed to Van Diemen's Land, which later received many prisoners. This was a material benefit to the free settlers to whom were assigned convicts in proportion to their holdings. At the same time it relieved the government of the expense of their support. (Page 16.)

6. There is no record of an institution by this name, although many brick buildings were used at that period which may have given rise to this appellation. (Page 17.)

7. Smith O'Brien was an Irish revolutionist, educated at Cambridge, who opposed the Irish Arms Act of 1845, and became leader of the Young Ireland

Party. In 1848 he was tried for sedition at Dublin and deported to Tasmania. (Page 21.)

### CHAPTER V

1. Crack my side, *"casse-côte,"* in the French text. (Page 23.)
2. There is now a popular drive known as Derwent Park leading past Government House and the Botanical Gardens. (Page 24.)
3. Apparently Bruni Island, a large island divided by a slender neck of land into North and South Bruni. (Page 24.)

### CHAPTER VI

1. Paul Scarron (1610-1660), a wit and comic writer whose satires were directed against the leading writers of his day. In 1651, although an invalid and old man, he married Françoise d'Aubigné Maintenon, who nursed him faithfully for many years. (Page 28.)
2. A tributary of the Dnieper River, known for its treacherous floods. Here during November, 1812, Napoleon suffered severe losses during his retreat from Moscow. (Page 30.)
3. Sir John Franklin (1786-1847), one of the notable explorers of the Arctic regions, had married Eleanor Porden. In 1836 he was made lieutenant governor of Van Diemen's Land, a post he held until 1843. (Page 32.)

### CHAPTER VII

1. The predecessor of Sir William Denison, and an extremely unpopular ruler who was constantly in trouble with the legislative council over the convicts. He was lieutenant governor, not governor. (Page 33.)
2. Pierre Dupont (1821-1870), a famous song-writer of France. His *Le Chant des Ouvriers* was extremely popular in France, as was his *Le Pain*. Dupont himself sang these songs at workmen's concerts in Paris, where he was universally known and esteemed by all classes. (Page 35.)
3. The *cordon bleu*, or blue ribbon, means in the popular vernacular, a superior cook. In court circles, however, the *cordon bleu* made the recipient a Knight of the Holy Ghost. (Page 36.)

### CHAPTER IX

1. These prisoners' barracks consisted of a series of brick buildings surrounded by a high wall, and were used by all convicts of the crown, as well as those who had recently arrived from England. (Page 46.)
2. Sir William Thomas Denison (1804-1871) was lieutenant governor from 1846 to 1854. After a distinguished career in England and Canada, he was sent to Van Diemen's Land to institute a more satisfactory method of handling the convict problem. He also materially improved public works and education. He ranks as one of the able rulers of that period. (Page 49.)

## CHAPTER X

1. Launceston is in the northern part of the island. The route lies through the land watered by the Macquarie River. (Page 51.)

2. Banks Strait is the small strait separating Tasmania from the Furneaux Islands. The main body of water crossed would be Bass Strait. Port Phillips, furthermore, lies somewhat east and not directly across from Launceston. (Page 51.)

3. Alfuros: the term applied by the Malays to all uncivilized non-Mohammedan peoples in the eastern part of the Malay Archipelago, meaning "wild" or "uncivilized". (Page 56.)

4. Jean François de Galaup, Comte de la Pérouse (1741-1788), one of the great navigators of his day, who was murdered at Botany Bay on January 26, 1788, while on a voyage around the world. The record of his travels, *Voyage de la Pérouse au tour du monde* (4 vols. Paris, 1797) recounts his amazing discoveries. (Page 58.)

## CHAPTER XI

1. Lord John Russell was an English statesman who lived from 1792 to 1878. (Page 61.)

2. See *infra*, IV, p. 234, *note*. (Page 61.)

## CHAPTER XII

1. This refers to the Maori and English war over property rights which began in 1843 and lasted until 1859. At this time Colonels Hulme and Wynyard with several hundred men were stationed at Auckland. (Page 65.)

2. The Maori term for a fortified place or stockade. The verb "pa" means to obstruct or block up an open space. (Page 66.)

3. These sepulchers were probably not places of defense, but burial grounds. (Page 69.)

4. Although these subterranean passages actually existed, there is no record of the slaughter of English soldiers at this time. (Page 69.)

## CHAPTER XIII

1. The journey from Auckland to the Bay of Islands could never have been completed in one day. By rail the distance is 183 miles, and by Maori trail only slightly less. (Page 70.)

2. Apparently North Cape. This was a trip of at least two hundred miles, a difficult, if not impossible, day's journey. (Page 70.)

3. On May 11, 1772, Captain Marion du Fresne in the ships *Mascarin* and *Marquis de Castries* reached the Bay of Islands. After a month of friendly relations with the natives the captain and sixteen men were murdered and eaten. (Page 70.)

4. Hone Heke. (Page 71.)

5. This refers to the Maori war led by Heke and Kawiti against the English over the natives' rights to land ownership. See G. W. Rusden, *History of New Zealand* (3 vols. London, 1855) I, 365 ff. (Page 71.)

6. On March 24, 1845, two hundred men from H.M.S. *North Star* reached the Bay of Islands and attacked the Maori warriors led by Hone Heke, who appears to be the Eki Eki of this journal. After losses totalling thirty-eight men, the English returned to Auckland. (Page 71.)

## VOLUME II

### CHAPTER I

1. The last known instance of this cannibalistic practice occurred in 1842, when one Maori tribe ate some prisoners of war. No white men, however, were devoured at this period. (Page 74.)

2. There is no record of a tribe bearing this name. (Page 74.)

### CHAPTER II

1. "Faire Longchamps" is a typical French phrase and has reference to the race course at the end of the Bois de Boulogne, Paris, which has long been celebrated as the promenade of smartly dressed Parisians during holy week, displaying French styles. (Page 76.)

2. Sir George Grey did not receive his title until 1848. At this period he was still known as captain. (Page 76.)

3. Major General George Dean Pitt was appointed lieutenant governor of New Zealand on January 3, 1848, and assumed office on February 14 of the same year. His death occurred on January 8, 1851. (Page 76.)

4. Another child's song, *"Sur le pont d'Avignon, L'on y danse,"* which is repeated over and over. (Page 76.)

5. A popular child's song, with music by Charles Widor, describing the promenade of a captain and colonel. (Page 76.)

6. This refers to Marion du Fresne, in command of the *Mascarin* and *Marquis de Castries,* who reached there on May 11, 1772. At first Du Fresne was warmly welcomed by the natives, then without warning killed with sixteen of his men by the blacks. (Page 77.)

7. The heroine of Goethe's *Leiden des jungen Werthers* which immortalized the poet's love for Charlotte Buff. (Page 78.)

### CHAPTER III

1. This appears as Lorafena and Orafena in the French text, but refers to Orohena, a lofty peak 7,349 feet high. (Page 81.)

2. The *pandanus spiralis* is a palm-like plant, typical of the island, belonging to the Pandanaceae, or screw pine family, which bears an edible fruit. (Page 81.)

3. The *gardenia florida,* or *tiraé.* (Page 81.)

4. The native costume was made of bark cloth with a hole in the center for the head. The loin cloth was worn by all men and women of the upper classes. (Page 81.)

5. Papeete, or "Vaiete" as it was originally known, means literally the "water basket". At this time it was primarily the resort used by the Pomaré family who had a retreat on the little island of Motuiti now used as a quarantine station. (Page 81.)

6. According to the French text *bois d'hisers,* apparently a local ironwood tree. (Page 81.)

7. This is the *hibiscus rosa sinensis,* known locally as the *aoutai.* (Page 83.)

8. Pritchard, English consul and missionary in Tahiti, was the leading adviser of Queen Pomaré, and the guiding spirit in causing the removal of Catholic missionaries from the island. (Page 83.)

### CHAPTER IV

1. These are not pure Tahitian phrases, for the natives had no name either for brandy or for time. "Ava ava" means tobacco. (Page 85.)

2. "Tiota" is an error for "toaeko", a sugar cane. The other words are not decipherable. (Page 85.)

### CHAPTER V

1. In ancient Greek legends the goddess Amphitrite was the wife of Poseidon. (Page 89.)

2. Bougainville sighted Tahiti on April 2, 1768 in *La Boudeuse* and *L'Étoile.* See Louis de Bougainville, *A Voyage Round the World,* edited by J. R. Forster (London, 1772), pp. 211-274, which describes in detail his sojourn at the island. (Page 90.)

3. Pedro Fernandez de Quiros (Fernandes de Quieros, 1565-1615) left Peru in December, 1605, and in February, 1606, reached one of the islands near Tahiti. See Clements Markham, *The Voyages of Pedro Fernandez de Quiros* (2 vols. London, 1904), I, 197 ff. (Page 90.)

4. Samuel Wallis in the *Dolphin* left England in 1766 for his Pacific exploration. From June 23 to July 27, 1767, he remained at Tahiti, which he called King George the Third Island. His sojourn is described in detail in his own narrative of his experiences. See Samuel Wallis, *An Account of a Voyage round the World* in John Hawkesworth Voyages (3 vols. London, 1773), I, 220-270. (Page 90.)

5. Among these natives, oddly enough, the will to die seems to bring swift death. (Page 90.)

### CHAPTER VI

1. In 1768 James Cook was appointed to conduct a scientific expedition in the South Seas and sailed in May in the *Endeavor* of 370 tons for the Pacific.

On April 13, 1769, he reached Tahiti. See *A Journal of a Voyage round the World in His Majesty's Ship Endeavor* (London, 1770), pp. 36-58. This rare and interesting account of Tahiti is believed to have been written not by Cook, but by one of his men. (Page 92.)

2. The mappa (*inocarpus edulis*), known locally as the chestnut tree, bears a fruit called *manaré ai*, a favorite with Tahitians. (Page 93.)

3. Apparently the *purau*, a type of wild hibiscus used by the natives for this purpose. Fire was produced by rubbing a piece of hard wood along a groove in the wood until a spark was produced. (Page 94.)

4. Queen Pomaré IV, known also as Aimata (1827-1877) was closely connected with French activities on the island. During her régime a French frigate, in command of Abel Dupetit Thouars, landed at Papeete, and forced the Queen to allow Frenchmen to settle on the island. In 1842 while Queen Pomaré was absent in France, her ministers ceded the islands to that government. Finally, in 1846, a French protectorate was formally accepted by Her Majesty. (Page 96.)

5. On March 5, 1797, thirty-nine missionaries on the English missionary ship *Duff*, sent out by the London Missionary Society, reached the islands. Their subsequent activities extended far beyond the realm of religion and into politics. (Page 96.)

6. Pomaré II reigned during a period of political strife, and for a time was exiled. Returning in 1812, he embraced Christianity and regained his power. He died of drink in 1824. His successor Pomaré III lived only until 1827. (Page 96.)

CHAPTER VII

1. In 1842, during the absence of the Queen, her ministers ceded her islands to France. This act, which she subsequently attempted to repudiate, led to political difficulties. During the upheaval the Queen attempted to enlist the sympathies of the English. (Page 98.)

2. *Puncho* in the French text. (Page 98.)

3. This appears to be the Curcuma (or cuscute) Longa, or Tumeric, an indigenous plant whose roots are used in the preparation of native curry and to produce a yellow dye. (Page 99.)

4. Mico: apparently an error. There is no plant in the Islands by this name. (Page 99.)

5. Taboo: a chief taboo can be placed on a house, bay, or man, which thus entails complete isolation. (Dumas' note.) (Page 102.)

CHAPTER VIII

1. Gardner Island. (Page 107.)

2. The Marquesas, or Mendaña Islands were discovered in 1595 by Alvaro Mendaña, and named in honor of Don García Hurtado de Mendoza, viceroy of Peru. Cook touched at the Marquesas not in March, but on April 8, 1774, spending several days at the various islands. For his account of this visit see James Cook, *A Voyage toward the South Pole* (2 vols. London, 1784), I,

298-312. Annexed in 1842 by France, at the time of Madame Giovanni's visit the native population was only a few thousand. (Page 107.)

3. Cook's second Pacific expedition with the ships *Resolution* and *Adventure*. (Page 107.)

4. This is an exaggeration; cannibalism never extended to Europeans. (Page 109.)

5. On September 5, 1774, James Cook landed at Balade, remaining there until the eighteenth. He gives a full and entertaining account of the island and natives in his *Voyage toward the South Pole*, II, 103-127. (Page 109.)

6. Bougainville visited this region in the Spring of 1768. (Page 109.)

7. Sequeba Island does not appear on modern maps. Possibly the reference is to the Sequeira, or Caroline Islands. (Page 110.)

8. This appears as Pomouton in the French, and Pomotu in the German edition. (Page 110.)

9. Also known as Annatom. The French version is Anatou. (Page 110.)

## CHAPTER IX

1. The spelling of this ship varies in the French text. According to contemporary newspapers she was known as the "barque Baretto Junior, Captain Huggins." Barratte Junior, in the French text. (Page 117.)

2. According to shipping reports, the bark *Baretto Junior*, Huggins, 78 days from Launceston, Van Diemen's Land, reached San Francisco on Dec. 27, 1850, consigned to MacKenzie, Thompson, & Co. See *San Francisco Alta, California,* Dec. 28, 1850. Her passengers were J. Williamson, H. and J. Dickings, A. Huggins. She cleared for Sydney on February 28. See *ibid,* March 2, 1851. (Page 123.)

## CHAPTER X

1. Telegraph Hill served to supply the first information about ships entering port. A high pole, on which arms, raised or lowered to indicate the type of vessel sighted, provided the so-called telegraph. In September, 1849, a house had been erected on the crest of the hill. (Page 123.)

2. The Contra Costa was the mountainous land lying east of San Francisco Bay dominated by the peak of Mt. Diablo. The San Antonio was one of the early Spanish land grants of 48,825 acres acquired in 1820 by Luís Peralta by whose heirs it was still held. The modern cities of Oakland, Berkeley, and Alameda are on the old San Antonio. (Page 123.)

3. A *real*, in the French edition. This was a small Spanish coin worth ten or twelve cents. (Page 125.)

4. Possibly William T. Barry. In 1850, he was living on Sacramento Street between Powell and Stockton. Charles P. Kimball, *The San Francisco City Directory* (San Francisco, 1850), p. 9. (Page 125.)

5. The slug was the fifty-dollar piece issued, after 1849, by the assay office in San Francisco. (Page 125.)

6. There were no great fires in San Francisco early in 1851. On September 17, 1850, what is called the third great fire broke out, followed by minor

blazes on October 31 and December 14. The fourth major fire occurred on May 3-4; and the fifth on June 22, 1851. (Page 126.)

CHAPTER XI

1. The leading hotels of San Francisco were the City Hotel, the Parker House, the St. Francis, the Dupont, the Union, and the Oriental. (Page 128.)

2. The Bella Union stood on Washington Street. (Page 128.)

3. Thirty-and-forty, a popular gambling game in which six full packs of cards are used and any number of persons plays against the bank, placing bets on two colors, red and black, indicated by large diamonds on the table. (Page 128.)

4. Gil Blas was the clever, but vain and weak Spanish hero of a famous romance by Le Sàge. Many of his nefarious adventures took place in haunts of vice. Dumas makes him the hero of his *Gil Blas in California,* translated and edited by *Marguerite Eyer Wilbur* (Los Angeles, 1933). (Page 128.)

5. Richard Ross and J. P. Sullivan. (Page 129.)

6. The Vigilance Committee, composed of the leading citizens of San Francisco, came into existence in June, 1851, not long after the Giovannis reached San Francisco. Its object was to check the wave of lawlessness following in the wake of the gold rush and to safeguard the lives and property of the citizens. Probably derived from a Virginian named Lynch, who first took the law into his own hands. In California the term meant the act of private persons who inflicted punishment for crimes or offenses without due process of law. Lynching played an important part in the history of this period. (Page 131.)

7. The so-called Sydney ducks were a group of criminals inhabiting an area around Clark's Point, in the vicinity of Pacific and Broadway. This haunt, known as Sydneytown, was a center of corruption and vice. See Theodore H. Hittell, *History of California* (4 vols. San Francisco, 1897), iii, 311-312. (Page 131.)

8. Probably the famous lynching on Sunday, August 24, of the criminals Samuel Whittaker and Robert McKenzie. The place of execution, however, was on the west side of Battery, between California and Pine streets. See Hittell, *op. cit.,* III, 329-330. (Page 132.)

CHAPTER XII

1. Possibly William Beatty, a commission merchant of Jackson Street. See Kimball, *op. cit.,* p. 11. (Page 133.)

2. Kandler (or Kaindler) and Bros. had a dry goods store at 193 Clay Street; Guerin and Co. were wine merchants located on Sacramento Street; Pommier was probably J. M. Pommares and Co., 177 Sansome Street. (Page 135.)

3. Felix C. Argenti, one of the six leading bankers of San Francisco and a prominent member of the Vigilance Committee who had offices on Montgomery Street, between Clay and Commercial.

4. Burgoyne and Company were located on the southwest corner of Washington and Montgomery streets. See map in H. H. Bancroft, *History of California* (7 vols. San Francisco, 1888), VI, 204. Their ad appears in the local newspapers of 1850-1851. (Page 135.)

5. B. Davidson, who was agent for Rothschild, had offices at the corner of Montgomery Street and Commercial. His ad appears in the *San Francisco Daily Herald*, No. 209, Feb. 1, 1851. (Page 135.)

6. El Dorado, run by Chambers and Co., stood on the southeast corner of Washington and Kearny overlooking the plaza, or Portsmouth Square. See Bancroft, *op. cit.*, VI, 204. (Page 135.)

7. The Roman Catholic Church stood on Vallejo Street, between Dupont and Stockton. Morning services were held in Spanish, French, and English. There were six Protestant churches in San Francisco at this period. Kimball, *op. cit.*, p. 127. (Page 135.)

8. The Adelphi, built in 1851 by French residents of San Francisco, was on Dupont Street, btween Clay and Washington. A comedian, Alexandre Munié, was its director. Such plays as *La Dame aux Camélias, Man about Town, Luke the Laborer,* and *Perfection,* were leading attractions. Daniel Lévy, *Les Français en Californie* (San Francisco, 1884), p. 116. (Page 135.)

9. Other places of amusement were the Jenny Lind, Dramatic Museum, and the American theatre. (Page 135.)

10. The post office stood on Dupont Street overlooking Portsmouth Square. (Page 135.)

11. Apparently Henry Herz, a celebrated pianist and French composer who reached California in April, 1850. Assisted by Madame Lacombe, pianist, and de Hennecart, a singer, he gave a series of concerts in San Francisco and Sacramento. He received considerable newspaper publicity at this period. See Lévy, *op. cit.*, p. 116, *note*. (Page 136.)

CHAPTER XIII

1. The first French consul of San Francisco was Patrice, or Patrick, Dillon, who reached California in 1850. His house stood on the corner of Jackson and Mason streets. (Page 139.)

2. Charles J. Brenham, of Frankfort, Kentucky, a prominent banker, was elected mayor on April 28, 1851, taking office early in May. Brahan in the French text. (Page 139.)

3. A popular actress, who toured the mining camps and towns of California in the fifties. See Oscar Lewis, *Lola Montez* (San Francisco, 1938). (Page 142.)

4. Probably C. K. Garrison. (Page 142.)

# VOLUME III

## CHAPTER I

1. Pierre Jean Béranger, a French lyric poet, patronized by Lucien Bonaparte. His first collection of songs, published in 1815, was very popular. (Page 144.)

2. *La bouchée de Jacques* in the French edition. Probably a small pâté made famous by Jacques. The word appears as suapjacks, snapjacks, and slapjacks throughout the French text. (Page 144.)

3. Dr. d'Oleivéra was a graduate of the medical school in Paris and one of the two French doctors in the city. See Lévy, *op. cit.,* p. 169 ff. (Page 148.)

4. In 1850 the Société du Lingot d'or, the lottery of the gold bar, was established. In addition to the major prize of a gold bar, many passages to California were offered. In 1851 and 1852 several hundred French men and women were brought to San Francisco on winning tickets. See Lévy, *op. cit.,* p. 72. (Page 149.)

## CHAPTER II

1. Micronesia, the third and smallest division of the Pacific Islands, includes the Marianas, Caroline, Marshall, and Gilbert islands. (Page 150.)

2. Some four thousand Chinese were living in San Francisco. Their quarter was known as Little China. (Page 151.)

3. James Duncan, whose shop was on Montgomery Street, between Washington and Clay. See Kimball, *op. cit.,* p. 39. (Page 151.)

## CHAPTER III

1. The old customhouse was a three- or four-story white adobe building that stood on the northwest corner of Montgomery and California streets. It was burned in the fire of May 4, 1851. Merchandise, however, was probably stored at the docks, and not at the main office. (Page 158.)

2. Perrette, heroine of *La Laitière et le Pot au lait.* (Page 158.)

3. Obviously a figment of the imagination! No major fire occurred until May of that year. (Page 159.)

4. Auction firms flourished at this period. Most of them, however, were on Montgomery Street, conveniently near the customhouse. Among leading firms were: Cronise Bros.; James B. Huie & Co.; Jones and Carter; J. L. Riddle; Payne and Sherwood; and Kendig, Wainwright and Co. Contemporary newspapers are filled with notices of goods offered for auction. (Page 161.)

5. The wife of John V. Plume, a leading banker located on Montgomery Street. The fire occurred on May 3 and 4, swept the entire business district, burned 1500 houses, sixteen business blocks, and caused a loss of seven million dollars. (Page 163.)

6. An exaggeration; the city had been rebuilt three or four times, however. (Page 165.)

7. These early fire companies, composed of volunteers, played an important rôle in early San Francisco. Organized shortly after the first major conflagration on December 24, 1849, by the following January three companies, the San Francisco, Empire, and Protection, had come into existence. They were seriously hampered, however, by a shortage of water. (Page 165.)

CHAPTER V

1. Probably the great fire of June 22, 1851, known as the Sixth Fire, causing a loss of several millions. This fire, however, probably started in a frame house on the north side of Pacific Street, near Powell. (Page 171.)

2. There is no clew to the identity of "M. V. B." San Francisco directories disclose only two names with these initials: M. Bochm, and Michael Brugeau. (Page 172.)

3. Possibly George N. Wood, who had a boardinghouse on the corner of Union and Powell streets. (Page 172.)

4. Dumas is probably drawing on his imagination. Indians were not numerous at this period in San Francisco. (Page 174.)

CHAPTER VII

1. Apparently the following spring of 1852. (Page 181.)

2. The spelling of proper names throughout the Dumas is notably inaccurate. *Comanche* in the French text. The *Camanche* left Pacific Wharf every Wednesday and Saturday at four o'clock. See *Parker's San Francisco Directory* for the year 1852-53 (San Francisco, 1852), appendix p. 25. Since the maiden voyage of the *Camanche* was in November, 1851, the Giovanni voyage must have taken place in the spring of 1852. (Page 181.)

3. The Oriental Hotel stood on the corner of Second and High streets and was not opened until the summer of 1851. See Thompson and West, *History of Yuba County* (Oakland, 1879), p. 137. (Page 182.)

4. Marysville was now one of the flourishing embryonic cities of California. Originally a portion of the 45,000 acres granted to Theodore Cordua in 1841, in the spring of 1849 the property passed into the hands of Nye, Foster, and Covillaud, and from them to J. M. Ramirez and John Sampson, who laid out a city. In February 1851 Marysville was incorporated. The opening of rich placers along the forks of the Yuba brought it swift and amazing prosperity. (Page 183.)

5. The Express was the major method of transportation, especially into the mining country. For its history see Ernest A. Wiltsee, *The Pioneer Miner and Pack Mule Express* (San Francisco, 1931). (Page 184.)

6. Apparently Nevada City. (Page 185.)

7. An error; undoubtedly Vallejo. (Page 185.)

8. Also written Greethouse in the French text. This was George Greathouse of Greathouse and Slicer's Express, one of the earliest companies operating

between Marysville and Downieville. See Wiltsee, *op. cit.*, p. 95. See also Fariss and Smith, *An Illustrated History of Plumas, Lassen, and Sierra Counties* (San Francisco, 1882), p. 454. (Page 185.)

### CHAPTER VIII

1. Ferdinand Delacroix, a well known French painter who lived between 1799 and 1863. (Page 190.)

2. Alexandre Decamps was a French contemporary of Delacroix. (Page 190.)

3. Oregon House, 24 miles from Marysville, was built in 1852 by Larry Young and was one of the leading hotels on the Camptonville Road. (Page 191.)

4. Nigger Tent was erected on what was known as the Gold Ridge Route by a negro in 1849 as a wayside station to Downieville. See Reusch and Hoover, *Historic Spots in California* (Stanford, 1933), p. 566; and "California's Bantam Cock", *California Historical Society Quarterly*, Vol. VIII, No. 3, September, 1929, pp. 202, 211, *note* 53. William Downie says it was called Negro Tent, or Hollow Log. See his *Hunting for Gold* (San Francisco, 1893), p. 71. (Page 193.)

### CHAPTER IX

1. Undoubtedly the Sequoia Washingtoniana, many of which are over 2,000 years old. (Page 195.)

2. Usually known as Goodyear's Bar. This camp, at an elevation of 2750 feet, had been opened in 1849 by Andrew and Miles Goodyear. See *An Illustrated History of Plumas, Lassen and Sierra Counties*, p. 465 ff. (Page 196.)

### CHAPTER X

1. The distance between Goodyear's Bar and Downieville was only four miles. The trail followed the North Yuba. (Page 203.)

2. Downieville, named for a Scotchman, William Downie, who settled there in 1849, had grown into one of the richest mining centers on the Yuba, and was the headquarters for the mines on both sides of the river. See *An Illustrated History*, etc. p. 456 ff.; J. D. Borthwick, *Three Years in California* (London, 1857), p. 213, ff.; and William Downie, *op. cit.*, p. 41, ff. (Page 204.)

3. The leading hotel of Downieville. See *An Illustrated History*, etc., p. 459. (Page 204.)

4. Apparently these were the Twist's Flats visited and described by Downie in the winter of 1850-1851. See his *op. cit.*, p. 71. In the German edition of 1855 of this Journal the words appear as Twists Flot. (Page 204.)

### CHAPTER XII

1. Probably B. Davidson. See *supra*, p 135, *note*. (Page 218.)

## VOLUME IV

### CHAPTER I

1. The distance from San Francisco to Honolulu is 2428 statute miles. (Page 226.)

2. Mauna Loa, on the island of Hawaii, the largest volcano in the world. It is 13,675 feet high. (Page 227.)

### CHAPTER II

1. Kamehameha III, who ascended the throne in 1833, reigned until 1854. An able monarch, his régime was marked by complications arising out of the aggressiveness of American and French missionaries in the islands. (Page 228.)

2. Prince Alexander Liho Liho was adopted by Kamehameha III and appointed his successor. In 1850 he toured Europe, where he was received by the reigning monarchs. The visit, however, was primarily political in character, two months being spent in an attempt to adjust French relations. On December 15, 1854, he was proclaimed King, with the title of Kamehameha IV. (Page 228.)

3. The Globe Hotel was located on King Street near Fort, and had entrances opening onto both streets. The manager was L. Franconi. The main building was wrecked in 1896 and Ehler's Block built on the same site. See T. G. Thrum, "Honolulu in 1853" in *Papers of the Hawaiian Historical Society,* Supplement No. 10, p. 19. (Page 230.)

4. The Hôtel de France, or Victor's, was an adobe structure, built in the thirties, situated on Fort Street above Hotel Street and extending through to Union. The lessor, Victor Chancerel, was a prominent Frenchman and his hotel was the center for the French colony of Honolulu. Later the building was used as the Foreign Office, the headquarters of the Board of Education, and finally as a Carriage Works. The building is no longer standing. See *ibid,* pp. 16, 17. (Page 230.)

5. King Street is still one of the leading streets of Honolulu. The palace, erected in 1846, has since been demolished. (Page 230.)

6. Nuuanu Street extends from the waterfront to the Pali, a distance of some seven miles. Pallis, in the French text. (Page 230.)

7. Paki, a highly respected man who was high chief, or Chamberlain, to Kamehameha III, died on June 13, 1855. (Page 230.)

8. Apparently an error. This great battle was led by Kaiana who, with Keao, King of Kauai, rose in revolt against Kamehameha I, not II, who had recently brought the Hawaiian Islands under his sway. The war culminated when the revolutionists were defeated after terrific slaughter in the valley of Nuuanu and their bodies thrown over the precipice. (Page 231.)

9. *Pulu* is a soft, wool-like substance that grows at the base of fern trees, which is gathered and sold for mattresses and pillows. In the fifties the *pulu*

industry flourished in the Islands, and *pulu* was even marketed in California. (Page 231.)

10. Mrs. E. M. W. Parker, principal of the Grace Church Seminary that stood on Powell Street near Jackson. (Page 232.)

11. John Young, better known as Keoni Ana, was Minister of the Interior from March, 1846, to June, 1857. His death occurred in July, 1857. His house stood on Richards Street, but was razed in 1879 when the Palace grounds were enlarged. (Page 233.)

12. This was Dr. G. P. Judd, whose stone house, on the corner of Judd Street near the Nuuanu cemetery, was the scene of many of the important political gatherings of that era. Dr. Judd reached Hawaii in 1828 as a medical missionary and, with the exception of the King, rose to be the most influential member of the Hawaiian government from 1842 to 1854. He served as Secretary of State for Foreign Affairs and later as Minister of the Interior. (Page 233.)

13. François Pierre Guillaume Guizot (1787-1874), a French historian, orator, and statesman whose histories were among the leading volumes published in France at this period. Entering public life he came into bitter conflict with Palmerston in England, being embroiled in the major political events throughout Europe. From 1840 to 1848 he controlled the destiny of France. (Page 234.)

14. Henry John Temple Palmerston (1784-1865) was an English statesman of outstanding importance in European political circles, primarily due to his attempts to prevent Russia from acquiring an outlet on the Bosporus, and France from seizing the Nile. At the time the Giovanni *Journal* was written, he was at the peak of his power. (Page 234.)

15. Clemens Wenzel Lothar, Prince Metternich-Winneburg (1773-1859), an Austrian statesman and diplomat, was also a leading force in European politics. Many of his activities centered around France and the rise and fall of the Napoleonic star. He was noted above all for his subtle and shrewd handling of diplomatic points and problems. (Page 234.)

16. This appears to refer to Armand Louis de Gontaut, Baron de Bîron (1747-1793), who played an important rôle in the American War of Independence. (Page 234.)

17. Alphonse Marie Lamartine (1790-1869) was a French poet, historian, and statesman, who played a prominent part in French political life, subsequently holding the post of Minister of Foreign Affairs. His various histories were classics of Dumas' day. (Page 234.)

18. Victor Marie Hugo (1802-1885), the celebrated French poet, dramatist, and novelist, was a close friend of Dumas and, with him, the most popular writer of that era. (Page 234.)

19. Probably the old castle. Near the waterfront were also the customhouse, the fort, Honolulu House, the courthouse, the armory, the Royal School, the Charity School, the Stone Church, the Catholic Church, Kaumakapili Church, and Bethel Church. (Page 234.)

20. Apparently the Catholic Cathedral. (Page 234.)

CHAPTER III

1. This stood at the corner of Nuuanu and Beretania streets and was owned for decades by the Macfarlane family. The site is now occupied by a Japanese store. (Page 239.)

2. The Varieties Theatre, destroyed in 1855 by fire. (Page 241.)

3. Bethel Church, which was built in 1833, stood on the corner of King and Bethel streets. In 1886 it was destroyed by fire. (Page 241.)

4. Charles W. Vincent, a wealthy resident of Honolulu who also owned the salt works at Pearl Harbor. His carpenter ship, a wooden two-story structure, stood on King Street, near Maunakea, and his mechanics, many of whom had been imported from San Francisco, were noted for the excellence of their work. His offices have been demolished. (Page 242.)

5. Elisha Hunt Allen, who was appointed American consul in 1850. In 1855-1857 he became a member of the cabinet of King Kamehameha IV, and later Chief Justice of the Islands. His death occurred in 1883. The United States Consulate stood on Queen Street, adjoining the Hudson's Bay Company offices, and has since been demolished. See *Papers of the Hawaiian Historical Society,* No. 10, p. 14. (Page 243.)

6. Ellen Fessenden Allen who married Patterson and, after his death, Judge Charles C. Harris. She died in 1881 in Honolulu. (Page 243.)

7. General Miller, who lived on Beretania Street near Washington Place, reached Honolulu in 1844. (Page 244.)

8. Louis Émile Perrin, who was originally sent to Honolulu in 1846 as special commissioner by the French government to negotiate new treaties, had returned to Paris in 1851. Upon receiving an appointment as French consul, he returned to Honolulu on January 8, 1853, remaining there until his death in 1862. His house stood at the corner of Chaplain and Nuuanu streets, and was of coral. (Page 244.)

9. Baron de Thierry, who was in the French consular service from 1852 to 1853, when he was removed from office by M. Perrin. (Page 244.)

10. This was D. Frick, a member of the Royal Society of Sciences of Paris, who later lectured in Honolulu. (Page 244.)

11. Felix Letellier, who was French consul in Honolulu in 1853. (Page 245.)

CHAPTER IV

1. This anchorage, now known as Kealakekua Bay, lies on the west side of the island. On Cook's maps the port is called Karakakooa Bay, and the island, O Whyhee. (Page 249.)

2. Probably the port of Lahaina, used by most ships at that period. (Page 249.)

3. Captain James Cook was born in England in 1728 and served in the war of 1755. From 1758 to 1767 he spent considerable time in America, subsequently being appointed to command an expedition to the South Seas. His voyages covered every corner of the universe and materially enriched the

geographical knowledge of that day. He was murdered by the natives at Kealakekua Bay in February, 1779. (Page 249.)

4. The native village, known as Kowrowa. (Page 249.)

5. The first foreigners to reach Hawaii were probably the survivors from one of the vessels in command of Alvarado de Saavedra, wrecked in November, 1527, while en route to the Moluccas. Formal discovery, however, is accredited to Juan de Gaetano in 1555, who called them Los Mahos. By Cook the beauties of these islands were first proclaimed to the world at large, and his extensive explorations in 1778-1779 and published records brought the country into prominence. (Page 250.)

6. Captain Cook's remarks, as quoted in his own Journal, are as follows: "At eleven o'clock in the forenoon we anchored.... The ships continued to be much crowded with natives and were surrounded by a multitude of canoes. I had nowhere, in the course of my voyage, seen so numerous a body of people assembled at one place. For, besides those who had come off to see us in canoes, all the shore of the bay was covered with spectators, and many hundreds were swimming round the boat like shoals of fish. We could not but be struck with the singularity of this scene; and perhaps there were few on board who now lamented having failed in our endeavors to find a northern passage homeward last summer. To this disappointment we owed our having it in our power to revisit the Sandwich Islands, and to enrich our voyage with a discovery which, though the last, seemed in many respects to be the most important that had hitherto been made by Europeans throughout the Pacific Ocean." See James Cook, *A Voyage to the Pacific Ocean* (3 vols. London, 1785), Vol. II, pp. 547-548. (Page 250.)

7. The following account, although considerably abridged, agrees in substance with that of James Cook in *Ibid, Vol. III,* pp. 28-82. (Page 251.)

8. See *Ibid,* p. 40. (Page 252.)

9. *Ibid,* p. 41. (Page 253.)

10. Upon Cook's death Clerke became commander. (Page 256.)

## CHAPTER VI

1. The *L. Stevens* departed on that date. See *San Francisco, Alta California,* for March 2, 1854, which gives a full list of her passengers. The name of Giovanni is not among them. In the previous chapter the sailing date is given as March first. (Page 261.)

2. Cornelius K. Garrison, mayor in 1854. (Page 261.)

3. *Pronunciamento:* an insurrection or uprising. (Page 265.)

## CHAPTER VII

1. General Juan Álvarez (1780-1867) had been an active participant in all Mexican revolutions since his youth. In 1847 he became governor of the state of Guerrero. His career culminated in October, 1855, when he became president. (Page 266.)

2. Antonio López de Santa Anna was born at Jalapan, February 21, 1795,

and died in Mexico City on June 21, 1876. In his youth he served in the Spanish army, later aiding Iturbide. After heading several major revolts, he became president of Mexico in 1833. In 1836 he led an army against the Texans. By 1843 he had deposed all rivals and become dictator of Mexico. History ranks him as one of the most dynamic and colorful characters of Mexico. (Page 266.)

3. In the spring of 1854 the political situation in Mexico was chaotic. Civil war was incessant; Santa Anna, opposed by the powerful Juan Álvarez, kept the state of Guerrero in turmoil. Acapulco, the west coast port of entry to Mexico City, was the scene of considerable activity, and the center of intrigue and rioting. (Page 267.)

4. Apparently a banker of Acapulco, as well as an agent of the steamship company. (Page 267.)

5. Ignacio Comonfort, an associate of Álvarez, was in command of the fortress at Acapulco. He had with him 7000 men. (Page 269.)

6. Apparently it should read:

El ciudadano, Miguel García, teniente colonel de ejercicio y prefecto del distrito. "Concedo libre y seguro paso darse á la Señora Doña María Luisa Giovanni, Francesca, para que pasa á Méjico y Vera Cruz por embarcarse. Por tanto, supplico á las autoridades si civiles como militares, no le pungen ninguno embarazo, asi tienen de facilitarle con auxilios que necesite, pagándolos por un precio dado en Acapulco.

I, Miguel García, lieutenant colonel of troops and prefect of the district, hereby order free and safe conduct be given María Luisa Giovanni, a Frenchwoman, to proceed to Mexico City and Vera Cruz, where she will embark. I request all civil and military authorities not in any way to hinder her, but to give her whatever assistance she may require, anything purchased to be paid for at prices current at Acapulco.

March 1, 1854,

Alexandre Ganina.

(Page 270.)

7. The headquarters of Álvarez and the center of military activity. Santa Anna's operations were conducted from the hacienda of Providencia. (Page 271.)

### CHAPTER VIII

1. Raousset de Boulbon, a prominent Frenchman of San Francisco, made unsuccessful attempts in 1853 and 1854 to invade Mexico with a small army of Frenchmen and Germans, but was captured and shot. (Page 276.)

2. La Fontaine's well-known fable *La Chauve Souris et les deux belettes*. (Page 276.)

3. *Arrieros:* muleteers. (Page 276.)

### CHAPTER IX

1. Pelion, or Plessidi, and Ossa, or Kissovo, according to Greek mythology, were the stepping-stones which, piled on top of one another, aided the gods to scale Olympus. (Page 278.)

2. The national bread of Mexico, a flat cake, made of ground corn and water, and baked on hot stones. (Page 280.)

CHAPTER XI

1. Baucher (1805-1873) was a noted French horseman and writer on the etiquette of horsemanship. (Page 291.)

2. Chilpancingo: an old Aztec name meaning wasps. At one time much gold was found near by. It lies some fifty miles from Acapulco, on the route to Mexico City. (Page 292.)

CHAPTER XII

1. In classical mythology, this couple entertained Zeus and Hermes who were traveling in disguise. They were rewarded for their hospitality by having their humble cottage changed into a palace. (Page 295.)

2. Apparently an error. Tomás Moreno and Ignacio Comonfort were his most important officers. (Page 297.)

# VOLUME V

## CHAPTER I

1. Zumpango Santiago, a small town on the shores of Lake Zumpango. (Page 300.)

2. General Zachary Taylor was the great American who defeated Santa Anna's forces in a series of battles in 1846 and 1847 that culminated in peace and the Treaty of Guadalupe Hidalgo which gave Texas, New Mexico and Upper California to the victors. (Page 301.)

3. The alcalde was a combination of mayor and justice of the peace. In small towns he was the final authority on all matters and the leading citizen. As inns were few in Mexico, it was customary for prominent citizens to extend the hospitality of their homes to total strangers. (Page 301.)

## CHAPTER II

1. A discoloration of the body found also in Panama, Colombia, and Venezuela known as the pinto malady, caused by a vegetable parasite, which is often contagious. At one time the villages of western Mexico suffered heavily from this infection. The Pintos were originally members of the now extinct Pakawa tribe of northern Mexico. (Page 308.)

2. San Juan Bautista, originally known as Tabasco, is the capital of the state of Tabasco, and lies on the south shore of the Gulf of Mexico. (Page 308.)

## CHAPTER IV

1. Iguala, meaning convention, or agreement. Here the famous Plan, or Guarantees of Iguala, was formulated by the Mexican Emperor Agustín de Iturbide and on February 24, 1821, Mexican Independence was proclaimed. (Page 318.)

2. Cespides: This may refer to General Martín Carrera, one of Santa Anna's most loyal followers. (Page 319.)

## CHAPTER V

1. On March 16, Santa Anna left Mexico City with Santiago Blanco to take charge of field operations against Álvarez who was stationed near Mt. Peregrino. See Herbert Howe Bancroft, *History of Mexico,* V, 650 ff. (Page 320.)

2. Sultan Mejid, ruler of Turkey from 1839 to 1861. (Page 320.)

3. He was made Minister of War in 1853. (Page 322.)

4. In 1852 the French Count, Gaston Raousset de Boulbon, outfitted an expedition in San Francisco to seize Sonora. Reaching Guaymas in June, 1852, on October 14 he captured Hermosillo. That year, and again in 1854, he made a series of attempts to invade Mexico. He was finally captured and shot on August 12, 1854. See Rufus Kay Wyllys, *The French in Sonora* (Berkeley, 1932), *passim,* and Bancroft, *California,* VI, 586 ff. (Page 322.)

## CHAPTER VI

1. The French expedition to Vera Cruz was an attempt to force Mexico to live up to the terms of an agreement made in 1827, and culminated in the blockade of Vera Cruz in October, 1838, by Rear-Admiral Charles Baudin. Under him were 26 vessels, 104 guns, and 4000 men. See Bancroft, *op. cit.,* V, 192 ff. (Page 325.)

2. Anastasio Bustamente, whose failure to send an adequate force against the French at Vera Cruz, stirred all Mexico against him. He was president of Mexico from 1837 to 1842. (Page 325.)

3. The conference at Jalapa took place on November 17, 1838, and although the French tried to press their claims, the Spanish, believing in their military superiority, refused to acquiesce to their demands. A reinforcement of 1000 men under General Arista was now rushed to Vera Cruz. (Page 325.)

4. The fort of San Juan de Ulúa, on a small coral island in the harbor, was poorly equipped and had a garrison of only 1200 men under General Gaona. The fort was captured without difficulty by the French on November 28, 1838. (Page 325.)

5. The abandonment of the fort to the French raised a flood of protest in Mexico City, and expulsion of French residents, as the *Journal* narrates, followed. The government, ignoring the recent agreement with France, declared hostilities and appointed General Mariano Paredés y Arrillaga Minister

of War. The question culminated in the convention of March 9, 1839, whereby France won the points for which she had long contended. (Page 326.)

6. Rear-Admiral Charles Baudin, who had been sent out with a squadron from France to arrange a settlement with the Mexicans, reached Vera Cruz in October, 1838. On the 27th he sent Captain Leroy with a note to Mexico City, in an attempt to arrange an amicable settlement. (Page 326.)

7. General Arista attempted to stop the French attack under Baudin at Vera Cruz with a thousand men but was defeated. (Page 327.)

8. Throughout Mexico, General Santa Anna succeeded in making the populace believe that he was a hero, and his amputated leg was actually carried to Mexico City with imposing ceremonies. (Page 327.)

9. Approximately one hundred dollars. (Page 328.)

CHAPTER VII

1. Apparently the Borda Garden created by the Frenchman, Joseph le Borde who came to Mexico in 1716 and amassed a fortune in the mines. The garden was purely classic, with terraces, arcades, pergolas, arbors, and fountains. Although neglected, the garden is still one of the beauty spots of Cuernavaca. (Page 333.)

2. Also known as the Gran Sociedad. It was under French management and rates were about $70 a month. (Page 334.)

CHAPTER VIII

1. Alphonse Dano, French chargé d'affaires. (Page 336.)

CHAPTER IX

1. See Duflot de Mofras' Travels on the Pacific Coast edited by Marguerite Eyer Wilbur (Santa Ana, 1937), I, passim. Dumas calls him Duflot de Mau-fras. (Page 340.)

2. General Mariano Vallejo, a leading Californian of this period, whose haciendas were among the most extensive in the west. (Page 340.)

3. Juan Alvarado was governor of California from December 7, 1836, until the appointment of Micheltorena, on January 22, 1842, as his successor by President Santa Anna. (Page 341.)

4. Manuel Micheltorena was appointed in 1842 as head of the Californias, and took office on December 31, 1842. His career was brief and spectacular, finally ending in disaster when, defeated in 1845 by the rival claimant for governor, Juan B. Alvarado, he was forced to leave the country. (Page 341.)

5. Luís Vignes, one of the pioneer French residents of Los Angeles, who reached there early in the thirties, and planted the Aliso Vineyard, near a great sycamore tree. His adobe house, surrounded by high walls, was long a famous landmark. (Page 342.)

6. Beecher and Co., according to the English records. The name also appears in contemporary records as Becker, or Jecker and Torres. (Page 342.)

7. General James Wilson, the attorney for Limantour, published a pamphlet in 1854 containing a full translation of the agreement, but the case was subsequently declared fraudulent and rejected by the courts. See *A Pamphlet Relating to the Claim of Señor Don José Y. Limantour* (San Francisco, 1853). Also John S. Hittell, *The Limantour Claim* (San Francisco, 1857). (Page 343.)

8. Erroneously called *casa fluidadora* in the original Dumas version. This should read *fundadora*, meaning house erected by Richardson. (Page 343.)

9. The translation is original, and not that contained in Wilson's *Pamphlet*, pp. 8 and 9. (Page 343.)

10. Limantour's claim to four square leagues south of California Street was filed February 3, 1853, confirmed January 22, 1856, and finally rejected by the District Court on October 19, 1858. His second claim, that included the Farallon, Alcatraz and Yerba Buena islands as well as one square league in Marin County, met the same fate. He also claimed ten leagues in Mendocino County granted in 1844, which was subsequently rejected, as well as three more enormous grants in other parts of the state. (Page 343.)

11. The Spanish league, used in California, was 2.63 miles. (Page 343.)

12. Guérande, an important French village in Canton Loire, whose cathedral houses a famous saint's image. (Page 344.)

CHAPTER X

1. Calle de Plateros was a leading shopping street at that period. On it were the shops of the leading goldsmiths, silversmiths, jewelers, milliners, and modistes of Mexico City. (Page 345.)

CHAPTER XI

1. The park lies about three miles from the Plaza Mayor in Mexico City. In the days of the Aztecs a fort and pagan temple occupied the summit of the hill. Under Montezuma II this was made into a summer residence and hunting lodge. The castle now standing was begun in 1783 by Viceroy Gálvez, and in 1866 remodelled by Emperor Maximilian. Its beauties draw visitors from all parts of the world. (Page 350.)

2. On September 12, 1847, Chapultepec surrendered to the Americans after a terrific battle. (Page 351.)

3. The blockading of Vera Cruz by Admiral Baudin, an affair rising out of claims by French citizens in Mexico for unpaid damages to property during revolutions, including some to bakers. See *supra*, V, p. 324 ff. (Page 351.)

4. Possibly Lake Texcoco, now dry. (Page 351.)

5. Popocatepetl, or smoky mountain, is 17,749 feet high and lies 50 miles southeast of Mexico City. (Page 351.)

6. Del Muerto, or Iztaccihuatl, known as the white woman, is 16,200 feet high. (Page 351.)

7. Dhawalghiri in India is 26,826 feet and Chimborazo in Ecuador, 20,498

feet high. Mt. Everest, 29,000 feet, is now believed to be the highest peak in the world. (Page 352.)

8. Cholula lies a few miles from Puebla, and its great pyramid is one of the most remarkable structures of New Spain. On its crest stood an Aztec temple revered as the Mecca of all devotees of the Aztec god, Quetzalcoatl. Cortés found a large native city built around this great monument, with a population of 20,000. (Page 352.)

9. Since the time of the conquest thousands of tons of sulphur have been extracted to use for gunpowder. (Page 354.)

10. A topographical error. The peak most closely answering its description is Colima. (Page 355.)

11. Possibly Mt. Malinche, 14,000 feet high. (Page 355.)

12. Known as *solfateras*, or breathing holes. (Page 355.)


### CHAPTER XIII

1. This is the famous Whitsunday festival of San Agustín de las Cuevas, or Tlalpan, which is still famous for its heavy gambling and municipal lotteries. It lies 11 miles south of the Plaza Mayor and was settled by the Spaniards in 1532. (Page 363.)


### CHAPTER XIV

1. Possibly Napoleon Rossi, a popular Italian operatic star. Pozzolini's name does not appear in contemporary records of that period. (Page 367.)

2. Henriette Sontag was a prominent Viennese singer. (Page 367.)


### CHAPTER XV

1. This structure, known as the Church of San Francisco, is located on the Avenida Madero. It was founded in 1524 by the Franciscan Order. (Page 369.)

2. Also near Avenida Madero. It was founded in 1595 by the Jesuit Order, and has long been the church of the most wealthy and aristocratic Mexicans. It is distinguished mainly by its leaning tower. (Page 370.)

3. Beggars, or low-class Mexicans. (Page 370.)

4. Still so called. On the north now stands the cathedral, on the east, the National Palace, on the west, the National Pawn Shop, and on the south, the Portal de las Flores. (Page 371.)

5. *Tertulias:* small gatherings, or club meetings. (Page 371.)

6. Colegio de Minería, or the Escuela de Ingeniéros (School of Engineers), near the main post office. The building was erected in 1797-1813, although the school was founded twenty years earlier by Velasco de León and Lucas de Lasaga. (Page 372.)

7. *Cuartillo:* one-quarter of a real. (Page 372.)

8. Now the Académia Nacional de San Carlos. Founded by Charles III in 1778, it was situated originally in the old mint and had one of the finest

collections of paintings in America. In 1791 it was moved to the present location near the Palacio Nacional. (Page 372.)

9. José Cordero, a nineteenth century painter of Mexico, whose work adorned many local churches. (Page 372.)

10. Luís de Morales (1509-1586) was a noted Spanish painter. (Page 372.)

11. Francisco de Zubarán (1598-1662) was another leading Spanish artist. (Page 372.)

12. Probably José Fernando Ramirez (1804-1871) who was closely associated with the Museo Nacional in Mexico City. (Page 372.)

13. About 28 miles northeast of Mexico City. They are the two largest artificial mounds in America and antedate the Christian era. (Page 372.)

14. The ruins of Palenque lie in the state of Chiapas on the Chimchivoi River. Here are the remains of a city of stone houses, *Casas de Piedras,* abandoned during the twelfth century. Many of the palaces reveal elaborate carvings, paintings and petroglyphs, and represent some of the finest architectural development of pre-Cortésian times. (Page 372:)

### CHAPTER XVI

1. The Alameda, or poplar grove, is over 1400 feet long and 700 feet wide. It is lined with poplars, eucalyptus, pepper, and cypress trees, and adorned with tiled fountains, flowers, and side paths. (Page 374.)

2. El Paseo Nuevo appears to be the modern Avenida Bucareli that merges into Calzada de la Piedad. (Page 375.)

3. Tacubaya lies a mile south of Chapultepec on the slope of the Sierra de las Cruces, and is now one of the fashionable suburbs of Mexico City. Originally the old Aztec settlement of Atlacuihauyan was located on this site. (Page 375.)

4. Usually known as the sombrero. (Page 375.)

5. Now known as Cazado de la Viga. This boulevard lies in the southeastern section of the city and was originally one of the ancient highways leading into the old Aztec capital. Nearby stood Montezuma's great palace. (Page 376.)

6. These floating gardens lie 15 miles south of Mexico City and date from the thirteenth century. (Page 376.)

7. Now the Canal Nacional over which fruits, vegetables, flowers, and other produce were brought into the city. (Page 376.)

8. *Trottoir de las Cadenas:* Footpath of the chains. (Page 377.)

9. Wooden rattles. (Page 378.)